L'America

Also by Martha McPhee

Gorgeous Lies

Bright Angel Time

Girls: Ordinary Girls and Their Extraordinary Pursuits

Martha McPhee

L'America

Harcourt, Inc.

Orlando   Austin   New York   San Diego   Toronto   London

Requests for permission to make copies of any part of the work should be mailed to the following address: Permissions Department, Harcourt, Inc., 6277 Sea Harbor Drive, Orlando, Florida 32887-6777.

www.HarcourtBooks.com

The author wishes to thank Hofstra University and the John Simon Guggenheim Memorial Foundation for their generous support. The author also wishes to thank André Bernard, Adrienne Brodeur, Pryde Brown, Sarah Chalfant, Heather Clinton, Jenny McPhee, Sara Powers, Andrea Schulz, Cullen Stanley, Mark Svenvold, Ana Livia Svenvold McPhee, Jasper James Svenvold McPhee, and Donatella Trotti.

Library of Congress Cataloging-in-Publication Data
McPhee, Martha.
L'America/Martha McPhee.—1st ed.
p.   cm.
1. September 11 Terrorist Attacks, 2001—Fiction.   2. Hippies—
Family relationships—Fiction.   3. Children of the rich—Fiction.
4. Americans—Europe—Fiction.   5. Aegean Sea Region—Fiction.
6. Islands—Fiction.   I. Title: America.   II. Title.
PS3563.C3888A84   2006
813'.54—dc22   2005020986
ISBN-13: 978-0-15-101171-1   ISBN-10: 0-15-101171-0

Text set in Columbus MT
Designed by Linda Lockowitz

Printed in the United States of America

First edition
K J I H G F E D C B A

For Jasper, my valentine
and always for
Mark and Livia

To an Unknown Poet, Dead at 39

Phil Perelson, 1956–1995

Love, it seems, when all is said and done,
kept you (maintained, withheld) indefinite.
In bits and pieces you offered your Te Deum.

To disappear was your "natural condition,"
but what to keep (guard, record) against the infinite,
when love, it seems, when all is said and done,

(so utter, complete) so obliterates someone?
Your "Five Keys to Anonymity," the ball & chain habits?
In bits and pieces you offered your Te Deum.

I still say "you," a mistake I see, for the third person
holds you (faithful, spellbound now) separate—
love it seems, when all is said and done,

need not answer back, or get a word in
edgewise, or feel at all compelled to speculate
in bits and pieces. You offered your Te Deum,

and what remains? What space along what margin,
what wisp in a rented room, what scrap, however delicate?
Love, it seems, when all is said and done.
In bits and pieces, you offered your Te Deum.

—MARK SVENVOLD

L'America

One

Campanilismo

Above the party a beautiful young man rises into a cloud. As he looks to the sky, a girl with black hair curled at her ears reaches toward him, as if to pull him back. He is naked, exquisite, revealing the entirety of what is being lost to her. His right hand, enveloped by the faint tracings of a claw (perhaps an eagle's but this is debatable), disappears into the cloud, and only the girl is aware—her upturned face lit by sun. She wears a beige silk gown with a dark brown velvet princess bodice bordered with small pearls, which hugs her full breasts; a pillbox cap snugly rests on the crown of her head. The full gown flutters slightly with her movement, her desperate step toward the sky. Rose tints flush her cheeks and a solemnity haunts her eyes. At the edge of a hill thick with flowering rhododendrons and azaleas, the party carries on around her. Girls in long velvet gowns cluster together like bouquets, coquettish turns to their pretty lips, awaiting the adoration of all the various men, men in velvet pants and elaborate vests brocaded and beaded with pearls and gems. With long curling hair flowing like the capes that drape their backs, they are as handsome and gay as the girls. The colors are rich and deep, burnt sienna and royal peacock blue and gold and golden greens and whites the color of the sky. Couples whisper sweet gossip, though no one yet knows that she is in love with him, except for him. And what is to become of her, of that love, overwhelming and futile? If you look closely, you can see her love fairly palpitating, throbbing under the swell of her breast, all fury and tenderness. The party unfolds at the edge of a town over which looms the bell tower of an imposing church, perched high above one of those cool northern Italian lakes. The party celebrates the flowering rhododendrons and azaleas and the completion of Fiori, the Cellini country house to which these flowering bushes belong. "May they flower for at least a thousand years," Signor Cellini might have said. He is there somewhere among the guests, the father of the lovelorn girl. Time is expansive like that. Fifteen hundred years have elapsed since Augustus ruled the world. A lute player plucks the strings of his instrument, perhaps the bells of the bell tower toll. The beautiful young man touches the cloud in all his glory. A wide ribbon runs diagonally across the girl's chest and on the ribbon in a swirling playful script of gold is the name of the artist who painted this fresco—Benvenuto Cellini.

He was nineteen years old, born in 1500, the age of the year, and had recently been banished from Florence for a second time for one of his many quarrels, the result of his proud and cocky temper. He had never painted a painting before, much less a fresco, and he never would again. He had sketched, he had practiced with paint and tempera, but his interest was in sculpture, working with bronze and on occasion gold. He thought painting an inferior art. A sculpture, unlike a painting, could be looked at from eight different angles and thus had to be perfect from eight different perspectives. But he had fun with this fresco. He made it for the girl, Valeria Cellini, his cousin and his love, too. It was Cellini family lore (you know the way that families have their myths, the stories that lend them importance and carve their place in history) that she would not have followed him even had he let her. She would not have left behind her family and her town—brave girl, she was the symbol of family loyalty and resilience. Of all the Cellini daughters, twenty generations of them, she was the first and she alone remained untouched by time and change: five hundred years old, perpetually beautiful and young, captured as if in amber while the other daughters of the Cellini line (the nineteen who followed her) had married and vanished into the myths of other families. The action Valeria would have taken, could have taken, didn't take, remains frozen in that one instant of after and before, frozen the way art can freeze something, after love and before all the potential of life. Valeria was fifteen years old.

Benvenuto danced into town, escaping Florence, to stay with his uncle Cesare Cellini in the town of Città in the foothills of the Alps. He stayed the summer of 1519. He stayed until he became well acquainted with the town and his uncle's friends and family. He stayed until he fell in love, until the shy half smile igniting Valeria's pale rose-tinted face flowered into something more complete. He stayed until he grew restless, impatient, bored even by romance. Then he left, traveled north to Switzerland, turned south and went to Rome, the city of his dreams, where a wealthy woman became his patron and where he stayed until he had the courage to return to the city that had exiled him but to which he unequivocally belonged. By then Valeria had faded to an insignificant detail, erased by the fullness and bravado of his biography.

In Città, though, he stayed long enough for Valeria to be seduced by hope, the depths of hope, its deep recesses and its wells, and to find himself basking in it, too, though they both knew that he was incapable of staying forever (that deceptive word) and that he would never have taken her away with him and that she would never have left. That is what she had loved about him, that from the beginning she knew their time together would not last. That was the draw, the pull, the urgency behind the love—the desire to conquer the impossible. The "if only" at that love's core, the "if only" triumphing to become all. But art trumped and Benvenuto left Città and he left Valeria and he left, as well, the story in the fresco, a token of his gratitude, an ode and a bow to exquisite pain.

For a long time, 453 years to be exact, the fresco remained in the dining room of Fiori, the villa in the hills above Lago Maggiore, thirty kilometers outside of Città. It presided over parties and dinners and the ordinary family meals of twenty generations of Cellinis (Sunday dinners of *polenta* and *uccellini,* tiny birds with bones as delicate and tasty as marrow, shot by the Cellini husbands in the estate's bird arbor) until Giovanni Paolo Cellini and his wife, Elena, at great expense, had the fresco removed and restored and fronted by protective glass and rehung in the more tempered environment of their Città villa. Humidity (the enemy of frescoes everywhere) was eating the lime plaster and corrupting the pigment, slowly devouring the picture, and the Cellinis wanted to save it. They wanted it to last. For twenty generations it had survived. Giovanni Paolo Cellini, a short elderly man (he had his first child at fifty) with a halo of white hair and a missing hand disguised by a stiff black leather glove that endowed him with the aspect of a laborer rather than the banker that he was, would not allow the fresco to die on his watch. Elena, tall, thin, dark-haired, big-eyed, good wife, wouldn't either. Through the centuries the job of the Cellini wives had been to preserve the Cellini family's rituals and customs, and Elena well understood her role. So in the 1970s, when

Elena and Giovanni Paolo's son was a teenager, the elaborate process of separating the fresco from the wall (digging out and destroying a good foot of plaster and stucco behind the picture) was undertaken.

Young Cesare was all but oblivious to this exercise. He was a boy caught up in history, studying Latin and Ancient Greek at the *Liceo Classico*. He read Aeschylus in the original yet preferred the comedies of Aristophanes because he liked to laugh and make others laugh. His little sister, Laura, had this same love of laughter, but she went even further. A funny little girl with thick curly white-blond hair, the source of which eluded everyone, Laura's ambition was to one day become a clown. Three years younger than Cesare, Laura already knew who she was and what she wanted, and one day she would run away to clown school in Switzerland; but that's later, much later.

Cesare liked music, could play the piano, was learning Dylan songs on the guitar, and had a passion for the harmonica. He listened to Italian music, too: Lucio Battisti and Lucio Dalla, and on occasion (strictly in private) Claudio Baglioni (but Baglioni was less hip, less cool, too romantic in a sentimental way, singing of "small, big loves"). Always Cesare dreamed of the big roads of America of which Simon and Garfunkel sang. America was his dream, just as Benvenuto had dreamed of Rome—a place where people did what they chose and anyone could become anything. In 1972, Cesare was fourteen years old, old enough to be aware that American boys were being blown to pieces in Vietnam. He watched this war on TV, watched it like a show each night, acutely aware, of course, that it was not a show. Aware that in France, one country to the north and west, the peace talks had been held, aware that Nixon had gone to China to speak with Mao Tse-tung, aware of the historic scale of it. He liked to know, Cesare did. He was a beautiful boy with thick dark hair so black that at times it almost seemed blue.

It was a year, 1972, like any year, filled with history. Ezra Pound died in Italy two days after his eighty-seventh birthday. Marianne Moore died, too, and the poet John Berryman jumped to his death off the Washington Avenue Bridge in Minnesota. So it goes and so it went and Cesare went with it. He watched the war protests on television, saw protestors gassed at American universities. Watergate began to unfold and Cesare began to ponder the consequences: one nightly drama replaced another. Being the boy that he was, fresh into adolescence, he had a girlfriend (named Francesca) and together they wondered mightily what would become of *Pioneer* 10 and the relics of human civilization it carried on its million-year journey into space, wondered if it would all be found and interpreted and how? (A million years from now, ten years from now, twenty, thirty, forty—where would they be? He would not be a banker like his father and his father's father and his father's father's father. Of this one fact he was certain.) Somewhere in the deepest part of him, he wanted to be a part of the bigness of all that was America—big musicians and big poets and big plans and big trips and big presidents and big protests and big failures and big wars and big dreams. Possibility, that was all.

He was a boy, a fourteen-year-old boy, when the fresco was removed, one year younger than Valeria when she was captured for eternity. But at fourteen he was unaware of her, only half aware of his mother, who ran around the house and the city nervously making the arrangements for the fresco. Nervous because she had a nervous energy that fueled her and that seemed to reveal that she knew there was not enough time. Long ago she had given up her passion for Russian literature and her fantasies of taking trips to Moscow and St. Petersburg, of riding in a horse-drawn sleigh in the bitter cold, wrapped to the nose in furs, of being surrounded by people capable of speaking half-a-dozen languages fluently, especially the children she would someday have. She spoke five languages herself: Italian, French, Spanish, German, and English. For a while she had studied Russian, but then she married Giovanni Paolo, a man who spoke no language other than Italian and who had never traveled (and never would) beyond the perimeter of northern and central Italy. He was a good ten years older than she, and though she had known him since she was young (her father was a lawyer for the Cellini bank), in the beginning he had felt like a stranger, if kind, and their marriage had felt like an arrangement that was intended to please her parents more, perhaps, than herself. In this new life, her ambitions had become decidedly less complex and her faith decidedly more profound.

Of her boy, of course, she was aware, more of his physical side (his skill at sports—soccer, skiing, tennis) than of his interior world (America, history, literature). She was acutely aware of his physical beauty. He was much more attractive than either she or her husband or their funny little Laura, though Elena could see herself in him: he had her height and Roman nose, long and distinguished. She was aware of Francesca, daughter of one of Città's richest and most prominent citizens, who had a thriving business manufacturing socks and whose accounts were at the Cellini bank; she was aware that Cesare and Francesca had a tight love. They went skiing together at Francesca's house in Cortina. They went sailing together from Francesca's house on the Costa Smeralda in Sardegna. The two would grow up together, falling in love at fourteen and staying together until they were twenty-two—eight years during which Francesca transformed from girl to woman, with her almond hair and her perfectly round face and her soft green eyes, and learned to expect nothing and everything.

Francesca's mother, Signora Marconi, younger than Elena by a good fifteen years, draped herself effortlessly in all her money, lots of gold and fine clothes, Como silk and Tornabuoni leather. She would invite Elena to their various villas, and Elena, in turn, would invite her to her own villas and involve her (she was named Caterina but was known as Cat, pronounced with a very hard *C*) with the elaborate process of restoring the fresco. Elena invited Cat to see the fresco in situ, before removal. She invited her to the restorer's studio in Milan. She invited her to the Città villa to elicit Cat's opinion about where the fresco should hang once restored. Elena lacked Cat's easy confidence and that is why Elena loved to be with her—as if Cat's confidence could some-how rub off. "Here," Cat said emphatically. "The fresco should hang right here." She was in the living room of the Cellini's Città villa. Cat was deeply tanned from an Easter trip to Sardegna. Smaller paintings hung on the wall Cat referred to, but it was a vast wall that would not swallow the fresco. And Cat was there when the fresco (restored) was hung in its new spot. Reaching her long and slender and tanned finger (bejeweled with one enormous diamond sunk in a thick band of yellow gold) toward Valeria's face, she drew a circle, targeting Valeria's expression. What she loved best about the painting, Cat said, was that pain. "It must be felt. Must. At least once, for some reason."

Elena watched the beautiful hand encompassing the pain that Elena had always felt in the figure of the girl but had never articulated—a ripping ecstasy tearing across the face, familiar to Elena from paintings of religious trials, from Anna Karenina's travails. Seeing Cat describe the pain, contouring it with the confidence of experience, Elena had the urge to ask private questions, to talk like free young girls, when all was whimsy and potential. She did not, of course, because it would have been impolite. Such subjects were not discussed, and she was a good

Catholic woman. But the pain, the heartbreak, it flourished in the privacy of her mind, Cat as the heroine with some lover, someone other than her small balding husband, emperor of socks—a ferocious kiss followed by tender bites on the back of a pale reclining neck, tender bites sending shivers of desire throughout her. Briefly this image cut across Elena's mind before she dismissed it and all such foolishness with an embarrassed prayer to Saint Jude.

"Just once," Cat repeated, and Elena burned again, an ember receiving a blast of air, "that love that rips through like a knife." And Elena nodded with a warm smile, hoping that Cat would not understand the depths of her ignorance.

"Is that a claw?" Cat asked, and the subject changed to a debate about iconography: was it God's hand or Zeus's hand or simply the hand of fate. "Oh, think," Cat said, "if those artists, all of them, Raphael and da Vinci and Michelangelo, Cellini even, if they could only have felt the freedom to paint secular subjects. Just imagine what their imaginations would have created. That ache, that pain, it is subject enough."

"It's fate all the same," Elena said suddenly, surprising herself. She was usually not so bold with her opinions. "If it is God's hand or Zeus's claw or the will of the boy to leave or be left—it is fate." And for an instant she imagined the world without the great religious works of all those artists and in that moment of emptiness she was certain that Cat did not attend mass every Sunday.

What Elena also knew was that her son would inflict that pain upon Cat's daughter. Francesca was the kind of daughter-in-law the Cellinis would expect and want, but Elena knew that Cesare and Francesca had found each other too young and their relationship would not last. She knew the outcome. She knew good-looking boys always had the advantage. In some small way, though Elena was not malicious, this knowledge made her feel triumphant.

The exquisite pain: the early hours of the morning, a calm Sardinian sea, a hundred little boats rowing off to the horizon, eager for the daily catch, all the faint noises of such movement, the bells of buoys, the swish and clunk of sailboats rocking in the sway of the water, the creak of ropes. It is a green Smeralda morning: seagulls ride on the back of a light breeze, calling sharply; the *forno* smell of brioche floods the dawn with the promise of something warm and a little sweet. Francesca is looking for Cesare. She has been up all night. Barefoot, she wears only her nightgown. Her round face and enormous eyes are marred by worry and exhaustion. It has occurred to her slowly through the night, the thought rising like the break of day, that this is the end. Eight years—a long run. She is innocent but no fool. He will be cold and mean because who knows how to end love well? It is the Dutch girl, Francesca knows, from last night's party. The one with the short black pixie and the strappy black dress and all the height, the one who spoke English to Cesare as they drank a little too much wine. The one who cocked her head with flirtatious drunken sloppiness. The one who laughed preposterously. The beauty of him, of Cesare, his smile widening for another girl—Francesca had studied it, noting his black hair receding at the temples, his dimples deepening with the curl of his lips as he bowed toward the Dutch girl.

Francesca's feet ache, the right one is scratched above the instep, enough to cause a little bit of blood to pearl. This romance will be insignificant for Cesare, for the Dutch girl, too, but not for Francesca. For Francesca it will mark the threshold of her adulthood. She sits down on the steps leading to the marina. Her hair is a mess. She has not brushed her teeth. She remembers being fourteen, imagining extraterrestrials finding *Pioneer* 10, the ship shipwrecked on some gorgeous star, the plaque inside with the picture of Man and Woman designed by Carl Sagan. The naked man waving his hand, inviting aliens to realize he is friendly. They had laughed, she and Cesare, at this simple notion and all the potential of such an expedition. Their futures rose just as bright and grand, full of the places they could someday be. All admiration and curiosity was she for Cesare's passion for America.

She has found him. She knows where he is. Down there in the marina, among the hundreds of yachts, in the sailboat belonging to her family, the cabin light is on. And he is inside with the Dutch girl, both naked like the figures on the *Pioneer* plaque, but intertwined, ruining everything and nothing. She sits on the cold cement steps, bougainvillea flowering hopefully all about, and the world smelling of brioche and honey, and she knows any ecstasy they enjoy is because of her, because of her sitting here watching them, their knowledge of her eyes on them, the pain of it ripping in her, how intense that makes their lust. She'll wait. She'll sit here until they have the courage to emerge from the boat into the bright Sardegna morning, the long limbs of the Dutch girl draping Cesare—her sly smile mocking innocence. And then Francesca will stand up so that Cesare can see her, rise above them and ride the back of a gentle breeze.

Of the year 1519, Cesare did not know much. It was the year that Leonardo da Vinci died (in France) and the year that Catherine de Médicis was born to the richest non-royal family in Europe. She was the granddaughter of Lorenzo the Magnificent and would become Queen of France and mother-in-law of Mary, queen of Scots. Among her many contributions to the world would be ballet, she its first patron. Ferdinand Magellan began his voyage around the world, sailing from Seville. The facts of a year knit time to make history. A young goldsmith from Florence fled to Città, was taken in by his uncle who brought him to Fiori, a small village in the hills above Lago Maggiore, and there he fell in love with his cousin Valeria. Her name means Strength. She was fifteen years old with a vitality that Benvenuto wanted to sculpt and make his own. In less than a year she would be married to someone else. The someone else stands among the guests, his eyes trained on Valeria, the only figure not oblivious to her ache. But you must look hard to catch this, the artist playing games, reading the future. Is he telling Valeria she will be all right? Or is he telling himself she will be all right? Trying to excise the pain, remove it as you would a thorn? No good way to end love, is there? That summer of 1519, when the pope and his bishops were carrying on trying to defend Catholicism and Catherine was born to so much privilege and da Vinci died, Benvenuto made a record of the pain, painted his fresco showing Valeria trying to both pull back and set free the ascending man too beautiful for mortal life. The pain would travel across time, being studied and watched and ignored by generations of a family, until in 1972 a gentle woman named Elena removed it from the Fiori villa, restored it, and placed it on the wall of the Città villa, where it still hangs today with a dull lamp suspended above it, illuminating it as gently as possible with the goal of immemorial preservation.

Now, sitting in a red velvet armchair, the velvet curtains drawn, Cesare studies the fresco. He studies it as he has many times before, pondering the debatable claw, the notion of fate—but tonight he looks at the painting as if for the first time because Beth is dead. He has just learned of Beth's death today in an e-mail sent by her husband. He had watched her death unwittingly and repeatedly on the television, over and over and over and yet again and would be able to do so for years to come. The little light perched above the fresco casts its glow on the anguish of the girl, the exuberance of the rising star, the fleeing artist, driven not by romantic passion or heritage or money, but by a desire to live untethered from the ground. He watches the fleeing artist enviously, watches the girl grab for his leg. Yes, as if to pull him back or be pulled up and taken away by him. "He wanted to be pulled back," Beth would say, standing there. "He wanted her to take a stand. Look at his left hand," she would say. "Just look at it. Look at the left hand." And Cesare did now, the longing curl of it, of the elegant slender fingers, perhaps, indeed, reaching back for hers. Willful American Beth, his beautiful rebellion.

Cesare is a forty-three-year-old banker in the town of Città. A rich prominent citizen, he lends money—as his father did and as his father's father did and as his father's father's father did, and so on and so forth—to big manufacturers of socks and shoes, who are trying to become bigger by inventing smarter, tighter, slicker, smoother socks and stockings and soles and heels. His father's big success, in collaboration with Signor Marconi, Francesca's grandfather, and later with her father, was with panty hose. Cesare's big success in collaboration with Signor Agnelli, husband of Francesca, as it turns out, has been with nonskid socks for toddlers. The Cellinis have mastered the art of money making more money, though the world is now in an economic slump and terrorism spreads like a cancer, metastasizing around the globe. And Beth, gone from him for fifteen years, is gone once again and permanently. Unwittingly he has watched her go many times. Behind her she has left a husband, a daughter, and a father. In their bedrooms, Cesare's wife and son are asleep. From time to time he peers in on them just to observe the gentle rhythm of their breathing, the rise and fall of their chests beneath the blankets. His wife's head, haloed by curly black hair, rests on her pillow, knowing only comfort. She peels her grapes, has the leisure to think of such stuff, the small silver knife and fork working intricately with the skin, slipping it off like a dress. She is the heir to an empire of fruit, ordinary fruits, exotic fruits, exported fruits, imported fruits—kumquats and kiwis and mangosteens, durians, and rambutans (favorites of the orangutan, as it happens). She breathes. In the morning, they will drive together to Fiori to oversee the construction of a swimming pool. *Pioneer* 10 has long made it past the edge of our solar system. He wonders what Beth imagined as she died? Did she know she was about to die? For how long, how many minutes, did she anticipate it? Who is her daughter screaming for now? The e-mail had been matter-of-fact: "*I wanted you to know…*" Did her husband know Cesare loved Beth still?

It is past midnight, September, a thick night of fog, the sort that Lombardy is famous for. The fog shrouds the Pianura Padana, dangerously suspended over the entire plain. From the Alps to the Dolomites, the fog is so dense it would seem you could cut it, so dense it makes the whole world dark. Zero visibility and highway pileups involving dozens upon dozens of cars and deaths, caused by a fatal combination of warm earth and cold air and a plain of land that creates stillness. Cesare can feel Beth; the soft smell of her fills his living room. His parents are out and it is late and she is there. His parents do not like her, or rather they indulge her as a whim of Cesare's. He is a student at the Bocconi in Milan. He fails his exams regularly because he doesn't study. He doesn't study because he doesn't care about economics, as he knows it must come to bear, eventually, upon socks and shoes. He does not want to spend his life thinking about feet.

Elena assures Giovanni Paolo the American is just a phase. Regularly (and in front of the American) he asks Cesare what happened to Francesca, why doesn't she come around anymore? It takes his parents months to learn Beth's name, to stop referring to her as the American. No matter that two years have passed since the Sardegna morning, no matter that Francesca is long since involved with (and intended to) the Agnelli relation.

Cesare's wife sleeps, breathing peace. He hears his son rise, five years old, a year older than Beth's daughter. Listens to the boy tiptoe to his mother's bed, listens to the boy lift himself onto the mattress. Imagines Beth's little girl tiptoeing to her mother's bed, each night, every night. He can hear her, her voice like his son's, howling for mama when she has only gone away for a day. For how long? How long before a child forgets? Cesare's father is dead now, a good ten years, died of lung cancer in bed at home. The last thing he said to Cesare was to put out his cigarette; he said it dismissively, offended by his son smoking a cigarette as he lay dying of lung cancer. Cesare was not smoking; he was not a smoker. Never is the answer. You never forget.

Not so many months after Giovanni Paolo died, Elena died, too; no cause but simple sadness. And here was Beth, cornflower blue eyes, short blond hair tucked behind her ears, nostrils that flare ever-so-gently, with her excitement widening the broad plains of her high and dimpled cheeks. He feels the brightness of her in the room with him, declaring that the fresco can be interpreted however we choose. "That's the brilliance of the artist. He leaves it up to us."

"You're so American," he says.

"Sei cosí Italiano," she counters.

"Benvenuto's father wanted him to play music."

"But he wanted to make art. He did what he had to do."

"He was the director of his own life," Cesare says. "Though in the end he returned to Florence."

"Campanilismo," Beth says. "No matter the depths of his love for Valeria, he would always have yearned for the bell tower of his Florence." She loves that expression, *campanilismo,* he knows, the intensely local patriotism of it. *Campanilismo:* love of one's bell tower, to die for one's bell tower. She loves the concept because it does not have an American equivalent and she loves the differences, the contrasts, of their respective traditions. Now, at the beginning, they do not pose a threat for her, but already he fears the chasm they will make. He will not think about that, though, preferring as always to push aside unpleasant truth, save it for a later date. She smiles, an adorable dimpled smile, pushes Cesare into the velvet armchair, and kisses him indulgently with a hundred small kisses. "Do you think they ever..."

"Signorina," said with feigned shock. Then, "I'm certain they did." And Cesare begins to kiss her, starting at her toes.

Exquisite Pain

She called him from phone booths all across America, standing at the edges of lonely gas stations by the sides of those long endless roads, while James waited patiently in the car, believing that she was only calling home. It was her grandmother's car, a black Lincoln boat with a gold inscription on the dashboard reading MRS. OLIVER CARTER BRANDT, III. She would watch the car lounging heavily in the hot summer sun. She would shut her eyes and wish that she could emerge from the booth as some sort of Superwoman and transform the world, wish that it were Cesare behind the wheel, acting the cowboy or Jimmy Dean, arm draped easily over the back of the long front seat the way he liked to do, his black-framed sunglasses resting on the bridge of his nose. He had loved driving the car, the sheer size of it, cruising the canyons of New York City, sailing the wide high-ways. The static crackled through the international line connect-ing them, reminding her of the distance. Even so she could hear his voice clearly, his accent bringing back all of Italy so that it seemed she was headed toward him, not away. It was a dare, that was all, this trip west. She hardly knew James. She was twenty-three years old and had just graduated from college.

It was 1987, a year like any other. The economy was strong, the Dow bullish. Many of those who had not voted for Reagan were secretly delighted that he was president. "America is too big for small dreams," Reagan declared. Indeed this was the year of Milken and Boesky and Gary Hart and Black Monday. The Iran-Contra scandal raged, making indelible the names of North, Schultz, Weinberger, Poindexter. With perspective and distance we know the outcome, the rise and fall, the tide. On October 1, James would be in his first year of graduate school at UCLA, feeling the earth move beneath his feet, Beth a gnawing memory. On October 19, Beth would be working at Lago, a renowned New York City restaurant, entry level, chopping carrots, watching the stories of people losing everything, glad she had nothing left to lose. But back in June things were heady. Gorbachev worked with Reagan to put an end to the Cold War, while Microsoft worked on CD-ROMs. AZT had entered the market. Yoko Ono was promoting peace around the world. Beth marched across this year with all the importance and obliviousness of youth, aware and unaware, the details and facts of the day seemingly irrelevant, relegated to the hazy background of the bright picture of her future that unfurled like a long red carpet for her to stride upon. The only thing that mattered to her was Cesare. He was in her, a ferocious, permanent love, eating her whole and alive.

In the beginning, the conversations were the same. "Are you coming?" Cesare would ask. "You know I'm not," she would say, trying on toughness. "You are," he'd respond with his cool confidence—a confidence that loved the conditional tense, the "if" that would make all possible. It was by now that she was supposed to have gone to Italy to marry him. At Christmas, however, Cesare had revealed an infidelity, giving Beth a green silk hat that a milliner lover of his had made. It was an exquisite hat, an oval pillbox with gentle tiers, reminiscent of Valeria's hat. Beth knew its entire story as she opened it, knew as well that the woman would ultimately be insignificant.

But at Easter, Beth did not go to Italy as planned. Then just before Beth's graduation Elena called to ask when she was coming. Beth could imagine tall thin Elena standing at the phone near the villa's kitchen, pressing the receiver to her ear as if to push away the static, her anxious anticipation, not of Beth's arrival but of her son's future. Beth was brave, bold even. She was in her apartment in New York City, fire engines screaming up Sixth Avenue, her roommates taking showers, walking around in towels. "Cesare has another girl," Beth had said to Elena to explain that she would not be coming soon, but also with a hope that Elena would somehow rise to her defense and make everything all right. *"O cara,"* Elena had said with tenderness, missing not a beat as if she had been waiting for some time to say this. "He always has another girl." She sounded exasperated, impatient, not with Beth, but with her son, with the fact that he was impossible, irresistible, that he broke hearts. Beth curled the long phone cord around herself, wrapping it round and round until the plastic pinched her skin. It was not the possibility of girls that concerned Beth most. Rather it was the truth of Elena being able to deliver the message to her.

In the phone booth now, Beth could see Cesare as if he were in front of her: his long Roman nose, his thick dark hair, his bright onyx eyes, his preppy clothes—docksiders, rolled khakis, oxford shirt—though the way he tucked the shirt, the fine cuff he made of the rolled legs, the unbuttoned collar, the sleeves pushed up his arms, all had nothing to do with the dull familiar look. After he returned from America all his friends in Città began to dress like him. He would write to Beth, in one of his many letters, telling her of his ability to clone Americans. He taught them to throw a football, too, taught them to sail it spinning off their fingers, taught them tackle not touch in a vast field at Fiori, taught them with a determination and a passion as if something quite important depended on their learning the game. His American-ness, the hybrid nature of him, grew like something magical, some sort of beautiful flower tenuously blooming, evolving until natural selection rendered it obsolete: the football was abandoned in a corner, lost to soccer.

"Are you still dressing like a preppy?" she asked. She remembered his inspiration a few years earlier to translate *The Official Preppy Handbook* into Italian, remembered the smile igniting his face at the idea big enough to build a bridge for them. He was a dreamer, too, she knew, and she would never give up hoping that he would allow his dreams to flourish. In the car, James turned on some radio music, a beautiful country tune that floated from the window, seeming to dress the blue day.

"Made in America," Cesare said.

"I'm waiting for you here," she said, looking down the long road, cornfields as far as she could see, feeling a slight ache at the emptiness, at everything that was not. But she believed, defiantly and somewhere, that he would arrive in the nick of time, blowing in hard on the breeze, hurting her in his arms.

She called him first from the outskirts of Hazelville, a little town outside of Pittsburgh that James had wanted to visit because he had been born there. James had been in Beth's graduating class at New York University, a good boy who detasseled corn as a kid, a geologist in the making whose subject was America, a poet at heart. Beth had been impatient with the sentimental notion of the detour to his birthplace. But she did not let him know that. What she did let him know was that she was falling in love with him—deeply, madly. In a field of sunflowers, she told him so for the first time.

Hazelville was a depressing town whose coal industry was long dead and whose character had remained frozen for decades—broad avenues with broad storefronts with long-forgotten names: Franklin's Five and Dime. A town hidden in the recesses and folds of this big land like a mole hidden in flabby flesh. Beth, too, had grown up in Pennsylvania, on an apple farm commune in Snyder County, four hours to the east, where hills rolled into more hills and all of it disappeared into wide blue sky. It was Amish and Mennonite country, the men and women in their plain black clothes with their buggies and their horses trotting over dale and hill. More than once, Beth had gotten stoned with a few Mennonite boys. She was the daughter of a hippie and a dreamer, her mother long dead, memorialized in the name her father gave the farm: Claire.

Beth and James had camped in some woods not far from the road, on the edge of James's birth town. In the middle of the night Beth had taken off in the Lincoln to call Cesare from a truck stop. The engines heaved and sighed; the massive trucks, lit up, sparkling and dazzling in the night, swarmed around her. She was silent, just listening to his voice. The night was cold with no moon and no stars. Knowing he was on the other end of the line was enough; she didn't need to speak. "I love you," he said. *"Ti amo."* *Ti amo* is different from *Ti voglio bene,* which means "I wish you well" but stronger, something a parent says to a child. *Ti amo* is reserved for lovers. Beth knew the subtleties, the moment in their relationship when one replaced the other. She adored the precision of his language.

Over the course of five years he had written her hundreds of letters. She had carried them back and forth from Italy to

America, from her father's farm to her grandmother's apartment, to her place on Sixth Avenue. She would carry them into adulthood, she would carry them for the rest of her life, stacked neatly in a box just the size to hold them closely, folded as he had folded them, tucked in their envelopes, the flap licked by his tongue, a proof, a testimony, a declaration of the absolute. *Ti amo sempre di più,* he wrote.

> *I will tell you the truth: I am andato for you, which in Italian means "I am out of my head for you," which means "I am crazy for you," which means "I am mad for you," which means "I would do anything for you," which means "you can rely on me," which means "my life only makes sense when I think of you," which means "you can do with me as you please," which means "you and only you can decide my fate: if I'll be happy or if I'll have to live the rest of my life remembering the time when you loved me."*

Why do you love me? Her response consisted of that one question, written on a long blank page. She was not beautiful, she had no style, her sophistication had nothing to do with that of Italian girls, she did not understand his way of life. She could not see herself as he saw her. Generally, she did not lack confidence, but early on she loved him to the point where it was almost unbearable. *Why?* She would ask. It was her perpetual question over the years. She was aiming for logic. Simply: the love was hard to believe. Love is hard to believe. Why do you love me? What is love? Why do people find one love out of all possible loves? What are the forces, the attractions, the causes, the consequences? What are the requirements, the shapes, the sizes, the measurements? Explain it. Why you? Why me?

She had met him on a small Greek island floating in the Aegean like a song. She had been eighteen years old. He was standing on some steps leading to a whitewashed pensione, struggling to speak with the landlady, to negotiate a price. The sun was on him, caught in his hair as if he could shake it free. Beth had watched him, the gesturing of his hands, listened to the odd and unfamiliar words. She had just arrived on the island with two friends of hers. Friends of his were there, too, laughing at his attempts to communicate. The old landlady was dressed in black, hunched over, and thick around the waist. The sun lit him, Beth would remember that detail forever, the way the sun illuminated him as if for her benefit. And then the way he turned, as if he could feel her eyes on him. His eyes locked on her, for an instant only, but long enough for her to feel a shock—a jab, a stab—and then nothing was the same.

The rich smell of oil and fuel floated through the night. Truckers with their bellies spilling over their pants waddled toward the buffet in the restaurant. In pulled a traveling chapel in the form of a semitrailer with JESUS SAVES in blinking neon on the roof. As a lover, a deceptive lover, caught between continents and cultures, separated by an ocean, she felt important, alive, standing there with the phone pressed to her ear in the cold night. James lay asleep in the tent, believing in her, in her declaration of love in the field of sunflowers.

"Dai, parla," Cesare said, begging her to speak. He waited for her to respond, but still she said nothing. *"Non essere scema,"* Cesare said with impatience now: Don't be yourself, don't be stupid, don't be irrational.

"Come get me," she wanted to say, but she said nothing, too proud. She remembered him once telling her that he wished he were her father because he would know for certain she would love him for his entire life.

"Cocolina," he said, suddenly tender.

"Be brave," she wanted to demand of him, blaming the whole mess on his inability to be brave. She wanted to blame— blame Elena, blame anyone. She wanted a culprit, wanted to point her finger, to indict the criminal. America spread out around her, engulfing her in the night. Without a word, she hung up. His voice receded like a measuring tape back into its metal casing and she wished she could be sucked back with his voice across all of those lines to him.

She drove back to the tent, slipped into the sleeping bags James had zipped together. He pulled her close against his chest and though her back touched his stomach she felt utterly alone and afraid and guilty because everything was wrong and this was not where she was supposed to be.

"I love you," she whispered, and she thought of Città: In the evenings the streets and the central piazza, Garibaldi, were alive with people out for an aperitif, greeting friends, carrying their packaged pastries neatly tied in paper with bows. They had been doing so for hundreds of years, perhaps thousands. After all, what was a forum? Stepping out among those people, it was as if she had been there all along as well.

She thought of Città: the Cellini bank advertised all over town, the Cellini name shouting from the streets, from the papers, from buildings and buses and bus stops. CELLINI. Betta Cellini. Bet Cellini. Betti Cellini. Never Beth. Signora of Città, Signora of Fiori. She could take Elena's place, become a Cellini wife, caretaker of the Cellini line, mother of more Cellini sons and daughters. Never Beth. Beth would become a thing of her past, a memory of her youth. That simple.

She was twenty-three years old. Beth had her own dreams, too.

She called Cesare from Gary, Indiana, and Peoria, Illinois. "America's so ugly," she said, staring at a sky filled with smokestacks and fuel tanks, the air thick with their smells. She knew he liked it when she found America ugly, as if this journey were an indulgence, a quest to get the country out of her system. She pictured the lakes of northern Italy with the Alps seeming to rise out of them, the small winding roads, clusters of stucco houses gripping the tops of small hills like colonies of barnacles and just as white. And the triumphant bell towers looming above it all. Hundreds of years in the same town, of course they loved their bell tower.

She called Cesare from Lake of the Ozarks and the rolling green of the Flint Hills; she was amazed as the country became beautiful and amazed because she had always believed that Kansas would be flat. The country didn't become flat, it seemed, until they got to Colorado. Flat like water just before a wave, shrinking, receding to nothing so that the wave could grow. And just like the wave, the Rockies rose into sight, cresting majestically, snowcapped (like foam) up there with the clouds. "It's so big," she said to James, loving him in the instant and the wonder. The wind raced through the open window, and James, enthusiasm lighting his blond smile, his voice ascending to beat the wind, explained to her how the Rockies came to be. His explanations of plate tectonics and erosion, of ancient oceans and sheets of ice made sense while he was talking, but Beth soon lost track as she imagined a tropical world of figs then covered over by ice, smothering the mountains, some many millions of years ago. "A nanosecond in the past, a blink of the eye," James said. He blinked then, his eyes hard on the road and then on her. As he began to describe the slow exhumation of the Rockies, the continent being flapped out like a sheet in a breeze to dry, the seas pouring off the surface to the Gulf of Mexico, Beth began to sing. "God bless America," she sang. Fields of lavender rolled by and she liked being on the road, the steady rhythm, the anticipation of what would be next.

"This land is your land, this land is my land," James responded, singing Woody Guthrie's answer to Irving Berlin.

Beth laughed but kept singing her song, though she only knew a few more of the words. "He wrote it in 1918 for a burlesque show but discarded it because it didn't have enough humor. In 1938 he rewrote it so that Kate Smith could sing it on Armistice Day to mark the twentieth anniversary of the war's end. He immigrated here from Siberia when he was five years old," she said.

"You like trivia," James said. "But not geology."

"A fat American man in Spain taught me that piece of trivia. For some reason I haven't forgotten it." She imagined their future. With James it could be anywhere, something designed together. James was generous, easy to be with and he loved her. He liked that she liked to cook. He liked for her to teach him food tricks, ways to cook garlic, which pasta to use for which sauce (he hadn't known it mattered). He liked to watch her concoct gourmet meals on a campfire—odd dishes from Iran and India learned during her strange childhood at Claire. The wind caught in his blond hair, mixing it all up.

At a state park James pulled over. "Where are we going?" Beth asked. He walked ahead of her, tall and slender, enthusiasm in his stride. He walked up a trail and then off the trail into the woods and tentatively she followed him, wondering where he was taking her. Beneath a big pine, needles on the ground, James told her to take off her clothes and she did. He told her to lie down and she did. She could hear other hikers, a child laughing, the sounds of the woods, some birds, some bugs. Rays of sun streaked through the canopy. She could hear a father shout. James let her lie there, naked, for a while, all anticipation. Her heart raced. She wanted him. He touched her gently, a seduction, her skin feeling the air, her body becoming thirsty. Cesare shot across her mind. She imagined him watching her here. Then she banished him. James continued to touch her until she was asking for him to touch her more. Then he stopped touching her. She needed him to touch her. It was essential that he touch her. "Please," her hips were rising, "please." He wanted her to plead. She would do anything. Please. He touched her. He kissed her. Please. He sank into her, right there for anyone to see. She could hear the child and the father as they unwittingly hiked by, hear them stopping for a rest. She wanted to shout. "This is going to take a long time," James whispered, cooing into her ear. She bit his shoulder, bit his cheek, he was pushing her head back. His hands were all over her, working her, and her skin was cold and hot and she wanted the father to walk off the trail and see her here and then she wanted Cesare to appear and watch, too. Leaves pressed into her back, twigs, a pebble. She arched to meet him and kept reaching until it seemed her body met the sky. Then she was thinking of nothing.

In Italian it was called *andare in camporella* or "fucking in the fields of the woods." Later, she told James this. One of the things she knew that James loved most about her was her air of being Italian. He would list the attributes that contributed to her aura: she spoke the language fluently (the day he met her she was reading Elsa Morante in Italian and he had let her know that he was impressed); she wore her clothes with some extra flair, even down to the dark liner around her wide blue eyes; she ate her salad after her meal; she cooked that meal with the ease and simplicity of a native. With James she felt exotic, rare, imbued with all the mystery of the other.

Then the conversations with Cesare started to change. "Tell me about him," Cesare said.

"Him?" Beth repeated.

"Him," he said. "I know who you're with." She had told Cesare she was traveling with a group of friends from college. On occasion she made up elaborate stories about their adventures, entertaining him with lies, of getting lost in the world's largest corn palace. It was true, somewhere in the Dakotas there was an entire palace made from cornhusks. (*"L'America,"* Cesare had said, just like that, capturing simply in the way he said the word the wonderful ridiculousness of a palace of cornhusks, the brash spirit of the country. He had loved, in particular, the super-markets with their wide aisles, their endless choice. Walking through the A & P, aisles upon aisles presented choice upon choice. In aisle five, to be exact, with, let's see, canned goods, SpaghettiOs, and baking needs, he declared, "I want to live here for the rest of my life.") But it was James she had lost in the corn palace and for an instant she had worried she would never see him again, that he had left her there because he knew where her mind was.

Lies encouraged more lies until she spun a fine filigree of untruths around her. "Tell me about this one," Cesare demanded. "Jason, Jeremiah, whatever his name is. Jack. Jerk-off." She could imagine Cesare in the living room of his parent's home, in the big velvet chair with all the lights off, sitting in the dark with a beer beneath the fresco of Valeria, waiting to be hurt like a patient waiting for surgery, begging for a wound to be cauter-ized so that everything could be that much easier.

"What about the hat lady?" she said. Then, "Your mother says you've always had girls."

"Come to Italy," he said.

"I can't," she said. But just then some truth that had been there all along acknowledged itself to her. She could go to Italy. She could, of course, why not? What held her back? She felt a little desperate inside, anxious, as if she would run there, fly there herself. Betta Cellini, heir to the Cellini line.

"Try," he challenged.

"You try," she said, getting mean. Once he had tried America, but was only able to imagine himself as a gas station attendant, pumping gas like so many other immigrants that he saw. "I wasn't trained to be ambitious," he had said. "Try," she had demanded. *Try.* It seemed so sensible, so easy—little word that it is. If he loved her, he'd do it for her.

"What's his name?" Cesare asked.

"Not this one," she wanted to say. Sometimes she would tell him about flirtations. Small details, enough to make him curious. It was a game they played designed to conjure jealousy or hurt, and ultimately hope—the hope that the other would come and put an end to all flirtations. She wasn't sure why she wanted to protect James, wished somewhere that she did love him so that everything could be that much easier. "You know who I'm with," she said. "We've just been to Mount Rushmore."

"Washington, Jefferson, Roosevelt—Theodore, that is— and Lincoln."

"Bravo," she said. "The wind was strong. We were almost blown away, clear to Kansas."

She met James in Washington Square on a brilliant spring day. He was juggling four oranges. He admired her as she walked by, tossed her an orange and told her to eat it, which she did. She liked the command. The juice dribbled down her chin, the sweetest she had ever tasted. He watched her carefully. The attention of his eyes released an entire box of butterflies in her chest. And for an instant and for the first time, she thought she could see beyond Cesare. Not a cloud in the sky. "Severe clear," James had remarked. "That's how pilots describe skies like this." The clarity made her laugh. He told her he liked her smile. He began leaving poems for her, tucked between the bell and the handlebar of her bicycle. ("I ride my bicycle," Cesare wrote to her, "all over Città, just like an American boy.") In the beginning, Beth intended James as nothing serious, just another flirtation.

"Him," Cesare said. "The *ragazzo,* tell me about him." Something mean and bitter infected Cesare's tone, as if there were a switch in him, too.

She remembered the first time they said good-bye, after a year of being together. They had been at the departures gate at the Zurich airport—sobbing, faces ugly with it, red and grotesque as if this were some sort of death. She had been nineteen years old. Shortly after she had returned home from the Zurich good-bye, four years before her trip west, just as she began her freshman year at NYU, he called her to say that he had learned that couples could marry through the mail. He made elaborate plans for their wedding, drew funny pictures of her crazy family—her father, her grandmother, and all the many people from the commune in all the funny clothes he imagined they might wear—alongside his small and formal family: tall mother, short father, sister with fuzzy blond hair.

She could hear the pull, the swallow as he drank his beer sitting in the dark. The receiver pressed hard against her cheek, becoming her cheek. On a street corner, in a filling station, on that road.

Sometimes they spoke of the ordinary: of his work, his friends; of his mother's plans for his cousin's wedding; of Fiori; of Valeria and Benvenuto and the azaleas and rhododendrons, flowering perpetually; of his evenings in the piazza; of what she wanted to do with her life; of her desire to be a chef and own restaurants; of how she wanted to turn a little chocolate cake into a massive wedding cake for a woman from Claire who was marrying there. Beth had been born to dream. Her mother was killed on a small Turkish road, dreaming with Beth's father about what their lives would be and mean. He had told this story to Beth countless times. His story of Claire's death (and the moments before it) became Beth's memory of her mother. It was one of his ways, she would later understand, of keeping the three of them, their family, alive. "I feel like dreaming," her mother would often say. "Let's hear them," Beth's father would answer. "What were they?" Beth would always ask even though she knew how he would answer. Claire dreamed of an apple orchard commune in Pennsylvania where anyone could live as long as they contributed, where parents could help with each other's children and no one person had to carry too big a burden. They had seen the property; when they returned from Turkey they had planned to buy it. Claire was twenty-five years old when she died, two years older than Beth was now. Beth could come up with thousands of dreams for her life with Cesare, but in the end he could only come up with one.

"Tell me about her," Beth asked, eyes stinging, looking down that road, a road made longer by more road and mirage. The game didn't work that way. This was a rule of her own making. She did not want to know the details of his flirtations. Road. She had never seen the rest of America. She grew up on the apple farm and then went to New York City for part of high school and for college. Her father never left Claire—a strange fidelity to his dead wife. Beth's maternal grandmother, a New Yorker with her own dreams, had wanted to save Beth from the apple farm and her father and had sent her off to Italy on a summer exchange with an Italian girl, Beatrice Nuova (nicknamed Bea), when Beth was sixteen. Beth had gone every summer since, had lived in Italy for two years. Beth had seen far more of Italy than of America. She had been to Sicily in every season, seen it green as emeralds in the spring. She had seen the lava of Mount Etna ooze a brilliant red, Day-Glo in the night, burning through the snow. James wanted to give Beth America, to show her all the beauty.

"You're the only her, Bet."

"I want to be the only her," she said softly. Then, pleading, "Come."

"I love you," he said to Beth as she stood in all those phone booths, semitrailers thundering past, blowing her this way and that. He was just in front of her, within her grasp. He was kissing her for the first time. Her top lip, then her bottom—softly, softly. His hands were on her ribs, as light as silk. His hands pushed back her hair—white oleander, grilled octopus, rosemary, and the Aegean Sea.

"Do you love me still?" he asked.

"Tell me about *her*," Beth demanded.

"I love you," he said. "I don't love her." Little shocks pricked through her, stabbing her here and everywhere.

"Her?" Beth asked. Of course, she knew there was a her, but she didn't want him to acknowledge the *her* just as he didn't want her to acknowledge the *him* out there on the road. It was hot inside the phone booth with the door closed. She didn't want James to hear. James was outside pacing back and forth, waiting for her to finish her call home. They were in the parking lot of Old Faithful in Yellowstone, some five thousand miles away from Cesare, five thousand miles away from the *her* who was buzzing around him like a bee, a fly. Beth wanted to swat that fly. The parking lot thickened with cars and tourists carrying their cameras, enthusiastic children racing across the sun-softened asphalt to watch the geyser erupt. *"Ti amo,"* he said again. "Let's not ruin anything. Let's be wise," he said. Goodbye. *Addio*—to God we go.

James pressed his face to the glass of the phone booth, peering inside, his hand making a visor above his eyes to block out the sun. He made a goofy, playful face that made him look ridiculous. She turned away. She didn't want him to see that she was crying. Two small children fought over a rag doll, each pulling at a leg. James knocked on the door. She wanted to tell Cesare everything. She wanted to be lying with him in the grass, smelling the mushrooms after the rains at Fiori. *Andare in camporella,* his lips beginning at her toes. She saw his family, nice ordinary family: mother, father, son, daughter—the family of his intricate drawing so many years before, their faces perplexed and funny as they greeted her family. She had wanted to be part of his family, as if it could make her ordinary. She wanted to be sitting next to him at the piano as he made up ridiculous lyrics to accompany a Mozart sonata, entertaining an entire party with the lark.

"Can you call your father back?" James pantomimed with his hands, an elaborate dance that she found somewhat endearing though she wanted to tell him that he was a fool for not seeing how desperately she loved someone else. She wanted to be brave (a different kind of brave) and get on the plane and fly to Italy and have this all be over with. "Call him back," James persisted, hopping on one foot, throwing her smiles, jutting his hands to the sky to mime an eruption. He did a lot of wrist tapping to indicate the time and then he swept his arm around the parking lot and then he crossed his arms to indicate they'd be waiting in this god-awful spot for another ninety minutes if she didn't hurry up. He would have been adorable if she hadn't been in love with someone else. Instead she wondered why he cared so much about a geyser? There was so much she wanted to say. She wanted to save her future. The two small children tugging on the doll managed to rip its legs off. And now the little boy was crying. The little girl held a severed limb in her hand triumphantly. "Let's be grown-up about this," Cesare was saying. He was speaking wisdom though it seemed he was speaking in tongues. She lashed out. She did not want to hear this talk; this talk was all wrong.

"Bet, be reasonable," Cesare said.

"Non posso," she whispered. "Her."

"How do we fix this?"

"Come."

"Bet," he said. Bet. Bet. It echoed throughout the hot blue day. The way he said her name. I can't, it said. You know I can't, it said. Understand, it said. "Greta," he said. Said the name with tenderness and warmth and as an explanation.

"Greta?" Beth said, the girl becoming real, taking on a form, a shape pressing into his shape. This was all wrong. Get rid of Greta, she wanted to say. Change the *a* and the *t* and you've got *great.* "Great," Beth said, as if Cesare would understand. Once he would have understood everything in her mind. Blame, wicked poisonous blame. It was Greta's fault. Tears pricked her eyes, burned down her cheeks. "I don't want to hear anything about Greta," Beth said. "Greta is irrelevant."

Then there was a silence, a long silence. Later, much later, for the rest of her life, she would think about this instant. Should she have allowed him to speak about Greta? Should she have spoken about James? Would the truth have been their ally? Outside, sweltering. The parking lot of Old Faithful. A gorgeous blue day. A geyser about to erupt. James impatient at the phone booth door. She a twenty-three-year-old college graduate in cut-off shorts that James had hemmed for her himself somewhere in the Rockies. Her hair in braids. Poindexter and Ollie North and Caspar Weinberger acting like cowboys, taking the law into their own hands. The stock market advancing crazily, stirring up a frenzy. Cesare sitting in his chair across from a stupendous fresco painted on a whim by a wild young man. Beth was waiting for him to say something that would resolve all this, waiting for him to make them whole again. She waited. She waited. She would be waiting there still. He could hear her tears, feel them on her cheeks. He could feel her fracturing, shattering like glass into a thousand different pieces. He knew everything about her. He loved her madly and inexplicably. Greta was nothing, an interference. He would love Beth for the rest of his life.

Then, "Tell me about him," Cesare said, bitter now—cool and distant, watching her not from a perspective of love. "How does he fuck you?"

"What?" she said. She was not sure she had heard him correctly.

"Does he come in your mouth?" he asked, dead serious, a solemnity to his tone, as if in that moment of silence he had truly transformed: her lover no more—a stranger. He was playing some sort of game. She began to shiver. It was ninety-eight degrees outside, hotter inside the booth.

"I don't want to play this game," she said.

"What does your face look like," he asked.

"I'll become Italian," she said. He laughed, almost sarcastically. "I'm coming to Italy," she said.

"Beth," James said, opening the door to the booth wide, seeing now her red face smeared with tears and drool. She tried to gulp back the tears. He pronounced the name well with his strong American accent. James was a Midwesterner who wore clogs and jeans. He had fine, almost delicate features, long fingers and big hands and a shock of thick blond hair. When they were in Kansas he wouldn't wear his clogs, afraid that people would get the wrong idea about him and give him trouble. He was aware of how far he could push. "Love, what's wrong," he whispered gently, concern spreading over his face like a stain. Looking at him, she saw hope dissipate. She knew James knew now where she was and had been.

"He's with you?" Cesare said. Then, as if it meant nothing, "The details," he said flatly. "I want to know what it feels like when he touches you." The truth now fueled and encouraged his change, made him more confident in his hatred of her. He hated her now not because she had betrayed him but because she represented defeat—the defeat of one part of himself by another: kind and cruel, ambitious and passive, willful and will-less.

No good way to end love, is there?

She covered the receiver and began lying to James, the filigree lies, so finely spun.

"Does he make you scream, do you beg?" Cesare asked. James stood in the doorway. The sun shone strong behind him, causing him to appear faceless. He put his hand on her head softly, gently. He loved her. She wanted to talk to him, to hang up the phone and explain it all, to have him excise all the hurt with his gentleness. Protect him, love him. He was a warm, good man. He would understand.

"He does," she said slowly, calmly. Cesare listened. James shut the door. She wanted to tell Cesare she was torturing James. She wanted him to help her figure out why, to dissolve the lie. "In the car," she said. Figure out that she wasn't such a mean, bad person, that she was still good and loveable—the sweet blond American Cesare had fallen in love with. "In the woods. I beg him. I take my clothes off for him and lie there so that anyone can see me and I wait for him." She watched James walk toward the geyser, shoulders slumped, in resignation, not defeat. He was a confident boy.

"What do you do when he touches you? What does your body do?" And she explained in explicit detail, describing the scene in Colorado when the father and child hiked by, describing the arching ache of her body rising to meet James. She was not injured, but her body felt pain just now, as if she were being cut, stabbed. She bled. She gave elaborate details, until she begged him to stop, but he wanted more. "He humiliates me," she said. "Is that what you want to hear?" She didn't mind now that he knew she was crying. What more could she say? Then, softly, "I'll come to Italy," she said. "Please let me come," she said.

"Putana," he said. Whore.

"I love you," she said. Her nose twitched. Her eyes twitched. A girl in a phone booth with braids.

"A lie?" Cesare said, as if that were the key, the justification.

"No," she said. "Her," she said quietly. "You knew he was here." There was another long silence. The booth was hot now, suddenly it seemed. A fly landed on her hand and stayed there patiently. The day was hazy with the heat; her foot could leave a print in the asphalt. The fly took off, finding the way outside through a crack in the door. Her mother flashed across her mind. Her mother's young smiling face, black hair windswept, was replaced by Cesare's, and then both were gone. Cesare was Beth's salvation. The booth was hot. Old Faithful began to erupt, hissing and steaming and spraying. She wanted to grab those faces back. Tourists not near enough yet began to run. The parking lot cleared, like water swirling into the vortex of a drain. The whole world empty. Do you want me to be a whore? she wanted to ask. I'll be a whore, she wanted to say. Italy vanished before her—swept into her past.

"Is this what you want, to hate me now?" she said, but even as she said it she knew he loved her still. She thought she could hear him crying, see him in the velvet armchair stifling tears, see him sitting there across from the brilliant fresco that seemed to spell their story, that had spelled it to them all along, as it had spelled the stories of lovers everywhere in their struggle against time. She saw the beautiful young man rising toward the cloud, the girl reaching in anguish, with determination, as if she could pull him back. Beth was in the middle of America. All around her were cars, a sea of cars leading to dozens upon dozens of places. Jets streaked across the sky. She saw his parents trying to stop the corrosive bite of time so that that party could carry indelibly on.

Three

Two Girls in Europe

Love is a victory over time. Love steals from death. The illusion of immortality for an instant blooms, a beautiful flower, and everything that is here is here and all that is, truly is. Beth went back to her story; for a long time she went back, held it like an object to the light, told it to friends. She would live it, dream it, breathe it. She would return to it again and again. She had heard that criminals return to crime scenes in order to gaze upon their deed, to make certain that it had occurred, to make it vivid, real, alive—to own it. She would return just as Valeria had returned simply by gazing at the fresco, as Valeria's family was able to return for twenty generations—return and relive and recall and remember—that instant frozen, stopped. Love is a victory over time.

When Beth returned, it was the beginning she liked to dwell on most, the clear dance with Fate, Fate's hand coming down, pushing her this way and that. The word *fate* is related to the words *fame, fairy, nefarious,* and *preface.* In common is the root *fari.* It means "to speak." Pause on *fairy:* enchantment, magic, illusion: *fata,* one of the Fates. *See* Fata Morgana, a fairy celebrated in medieval tales of chivalry. In Arthurian legend Morgan Le Fay is the half sister of Arthur, the wife of Uriens, King of Gore, and is a great necromancer. She tries to procure the death of her brother and attempts to slay her sleeping husband. She is evil; she personifies fortune living in the bottom of a lake in the *Orlando Innamorato* of Boiardo. She is a mirage, one seen especially (and frequently) at the Strait of Messina, between Calabria and Sicily. She is enchantment, magic, illusion. She is Clotho spinning her thread; she is Lachesis determining the direction and the length of our respective lots; she is Atropos inflexibly cutting off that lot; she is the Weird Sisters of Norse myth. Think divine foreordination. Think that which is destined or decreed. Think final outcome, end, ruin, disaster, doom, death, as in "to bemoan a friend's fate," as in "the fated day" or "the fated sky" or "the fateful cawings of the crow." Think, fairy: enchantment, magic, illusion. Think fortune lying at the bottom of a lake, shimmering dreams on a body of water, illusions in rose and lavender skipping upon the slight waves. For how long have we been searching for a pattern, a meaning, an interpretation, a reason—reason?

Beth was no different: she was a girl, a woman, who wanted to know why. She was as susceptible as the rest of us to the what-ifs, to the romantic notions of something personal having implications larger than the personal, some divine pattern or at least purpose. It was there within her, this story, her myth; its power receded with time, but the questions persisted like wonderful rare butterflies we are eager to capture and preserve. Did he love her? Does he love her still? Will he love her always? What is the relationship between Fate and Chance, does the one differ from the other? Is love simply, as Dante said, an accident? If, instead, Fate does exist, for what purpose did it lead her there?

Who among us doesn't have a story that she loves to repeat simply because it brings back something—life?

————

There. Summer of 1982. Hot. Beth is in Europe with her friend Sylvia Summerhaze, who has never been to Europe before. Sylvia is a country girl from Snyder County, Pennsylvania, and has been Beth's friend since the second grade. Even after Beth moved to New York they stayed friends, seeing each other whenever Beth visited her father, spending extravagant weekends in New York together with Beth's grandmother. Beth is the leader. (Secretly she loves the role of the sophisticated guide. She has been to Italy two times so far. Some small part of her thinks of herself as Italian. She speaks the language fluently and thinks she has more style than she actually does.) They are traveling around on EurailPasses for two months, at the end of which Sylvia will return home to college and Beth will go to Italy to live with Beatrice Nuova and her family in the northern Italian town of Città. Beth is taking a year off before college funded by her grandmother and from money Beth earned as a waitress in Manhattan's West Village. Now the two girls are in Spain. Spain is sponsoring the World Cup. Italy will win for the first time in forty-four years, beating West Germany and making of Paolo Rossi a big star on the world stage—star striker. Beth and Sylvia have just graduated from high school. Reagan is president. John Hinckley Jr. is on trial for attempting to murder him. In March, John Belushi died of an overdose. Israel has just invaded Lebanon, stirring up the Middle East. But Europe, for the summer anyway, belongs to Beth and Sylvia. They are eighteen years old, giddy with possibility, traveling with their backpacks, their Indian print skirts and Jesus sandals, a little bit of money in their money belts, and a guidebook entitled *Europe on $5 a Day*. The dollar is strong—a very important detail for two American girls in Europe.

The story begins really (the beginning of *there,* that is) in San Sebastián, where the Golfe de Gascogne meets the Bay of

Biscay in that gentle curve of land as Europe turns west from France to Spain, reaching toward America. The mouth of the Urumea River opens into the particularly protected Shell Bay, and rising through gardens and promenades, tamarinds and railings, are Mount Urgull and Mount Igueldo with views of the sea and the islet of Santa Clara that floats just offshore. Beth had remembered reading in a novel about San Sebastián, a popular seaside resort for the royal and the rich, known for its balconies and its food. She didn't remember which novel—she believed it was something by Hemingway—but she wanted to visit the town simply because she had read about it.

She wanted to hitchhike from Deva to Bilbao, visit Bolívar and Guernica and also the birthplace of Saint Ignacio, founder of the Jesuits. She wanted to be in the heart of Basque country, land of Euskera, a language with unknown origins. Of the two of them, Beth was the dreamer. She was driven by romantic notions and whims, a desire to make the impossible happen. Sylvia was the pensive one and the planner, infinitely practical. She read the guidebooks. She had notepads and pencils, knew how to spot gypsies (cute little kids with dirty faces and dirty clothes who'd take you for everything you had with a piece of cardboard as their tool), knew how to read the train schedules and find hotels cheaper than youth hostels. Beth loved exploding Sylvia's plans and Sylvia loved Beth for doing so. In Innsbruck at the train station, way past midnight and everything closed, it was Beth who met Hans, a nice man with gentle eyes and a gentle face and a slight stutter who offered them his grandmother's bed for the night because she was out of town for the season. "He might be a murderer," Sylvia said. "Oh, come on," Beth said impatiently, looking her in the eye and then looking around the sad, quiet train station. "Would you rather sleep here or in a bed?" It was a big warm bed with a huge soft goose down comforter. He fed them soft-boiled eggs at 4 A.M., using his grandmother's silver spoons. Then he let them sleep well into the afternoon.

"How did you know he wouldn't murder us?" Sylvia asked, curling up to Beth in the grandmother's bed. The bed and the room smelled like rose petals and old age. "He still could," Beth said, and fell asleep.

The next day she said, "Season! Murderers don't have grandmothers who go away for the season."

From Austria to Paris to Nice to San Sebastián they zig-zagged their way, the itinerary designed by their whims. In Nice they met Chas, an American who serenaded them from the street beneath the tiny balcony of their tiny pension, singing Cat Stevens songs.

"It's him, it's him," Sylvia said, lighting up. She had a large smile that opened her entire face.

"Who?" Beth asked. They were having a midnight snack of *pain au chocolat* and white wine that tasted a little like whiskey. They could buy all the wine they liked and no one ever said a thing. They could sleep late and no one ever said a thing. They could eat chocolate for dinner, lunch, and breakfast, and no one said a thing.

"The cute man from the single down the hall." Sylvia leaned over the balcony and smiled down to him on the street, his songs rising up to them as if the three of them were the only people in the world. From the balcony the girls could glimpse the silver Mediterranean seeming to hold the moon. Beth thought he was singing to both of them, but learned, when he changed his easy plans to come with them to San Sebastián and climb 425 feet up the famous Mount Urgull (presided over solemnly by the imposing statue of the Sacred Heart) that Chas was serenading Sylvia alone—beautiful Sylvia Summerhaze, with her long auburn hair and her sea green eyes (set just a fraction too close together).

Sylvia was Beth's best friend and Beth was jealous, the way a lover might be. Freshman year in high school they had once contemplated sharing a boyfriend simply so they could experience everything together. The boy was Jacob, a blond drummer in a band called Random Joe. Random Joe played a lot of the Police, and Jacob sort of looked like that band's drummer, Stewart Copeland—tall and lanky with dusty blond hair that framed a long angular face with lips as red as lipstick. "He has a strong jaw," Sylvia liked to say. And she kissed him and shortly thereafter Beth kissed him and, lying in bed at Beth's farm, the girls compared notes. Sometimes what Beth wanted most was simply to kiss Sylvia, one of those unspoken ideas that even she herself did not fully comprehend. Jacob sang "Walking on the Moon." He sang it often for Beth and Sylvia. He said he loved Sylvia for her mind and Beth for her body. For a while Beth liked the idea of being liked for her body. She had confidence in her mind.

On Mount Urgull, Beth was admiring the view, her face turned away from Chas and Sylvia, feeling quite light with independence and with the excitement of Chas's company. Chas was four years older than the girls. He had just graduated from Harvard and was working his way around the world before getting serious with a job. He spoke of trekking in Nepal, riding elephants in India, teaching English in Taiwan. He was a good boy, a gentleman in the making, but a type all the same, with his guitar and easy manner. The kind you see traveling the world, privileged and rich, trying on poverty for a year or two before settling down to earn millions in some banking job or other, this excursion a reminder for the rest of his life of what he had seen of the world and of what he didn't want, though he would never admit it. This type, he spoke of eating dog in China just as enthusiastically as he spoke of camel treks, eager to let people know he really had been adventurous—once upon a time, long ago. Back then he had slept on thin mattresses with bedbugs and cockroaches, slept in huts on dirt floors, lived without water for a week, contracted giardia and hepatitis. Oh, but the Taj Mahal was stunning, shining in the heat of Uttar Pradesh with all those cute poor children begging for bonbons and school pencils. Through the young eyes of Beth and Sylvia, Chas was simply an adventurer, all bravado and fearlessness, traveling in the footsteps of the great explorers who came before him, from Marco Polo to Vespucci to Kerouac. And the girls loved that about Chas, that stories and ideas spilled from him— exotic expectations, a desire to experience everything and all. The world was his and the girls found that seductive; at night, curled up together in their bed, they would dream of their own adventures, of taking a world tour, of being brave enough to head to Africa.

But up there on Mount Urgull, determined Chas took Beth's turned back as a chance to sneak up behind Sylvia and kiss her. (Later, Sylvia would tell Beth that she had not been surprised by the kiss, that indeed she had been hoping for it and would have kissed him herself if he hadn't first. "The desire," she said, "had been visible." "Desire?" Beth asked, wanting to laugh. What did they really know about desire?) And just as their lips met, Beth turned toward them. Then, before they could see her seeing them, she turned away.

The kiss hit her like a slap. A rush of envy and fury pushed against her chest, caught at her throat. She saw Chas stealing Sylvia from her. That was the only picture she could see. Suddenly she hated Chas, understood him (just as suddenly) not as an exotic adventurer but as a fraud, a thief taking Sylvia for his own, seducing her with his guitar because she was an easy sweet girl. He would carry her along until grabbed by some other whim. The picture was there, developed in that quick glimpse of Sylvia's head leaning back, her lips reaching up to his. Beth saw them skipping across the world, from elephants to tall mountains to little Chinese men eager to learn English. His lips so gently on Sylvia's, his hands so lightly on her back, as soft as the light summer breeze, which caused her long auburn hair to dance. Their embrace was gentle, it was loving, it was romantic. Beth could feel it as if Chas had been kissing her. She wished Chas had been kissing her.

For a long time Beth would think about this moment. She would think about it once she met Cesare in Greece and everything and everyone became easily dispensable, sacrificial even, and nothing mattered but more of Cesare. She was struck by the uncontrollable will of love, the awesome force of it, which created indifference and undeniable selfishness in regard to others, yet exquisite selflessness in regard to the other, the lover. She and Cesare would be together in Greece for just four days, on the Aeolian island of Páros. They would meet on that first morning as Cesare spoke ancient Greek to the landlady of his pension and as the sun lit his black hair, turning it almost blue. Have you ever been watching a movie when the film burned? It starts as a small hole and then grows. As it grows, it devours the image, takes over the entire screen, blotting out the picture with white light until the film snaps. Do you remember how quick it is, how all encompassing, nothing matters but that hole, the increasing size of it, the triumph of it?

Beth gave Sylvia the silent treatment as they drifted back to the hotel, Sylvia all but oblivious as she floated along at Chas's side, believing they held a secret from Beth, a secret that made the intensity of their desire all the more powerful. Walking ahead, Beth hated both of them. She was fury itself—irrational fury, she realized—threatened, afraid, as if somewhere she did believe that Sylvia would abandon her, leave her there in Spain by herself.

"But what's wrong, Beth?" Sylvia asked once they were back in their room and a good ten minutes had passed without a word from Beth. Sylvia danced around trying on dresses. She wanted to tell Beth about the kiss, but was afraid. She had only a vague understanding of that fear; she simply understood that it would be better if she didn't mention kissing Chas. All that was on her mind was seeing Chas again, kissing Chas again. She had even liked the smell of his breath. It was as if she were still inside that kiss, a bubble surrounding just the two of them. She imagined she could sneak out for a midnight walk once Beth was asleep. Seeing him again was an urgent need. She wanted to be free of Beth. She wanted to know everything about Chas, to reexperience that wonderful jetting sensation.

"What's wrong?" Beth snapped, mocking Sylvia's question. Sylvia looked at Beth, holding her with her eyes to make sure. Beth's face revealed everything, though she tried to pretend it did not.

"It doesn't mean anything," Sylvia said.

"What doesn't mean anything?" Beth persisted. She wanted to be cruel, wanted to make Sylvia tell her everything, admit to the kiss as if there were something fatally wrong in it.

"You know what I'm talking about," Sylvia said.

"I do?" They studied each other for a long time and then Beth conceded. "He's a fake," she said.

"Are you going to try to convince me he's awful when just a few hours ago you adored him, too?" Rarely did Beth see Sylvia mad. Then Beth decided she wanted to see Sylvia really mad. Beth wanted to be mighty and evil and say wicked things.

"He'll eat dog in China, get an awful disease in India, come home and brag about it for the rest of his life and think he's somehow more enlightened for it. And meanwhile he'll dump you when something better comes along." She'd heard her father talk about this sort of fake. She knew the mantra.

"This is more than one kiss deserves."

"I'm leaving," Beth said. "I'll go to Italy," she said, wanting to make Sylvia feel the way she felt now—choked, abandoned. She knew she was being irrational, but she couldn't stop herself. She was prone to slamming doors and bursting into flames. A temper, her grandmother called it. "To Beatrice and we'll—"

"And you'll what?" Sylvia said, her green eyes turning angry even though she knew Beth was bluffing, that Beatrice was in Italy studying for her final exams. But the truth didn't matter. The mention of Bea's name now was enough to get them fighting. Beatrice Nuova was Beth's other best friend and Beth had tried to make them a trio in the summers when Bea was in America. But it never quite worked. Beth always remained in the middle with Sylvia and Bea vying for a greater share of her. At Claire, Sylvia would lord her knowledge of the place over Bea, showing Bea where everything belonged, introducing her to the people, making knowing comments to Beth that Bea wouldn't understand. Then Bea would make a suggestion that actually, coming from her, was more like a command: "I would like to go to New York." She would say the words slowly in her accented English. Each word enunciated, each word saying to Sylvia: To Get Away From You. When Beth went to Italy, Sylvia was left behind, envious of her friend's experience, as if it were some sort of tryst that necessarily excluded her.

Sylvia and Beth fought hard now, as if fighting could release the grip. They fought about Sylvia's annoying plans and constant suspicions of everyone, all her gypsies. They fought

about all Beth's impractical schemes. They fought about anything and everything, including the shoes of Sylvia's that Beth
wore without asking. They fought until they started crying, and
then they lay down on the bed and sobbed. They were eighteen years old, overwhelmed by a new and inexplicable longing. Something grand was about to happen to them that they
didn't fully understand. For the first time in twelve years they
would be separated for more than a few months. They were on
the threshold of life and though they would never have been
able to articulate it in so many words, it was pushing forth of
its own accord—the understanding that they would fall in love
and grow up and their friendship as they had known it and
their lives as they had known them would be over.

"I'm jealous," Beth confessed.

"For once," Sylvia said teasingly, and then quietly, "I'm the
jealous one." They lay on the bed, side by side, Beth in her underwear and Sylvia in a pretty pink sundress with white eyelet
at the bodice, especially selected for Chas.

"You look beautiful," Beth said. The ceiling fan stirred the
hot air, cooling them slightly, but enough.

"We'll leave," Sylvia said, perking up, rising above Beth on
one arm. A late sun leaked through the slatted blinds, pushing
in the heat and the smell of paella. She was returning to herself. She liked drama. They both did; they needed drama, fed
off drama, created it for their fuel.

"We'll flee in the middle of the night," Sylvia continued.
"It'll be fun. Where would you like to go? Africa? Portugal?"
Sylvia was a sweet girl. There was no friend she loved more than
Beth. She could banish her own dreams if her sacrifice would
make Beth happy. Countless times she visited Beth in New York
City, forgoing dances and parties at home simply so that she
could be with Beth. Indeed, she was in Europe with Beth now

instead of on a biking tour of Alaska with her senior class. She had been following Beth's lead since the second grade. A fact that alternately made Beth feel terrible and wonderful. Beth expressed her selflessness in other ways—ways that weren't always so visible and that she couldn't always enumerate but that had to do with her belief in Sylvia, in her ability to be more than a quiet girl from Pennsylvania.

"But you love him," Beth said (trying for that selflessness). And she did believe that Sylvia could be in love. It was possible, then, to fall in love in an instant. That's what love was to them, instantaneous and all encompassing. A shock. A stab. And infinitely important. They were reading *Anna Karenina*, Tolstoy introducing them to the consequences of illicit adult love. All across Europe they had been reading the book—Beth first, tearing out the pages as she finished and passing them to Sylvia, who tread close on her heels. "Don't cry, don't cry," Sylvia would say. "You're giving it away." And Beth would try not to cry.

"I'm not sure that I do love Chas," Sylvia said, with all the earnestness of her age. "I only just met him."

"Don't you want to find out?" But Beth knew what she wanted Sylvia to do. Beth willed it. Sylvia couldn't betray her. They were best friends. Sylvia Summerhaze, she was Beth's first love. Beth loved Sylvia's pale skin, like her name—that pale creamy haze that veils a summer's twilight. Sylvia loved Beth more than she loved her own sister. She had told Beth that emphatically. How important this had all seemed.

"We'll flee," Sylvia said, more urgently now. "I want to flee." She started stuffing her backpack with her clothing, and then so did Beth, infected, too, with the sense of urgency that fleeing commanded, as if their lives depended on it. They were fast and anxious in their flight. "If this is meant to be," Sylvia said, "we'll meet up with him again. Consider it a test of fate." Beth liked that notion, tempting the gods.

Just before dinner, the two girls fled, tiptoeing past Chas's room out into the street, running to the train station, hopping a train for Irún where all the big trains converge to take you north, south, east, west. In Irún they chose a train to Madrid; from there they could go to Portugal and maybe even Africa. They were giddy with fear, a fear that Chas would miraculously appear on the platform as they waited for the great southern express. At midnight they boarded the train. They loved that the town was called Irún. *I run, I run, I run.*

"It should be called Werún," Sylvia said.

"Are you sad?" Beth asked.

"Do I seem sad?" Sylvia smiled. The two girls stood there inside the train, the atmosphere thick with that drama pounding heavily in their chests.

They looked out the window, saying good-bye to Irún, as the metal wheels began turning over the metal tracks. Sylvia's name suddenly rang through the night, rising over the bustle of all the many travelers escaping Irún. Her name floated through the darkness and the smoky light of the station's lanterns. "It's Chas," Sylvia said brightly, as if she had hoped also for the drama of this, as if fate had indeed made its message clear. Chas's round, handsome face bobbed above all the other faces. *Unbelievable,* Beth thought. *Pick up speed,* Beth urged the train, feeling astonished and a little manic, her body surging with the power of the train's gathering momentum.

"I'm sorry," Sylvia yelled back, throwing one hand out to him, gripping Beth hard with the other. The grip said, *Look, he did this for me.* The grip relished, enjoyed, devoured, the meaning of a man running for her alongside a train.

"Meet me in Corfu," he said. His eyes caught Beth's, telling her to promise to bring Sylvia to Corfu. Beth wanted to disappear. Had she had a hand in ruining something? she wondered. Could she be Atropos herself, in disguise. "August first," he added. "Promise?" beautiful word that it is.

"We'll be there," Sylvia said. She threw him a kiss.

"This is just the beginning," he said to her. To Beth he said, "Good-bye, Beth," catching her again with his smile, understanding everything but generous just the same. Where is he now, that boy? Chas. The night he serenaded them in Nice they let him come up to their room. He helped them finish off the cheap wine and they talked until dawn about their brief lives and his exotic plans. The four years that separated Chas from the girls and the sea of experience that is college didn't seem like a lot to them then. Traveling you are outside of time.

The girls told him about Beth's father's commune in Snyder County and about growing up there and all the odd folks from all over the world who had passed through at one point or another. "I could just stay there and see the world," Beth had said, and explained that that's what her father did, that he never left because according to him there was no need. Beth knew her father's attachment to Claire was deeper, more paralyzing, but she didn't speak about that.

"You could just go there," Sylvia suggested to Chas.

Indian scientists, Chinese doctors, herbalists from Africa, a scholar from New York, a French chef, an Italian fashion designer, a Spanish engineer—at one point or another every type passed through Claire. Claire was a colorful place with colorful notions of idealism, built on extravagant dreams and fantasies, and Sylvia (as observer) loved to describe it: all the apple trees and berries grown organically; the chaos; the pantry with its sheer abundance of food; Beth's father's penchant for allowing Revolutionary War aficionados to stage reenactments on the front lawn (cannons, muskets, and all); the vast games of foot-ball (tackle not touch) that they had been playing on the week-ends since the girls were small. Sylvia loved Beth's father, Jackson, too—ambitious dreamer, big round head suspended on his shoulders like a globe, sitting at his desk at Claire, writing to the government to tell them about the potential of hydrogen for fuel, disseminating information to schools and businesses around the world, hoping he would be heard. He always had time for Sylvia, even with all the business of the farm. He'd squat down so that he could look her in the eye to explain what it meant to drive a hydrogen-fueled car (an idea that her own father, who was suspicious of Beth's father and Claire, described as bunkum); he showed her clippings of a van that actually did use this technology (albeit a funny-looking van with hardly any room for passengers). Jackson taught her to throw a football, he taught her to build a fire, he taught her to pay attention to the sky, to lie in the grass and look up at it, so that she could learn to read it and know what kind of day it would be. Mostly, she loved the attention he paid her, as if her curiosity really did in-terest him. She envied Beth for how important her father must have made her feel.

But she didn't say all this to Chas. To Chas she simply described the funny romance of Claire, exaggerating details enough to make him laugh even if at Claire's expense as she al-ways did when describing it for strangers. Beth didn't take of-fense; she adored listening to her friend describe her world, appreciated the intimacy with which Sylvia knew Claire, her humor about it as if it were her world, too, as if they shared it like sisters. In contrast, Sylvia had one sister and a mother who stayed at home and a father who was a lawyer for the local uni-versity. Theirs was a life as foreign to Beth as another country but one that she loved to visit for the sheer reliability of it.

Sylvia's home was like Switzerland—everything functioning, well oiled, on time.

"And your mother?" Sylvia asked Chas, and perhaps that's when he fell in love—because her mind missed nothing. Her auburn hair fell across her left eye and she tilted her head, giving him all of her attention.

"She's dead," he said. He lit the two candles on the small balcony table. Sulfur sparked the air, then vanished. The flames reflected in their eyes.

"So is mine," Beth said matter-of-factly. There was no hole or pang of pain, just an instant of recognition, though Beth realized she had never known another person whose mother was dead.

"I'm sorry," Sylvia said. She was addressing Chas, but her sympathy extended to Beth. It had always been that way for Sylvia; she felt sorry for Beth because she knew what Beth didn't have. She saw it every time her mother hugged Beth, felt it viscerally. In some ways, it's what made Sylvia's love for Beth ferocious—as if she could give her just a little of what she was missing.

"No need," Chas said, and Beth knew his mother had been gone a long time, too. He played old country tunes, singing the girls to sleep. He blew out the candles and tucked them in and disappeared to his room just before dawn.

"Good-bye, Chas," Beth said to him as he ran alongside the train. She felt ugly and greedy, like a selfish two-year-old unwilling to share, but she was also content to have Sylvia again for her own. The train picked up speed.

Choice: one of the great mysteries of love. The Surrealist thinker, André Breton, was kept up at night contemplating the meaning of choice and love. Exclusive love is the result of choice, but isn't that choice the result of a series of coincidences? Might those coincidences have a meaning, obey a hidden logic? Breton well understood the moment when chance transforms the world into something rich and strange. Objective chance, he called it—that moment of recognition of the extraordinary in the ordinary, the moment when coincidence—Fate?—offers up the answer to a question that hasn't yet been asked; the moment when love finds its object and two lives are bound together forever.

The train south on that Spanish night is entwined with Fate—the great hand of Lachesis, sister of Clotho and Atropos, daughter of Themis—spinning human destiny. Her hand comes down and we are simply playthings, instruments in her delightful little game. Her hand came down and gently set Beth on a different course—for this is Beth's story. You can see it clearly in retrospect, there like an old roadmap to your life. Do you remember that moment, that time, when the world felt perfect and the future impossibly easy and there was only one inevitable direction?

Chas was a part of the past, behind them now, and it was dark and late and the girls were tired and suddenly aware that the train was crowded. Travelers lined the corridors and even the entrance wells near the bathrooms; many of them were as young as Beth and Sylvia, lugging backpacks, smoking, looking older than their age but tired like the children that they were. Beth, feeling guilty about Chas, tried to make Sylvia comfortable. "Are you sorry we left?" she kept asking, and Sylvia would smile her winning smile. The thing about Sylvia was that once she made a decision she didn't regret and she rarely held a grudge. Sylvia was already flipping through the guidebook, ready to start with her plans. But Beth knew that she had been bossy and demanding and she had forbidden her friend a chance. She got up and opened all the compartments to see if they were actually filled, which they were, overflowing with entire families—children, uncles, grandparents, many of them snoring. Walking down the narrow corridors as the train bumped along, she had to be careful not to step on sprawling limbs, fingers, and toes. So many travelers had made themselves comfortable just as if they were in the privacy of their own rooms, mouths agape. She didn't want people looking at her while she slept. She slid open another door, poked her head in, and saw a group of six nuns who were eating rice from tins and drinking water from metal cups, the cheap kind that leave a metallic taste on your tongue. They spoke quietly in some unfamiliar language that Beth imagined was Euskera. She studied them for a moment and they her, then she shut the door and turned back to Sylvia, who was squatting in the corridor. The car swayed, catching Beth off balance, and she stumbled against her friend.

"We can sleep here," Sylvia said. "An adventure." And she opened her eyes wide and invitingly. She began to unfold her sleeping bag and Beth helped her. "I'll keep watch," Beth said. One of the nuns slid open the door to her compartment and looked at the two girls. The old lady's mouth puckered and her lips trembled involuntarily. It seemed a long time passed, as if she (in her habit and her veil) were studying them, as if she herself might be Lachesis. Then indeed with her hand she beckoned the girls in.

The nuns welcomed the girls into their compartment. They helped them stow their backpacks on the racks overhead; they made space for the girls to sit; they fed the girls rice and water, murmuring to one another in their unfamiliar tongue. One of them opened the window a crack for air, letting in as well the whistle and cries of the train. Cradled against the soft laps of the nuns, the girls fell asleep, rocked gently as the train hummed and swayed through the moonless night.

In the morning the nuns were gone. Sylvia was stretched out on one side of the compartment and Beth on the other, all the seats to themselves, their sweaters wrapped neatly around their shoulders.

"Was that a dream?" Sylvia asked. The only sounds belonged to the rhythms of the train.

"Where were we yesterday?" Beth said. Light pushed around the edges of the curtains. Sylvia pulled them open. Sun alone filled the crowded corridor of the night before.

"Yesterday's gone," Sylvia Summerhaze said.

"I suppose," Beth replied, as if that fact were debatable.

"Is Madrid on the ocean?" Sylvia asked, standing at the window.

"It's definitely not on the ocean," Beth said, still lying down, not paying much attention. She loved being rocked by the train. She could have lain there forever.

"Is there a lake in Madrid?" Sylvia persisted.

"There's no lake in Madrid," Beth said, getting up to see. But she had only a vague memory of Spain's geography. The train was traveling parallel to a huge body of water.

"Where are the nuns?" Sylvia asked abruptly, as if their disappearance was somehow linked to the appearance of water outside. Beth looked under the seats, pretending to hunt for the nuns. Sylvia laughed.

"Do you have your money belt?" Sylvia asked, clutching at her waist.

"They were nuns," Beth said.

"They could have been gypsies," Sylvia said. "In disguise." But everything was where it should be except that body of water, the Mediterranean, vast and cornflower blue, like another sky.

"You and your gypsies," Beth said.

The train had divided in the night, half of it heading to Madrid, the other half to Barcelona, the conductor explained to them with a Spanish smile in a tangle of broken languages. Rome, Athens, Istanbul replaced Portugal and Africa, and the girls' imaginations became rich with new possibility.

When Beth and Sylvia left the train station in Barcelona, a group of Americans with toy drums, guitars, balloons, and American flags marched by, singing the "Star-Spangled Banner." They were drinking cheap wine and offering some to all the Americans they passed. Beth and Sylvia, shouldering their backpacks, joined the parade as it snaked its way across the city, down the Gran Via, through the Parc de la Ciutadella and the Portal de la Pau to Las Ramblas, where the street came alive with folk dancers and living statues, musicians and magicians, vendors selling a bit of everything. A paunchy old American man marching next to the girls offered them more of that wine that tasted like whiskey as he gave them a lecture on patriotic songs. He was shirtless and he smelled of sweat and garlic. He told them the story of Irving Berlin's "God Bless America," of how he wrote it for a burlesque show initially. He asked them if they knew who wrote the national anthem (they didn't) and told them about Francis Scott Key, poet-lawyer, inspired to write the poem by "the valiant defense of Fort McHenry from the British on September 13, 1814." Beth remembered pledging allegiance to the flag every morning when she attended the public elementary school, saw her little self with her right hand to her heart. Even so, she never thought about patriotism or being a patriot, of dying for love of land and country. And she could not, for the life of her, remember the pledge. "But nothing," the old man said, smiling at the girls, "beats Katharine Lee Bates's 'America the Beautiful.' 'Thine alabaster cities gleam…'" he sang, flashing his yellow teeth. New York rose before Beth and Sylvia, shimmering buildings emerging from the sea. It was hot. They had had too much wine. "She began writing it on top of Pike's Peak, for goodness gracious." He spit the words.

"I get it," Sylvia said, nudging Beth. "It's the Fourth of July." They burst out laughing from drunken silliness, and then, gesturing to each other in their private language (more ridiculous than specific, involving raised eyebrows and crossed eyes), decided to escape, as if leaving the parade would involve a plan more complicated than merely slipping away. The old man started giving his lecture to some other young girls.

Just off Las Ramblas, Beth and Sylvia passed a little hotel advertising cheap rates. (It was a brothel, but they didn't know it.) Pretty Spanish girls with long hair and dark made-up eyes sashayed by as Beth and Sylvia waited at a small table in the courtyard for their room to be cleaned. Red geraniums with creeping ivy cheered up the interior balconies. Two cats arched their backs in unison and then began to lick their paws, lounging in a cool spot of shade. A dark burly man sat opposite the girls, wine in a water glass on the table in front of him. He took a sip, looked at the girls, and offered them a drink by raising his glass. He seemed old to them, in his thirties or so. Beth couldn't decide if he was handsome or very ugly. The girls looked at each other, conferring silently, and decided to accept the offer. In Spanish he called for a bottle and some glasses. The girls could always drink more, even though by now, after marching all over Barcelona, they were decidedly drunk.

"Me, Carlos Alberto," the man said, pointing to his chest. His accent was thick. He had a leer to his eye, a bit too eager. "Brazilian football star, World Cup champion," he added.

"Me Jane," Sylvia said, pointing to her chest. Beth laughed hysterically, far more than the comment warranted. Her cheeks and nose flushed.

"Y tu?" Carlos said to Beth. She drew a little mirror out of her bag and put on some lipstick and powder to cover up the heat she felt on her face.

"Me Beth," she said.

"Me like Beth," he said.

"Me like Beth, too," Sylvia said, and hugged her friend and kissed her on the lips. Beth felt a thrilling sensation race through her and then a little shock. He poured them more wine.

"Nice," he said. "Very nice. What's your country? German?"

"Ich bin ein Berliner," Sylvia said. He didn't seem to understand the reference.

"Tedesca," Beth agreed. She didn't know how to say *German* in German, but she knew the Italian. Beth and Sylvia looked at each other again with that knowing look, a look that indicated they liked the idea of being German for an instant, liked being something—anything—other than what they were.

"USA?" Carlos guessed again, pronouncing it *"oosa."*

"Football is soccer," Sylvia said to Beth.

"I'm not stupid," Beth said, and they burst out laughing again. The World Cup was being played all across Spain. Tomorrow Italy would play Brazil. Star striker Paolo Rossi would lead Italy to a three–two victory. The girls were only vaguely aware of the World Cup and knew very little about soccer. But they liked the idea of a soccer champion. Beth decided he was sort of cute in that burly, athletic way. And she found the eye attentive rather than leering.

"We'd have to share him," Beth whispered to Sylvia. "After Chas…"

"You can have this one," Sylvia said.

"Oosa," Beth admitted.

"Land of the free," Sylvia said.

"It's the Fourth of July," Beth said.

"Your birthday. *A votre santé,"* Carlos said in French, and raised his glass. He seemed, to the girls, to be trying out a bunch of languages.

"Don't they speak Spanish in Brazil?" Beth asked Sylvia.

"Or is it Italian?" Sylvia said.

It took a long time for their room to be made up. Carlos entertained them with soccer stories and wine and with pictures of himself standing next to his brand-new red Ferrari. It was when he got out those pictures that they believed he really could be a soccer star, although they couldn't understand whether he was playing tomorrow in Brazil's game against Italy, or if he was a former star. If he was playing, why was he staying in this hotel and not someplace nicer, and if he was so rich, why was he staying in this hotel, which cost under ten dollars a night? All these questions and more swirled through their heads, but they liked his attention. "My baby, this car. It killed a little boy. Accident," he explained in his broken English, as if the car had acted alone.

"Oh, that's awful," Beth said. When Beth's mother was killed by the fast car in Turkey, Beth had been with her grandmother in New York City. Claire had not been killed instantly. Indeed, Jackson insisted that had they been in America she would have survived, a mantra Beth heard across her childhood but that she did not believe. Those small, slow Turkish roads were to blame, he would say; it had taken too long to get her to a hospital. This image of her mother shot through Beth's mind then vanished as it had thousands of times before, and she simply saw the boy standing on the road, fine one instant then gone. Then, for some reason, she thought of Anna Karenina screwing up her eyes, high on morphine and grand passion. Carlos poured her more wine. She noticed that his hands were very big.

Sylvia excused herself and went to the bathroom, and while she was gone Carlos tried to kiss Beth. "You're soft, so tender," he said. But she wouldn't let him kiss her because instead of seeing his face she saw the boy's face as if Carlos had shown her a snapshot of the boy as well as of the car that killed him. Then the boy's face became Chas's. "I'm tipsy," she said, and sank against Carlos's shoulder, feeling a desire to be protected. Somehow she wanted to cry. She thought she could start crying and never stop. She was a mean ugly awful person. She wanted her father, her funny father who lived in his dreams and would never leave Claire. She wondered for an instant, and then banished the thought as she had so many times before, what her mother and father had been like together. Like Chas and a pretty smart girl eager to know and devour the world? Chas and Sylvia marching into the light of the rising moon?

"You should have kissed him," Sylvia said later in their room. "He's famous." Beth had been thinking the same thing. Then she thought they were acting like silly eighteen-year-olds. They *were* silly eighteen-year-olds, desperate to understand passion, delighted by the attention of men, thrilled to discover the alluring power of sex. They had both had boyfriends, nothing serious though, no one who kept them up nights wondering.

"But we're in Barcelona," Beth said, wanting to be serious and not silly. "City of architecture." She thought of the Gaudi buildings—Casa Battlló, La Sagrada Familia, Casa Milà—and she wanted to see their weird surrealistic contours, colors, shapes, dimensions, like a cartoon city. She put her head back on the pillow. She was tired. She didn't feel like crying anymore. That had passed quickly as the desire always did.

"Let's be silly just for tonight," Sylvia said.

"Let's get him to take us out to dinner," Beth said, sitting up suddenly. They both realized they were starving and that it had been a long time since they had had anything proper to eat. They liked that about traveling though. You lost weight.

"Good idea. But then you'll definitely have to kiss him, you know."

"Do you think that's all I'll have to do?"

"He'd probably like it if you"—she made an obscene gesture.

"Think so?" Beth stood up and looked in the mirror. The little room was small, windowless, and dark. The walls were thin. You could hear everything, but the girls didn't notice because they were drunk. Beth let her shirt drop off her shoulders and she looked at Sylvia in a coy alluring way, thinking as she did about Jacob liking her for her body, and of the power of sex. She wanted Carlos Alberto, soccer star she had never heard of (but whom she would discover before too long was indeed very famous), world champion of the world, to want her for her lovely body.

"A kitten," Sylvia said. "One hundred percent sex kitten. We should get a great dinner for that body."

Beth inched her skirt all the way up her thigh and then jumped up and down on the bed and started laughing uncontrollably; on some level she liked the idea of using her body to buy Sylvia dinner and without quite realizing it Beth wanted to see how far she could push a situation and still get out unscathed.

"They were Carmelite nuns," Sylvia said, trying on a sudden seriousness that made everything quiet, even their racing heads. In the new quiet the muffled sound of Spanish music floated to them from another room.

"What are you talking about?'

"The nuns on the train. You know a group of them were slaughtered at the end of the French Revolution—guillotined for being enemies of the people. Poulenc wrote an opera about them. I heard it at the Metropolitan Opera House with my mother." Beth imagined them, Sylvia's mother in sturdy white walking shoes, carrying a pocketbook, trudging through New York City arm in arm with her daughter, a little scared by the bad things that could happen there, her coiffed hair protected by a scarf.

"Quit being serious," Beth said. "You're scaring me. Shut off your brain. We're talking about my body now."

Carlos Alberto, Brazilian soccer star, bought them dinner, and then he kissed Beth and she kissed him, in the street beneath the brothel. He was big and strong and the kiss was long and wet and full and a little like he was trying to eat her. Beth felt tiny as his arms wrapped around her, pulling her into his hairy chest. Then he held her away from him and looked her in the eye and told her that she was beautiful, the most tender thing he had ever put hands on. She thought about the little boy hit by all the metal of his red Ferrari. They both smelled of smoke and, of course, all that wine—more even at dinner. Cars zipped past on the streets. People bumped against them accidentally— two lovers in the night beneath a streetlamp. (Or was Beth mistaken for a prostitute?) He asked her to come to his room.

"I'll come," she said, and then she tried to slip away, but he wouldn't let her. He kissed her again, almost as insurance. This time he kissed her softly as if his lips, his kiss, were serving to open her up to him. She was opening. He traced the edges of her ears with his fingertips. She could feel sensation shoot through her like ecstatic currents ricocheting this way and that, all the way to her toes. She had never made love before.

"We're leaving," Sylvia said, bursting onto the street with much clamor. She stood before Beth and Carlos with both backpacks, one draped over each shoulder. Carlos scooped Beth possessively closer to him. But the spell was broken and all Beth could think was thank goodness. She smiled an enormous smile and looked at her friend. "Bea's waiting for us. She's passed her exams and she wants us to come travel with her."

"You called her?" Beth asked, surprised. I thought you hated her, she wanted to say.

"I called her and she's waiting." A train schedule flopped in Sylvia's hand. She wore black capris and delicate shoes that looked like ballet slippers. The pants and shoes belonged to Beth and had been hand-me-downs from Beatrice.

With many apologies they disappeared, leaving Carlos standing alone, illuminated by the streetlight at the hotel's entrance.

Later on the train to Milan, "It was a brothel," Sylvia said. "I realized when I paid."

"And to think he would have gotten it for free when I could have charged him," Beth said.

"Would you have fucked him?"

"Watch your language, young lady."

"I knew I needed to save you. I didn't want you paying for my dinner with your body." It all made sense to Beth now, Sylvia's arrival, deus ex machina-like, with her new plan.

"Isn't there something about brothels and Barcelona? Something famous?" Sylvia asked.

"Picasso," Beth said. "Yes. Something about brothels and Barcelona and Picasso. All my Gaudis, we didn't see a one."

Later, Beth asked, "Are we even now?"

"Nope," Sylvia smiled.

Before all this, before the train divided in the nun-filled Spanish night, there was another chance in Breton's series, a chance which could have been, as well or in addition to or purely and simply, that hand of Lachesis. The other chance, or rather the first, was Beatrice Nuova. It was only by accident that Beth met Beatrice (a literal accident), and had she never met Beatrice, she would never have gone to Città or to Greece and she would never have met Cesare. And had she never met him, she would not have become herself.

Beth enjoyed looking, from the perspective of time, at the sequence of events that lead to the unfolding of a life. Not just her own life but any life, any story in which something grand (or at least big) happens because of something seemingly inconsequential.

Her daughter, Valeria (born in 1997, fifteen years after Beth's European journey with Sylvia), would have a penchant for this, too. Valeria obsessively traced the path of her mother's life—Beth's love affair with Cesare; her marriage to Valeria's father; her death. For example, on September 10, 2001, Beth had an appointment with a very rich bond trader named Bear who intended to loan her money for a new restaurant that she wanted to open. He had been a silent partner in her other restaurants (Como and Matera) and had always had private ambitions to be a chef and restaurateur. He lived vicariously through Beth and intended therefore to bankroll the new one—Preveena, a foray into Indian cuisine inspired by and named after her half sister's mother. Bear's daughter, a playmate of Valeria's, got sick, and this delayed the family's return from vacation in France by one day. The meeting was rescheduled for the eleventh—the morning instead of the afternoon because his afternoon was filled already with a house-hunting expedition in East Hampton (he'd planned to get there by helicopter) with his wife.

Valeria would look nothing like her mother: she had dark hair instead of blond, big brown eyes set wide apart in a perfectly round face, and she was a good four inches taller. Indeed, she looked more like Claire, her grandmother, than Beth. But if Valeria looked carefully at her face she would be able to distinguish attributes there that were unequivocally Beth's—her large forehead, the perfect shell-like curl to her ears, the swirling pattern of her hair, which caused it to fall gracefully. These were her mother's gifts to her and she would only see them as beautiful. What else belonged to her mother? Her father would say her determination, her will, her capacity to dream; her full cheeks, her smile, the very tone of her voice. Her father would remark, "I thought the tone of one's voice was learned." She loved the sound of her voice, loved to speak since she had been told her voice was her mother's.

Valeria would remember a few things about her mother—her mother's long nails scratching her back, her arms, her legs. "Scratch," Valeria would command. She'd remember loving to be scratched gently by her mother before she fell asleep. She'd remember her mother watching her as she played make-believe by herself in her bedroom, her mother standing in the doorway for a good long time simply watching her child's imagination at play. In memory, a scrim of light would filter through the window to create a golden haze around the play world. Valeria would remember cooking with her mother, baking endless almond cakes, being reprimanded for eating too much of the batter. Valeria would hold on to these shreds, little seeds that grew into a mother, her mother. What else would Beth have given to Valeria, if? What if? What if? Maddening combination of words—all that promise and all that reality swirled together. What if the daughter of Bear, the rich bond trader (he had fiery red hair and a jolly smile), had not gotten sick (a slight fever as it turned out, not worth delaying a trip home, an appointment, a life)? What if?

It would take Valeria a good fifteen years, the discovery of some letters (folded neatly in a box), the learning of Italian, several trips to Italy during high school (traveling with her father), and the meeting of Leonardo (Cesare's son) before she would fully understand the meaning of her name.

Beth grew up at Claire in Pennsylvania, moving to New York in high school. In New York, Beth lived with her grandmother in an apartment overlooking the Hudson River on the Upper West Side. Her grandmother was a handsome woman with a strong jaw and pure white hair that had been white since her forties and that she kept in a bun on the crown of her head. She was active with the opera and gave tours of the Metropolitan Museum of Art's Baroque rooms. Bernini was her specialty, though she was only an amateur. She liked to tell people that she was a novice so they would be all the more impressed by the vast expanse of her knowledge. She had been married to an engineer who died of cancer before Beth was born, leaving her with a nice monthly pension and social security, but she acted (and spent) as if she had a whole lot more. Her apartment was rent controlled and thus cost her very little, but it was grand and allowed her life to seem quite rich. She was an ambitious woman, especially for Beth.

In Pennsylvania Beth lived with her widowed father at Claire, the commune he started with a loan from Claire's mother (the collateral for which was his life insurance policy). He came home from Turkey with Claire's body in a coffin and he cremated her and took her ashes to the apple orchard they had fallen in love with, and he spread the ashes there. And though he since had had his share of love affairs (Beth gained her half sister, Rada, whose mother, Preveena, was her father's lover for a few years), he never left Claire and vowed he never would. Beth went to school at the commune from fourth grade through eighth grade, but after her freshman year at the local high school her grandmother insisted that she go to private school in New York (a girl's school—uniforms and Latin and horseback riding in the park). It was a heady time. Friends taught her to befriend the doormen in her building so that she could sneak out late at night. ("Tip them, that's all," they wisely explained.) In the middle of the night, New York belonged to teenagers and bums. They went to the theater and to fancy restaurants. Sometimes they even went to clubs—Studio 54 and The Volt. They ate at all-night diners and slipped back into their homes just before dawn, their families unaware. The trick was to be bad in a sweet sort of way. Sometimes drugs were involved, pot and, on occasion, cocaine.

In some ways Beth liked New York better than Claire. She liked the sophistication, the maturity, of her new friends, their curiosity about the world. After being in New York for only a short while, Beth found that Sylvia seemed so much younger than her New York friends. Eminently naive, Sylvia would chatter on about Friday night football games and Jacob's band, while the kids in New York engaged in serious subjects such as the new painting the Met just bought for millions of dollars (*the most ever spent* and *was it worth it?*). They played a game of who knew more, a game they didn't realize they were playing, but Beth could see them trying to outdo one another with their knowledge about everything, from art to clothes to countries to food. Though Beth dressed, when not in uniform, like she came from the country (jeans, Indian print skirts with work boots, bulky sweaters), and though the slick life of clubs and late nights and so much money was new to her, she could keep up with the conversation game. And she liked that because it was familiar and in some ways she had been playing it since her mother died and her father moved to Claire.

But the person of concern here, for the purposes of this story, is Beatrice Nuova (*Bay-a-tree-chay New-whoa-va*), and *nuova* does mean "new." Bea came to Beth from Città in the summer of 1980 on a Rotary exchange and Beth loved her as much as she loved Sylvia if not (in some ways) more.

The summer after Beth's first year of high school in New York City she and Bea did their first exchange—three weeks in each other's countries with Bea coming to America first. And just as New York had transformed Beth from a country girl to a city girl, Bea transformed Beth from an American girl to an Italian— or that was Bea's ambition, anyway. Bea with all her dark hair and her long nose and her voluptuous figure was a force with a will even greater than Beth's. She was bossy and demanding and loving and wanted Beth to learn Italian immediately. (Bea's English was perfect.) Beth became her pet, her project, and Beth was happy to comply. While Bea remained a spectator in America, happy to be the exotic dark creature from a foreign land of whom Beth's friends (especially those in Pennsylvania) did not know what to make, Beth adapted in Italy, eager to be transformed. With Bea, Beth wore her first string bikini, visited her first Mediterranean island (she had not imagined that water could be so many shades of blue, as if created simply so that it could be enjoyed by the human eye), learned her first foreign language (Italian) fluently. Bea began teaching it to her as they lay in the grass at the community pool in Orchard Hill, a town near Claire, with Sylvia and some other friends of Beth's. People gawked at Bea, lounging in her string bikini. "They're lucky I'm wearing my top," she had said, and continued with her lesson: *"E' la vacca una persona?"* Is the cow a person? And Beth: *"Si, la vacca e' una persona."* With Bea, Beth discovered her love for Renaissance art, wandered for days in the Uffizi and the Vatican, studied the Belvedere Torso to discover why Bernini loved it best of all: it seemed in motion as if the missing limbs were still there. She learned to twirl (never cut) her spaghetti, learned to make her own pasta (of all sizes and shapes and colors). She learned not to be self-conscious topless on a beach (an Italian beach, that is). Beth learned about waxing versus shaving, though waxing hurt so much on the first attempt she preferred to leave one leg hairy for the days it took to gain the courage to rip the hair from the second leg. She learned (eventually) to ski and to sail and how to dive from rocks into the clear blue Mediterranean without losing the top of her string bikini. Beth learned to make cappuccino and to flirt even. She learned that staying up all night could be innocent—eating watermelon at a fruit stand at 2 A.M. with a large group of friends, spitting seeds. She learned about large meals in the middle of the day and a touch of grappa in the evenings—something special to help you digest.

In the evenings Bea dressed Beth up in some of her smart Italian clothes and they rode to town on Bea's Vespa just like all the other elegant girls in their high heels, the boys nicely cleaned up and fragrant—nothing like Beth's male friends from Pennsylvania who took pride in their long hair and scrappy jeans and scruffy beards and who spoke incessantly about traveling the country in pursuit of Jerry Garcia and the Grateful Dead and bragged about who could drink the most. Nor were the Italian boys like Beth's male friends from New York, who dressed in wrinkled khakis and oxford shirts, and were always eager to have deep conversations about existential angst, even if they didn't quite know what that meant.

Bea would take Beth's hand and they would walk through the streets of town. Bea's hand was soft and warm in hers. Beth wanted to walk down an American street holding hands with Bea or Sylvia, simply because it was foreign and unthinkable and would cause people to make incorrect assumptions. Bea's friends admired the blond American (whose long hair had been freshly cut by Bea into a more sophisticated shape: layers and wispy bangs). In Città, Beth felt a little like a celebrity, a curiosity—rare, unique, prized—and she adored the sensation of being at the center of things. She loved the history, the vast extent of it. She could feel the expanse of time and experience life across centuries by simply walking along a narrow street.

The first summer when everything was new, Beth could not rest. She wanted to drink it all up: the pretty girls, the fragrant boys, the delicious smells of baking bread, the stores with their neatly arranged merchandise, stores you didn't dare enter unless you intended to make a purchase. Città made sense. Everything was so well cared for, flowers in all the windows, clean streets, sleek Citroëns and Mercedes and Peugeots that glided easily out of driveways barred with big electric gates behind which loomed well-shuttered villas in the midst of gardens thick with apricot trees. She loved the very shutters: heavy metal blinds that came down, with the big sound of metal rasping against more metal, each noon to keep out the sun and the heat so that siestas could be enjoyed in the cool dark of the home. At siesta-time Bea's home became a dim and fragrant trove, scented by the aromas from the risottos or the pastas, the roasts or the fillets, the blanched vegetables, which lingered long after the big noon lunch had been cleared away. Each day Bea's extended family gathered around the table: Bea's father's father—a little, very old man who lived in an adjacent villa that had a basement filled with prized sausages and salamis hanging from the ceiling to keep dry, including a very rare salami made from horse-meat—and Bea's mother's sister and mother, and Bea's older sister. But after lunch the house fell silent while everyone slept. The whole town slept. The stores closed their shutters and the streets became quiet. Beth lay on her bed impatient for the siesta to end so that she and Bea could be out once again on the Vespa in this fascinating new world.

Most of all Beth learned about the beauty of and the seeming simplicity of an ordinary family: Bea's family, like Sylvia's, was conventional and small and predictable but even closer than Sylvia's because of the proximity of both sets of Bea's grand-parents. Sylvia's grandparents lived far away and rarely came to

visit. And though Sylvia's family loved Beth, she had never lived
with them and had not witnessed intimately their life as a family. (Beth also knew that Sylvia's father was suspicious of her
own, so of course she disliked him.) Bea's family was different.
It was the family she had always dreamed of having. Bea's
mother adopted Beth immediately, her American daughter, and
Beth wanted to be polite and good and make Signora Nuova
proud with her new Italian words. Through Signora Nuova she
learned what it might mean to have a mother though Beth
knew Claire would never have been like Bea's mother with her
long protective arms wrapping you up in the scent of a fine and
subtle perfume, teaching you about all the pretty things of the
world. Bea's mother loved to iron, loved the order of making
wrinkly things smooth and neat again, and she would iron for
hours in the basement, which always smelled of detergent and
freshly washed laundry. She busied herself with errands: shopping for food, doing laundry or running to the dry cleaner with
clothes for the girls, preparing the meals. Beth took a great interest in the latter. Though neither spoke the other's language
very well, Signora Nuova enjoyed teaching Beth how to make
risotto alla Milanese, say, or *un piatto di funghi di bosco al salvia;* she
taught her how to make fresh pasta and desserts: *salame di cioc-
colata* and *dolce di Città* and *zuppa Inglese* and *crostata della nonna
ai fichi.* Beth's first summer in Italy she gained ten pounds.

Bea became the older sister Beth had always wanted and
she loved everything about her and wanted to be like her, down
to the way she packed her suitcase: all her shoes in their own
small felt bags; her underwear (matching bras and panties of a
crisp white cotton with the smallest red strawberries) wrapped
in tissue paper as if each set were a gift; her dresses, somehow
still neatly ironed after all the travel; her towels soft and even
warm-seeming and smelling of lavender. Watching Bea unpack

was like watching a princess. Bea had an inherent elegance and self-respect, and each item of clothing was more adorable than the last. Bea's suitcase had nothing to do with Beth's, which was an indelicate mishmash of torn Levi's and Indian print skirts and T-shirts, items she cared about deeply until she met Bea. With Bea, Beth could surrender her will and stop being in charge.

Beth had heard about the Rotary Group's Summer Exchange Program during the daily assembly at school. A man came to tell the girls about an exciting opportunity in Venice, Italy. When he asked for volunteers, Beth's hand shot up, and then so did another girl's hand. She was a year older than Beth. Her name was Larissa Lord Jones. They filled out applications, wrote letters of purpose, submitted recommendations, and waited and waited and waited. All the while Beth's grandmother drew pictures for Beth with words—pictures of palaces and canals and gondolas and Italian princes waltzing her across vast marble floors. This was what she wanted for her granddaughter. This was what she had wanted for her daughter, not for Claire to have married a hippie dreamer with ambitions she could not, for the life of her, comprehend. For Beth's grandmother, known to all, even to Beth's father, as Grammy, Europe was older thus better. Europeans had figured out how to live. Grammy would support Beth in style with trunks and new dresses and letters of introduction from people at the Met to people at the Vatican and the Uffizi. The larger Grammy's pictures grew, the more Beth wanted to go and the more she came to hate Larissa Lord Jones. The hating was mutual. Larissa hated Beth. Then Beth hated Larissa finally and completely because Larissa won. She was older, Beth was told; Beth would have another chance next year.

And here again comes that hand, sweeping down quietly but with finality: A few weeks before Larissa Lord Jones was to begin her exchange with Beatrice Nuova (Beth hadn't stopped thinking about Larissa floating through the Venice canals with Italian princes), her older brother was killed by a semitrailer on one of those fast western roads. He had been riding a motorcycle when he was hit; he died instantly.

The Rotary man was wrong about the city. It was Città la Venice (pronounced *Ch ee ta la Ven-ee-chay,* but known plainly as Città) and definitively not Venice or Venezia. Città, a small rich town, nestled into the foothills of the Alps, garnered fame not for its history or its art or its beauty but for its industry of socks and shoes: Bianchi, Macchi, Ghiringhelli. Città: capital of Italian wealth and feet.

So Beth and Sylvia were blown to Città. Bea met them at the station, took them back to her house, fed them abundant amounts of pasta, listened to their tales of Chas ("We'll find him in Corfu!" she declared. And indeed she would make sure they were there on August first, renting mopeds and circling the island, asking other Americans if they had seen Chas, but to no avail), and of Carlos (Bea would inform them of his fame but was skeptical about whether the man they met was the real Carlos Alberto. "But the Ferrari, the Ferrari," the girls would persist). In her basement, Bea stored their backpacks and their clothing. She loaned them green leather suitcases, which she filled with clothes from last season, along with a blow-dryer and a curling iron. She taught them to wear mascara properly and trimmed their hair, giving them both bangs. In her own country she was not threatened by Sylvia, just bossed her and led her as she did Beth. And somehow this worked beautifully.

The next day they drove to the Tuscan coastal resort town of Forte dei Marmi in a Maserati with two of Bea's friends, Miki and Dario. The Maserati was red, of course, and it belonged to

Miki, a very rich, very tall (awkwardly so) heir to a newspaper delivery empire. He was the kind of man that gold-diggers prize: incredibly kind and sweet, though none too attractive, with bad teeth and a weak jaw, stumbling over himself to be polite. He drove his car fast to impress the girls. Their suitcases bobbed in the back and Sylvia held on tightly to Beth, pretending to be afraid, but they were too young to have that sort of real fear. In nearby Pisa, Miki arranged for a private tour of the Leaning Tower by moonlight. When they were hungry, he made sure everyone was well fed with whatever she desired—*tortellini alla panna* and *bistecca alla Fiorentina* and brioche at 4 A.M. fresh from the bakery, paying the *fornaio* extra because she opened her door for them so early in the morning (white smock, flour on her face). He took them to Parma so that they could try real *prosciutto* and real *parmigiano.* "You must. You're in Italy" (*Ee-ta-lee*). They would not sleep. They barely slept that summer. Over two hundred kilometers per hour, all of them squashed into the Maserati, Sylvia singing—you can guess what—about a Maserati doing 185...

Dario was a printmaker, none too wealthy, and Miki's side-kick, small and dark and wiry, Miki's exact physical opposite. Soon he was smitten with Sylvia (who found him a fun diversion), kissing her in the dark as they walked along a rocky jetty, fringed with crashing waves, that jutted far into the Mediterranean. He spoke only a few words of English and Sylvia only a few of Italian. "They communicate through the language of love," Miki said. It was funny to watch them. Beth didn't mind losing Sylvia to Dario because she had all of Miki's attention. It simply seemed to Beth that in Europe romance was everywhere and women had their pick of men.

After two days of sunbathing at the edge of Forte dei Marmi's thin beach, with the Mediterranean lapping at the shore and *ombrelloni* for shade and *lettini* for comfort and fresh brioche and tortellini and the fast Maserati and stories of what it means to be in charge of getting everyone in northern Italy their newspapers on time in the morning, Miki declared his love for Beth (and Dario his for Sylvia), and the boys asked them to come to Greece where they were going in ten days with some other friends to windsurf on the island of Páros. This was the way in which Italians vacationed: in packs, traveling somewhere warm and watery that involved fun and exercise and staying at least a month. They didn't travel like Americans in Europe: long distances, many destinations, cultural devouring, backpacks, long letters home. (In fact, postcards home from Italians included at best the signatures of the vacationers.) But every night Bea and her friends would call their parents. Even if their parents knew exactly where they were and that they were not leaving the chosen spot, said island, they needed to hear from their children, otherwise they enlisted the parents of others traveling in the party, the law, the national guard, in order to locate them, nervous until they heard the voice of the twenty-year-old daughter, the twenty-six-year-old son. Watching the evening ritual of the phone call was always amusing and touching for Beth: her father or grandmother would have thought something tragic had happened if a call came in from overseas. Rather, once in a blue moon, she wrote a long descriptive letter detailing all of her adventures, every single one of them.

"I'm in love with you," Miki had said. Waves splashed them on the jetty, soaking them entirely. His kisses were salty and he was so tall and so thin and so rich. His feet were enormous. The kisses, salty as they were, became intoxicating, the kind that send chills rivering through your body. Beth thought she loved him, too, except that he was so tall and those feet. His feet! "You're so tall," she said. "But he's so tall," she'd say to her friends. He stuck his hand down her shirt and gently held her breast. The brilliant moon blocked out the stars and lit up the water, a shimmering silver surface. "You're beautiful," Miki said, "and I'm in love." He unzipped his pants and placed Beth's hand on his penis and she had no idea what to do with it so she just held it and said, "I can't do this. I can't betray Sylvia," acting dramatic, half pretending that this was too big and complicated and confusing for her until he simply held her and told her it was okay, that they had time—indeed all the time in world. Beth looked around for Sylvia in the dark, couldn't spot her anywhere. Wet with the sea, Beth skipped back across the rocks toward shore, and Miki following awkwardly with all his size and feet. "Come to Greece," he yelled after her. "Come to Páros."

Bea watched her friends, feeling a little like a matchmaker, or a puppeteer, proud and happy with her success. She was delighted by the invitation to Greece and happy to have established these little romances. She wasn't afraid of being a fifth wheel; Bea was too confident for that. And besides, for a while now, in Città, she had had a small flirtation going with a boy named Cesare, a handsome boy who made her laugh when they met in the center in the evenings for a *Prosecco* before dinner with all their friends from town. He made her laugh because he liked to observe the odd details of the other people collected there and did so in a way that was also self-deprecating. At the same time he exuded a confidence that somehow lifted him high above everyone else. He was sort of an Italian Peter Pan, loving to have fun, treating the world as his playground. He was tall and slender with black hair that receded gently at the temples and he came from a prominent Città family who had been bankers in the town for five hundred years. He loved everything American—Levi's and Bruce Springsteen—and though he had never been there, when he and Bea spoke, it was about America. Bea regaled him with her adventures on a commune there. The more stories she told him, the more she loved America herself, remembering how she had been both exotic there and utterly invisible, allowed to observe. But for the sake of entertaining Cesare, she made herself an active participant in American life: she had played American football, had milked goats with her bare hands, had picked apples and raspberries, and even sold them to fancy New York restaurants. She had been a part of the Claire community, had helped build a yurt and cut a road (not true), had taught Italian at the commune school, had been introduced to American literature. "Books?" Cesare asked. He was a reader, too, liked books in English. The flirtation was just the smallest inkling of a flame, but it flickered with promise in Bea's chest, occupying a large percentage of her thoughts—only a fraction of which she would share with her friends because she did not like opening herself for all to see; such unselfconcious candor was a characteristic she noted as particularly, endearingly, American. Cesare, one of Miki's friends, was headed for Páros as well; Bea imagined Beth and Sylvia and herself all paired off and felt exhilarated by the prospect of the summer and this vacation.

After the declaration of love, the Maserati drove back to Città with two happy boys eager for the ten days to swiftly pass. The girls were happy, too, to be on their own again, in charge of their own adventure, though Bea took command and led them, lugging their green leather suitcases first to Florence, sweltering in the July heat, to see Michelangelo's *David* and the *Slaves* and Botticelli's *The Birth of Venus* rising from the foam. The girls felt nourished by culture and less guilty for at least having seen something. It didn't matter that Beth and Bea had seen all this "stuff" before. That knowledge simply allowed them to hold forth, which they did, as if they knew so much more than Sylvia about Michelangelo and Botticelli.

After Florence they traveled to Rome where the biggest attraction, aside from the Vatican and the Forum, was the Porta Portese market. They each bought a string bikini and here

Sylvia saw plenty of her gypsies and even had the chance to thwart a robbery. "I caught him! I caught him!" she screeched, holding on to the arm of a dirty little boy who had tried to snatch her wallet. He struggled with a fiery energy to free himself from her grasp. No one, not a single person, seemed to care.

It was in Florence though, in front of the *David*, in the heat with hundreds of other bodies sweating and pushing against the girls, that Bea first mentioned Cesare. "Cesare has a body like that," she said. "Who?" Sylvia asked. "Who?" Beth echoed. Beth knew intimately the details of Bea's love life, knew that for two years she had been having an affair with a married man. Bea would write Beth long letters about him that Beth would read and reply to during English class or say, history, while pretending to be taking notes, riveted by her friend's escapades because they were so much more daring and grown-up than anything she or her American friends even dreamed of. Bea liked being with a married man because she always knew what to expect, knew that someday he would leave her and knew in advance that the reason would be the wife and not some flaw of her own. (Italians rarely leave for the other woman.) She never wanted anyone, especially a man, to identify her flaws. She was overly proud that way, wanted to keep her flaws to herself. Above all, Bea loved spilling her insides out to Beth in a letter, something she could never have done in person or with any other friend.

"Cesare," Bea said. *Chey-zar-ay*. Just from the way Bea said his name with an uncharacteristic warmth and a tenderness, Beth knew. "He has a body like that?" Sylvia said. "He's so big," Beth said, feeling a little jealousy creeping up her throat that she tried to quell like one does an overexcited dog. Most of all she wanted to know the details.

And as they floated toward Greece on their bubbly cloud of youth, the details of Cesare would emerge, a bit like treats to reward the girls. Cesare was generous, warm, handsome, playful, studying economics at the Bocconi in Milan, and he came from an old family with a name in her town. "Old family" was an idea that meant nothing to Beth and Sylvia, but to Bea it meant a lot; it was better to be aligned with a good old family with a name just as it is better to go to Harvard, say, than to a state university. Her family, though good, was not old and did not have a name. The Nuovas had been transplanted to Città from Verona and Genova—towns not a great distance from Città, but far enough all the same to make the Nuovas a new family (even though they had been in Città for over a hundred years). And their wealth was new, too. Bea's grandfather, a manufacturer of dyes for stocking threads and sock fibers, had been a factory worker who happened to be educated and lucky. He rose within the company until one day he owned it (an extraordinary feat), and was thus able to give to his son, Bea's father, a fortune and a job. In Città the new families were distinguished from the old families and the new families carried a certain unspoken stigma. For example, Cesare would be a good match for Bea. He would lift her from her unspoken lower status (within the upper echelons, of course) to one equivalent to his own. Bea's parents were delighted by this flirtation not only because they did not approve, needless to say, of the married man (whom they knew about even if Bea told them nothing), but because Cesare had a good name and was known as a nice boy—if not an all-too-serious boy. For Cesare's family the match with Bea would be a bad one. The family's status was solid and a match with Bea would not lower it, but these things mattered, and all things being equal a marriage between Bea and Cesare would not be desirable. She would be a freckle on the complexion of the family name. (Heaven forbid an American!) Of course, Bea as a match had not crossed Cesare's family's mind, nor even Cesare's, to be truthful.

His family did not even know who she was. But Bea knew all the subtleties of class, of new and of old and of how they existed, thrived even, in late-twentieth-century Italy like some sort of burden from the past. Thus Bea's last name always felt to her like a mark, a scarlet letter. And though she had mostly observed in America, she loved the freedom of being there, of being anonymous, of being free of the burdens and expectations conferred by her family name. But most of all, Bea loved Beth madly simply because this vast web of name and stigma and class that ran beneath the surface of Città like a complicated power grid supporting the infrastructure meant absolutely nothing to her and wouldn't even if Bea bothered to explain it.

"But how long has this been going on?" Beth demanded. "I never received word."

"Never received word?" Sylvia said, laughing at Beth's stilted sentence construction, which seemed the result of too much time abroad.

"New new new," Bea said. "Brand-new."

"Have you kissed?"

"Almost," she said, and told them how she had been introduced to him in town one night. They did not share the same group of friends and she only knew him vaguely by face but that night he rode her home on his motorcycle and would have kissed her had the married man (his name was Giorgio) not been waiting for her in his car outside the gate. "I have never more not wanted to see Giorgio."

Beth had never met the married man, but she had this image of him as tall and dark and cloaked in a black cape so that he never emerged from the shadows, a sort of hooded Darth Vader (Bea had described his black hair, deep-set eyes, strong jaw pocked with shallow dimples, and his hands—hands that could hold a lot, all of her).

At this particular moment the girls were in their hotel room in Florence, Bea on the bed in her underwear with tweezers, leaning over her left leg, from which she plucked newly emerging hairs. She could do this for hours and she would try to get Beth and Sylvia to do it, too, but neither one had the patience. In fact, they had given up on waxing and gone back to shaving. Their beauty treatments involved gentle tasks like facials and deep conditioning of the hair.

"Are you in love with Miki?" Bea asked Beth, still with her eyes hard on the project of her left leg. She did not like to talk much about Cesare and didn't mention him very often as it made her feel too vulnerable. Indeed, by the time they arrived in Páros, when Beth would see him for the first time on those steps, Bea's romance, lived vividly in her own mind, was only a faint memory to Beth and Sylvia.

"He's too tall," Sylvia said. "And those feet."

"He is tall," Beth admitted, and remembered him leaning down, way down, to kiss her. "Plus I don't think he knows what he's doing. He cupped my breast and just sort of held on to it as if it were a knob. I was afraid he might turn it to see if he could open something." Then she told them about his penis and how big it was and how he had put it in her hand, but that she realized once she was touching it that she didn't want to be. She didn't mention that she hadn't known what to do with it.

"Yick," Sylvia said, but they loved talking about sex. They wanted to talk about the really juicy stuff, and of the three of them Bea had had the most experience because of the married man. Beth would get Bea to describe her escapades for Sylvia, how she and the married man (they liked to call Giorgio that because it sounded so sordid and adult) snuck around late at night, making out in dark parks and in the back of his Mercedes. "His wife is always there," Bea would say. "And I like that." His wife looming over them like some sort of aphrodisiac made the encounters one hundred percent satisfactory.

"What about Cesare?" Beth asked now.

"I love my married man," Bea said, turning the attention away from Cesare. She did not want them to know how much she thought about him. Beth and Sylvia had no idea yet that he, too, was one of the friends coming to Greece.

Their suitcases were heavy but Bea always found some kind stranger to carry them, and when she didn't, they dragged them, destroying the rich green leather. From Brindisi to Patras they took the ferry, sleeping on the deck beneath a shower of soot from the ship's smokestack, feeling like real travelers. They danced Greek reels in the discotheque and played slot machines, getting rich on worthless drachmas. They were well dressed in Bea's adorable clothes, miniskirts, cropped pants, cropped tops, delicate strappy shoes in gold. The clothes featured last year's color, mandarin. "Orange," Sylvia would say in that direct way of hers. Poor and in Athens, however, they slept in Zappeio Park in order to save a few more of those easily won drachmas and because Sylvia read in the guidebook that it was safe as long as you secured your luggage to your body so that thieves couldn't snitch it in the night. Beth and Bea were skeptical and this excursion was truly slumming it for Bea. After all, her money problems were not the same as Sylvia's and Beth's. Bea's parents paid for her entire trip. The idea of an Italian child waiting tables to earn spending money of any sort was anathema in their world. In Italy waiters were waiters and had always been waiters and would always be waiters. But Bea enjoyed the adventure of traveling on a budget and knew that with Italian friends she would never have slept in a park. With Beth the world was always just a bit bigger for Bea, and for that she loved

Beth all the more. "Can you imagine sleeping in Central Park?" Beth asked. "Or the Cascine?" Bea said of Florence's big park, thick with transvestites and transsexuals who had had operations in Casa Blanca—a detail the girls had found unbelievably curious, so they had taken a midnight tour of the Cascine (in a taxi) to observe these "ladies" strutting about in their high heels and sleazy skirts, thinking of them all the while on an operating table in the depths of Africa with doctors magically transforming them from men to women, chopping here, adding there. "Gross," one of the girls had said.

Zappeio Park was in the center of Athens and part of the National Garden, which was once part of the royal family's palace grounds. Signs at the entrance said (in English, quite clearly) that the park was open from dawn to dusk. "But this isn't Central Park, or the Cascine, and the guidebook says it's fine," Sylvia insisted, pointing to the passage. They indulged her, allowing her to thread a long cord (they had no idea where it came from, but Sylvia somehow produced it) through all the handles to all the suitcases and then through all their clothes so that they were neatly bound together like some bulky, but precious, package. "If anyone tries to snitch a suitcase they'll get all of us and that will be too heavy to carry away. We're anchored here," Sylvia said. Beth and Bea rolled their eyes, but Beth was happy to save the price of a night's room. They also noticed other travelers, with backpacks, beginning to emerge from the shadows to find a spot for the night beneath the orange and the lemon trees. The new company made Sylvia more confident, and she gave Beth and Bea a "see" look—squinting, pursing her lips. It was dusk and the city was hot and dry and smoggy (smog was the detail the girls noted first and foremost upon their arrival), but the park was green and fragrant. A breeze rippled the air.

Beth felt guilty about her suitcase as she watched the back-packers, as if somehow the suitcase made her a less serious traveler, and she wished she had brought her backpack. It was also much easier to carry. One of the long-distance travelers camped nearby approached (long beard, bare feet, tie-dyed undershirt, cute in a Jesus hippie sort of way, definitely an American) to ask them if they had any spare rope, and this request made Sylvia's afternoon. "I just don't understand the attraction of American men," Bea said, as the young man walked away. Secretly, though, she did: they seemed to belong to a world of no cares. And when the birdsongs died down and the late sun finally disappeared and when there was no more conjecture about the other friends Miki and Dario might be bringing along to Páros (a subject that occupied a good portion of their conversation), the girls drifted easily into sleep.

In the middle of the night, to Sylvia's great delight, a thief tried to steal their bags. Instead of the suitcase, the thief got the whole bundle and was scared away by the three screaming girls. (For the rest of her life, Sylvia would love to tell that story.) Then at 5 A.M. when the orange light of dawn began creeping into the lemon trees, the girls were awakened again, this time by a shower of water as all the park's sprinklers turned on.

Ambitious, feeling confident, if a little tired, that morning they planned a tour of the Acropolis, the Agora, and the Plaka. They left the heavy suitcases on the sidewalk near a busy outdoor café, agreeing that no one would steal them, because any thief would believe the owners were sitting nearby sipping coffee. "Who would be so stupid as to leave their bags on a street in Athens?" Bea asked. "No one." "Precisely," Sylvia said. And after a hot morning of drifting through the Temple of Athena Nike and the Parthenon and of imagining them as they must have been two thousand years ago, painted brightly and active with life (everyone in white togas as in the movies), the girls went shopping at the Plaka and returned to find their bags almost exactly where they had left them (though moved a few feet farther toward the street by a waitress because they were in her way).

Funny about that age, you're invincible. Death is a long way off, something that happens to others. Risk is less risky. That summer a boy Beth and Sylvia knew from high school in Pennsylvania died. Likely, he was dying at the moment they left their bags on that crowded Athenian street; the night before while they slept in the park, he was doing the damage that would later kill him. He had driven too fast in his car with too many drugs and too much alcohol in his system, believing, like everyone his age, that he was invincible. (Do you remember all those high school nights when you rode fast in your Camaros, your Mustangs, your cute VW Bugs, when you got home without even knowing how, how you would laugh about it later, boasting to friends?) Beth and Sylvia's friend was Paul. He had been the guitarist in the Random Joe band, the band whose drummer both Beth and Sylvia had kissed. When Beth later heard that Paul had wrapped his beat-up old LeSabre around a sycamore tree, she imagined the accident literally—his car curling around the tree like a snake, Paul inside, the metal slicing into him. Paul had actually been thrown into a blackberry thicket, where he was found by a fireman, who took snapshots of the scene to warn his kids about the dangers of speeding and drunk driving. This was one of the worst accidents the fireman had ever seen. Rescue workers had to pick parts of Paul from the blackberry thicket. Even so, he somehow lived for half a day more.

Paul and Beth had kissed once at a party. He had put the gum he had been chewing on the back of his wrist and they had kissed, a sloppy wet kiss that left her lips and her chin sore and chaffed. He had driven too fast a month after graduation with the Grateful Dead blasting away on the cassette player. Somehow it was still playing "Sugar Magnolia," so the rumor went, when the fireman found him. The girls slept in an Athenian park, thinking themselves just as invincible. Beth would picture their luggage at the edge of the café while the three of them marched up the hot hill to the remains of ancient Greece.

"Do you think you'll sleep with Miki?" Bea asked as they rose to the Parthenon, history and its ruins all around them. Paul had asked Beth to go steady that night when he put the gum on his wrist. She had said yes, and they had walked around the party hand in hand, trying on love, trying on the grown-up world with all its formulations and rules—a dear boy with long black hair that he let cover one eye in a way he believed made him look dangerous. He did not want to be a nice boy, a good boy, but he was. For years Beth would see those kids from her Pennsylvania high school, her New York high school (more sophisticated though they were with their cocaine in the bathrooms of clubs), and she would see Bea and Sylvia and herself, all of them invincible, all of them waiting impatiently for the *real* (definitely emphatic here) to begin. What was it? Where was it? Won't someone show us the way? Take us there now? Guide us. Lead us. No wonder Beth and Sylvia surrendered so easily to Bea.

Going steady had felt awkward and uncomfortable, a shirt that didn't fit right. At the end of the party, Beth broke off the affair, explaining the news to her friends who were only just beginning to celebrate. The drama of their reaction was as far as she wanted to push adulthood. The relationship had lasted four hours. Paul hit the sycamore tree at ninety miles per hour. Despite his mangled body, it took him a good twelve hours to die. "How are they going to fix him?" his mother kept crying, repeating the words into the enormous chest of her sad-eyed husband, wondering how the doctors would make her son whole again. When Beth learned about the accident, she would think of the Maserati speeding along on the Italian highway. She would think of her own mother, so deeply dead she was as much a part of history as George Washington. Beth would think of Paul's gum stuck to his wrist, his sloppy wet lips kissing hers, his black hair falling in the way of their mouths. By the time she learned of his death she would be well initiated into adult pain and deeply ensconced in the early days of her life's most central myth.

It slipped out, on the tiny island of Antiparos, that Bea's Cesare was a friend of Miki's and that he was a big windsurfer and that he, too, might be coming to Páros. The detail was just one of many details that occupied the girls as they passed the hot days beneath the fierce Greek sun on their own small nude beach. They camped on this beach for three days, which felt more like an eternity, dreaming of when they would get to Páros and wondering if they would still be keen on their men, inventing instead some new men they would meet—Frans, Hans, and Reinhold, rich Germans (heaven knows why they were German) who drove a Mercedes. And, as they starved on their beach, waiting for the days to pass, they told each other ridiculous stories about the things they would do with these men. The girls had only brought some melons (which turned out to be round cucumbers) for food and Antiparos's main town was a good ten miles by mule away from their beach. They had wanted to eat melon for three days in order to lose weight. On the third day of starvation, as if an apparition, an ice-cream truck appeared on a rocky dirt road above the beach, a road they had thought was intended only for mules. But it was no apparition.

It was the real thing and all the weight the girls had lost eating cucumbers they gained back eating ice cream. The ice-cream truck gave them (and their green leather suitcases) a lift to the ferry and from there they sailed across a small gulf to Páros, adorable in Bea's clothes, carefully manicured, and deeply tanned (even their boobs and butts).

Miki and Dario and Miki's car, a Land Rover this time, waited for them at the Páros dock in Parikia. Awkwardly, but possessively, the boys kissed their girls and then whisked them and Bea and their luggage off to the small fishing village of Naoussa, the road winding through eerie magnificent rock formations and gentle terraced hills, some laced with vineyards. In the front Miki and Dario spoke nervously and fast to Bea, and in the back Beth and Sylvia were suddenly exhausted. Beth couldn't keep up with the Italian and didn't bother trying. Though it was late afternoon, the sun was still high, shining red and magnificent against the aquamarine sky. It felt as though the ten days since Forte dei Marmi had passed as fast as a breeze, blowing them all to this moment.

And then there was Cesare, standing halfway up the steps of one of those traditional Cycladic homes—whitewashed with a deep sea-blue trim. Above the stairs wisteria draped a latticed balcony and here and there stood pots of brilliant red geraniums. Cesare was struggling to communicate with the landlady, attempting to negotiate the price of a room for the girls—his friends' friends—using his best ancient Greek learned several years before at the Liceo Classico. The landlady, her bulk draped in a black housedress, that revealed only her thick ankles and bare feet, did not understand a word but seemed to understand the topic was money and was thus keen for the conversation. The light of the afternoon sun caught in Cesare's hair, illuminating him, while his figure cast a shadow over the landlady. He gestured with his hands and smiled, clearly flirting. On the small road upon which the car was parked, a mule led by a hunched-over old man clomped by. Beth stood at the car door, green leather suitcase near her feet. She wore a mandarin-colored sundress and her Jesus sandals and she looked up at Cesare, thinking that he wasn't as attractive as Bea had suggested. His features were too sharp—angular jaw, Roman nose, even chiseled temples, making the lines of his face seem harsh. And there was something funny to his look, something strange, perhaps only the result of being animated by his conversation. Just then, as if he had heard her thoughts and wished to prove them wrong, he looked at her. She looked away, but felt the shock, the stab, a sensation she had not felt before and that struck her just as swiftly as something randomly falling from the sky. It was utterly intoxicating and seemed to have nothing to do with anything that made any sense, and she wanted to look at him again. Indeed, she could feel her face flush, a very hot and brilliant red. He's not that attractive, she thought again, as if to excise something uncomfortable—a thorn from a toe.

I will never go back to Páros. White houses trimmed with blue, small towns at the edge of the water with outside cafés serving fried squid and other fresh seafood—the smell of it, grilled fish and salt air and corn—the corn on the cob dressed still in its silk was grilled, too. On that island Beth and Cesare are perpetually falling in love—over and over and over again. It's a level in Dante's Paradiso *out there in the blue sea where this blessed young couple are forever able to reenact their first moment of love, when everything is absolutely possible and you're blissfully unaware of the destruction that lies in your wake, of the cruelty and pain you'll inflict on each other in the name of love at some unforeseen and distant time. You trust. You trust your body, your future, the*

*mysterious laws that say everyone will receive love. You trust, you
have no experience yet to teach you otherwise. I will never go
back to Páros.*

A fragment of Valeria's mother's life. Dated 1992, written by her
mother in her mother's diary, in her mother's neat, careful,
swirling script, her mother trying to tell a story, her mother,
perhaps, trying to be indelible, poetic even, her mother speaking. It was all she ever said about Páros in her journals because
she didn't start writing them until well after the Páros trips were
over. (She and Cesare went to the island several times because
they loved to windsurf and because the nature of their vacations
were decidedly Italian rather than American.) And that was also
the last passage Beth wrote about Cesare. She had just been to
Italy to see him for the last time, Valeria knew from the letters.
They started breaking up in 1987, but the drama endured until
1992, for five years—telephone calls, letters, fast and secret
trips to somewhere. Years later, after Beth's death—fifteen, sixteen years later—Valeria, a twenty-year-old woman living in
New York, wished her mother had written more. Beth had written plenty in Valeria's baby book, written not just about her first
smile and bite of food but also about the politics of the time—
some sex scandal, an impeachment, a stolen election. Valeria
wouldn't care so much about her mother's views of her baby
years (sweet, yes) as she would about her mother's life. You see,
Valeria, unlike Beth, would have memories of her mother. Simple
things, her mother cooking with her, her mother helping her to
brush her teeth, her mother dressing up like magic for an evening out with Valeria's father, the wonderful scratching. Thus
for Valeria her mother would not always be dead (like George
Washington). But because of the way in which Beth died, the
memory of her would not be about her life but rather about her

death. She would become for Valeria someone who was always dying. Perpetually she died. For eternity Valeria would be able to watch her mother's death. For years and years and more years still she would be able to see it on television. Thus she would love digging into Beth's life, retracing it, finding in this passage, written in her mother's hand, a moment where her mother is doing something fabulous and dangerous just as perpetually, just as permanently, just as indelibly. In this passage she breathed, alive, a person feeling, immortal. *On that island Beth and Cesare are perpetually falling in love—over and over and over and over again.*

Cesare came down the stairs, smiling, "All I know is the ancient Greek," he said in English, apologetically, to his friends and the American girls. He had a big smile, not one bit harsh. His accent was clearly Italian but with a hint of British English (from having studied in London, Beth would later learn). He didn't seem surprised by the arrival of the three of them and Beth wondered what he had been told by Miki, hoped it wasn't much. "She doesn't understand it though," he said, shrugging. He kissed Bea on either cheek and, in Italian, asked her about her adventures getting to Greece. Beth noted that they did not seem like lovers. Miki appeared behind Beth and introduced her to Cesare with a certain amount of pride that made Beth feel both possessed and annoyed. Beth smiled and so did Cesare and she wondered if he had felt the shock that she had and then hoped that no one could hear the way her heart thumped. Miki, as if he could sense something, swept Beth upstairs to see the apartment and his room. She could still hear Bea, her big flirtatious voice carrying on with Cesare. The room had a vine-covered balcony that offered a view of the sea. Miki's clothes were neatly unpacked and arranged in his closet, and Beth wondered if he packed like Bea did, if all Italians were taught to pack so precisely. Somehow she didn't find this habit as attractive in a man. More than that, she didn't want to be in the room alone with him. She wanted to be outside with the others. She wanted to know if she would feel that shock again. She wanted to feel it again. Just then Miki tried to kiss her. She told him she had to pee. Alone, in the bathroom, she studied herself in the mirror. The shock was palpable. She could see it. She felt it again, aftershocks trembling through her, making her somehow feel beautiful though she knew she was not a beautiful girl. She went back to Miki's room. She heard nothing that Miki said as she sat down on his tidy bed. She saw nothing. She tasted nothing. She was blissfully and completely and absolutely and marvelously empty. Miki kissed her. Cesare entered the room. She pushed away from Miki, almost meanly. Medium tall and dark and slender, Cesare had a body like the *David,* but he was dressed in American-style swimming trunks, a T-shirt with the words NEIL PRYDE beneath a picture of a sailing windsurfer, and flip-flops. Italians never go barefoot. *"Scusatemi,"* he apologized, and backed out of the room. His eyes were big and dark brown with a spark. "No no," Beth said fast, as if her words could yank him back. And they did.

"Cosa vuoi?" asked Miki. What do you want?

"Will you come to dinner with us?" Cesare asked, reentering but only just slightly. Such lovely English. He was all grace and humility and elegance. And Beth said yes before Miki could answer, and the big group of them went off to a café at the edge of the water in Naoussa for red snapper and grilled octopus and tsatsiki and something else and something else...but Beth barely noticed. Despite the daze and the shock and the desire to watch this boy talk and smile, she had no idea what she was experiencing, and that night, after a little too much wine for all of them, they would be paired off by Bea's design, and not by the direction of this wonderful new sensation of Beth's, which made her eager and anxious and pretty and giddy and the whole evening smelled of jasmine and rosemary and citrus and was filled with the rhythms of the little fishing boats knocking about in the port and the Greek wine was terribly good and she loved Greece and never wanted to leave.

Valeria would find this fragment of a letter, dated 1987, written in English:

> *My dear little Americanina. My America. My future. My dream. My impossible dream. Your body so soft, so like velvet your legs. I detest the thought of you with another man and love the thought that others should experience you. I want to know every detail by name. It is good and right for you to be with others. Perhaps I am repenting for my sins. But let me know. Spend one hour each day, at least, to let me know. If you are to be my wife, if we are to realize this love—you must. But don't be cruel. Don't torture me. Not with someone young, not with someone you could love. I love you more than ever, more than life. I'll love you when I'm dead.*

Mom, Valeria would have said, had she been able to speak directly to her mother, *Ma-omm,* in that drawn-out disbelieving tone in which her friends called for their mothers, taking them so guilelessly for granted. (*Mom,* she would love the word.) You what? Do you see, Mom, what this letter implies? Did you really? But why? If you loved each other? That's sick, perverse. But look at how this person loved you. How can you stop loving someone if you loved her this much? What is this twisted love, twisted into knots? *I'll love you when I'm dead.* Did he love her still?

Beth's life. Valeria would feed upon Beth's life. It would nourish her own. What Valeria would give to read her mother's letters to Cesare. Beth would be with Valeria always, standing by her side. Picture this: just now they are in the kitchen together making pasta with tomatoes and basil and mozzarella because it is a hot July day in New York City with those fire engines racing up Broadway and car alarms and police cars and the stench of garbage on the streets just the same as always. The Hudson flows carelessly by; Valeria can watch it from her window. It flows both ways, the river an estuary here, flowing backward, defying Heracleitus's notion of time moving in one direction only. Here, a young woman can, in fact, step in the same river twice.

Picture this: the year is 2017. Catastrophes happen, former presidents die, pop stars die, even a famous singer from Beth's youth, known for turning her life into fodder for songs that rocked the charts. Future kings and queens and dictators are born. Men are still in power doing powerful things, not for the right reasons but simply because they can. All of us skipping along in tandem with the parallel world of history. Valeria is twenty years old. She has an adoring father in New York City, a lovely stepmother, a younger half brother of whom she is ridiculously fond. She has a crazy old grandfather on his commune in Pennsylvania, which struggles, a bit, to stay afloat. He reminds her of Miss Havisham, preserving the wreckage—and why not? The man who killed Valeria's mother is long dead. But Evil still lurks as it always will, people seizing power because they can. God bless her grandfather for his utopia, for trying to make something right of all that has gone wrong. Her mother had been wildly in love. Valeria wants to know the size and shape of love, wants to quantify love's power, understand its capacity for endurance. What has Cesare made of the wreckage? Would he love Beth when he was dead? Does she, dead, love him still?

Bea and Cesare kissed that first night on a beach in Naoussa near a bonfire they built of driftwood, oblivious to the other pairs and their whereabouts. They stayed out all night and at dawn Bea floated back to her room and her friends and flopped on the bed in a dreamy sort of way and they exchanged stories about their midnight escapades (barefoot walks in the sea, salty kisses, and the like), giggling, posturing for one another, stretching their legs into the air, giddy with romance and the notion of feeling sexy. It was summer and they were in Greece and the moon, if inconstant, was always bright. Of the three of them, Beatrice's glee radiated the most and the other two tried to drill her, tried to extract nuggets of her adventure as if each detail were a jewel. Finally, the conversation dropped off and the girls fell asleep, until they were wakened at noon by the loud arrival of Miki who wanted to take them windsurfing at Santa Maria beach.

The next night on one of those small labyrinthine streets, not far from one of the many churches of the town, not far from Cesare's apartment that he shared with his friends, not far from Bea's room that she shared with her friends; that next night when the sun was well down and Bea and Sylvia and Dario and especially Miki were searching the streets for the missing pair, afraid that Cesare and Beth were lost, calling their names with perhaps too much wine in their tones; that next night, hearing their names and sneaking farther into a nook in a wall, a secret hiding spot illuminated ever so gracefully by the moon and all those stars; that next night feeling the exhilaration of the new and the secret and the illicit and the mystery of choice; that next night with the distant sounds of a discotheque and people eating, the clatter of silverware and glass; that next night, cool from the wind and too much sun, caring not a whit for Bea's feelings, for Sylvia's whereabouts, for Miki's probable pain, Beth and Cesare kissed.

A first kiss, do you remember? Gentle at first, his lips exploring every delicate curve of her neck and face, the hollow of her throat, her eyes, the ridge of her nose, the curl of her ears, as if reading her face, deciphering there some complete, some absolute, truth. His lips in her hair, his hands so gently on her back, his fingers on her arms, then the kiss. That way that desired lips feel. Voices calling their names, a brilliant night sky, moonlight dancing on the Aegean Sea. Thieves stealing kisses. How fun it can be to steal. The smell of fried something or other. Then hungry, then greedy, then desperate for those lips. Their names so clear; the voices so close. Their bodies pushing together, hiding. *"Tu sei perfetta,"* Cesare whispered into her ear, and his words became all of her body. This was dizzying, this hurt, this she did not want to tell anyone, this she did not want to leave. No wine, no ouzo, she was drunk just the same. *"Io sono perfetta,"* she repeated in his ear, drawing out the words in order to believe them, loving the confidence, and he pulled her into him again and up to him and they were both so light, ethereal as if shades, barely there. Their names rang out again, a little more urgently this time: Bea calling for her friend—not even for Cesare but for her friend—all concern in that tipsy tone. But Beth did not care. Indeed, she was annoyed by their persistence. She cared about nothing beyond his kiss. The voices, thank god and finally, disappeared as if the friends had given up. Beth and Cesare were alone within the kiss. Beth thought of all previous kisses, gum-on-wrist kisses, Carlos beneath the lights of the brothel. Beth had never kissed or been kissed before.

They had spent that day paired in their pairs on Santa Maria beach, a gentle curving beach with a predictable wind, onshore, good for windsurfing. Other friends were there, too: rich boys of sock-and-shoe fame and money, all with their windsurfing paraphernalia of boards and sails and wetsuits. This crowd simply added to the mass, if not the story. These were boys whose families made incredible things like the thread that is woven into fine silk stockings or more mundane things like shoelaces and the little metal rings that fit into the eyelets of shoes. So many jobs Beth had never thought of. The boys attempted to windsurf, tried to teach the girls, but they all gave up for lack of wind and spent the day talking and eating Greek salads and playing endless games of backgammon at a small taverna at the edge of the beach. Bea and Sylvia had entertained the group first with stories of their adventures en route to Greece and then with stories of Beth's commune and of Beth's father, making everyone laugh and ask even more questions about the logistics of the place and about the reality of the place. Beth's was truly the strangest family life any of these Italians had ever heard of; they were astonished by the idea of a dead mother memorialized in a farm, Mother Earth, Beth raised on the back of her mother. "I'll admit," Bea said, speaking in Italian, "my first summer in America I was terrified of the place. All these children, all these people all over the place, and this one big man leading them and not leading them at the same time—all living together in chaotic orderliness. By the second summer I realized you could go unnoticed if you chose, that no one was watching. As long as you helped, that's all anyone cared about. And Jackson, the interest he took in you was inspiring, made you want to try things you'd never have thought of. I milked a goat even, can you imagine?" To outsiders, life at Claire was a curiosity, as if Beth and her strange home were like some sort of object that could be picked up and examined and admired. Sometimes she became tired of this song and dance, but mostly she was proud. She looked across the flat waters to the island of Naxos. It rose, awesome, to the sky. Beyond it, she knew, lay Turkey.

"You grew up there?" Cesare asked, sitting down beside Beth. He seemed to be searching for something to say. His voice faltered: the question need not have been asked. She smiled. All over again she felt that sensation. She liked that he wore American swimming trunks instead of the Italian kind that Miki wore. Miki nudged himself a little closer so that they formed a triangle and he leaned in as Cesare asked for an example of what someone like himself could do at this commune.

"What would someone like yourself want to do?" Beth asked. It was a pretty simple question, a pretty simple notion, for an American girl. There was very little to it but the obvious. "What do you want to be when you grow up?" was the big question for children in America. The possibilities for girls had evolved since Beth was very young, when schoolteacher, nurse, or mother ran the gamut of female choice. But it was a question asked regardless and equally and all the same, and it made each child dream of potential, revel in fantasy. Beth was asking this simple question, asking it innocently and sweetly, without any understanding of Italian tradition, a chasm that would always divide her from Cesare.

He repeated the question aloud, turning it over, it seemed, in his mind as he said the words, *"What would someone like yourself want to do?"* He was not making fun of her. She understood that. Rather, he enjoyed the question, the possibilities of it. She studied his face, his eyes looking into the bright blue sky. She wanted to ask him a thousand questions. "I suppose I'd like to be a writer," he said. "Would they ever have a writer at Claire?"

"We've never had one, but I'm sure my father would know how to use a writer. A writer could help him write his long doctrines and letters to Washington." She raised her eyebrows with an affectionate smile, thinking of her father hard at work at his desk. She imagined Cesare at his side, helping him with the letters. No one had ever come to Claire to stay on her recommendation. The idea that she would meet someone who would wind up living at Claire had never occurred to her. She liked the notion. For a moment it made her feel proud of Claire, closer to her father.

"Are you a writer?" she asked.

"I study economics and I don't like it," he said honestly.

"Then why do you study it?" This made no sense to her.

"I'm in training to take over my family's banking business," he answered. And he pointed to his friends milling about on the beach. "So that I can finance their dreams of better shoelaces and eyelets and dyes and designs. So that I can help them become richer."

They were both only partly aware of Miki. His English was all right but not good enough to keep up with the speed of their conversation. He smoothed the sand with his hands, as if ironing it into something neat and orderly. Beth and Cesare threw him smiles as if to suggest he was part of the conversation, but if he had asked a question they wouldn't have realized it.

"But you'd rather write."

"I love to read." He noticed just then that she was reading *Middlemarch*. He picked it up and told her he had read the book in English during one of his summers studying in England. Miki grabbed it and asked Cesare in Italian if he'd really read the whole book in English, declaring it long. Beth wished Miki would go away. She was impressed that Cesare had read the book. It was difficult enough for her in English. She had been sharing this one with Sylvia, too, having finished *Anna Karenina*. Beth wasn't very far along, but Dorothea had married Casaubon and was honeymooning (sort of) in Rome, a city she found claustrophobic from the pressure of so much history and time. Beth loved that Dorothea hated the weight of all that history since tradition taught you to love it no matter what.

"The weight of history," she said, suddenly understanding why he'd found her question amusing, why he'd repeated the words.

"For that reason especially I enjoyed those summers in England reading. Now I read only American books." He was reading *On the Road,* a book Beth had not yet read. She liked Cesare just a little more already simply because he was a reader. Their enthusiasm for literature is too banal to describe beyond the rush that such a connection triggers, a sense of sharing something big, important yet undefined—a vocabulary, if not a language, of their own.

Miki said something about what he was reading and then about what he would become at Claire, but neither Beth nor Cesare heard him.

They talked and they talked and the wind never came and she stopped feeling that shock of nerves, just the exquisite desire to hear him ask her questions and to make him laugh and to be made to laugh by him. His sister, Laura, was just now in America, he said, in Alabama of all places—a state Beth had never been to—on an exchange with a family down there. Unlike Beth's arrangement, it was a one-way exchange, since no one from Alabama would come home with Laura to Italy. She wrote long lively letters home (in the American fashion), describing the trailer she lived in, the room she shared with the four daughters, the bunk beds they all slept in. Late at night the girls would ask Laura to help them spell American words, help them read English books, and carefully and patiently she would teach these American girls English. Beth imagined a female version of Cesare as Beth tried to comprehend the implications of an Italian teaching English to English-speaking girls. "She has warned us that she has gotten fat on hamburgers," Cesare said. "That is all they eat and she loves them." Beth loved the way he didn't make conjunctions of his words; she loved the rhythm it gave his speech. When Laura's boyfriend came to visit, they rented a big American car and traveled all across the country following Bruce Springsteen on tour. They covered three thousand miles and received over two thousand dollars' worth of speeding tickets.

Beth and Cesare spoke about everything and anything, each one comfortable, eager to unfold for the other, and the deeper they went, the more interested each became to the exclusion of all the others. The others did not exist: only this beautiful man and this adorable girl (not a great beauty, but adorable all the same, especially when she smiled. Later, in Città, none of Cesare's female friends would understand what he saw in the American: *"Non e' neanche bella,"* they'd say to one another: She isn't even pretty). Dario, small and wiry, approached them and tried to ask Beth if she believed he had a real chance with Sylvia. But Beth couldn't be bothered by him. She was becoming selfish in a way she had never been before. She teased him kindly so she wouldn't seem too awful, but he could hardly speak English and Sylvia didn't speak Italian and Beth simply didn't care. So the afternoon passed on the shores of Santa Maria beach with no wind and Naxos looming across the water hiding Turkey and the sun baking them to a delicious brown. One by one, the others started to leave. First Miki, then Dario; then the other sock-and-shoe boys; then Sylvia and Bea, unable still to believe the worst of their friend; Bea still high on last night's excursion and kiss. Bea bent down, all her dark hair swinging, and kissed Cesare on the cheek and told him, in English, to take care of her friend and to bring her home before too long so that she could have time to dress before dinner. Teasingly, Bea admonished him to be good. And then the two were alone and they stayed there until the sun slipped to the other side of Páros, talking, wanting to explore each other inside and out, like a country you visit and never want to leave.

———

The first time that Bea and Beth said good-bye to each other they cried. But actually Beth was glad to go, and Bea was happy to see her go. They liked each other a lot and wanted to see each other again, but they weren't in love. Sometime during the winter Bea proposed they do another exchange the following summer. They decided to do six weeks in each other's country instead of three. When they said good-bye the second time, at JFK International Airport, Bea's aunt by Bea's side (she had come for the last two weeks of Bea's trip because she had just lost her husband to brain cancer and had discovered a lump in her left breast and hoped a vacation would do her well), it was as if one of the girls were going off to war to be tortured and then murdered and the other would have to endure the pain for the rest of her life. They cried the whole day before, during the entire drive to the airport, and for three hours while they waited for the plane. At customs, where the final separation occurred, Bea's aunt, a slender slip of a woman who had little patience for all this crying given her current woes, had to physically pry the girls apart and ask them to stop causing such a scene. But it was heartbreaking watching the two clinging to each other like answers. Even Bea's aunt could recognize this.

Upon arriving home, their love letters began in earnest. (Beth saved these, too; they took their place among the papers spoken of when we speak of going through a dead person's papers. Of course Valeria read them, but Bea was no mystery to her. Bea was Valeria's godmother and had settled in New York many years before Valeria was born, wanting to be far away from all that she found confining about Città. In the months after Beth died, Bea saw Valeria every day.) In the first letter Bea invited Beth to come live with her in Italy for a year; she couldn't bear the separation, and looking forward to a year together would make this one pass the more swiftly. Beth agreed, and she came. And she fell in love immediately, madly, irreversibly, with the very man Bea was keen on.

The day following Beth's disappearing act and the kiss, Bea, no fool, understood the betrayal and hated her friend. But being proud, she remained aloof and cool for a day. She watched Beth pretending that Cesare was of no interest, listened to Beth asking leading questions about Bea's feelings about Cesare, heard Beth lying about where she had been the night before, and observed Beth trying to be sweet to Miki when it was clear Miki repulsed her in the way a spurned lover always repulses the deserter. For the first time since she had known Beth, Bea's world started to become a bit smaller.

On the next day, when it became clear that Beth and Cesare couldn't even be bothered to hide how they felt, when pretending they wanted to was impossible, Bea turned to Sylvia. Strong, radiant, proud Bea broke down and cried. She and Sylvia sat together in their rented room with their suitcases spilling several seasons of Bea's beautiful clothes, their skin prickly with the sand and the sun. Bea was heartbroken, not for the loss of Cesare but for the loss of Beth implicit in the betrayal.

"I should be worth more," Bea cried.

"I know, I know," Sylvia kept saying, rocking Bea in her arms, glad that Bea felt close enough to her to be able to cry. Sylvia felt very grown-up and mature, comforting Bea. At the same time, she felt betrayed, too, thinking of Chas. Perhaps Sylvia was realizing that people change, becoming something other than what we know of them. As Beth was blossoming into the great love of Cesare's life (and he of hers) she was wilting before her friends. What Sylvia didn't yet understand, because she didn't yet have the experience, was that people just as easily turn back into who they were, that all this change is nothing special, indeed quite ordinary, and the little fissures don't amount to much in the larger scheme of things.

"Did you love Chas?" Bea asked. She, too, had no idea yet of the elasticity of friendship. Sylvia continued to stroke Bea's thick dark hair. How had Sylvia felt about Chas? She thought of the fight in the small San Sebastián hotel room. They had been scared, lying there on that bed, of something they couldn't articulate. If she had loved Chas, would she have run off, abandoning Beth? Was there a reason she had fled so fast to Irún, a reason, which did not involve Beth, that would explain why she had chosen not to see Chas again? Would that reason explain their fear?

"I don't know. I don't think so. I didn't let myself find out."

"I hate her," Bea said. The afternoon sun illuminated her face, which glistened with tears.

"No, you don't," Sylvia said, and they rocked there, trying to negotiate everything they felt. Yet even though the girls took great comfort from each other, it was really Beth each wanted to be holding and to be held by. And they wondered, more simply than this, because once again they would not have been able to articulate it quite so clearly, if their friend had crossed the divide into that new region looming ominously in front of them. Each was bewildered, perhaps even jealous, that Beth was crossing the divide first, without her. A long time passed and then they began to scheme.

When Beth returned to the room, Bea was silent no longer. She was not mean; she did not yell. Rather she was direct and clear. Sylvia let Bea speak first, but it was clear to Beth they were united against her, and she had a terrible sinking feeling because it seemed that all the beauty of the last three days was now to be paid for, and she could only think of that injustice, not of her friends.

"You have a choice," Bea said. "We are leaving tomorrow. You can come or you can stay."

It was two in the morning. Beth noticed their packed suitcases, standing side by side like soldiers or simply like her two friends, standing united now in their disappointment in her. Still she did not care.

"The ferry is at six in the morning," Sylvia said.

They never discussed Cesare or betrayal or Chas. All of that was perfectly clear, implicit. There was no way for Beth to tell Cesare anything. The girls would be long gone before he awoke. She couldn't go to his room now, not with Miki there and all of the others asleep. Beth looked at her friends. Oh girls, they can be so punishing, so mean and cruel. Bea and Sylvia enjoyed this test, though perhaps they didn't fully know it or admit it. Either Beth chose them or she chose Cesare. She had known Cesare a few days; what would he do with her if she stayed? What would she do with him? What if all that had passed between them—that shock, that stab, the giddy desire, that kiss—was nothing? Bea and Sylvia stood like two shades in that moony night. Beth got their game. Checkmate. She hated them now but knew she was in no position to fight and scream and carry on. Instead, there was just a vast silence in the room. Sylvia and Bea prepared themselves for bed as if nothing were wrong, saying little things to each other about toothpaste and nail scissors, talking comfortably as if they had always been great friends.

"Of course, there's no decision," Beth said. She sat down and started packing and did not let them see her cry.

The night of the kiss, Beth and Cesare walked all over Naoussa. A tremendous wind had settled on the island, the one they had been waiting for all day; it whipped every tree and every shutter, sending litter aswirl. They are called Meltemis, these winds.

The couple was blown miles, it seemed, up into the hills, down to the water, electric, in that state where selfishness reigns. Part of the beauty is that you are sacrificing everything—your friends, your family, your country—for this love, and you're young enough not to really understand that you're hurting others, a concept you can't quite get because you've never been hurt. After the realization that Cesare and Beth were likely together, Sylvia comforted Bea, Dario comforted Miki, then they all comforted each other. They all hated Beth and Cesare. When the sun started coming up, Cesare and Beth, realizing this might be the case, decided to just keep walking, and so they did—walking and laughing in that Meltemi wind. The wind was causing its own private destruction. Branches snapped, flying this way and that. The town started to wake up, little Greek women in black, hunched over, carrying enormous shopping bags. Church bells ringing. *"Tu sei perfetta,"* he whispered. *"Io sono perfetta,"* she whispered back, and nothing really seemed to matter much even if it did. At the harbor the fishermen were just coming in with their catch.

"Are we even?" Beth asked Sylvia with a smile, lying beneath the shower of soot on the ferry back to Italy. They were headed now to Favignana, an island off of western Sicily where Bea's parents were vacationing. The girls had inevitably warmed to each other again. But it took Beth a good four days after the Páros departure, four days of roaming all over Corfu on mopeds in search of Chas, to ask that question.

"Yes," Sylvia said, with her equally winning smile.

Beth saw the train. She would always see the long train dividing in the middle of a Spanish night with two girls on it cradled in the broad expanse of some nuns' laps. These girls have never been in love, have never known anyone their own age who has died; their futures are filled with promise and the train is dividing to take them toward it, dividing in the middle of the night with the rumbling of so much metal over so much metal. And though there may seem to be a choice, there is only one inevitable direction.

Four

You Must Change Your Life

A fast car on a wide American highway. A free soul from an exotic land of deserts with blood-red canyons and buttes and mesas that scrape the sky; a land of strip towns with drive-thru-just-about-everything, seedy hotels, and lonely phone booths on long lonely roads. A drive-in movie theater, jazz, and alligators in the bayous, the heaving and sighing of semitrailers lined up and glinting in the night. New York City, Los Angeles, Las Vegas. A wide-aisled supermarket flooded with choice. McDonald's, fried chicken, apple pie—simple things Cesare had never tried. Cornfields and wheat fields and soy, shifting loess hills, rolling into more fields, then pastures dotted by cows and sheep, and farmyards with barns and silos and grain elevators, and wide-open views the size of Texas. Beth was all of this for him. Twenty-one years old with a gap between her teeth and blond hair, blue eyes, and the longest darkest lashes he had ever seen, she was abundance and risk, experimentation and discovery, and she had fallen sweetly, deeply, permanently for him. Her name, ordinary American name, he pronounced it *Bet* with his Italian accent that didn't know that foreign *h*—*Bet* as in "to gamble everything," his tongue transforming the name (and her) into something different entirely, extraordinary even. She was the Statue of Liberty, the Empire State Building shooting into the sky like hope. She was America.

"If I'm America," she said to Cesare, "then you're the Roman Empire." She lay beside him in the soft summer grass of Fiori, his parents' country house in the hills above Lago Maggiore. She was leaving Italy soon and had been trying to convince him to come to America and he was trying to convince her to stay, to put off returning to college for another year. They had been together three years already and he had not yet been to America. There were excuses, of course, but even so she was becoming impatient. For the first year she had lived in Città. The second year, while she started college at NYU, he began a two-year tenure of military service, which he spent in the Servizio Civile because he did not believe in firearms, and during this time he was forbidden to leave the country. Thus for their third year she took her sophomore year away from NYU to study economics at the Bocconi in Milan so that she could live again in Città, always with Bea's family, who welcomed her as if she were a daughter. The Bocconi would open up for her the economics of business, fueling what would become her calling. The Bocconi became part of her life plan.

Now, however, her year was coming to an end and she was going home. His service finished, he was free and she wanted him to come. He knew that. She wanted him to come not for a few weeks or a month or two, but for an entire year. She wanted him to give America a try. She wanted him to prove that his desire to construct his own life, separate from the life being handed to him by his family, was authentic. It was a test of sorts, and he knew that as well.

"Why am I not simply just Italy?" he asked, curious about the way of her mind. He liked to explore every inch of her as if he could find in her the answer. There was a lot to excavate even after three years; she had the weirdest family he had ever heard of. He had met the grandmother, Grammy as she liked to be called. He had shown her all over Città and Milan, taken her to Como to buy silk. She was a handsome woman who wore sturdy shoes. "Hand stitched," she informed him because she knew he had an interest in shoes. "My husband's relatives were of Buster Brown fame," she added, "beautiful hand-stitched shoes. Ruined, they were, by Bata which came in from Czecho-slovakia—or some such country—and were cheaper because the soles were glued!" Grammy was one who liked to know a bit about everything and enjoyed letting her company know the breadth of her knowledge. (It is debatable whether or not her husband's relatives were attached to Buster Brown, but that's another point and one that didn't concern Cesare because he had never heard of Buster Brown anyway.)

She made a fuss about being an "opera buff," wishing it were the season to go to La Scala because there was nothing in the world she would have preferred more. "I'm a patron of the Met," she said to him, fixing him with her sharp and penetrating eyes, which seemed to delight in absolutely everything he took her to see. At four in the afternoon she liked to have her tea, "Piping hot," she would say. He learned the term and its definition well. He enjoyed the eccentricities of this woman. She referred to Cesare as a prince and Fiori became his castle. She was impressed with the azaleas and rhododendrons and returned to Europe in Beth's third year especially for the annual party to celebrate their flowering. Of Benvenuto's fresco depicting Valeria she said, "I have an eye. I have a discerning eye. I know art history and this picture is worth a lot." Never did it occur to her that its value to the family was beyond recognition and money, that the last thing they would want was a bunch of art historians claiming it for history, no matter the price. ("So American," Cesare had said to Beth, not as a reproach, but rather with a certain wistfulness at how easy it is for Americans to let go.)

"You're a Renaissance man," Grammy said to him, looking him up and down. In his hand he held a book (he always did), *Revolutionary Road.* She had never heard of it, but was impressed, nonetheless, because it was in English.

"Made in Italy," he said, with his smile catching her smile. And she laughed that bright all-knowing laugh of hers.

In Città Grammy spent oodles of money at the best shops, buying clothes for her granddaughter, using credit cards instead of cash. (At that time credit cards were not so widely used in Italy and still a bit of a curiosity.) She often noted the quality of Cesare's shirts, fingering them and declaring the fabric authentically Italian. "The best workmanship in the world comes from Italy." His parents hosted her. His father spoke no English and she spoke no Italian, so she had Cesare and his mother translating endless stories of her youthful adventures traveling Italy with her trunks, stories that involved small dramas on the Bridge of Sighs and escapades in the Vatican (not romantic) with a priest. Even stern little Giovanni Paolo smiled at her tales. When she arrived in Città, she always carried three trunks though her visits never exceeded ten days. "When you come to America...," she would say to Cesare. "When you marry Beth...," she would say. And she would describe the big parties she would have for him in New York to introduce him. She never defined to whom he would be introduced. That was implicit: the finest crowds. Of Beth's father she said little, and though Cesare wanted to know her opinion of him and hear her description, it was not in his nature to pry. All she said on the subject was that getting Beth away from Pennsylvania had been her life's work, and now that Beth was safely in Italy, on the "Continent," she felt she could go to heaven. Of her daughter she spoke often, saying simply that she had been a beautiful, smart woman, and had she survived, Pennsylvania would not have been her path.

Cesare liked this woman, liked her energy and her enthusiasm. She was over seventy and had the strength of a hundred mules, mules because she liked to describe herself as "an old threadbare mule going round and round the katydid." Of the phrase he only understood mules. However, her airs were not missed by him. (And the fact of these airs endeared Beth to him all the more completely because Beth had none.) In an Italian he would find this characteristic pretentious and annoying. With Grammy, however, he did not because he could tease her and make fun of her and she would laugh along with him at herself because, of course, she, too, was well aware of the airs. "The airs," she would say, "are so fresh. What a pleasant day." She knew who she was and where she came from: a cowgirl from Montana who was smart enough to make her way east to Vassar, to marry well so that she would be provided for for life. But her roots were her roots; her parents had been uneducated. Everything she knew she learned herself, including her airs.

Grammy visited Città three times, going to church with Elena, eating daintily, shopping mightily, pretending to be a grande dame from New York with not a financial care in the world. Cesare would take her to the center of Città in the evenings for *prosecco* and to show her off to his friends, who would gather around her and smile and try out their varying abilities with her language, and somehow she would make them all smile and laugh as she sipped the bubbly wine, flushing from its influence, inviting everyone to visit her in America.

"Your bedroom is waiting for you in New York," she'd say to Cesare, whom by now she considered her pal. "Of course, it is separate from Beth's. There'll be none of that in my household. Not until you marry her. You'll have to go to Pennsylvania if you relish monkey business." And she lifted her left eyebrow and pierced him with those sharp green eyes and then lifted her lips in a gentle, knowing smile that said, I like you, son. (She called him son.) And then she was gone.

As for the rest of the people in Beth's family, those at Claire, they were a mishmash. Over the years Cesare got to know them through pictures and through the stories Beth told: he heard about the people who came, the ones who left, the ones who seemed to stay forever. The father took in anyone who needed a place to live, and they could stay as long as they contributed. There was a Russian carpenter named Mash, who erected yurts and teepees in the woods. There was an out-of-work investment banker named Hunter, who helped with finances and kept them flush with champagne and had an exquisite eye for antiques. Sometimes the way Beth paused on Hunter made Cesare jealous, wondering if Beth liked this Hunter more than just a little. "What kind of name is Hunter?" he asked, though he knew well of Hunter Thompson. "Jealousy doesn't become you," Beth responded, and then kissed him. "Besides, I hardly know him. He's only just come to Claire. All I know is that he's rich." Beth's noting that detail struck Cesare as particularly indiscreet: that Hunter's wealth would be the defining attribute, the one thing she'd recall and share, revealed in her that American fascination with any kind of money.

Beth's current stepmother's name was Sissy Three. (Yes, her last name was like the number; Cesare had checked with Beth several times to make sure he had heard correctly.) She referred to herself as Beth's stepmother, but she wasn't legally married to Jackson. "He'll never marry again," Beth explained. "He would see that as a betrayal of my mother." The man made no sense to Cesare, and thus Cesare became curious, especially because those who spoke of him (Bea in particular) admired him and his Claire, remarked on this visionary with two thousand acres smack in the middle of Snyder County, Amish country with horses and buggies rolling busily across the rippling hills of orchards. Of course, Cesare knew about the Amish. Later, when he finally visited Claire, their presence would make him feel like he had gone back in time, as though he were walking through a Thomas Hardy novel. Seeing them and seeing Claire juxtaposed, he couldn't help but reconsider his notions of the preservation of the past. Who doesn't try to preserve the past in one way or another?

Grammy claimed she hated Beth's father's haven, but she couldn't stay away. She drove out there often in her long black Lincoln Continental to try and "convert" them to ordinary souls. *Them*—the members of Claire—they came from everywhere bringing along their talents and knowledge. Sometimes Cesare would have Beth draw a diagram of the people and the place so that he could understand how it all fit together. Mostly Claire was just too weird and he wanted to save Beth from all that. Though another part of him, in truth, wondered, if he ever went there, would he ever leave—an idea that both excited and terrified him from the moment he first heard of Claire as he sat beside Beth on Santa Maria beach, imagining himself a writer. Writing for a living was the one dream that burned in him but that he rarely allowed himself to acknowledge. Even so, he always wrote: journals, letters, letters to editors. He was the rare Italian who filled up every inch of space on his postcards home, describing in explicit detail his adventures. Secretly, he wanted to be a nonfiction writer in the tradition of all those Americans who wrote real stories like novels. His hero was Tom Wolfe—

The Electric Kool-Aid Acid Test; The Right Stuff. Perhaps, he thought, he could write a book about Claire.

"Why am I the Roman Empire and not just Italy?" he asked again as they lay together in the summer grass.

"Italy would be too obvious and I prefer the idea of Rome because you're Caesar, emperor of my country." She held her eyes to the clouds and let her right hand drift the length of her to indicate the borders of her country. Sunlight coming through the trees dappled her skin with golden spots as the wind rustled the leaves. *Caesar Not Exactly,* he thought, imagining the three words as a name. He was an ordinary Italian man at twenty-seven, living with his parents who were desperate for him to finish the Bocconi so that someday he could take over his father's position at the bank, taking the baton and leading the family forward in a journey that started five hundred years ago. But then came Beth like a revelation. Cesare loved how large she could make him, as if through her there really could be more to who he was. He was in love. She was in love. Possibility seemed infinite. "As emperor I command you to stay," he said, and began to kiss the length of her.

Cesare's English was perfect, better than Beth's Italian. He had studied in London during high school summers, had had an English governess at one point, had read many English novels. The slight hint of an English accent hid behind his words, hard *t*s and strange pronunciations—shedules, tom-ah-toe, and the like. He was lit by hidden dreams and unending enthusiasm for anything and everything. He loved to cook with Beth, teaching her about why certain pasta shapes went with certain sauces, which pastas held which sauces best. For example, *farfalle* worked well with smoked salmon because the little flakes of fish caught in the butterfly wings. Cheese never went with

fish. (This was at a time when many Americans were still unso-
phisticated about pasta, when it was most often referred to as
noodles.) The names of the various pasta shapes alone was
enough to ignite her imagination: twins, weeds, snails, little ears,
priest stranglers. She wanted him to teach her to make a dish
with each shape. He taught her to revere and thus eat with the
seasons: onions in the spring, asparagus in early summer, then
mushrooms (hunted in the woods at Fiori). She taught him all
about chocolate and chocolate desserts; she taught him the bit
she knew about Indian food. Together they made elaborate
meals for his family and for their friends, who feasted together
in the Fiori gardens. Cooking and entertaining, Beth was in her
element—confident and generous and gregarious. She brought
people together with the food, fitting as many as she could
around the table, sparking conversations on any topic, making
certain everyone felt comfortable. Even his parents acquiesced to
her authority (though they only pretended to enjoy her Indian
dinner). Together Cesare and Beth played. He taught her to
windsurf and to compete in ski races and to vacation like an
Italian—long months at Santa Maria beach waiting for the
wind. He introduced her to Wolfe, who, in truth, she did not
much care for, preferring fiction. She didn't tell him this, but
he noticed her leaving the books he recommended half read.
He cared not a bit for shoes and the Bocconi and exams,
though on occasion Beth would try to help him care, encouraging him to study, accompanying him to Milan for the exams
so that his parents would leave him alone and so that she would
endear herself to them. She tried to fit in. She tried to adapt to
the traditions of his life in Città—the pattern of the days and
weeks and years. She learned to buy the daily bread at noon,
learned to eat a big meal in the middle of the day, learned to
drink her aperitif in the town center at dusk, making conver-

sation with his friends even if they (initially) were suspicious of her. Sometimes he wondered how long she would be able to keep this up.

Città with all its Bianchis, Macchis, Ghiringhellis, and Cellinis was his world, a world that few ever left permanently. *Cittadini* and *Cittadotti* crossed the nearby Swiss border to deposit money (all the money they had made on socks and shoes) in Credit Suisse banks, buy cigarettes and chocolate, and fill up their cars with gasoline, but they always hightailed it back to the beauty (and certainty) of their prosperous little town. From the top floor of Cesare's family's villa, which loomed above the town, you could see the snowcapped peaks of the Alps. What he wanted, deep down, was to be able to wander away from here, free to be a writer, a cook, a farmer (God forbid), and at the same time never to leave—to take his place in Città as master of Fiori, raising children with Beth. Indeed, he had never been to Rome.

For five hundred years his family had been bankers in this town. And for five hundred years his family, the Cellini family, had produced at least one son and a daughter or two. The firstborn sons were always named after the grandfathers, which allowed them two alternating names, Cesare and Giovanni Paolo (one Roman name, one Catholic, anchoring them quite squarely in the secular/religious duality of their country). For the names of the daughters they were allowed to choose anything: Valeria, Federica, Livia, Claudia, Isabella, Caterina, Laura. Beth thought of the women as the precious jewels of the Cellini line, the Cellini's gift to the world. The Cellini women were not bound to a single destiny. Cesare's sister, Laura, could do almost anything she wanted with her life except be a clown (which was, as it happened, what she wanted to do most with her life).

With Cesare's help, she ran away to clown school in Bern, Switzerland, when she was eighteen. He was twenty-one. He organized admissions to the school and train fares and an apartment rental. "My face is a funny one," she told him, looking him in the eye. "My face is absurd. When I smile, I can make people laugh. I like the way that makes me feel." He told her not to be ridiculous, but even as he said the words he couldn't help but agree. Her broad, puffy cheeks, her bright round eyes that seemed to jump forth with her animated smiles, her tight curly blond hair, her button nose, she had used them all to make him laugh many times. So, because he loved her, he took on her escape as if it were his own, awed by her determination and passion, curious to see how far she would get and whom she would become. He had visions of her tromping across the world, leaving happiness in her wake. A small part of him wished he had been born female because he believed he would have been allowed the freedom to make himself.

Alas, however, her parents learned the news and Signor Cellini, throwing all banking obligations aside, tore off to Bern to save his daughter from clowns and from all that clowns implied. (He gave the silent treatment to Cesare, knowing he had facilitated Laura's plan. Elena only asked, "But why?") Giovanni Paolo found his daughter wearing a clown costume—red and white polka dots and a big red nose—in a class that taught the art of laughter. The grotesque animation of her laughing face destroyed her beauty. Her luscious curly blond hair, a bob above her ears, had been dyed green. He simply held her, tightly and with everything he had, hard tears forming in his eyes. And that was that.

Bea had long since forgiven Beth for falling in love in Páros. "When I realized how serious this was," she said, there was nothing she could feel but happiness and a hope that someday this relationship would mean that Beth would live permanently in Città. Years later, after Bea had abandoned Italy for New York, she admitted that she had been stupid to hope that Beth would have come to live in Città. "It would have been wrong for you and would have destroyed you. Cesare, dreamer that he was, would never have been capable of being anything but a spoiled boy from that town." In the end, after knowing him longer, Bea did not like Cesare. She saw that he was entitled in the way that rich boys from Città were: arrogant and unaware of their privilege. Sure, they had secret notions, but for all their confidence and all their resources, they couldn't break away. But that was later. For now, in Beth's second year of living in Italy with Bea's family, Bea hoped. She hoped along with Beth's grandmother, who helped fund this year because she was determined that Beth lead a "normal" life far from her father's ideas of "joyful" communal living in which talent was liberated from the pesky details of everyday life.

"Hogwash," Grammy would say to Beth. "Someone has to wash the dishes." But Claire did work as far as Beth could tell. If you liked to cook you cooked, if you liked to farm you farmed, if you liked to sew you sewed, if you liked children you taught, etc. It was a thriving farm that fed itself, taught itself, paid for itself—a think tank of sorts, too, from which some quite clever ideas were emerging about the use of alternative fuels. Indeed, by the year 2017 many cars would be using hydrogen and Jackson's role in this transformation would be acknowledged. And though Beth would be sixteen years dead, her daughter Valeria would witness the fruits of this dream, invited with her grandfather to Washington to celebrate the milestone and his contributions, his sheer persistence and determination in spreading the word, putting a face on the idea. Now, however, Beth was alive: she was twenty-one years old, lying in the grass at Fiori with the summer against her skin and a future looming beautifully in front of her. Cesare lay by her side, pondering the idea of a year in America, which he liked very much but only cautiously so because he knew his parents would not approve, that they would want him to finish university first, and even then they would find the year an extravagance and a waste. "Tell me what I would do," Cesare said. He wanted to hear the flood of her ideas for him, how easily they came from her lips like all those soap bubbles blown by a child.

"We'd be in New York," she said. "You could do anything there." The possibility, an ever-expanding universe. "You could study at Columbia's business school, get a job on Wall Street. Your father must have connections." She paused, thought deeply. He could see the answer occurring to her. "Or better yet, you could study American literature, write for a newspaper. You're a brilliant writer." He thought of all the letters he had written to her, the stacks she had at home, neatly preserved in a box, of how she would tell him this, that she loved being away from him, in part, simply so she could receive those letters with their detailed reports of Città, the people, the intricacies of his love for her. "Write more," she often wrote to him, and the knowledge that she liked his letters made him work harder on the next.

It was life at Claire that Cesare liked to imagine. What talent of his could he really offer? Certainly not banking. During Servizio Civile, his job had been to work with paraplegics and spastics and other severely handicapped teenagers. They adored him simply because he was not afraid to tease them, not afraid to carry them about with him with all their complicated equipment, wheelchairs and breathing tubes, and to entertain them with his friends. He had liked that job; it had given him a sense of purpose.

"You could go to Claire if you wanted," Beth said. "You could help out as a nurse, the way you help with the invalids."

"Be reasonable, Bet," he said, and he laughed imagining himself as a nurse. He explained that a career as a nurse would humiliate his family, that there was very little he could do that would not humiliate his family, and as he watched her bright eyes he realized how little she allowed herself to understand even though she tried. "It's already been decided for me," he said.

"But you can change that," she said. And with her will, pure American will, the will of a new country that believed irrefutably that the best was still to come, she persisted. He loved all sports. He could farm. Farming was another career that would humiliate Cesare's family, but he did not tell her that. He did not tell her, either, that the gift of having his life decided for him had made him lazy.

During the first weeks of their romance in Città, once they had found each other again after Greece, every time Cesare saw Beth she became light and impatient as if every nerve had wings, so apparent was her infatuation that it was as if she were made of air. Now in the grass at Fiori, he wondered if she would ever leave America permanently for him, or he Italy for her? He wondered if somehow they could merge in their children, create a magical combination of stability and freedom. He was romantic that way. Cesare had been in love a few times, but when he met Beth it seemed to him he had been wrong before and that he had never actually been in love at all. She was a prism, always refracting a new light. His other girlfriends knew the path they had to walk and walked it with elegance and style in their fine Italian clothes, believing in the good alliance of the Cellini bank and Macchi socks. Beth wore jeans and Jack Purcells and got fashion wrong when she tried on Bea's hand-me-downs.

"Come see for yourself if the great experiment of America works," she was always saying to him in her persistent way.

"Oh, Bet, I would like to," he said.

"Would?" she said. He was, as were all Italians, good at using the conditional tense. The list of things they *would* like to do was much longer than the list of things they actually did. *"Vorrei, vorrei, vorrei,"* she said, daring, bold, unafraid to draw attention to herself. It was way past midnight and they were eating watermelon with friends at a farmer's stand by the side of the road—long picnic tables beneath bright lights and plenty of other people both old and young, slurping up the fruit, spitting out the seeds. She loved the innocence of all these people gathered over the jolly slices of watermelon so late at night. Cesare had been doing it since he was a child, part of that pattern of his days and years. Classes, siesta, work, study, a stroll before dinner down the arcaded *Corso Roma* in the center of town greeting his friends—friends he had known since childhood. His parents and their parents had played as children, too. On weekends Cesare and his friends played, enjoying big picnics and soccer, windsurfing on the lake. For a week in the winter they took a *Settimana Bianca,* skiing in the Dolomites, a month in the summer at the beach. The Cellinis spent the month of September in Marmi on the island of Elba in a humble beach shack. (For all their money they were not extravagant.) How Beth loved these patterns; she was fascinated by the notion of knowing—day in, day out; year in, year out—what to expect from a day, a life, for five hundred years, like threading time, stitching up all these lives. Beth saw it clearly, this life in perpetuity, and had a great respect for such continuity.

At the watermelon stand Cesare's friends watched them; they always watched the couple, wondering how long this affair would last, making private bets on who would take whom away from what. And, of course, that was the issue here: not a simple year abroad or a vacation to his girlfriend's family. In town one night someone spray-painted, GO HOME, AMERICAN on the walls beneath the portico along the *Corso Roma*. America was ugly and new and powerful, dictating to the world in the guise of spreading freedom. But really most of Cesare's friends loved Beth and loved things American: Nikes, Levi's, Bruce Springsteen, Simon and Garfunkel. One friend had her write down all the words to an entire album of Simon and Garfunkel songs so that he could learn them to sing along with his guitar. He spoke no English. Whenever Beth came from America, Cesare's friends would ask her to bring Vibram-soled shoes—Timberlands, L. L. Bean boots—and her suitcases filled with the orders. Cesare taught them all American football and baseball, presiding over his friends with the confidence of a politician, all charisma and charm. Emulation. Cesare, without having been to America, brought America to Città. As a result there was a trend: they wanted to look American, be American, and never leave Città.

Cesare cleaned the paint up so that Beth would never know. But she had known. She had seen it, impossible to miss, a bright blue beneath the portico, when she was shopping on the *Corso* with Bea.

"You're popular," Bea had said, her arm linked in Beth's, standing in front of the graffiti.

"Oh very," Beth had replied. Suddenly she hated Italy. She wanted to go into a store and try on many items, leave them all unfolded and buy not a one, demolishing the unspoken law of trying on only what you intended to buy (which, even so, was an imposition on the sales help). "It's the most absurd idea," Beth had said to Bea. "How can you possibly know if a sweater looks good unless you try it on?"

After occasions like these, Beth would write long, tearful letters to Sylvia, sitting in Bea's dark room with the shutters drawn, everyone else about their business. She would describe the painted sign in detail, complain about how faraway and alone she felt. Cesare's crowd of friends was very different from Bea's so they rarely went out together. Bea was always caught up with some new lover or other, anyway—some dangerous and illicit situation that Cesare didn't find very amusing. Cesare didn't like Bea, she would write; Cesare's family didn't much seem to care for Bea's, though Beth couldn't understand why, knew that there was some deeper social complexity that was beyond her desire to comprehend. The Cellinis never once asked about the Nuova family, referred to them as "the family from Genova" (it didn't matter that a hundred years had passed since the Nuova family had lived there) when Beth mentioned them. By the time Sylvia's response arrived in the mail (soothing letters, mostly filled with details of college life in Boston, escapades with boyfriends that made Beth long to be in college herself), Beth would be vibrant again, the insult forgotten. Then something else would occur and once again she would write.

Of the graffiti incident Cesare said tenderly, *"Non essere triste,* Bet." She thought of all the friends, the meals and conversations, the Vibram-soled shoes, the ease with which they seemed to accept her, understanding it all now as a charade. "It does not mean anything, just jealousy." That's what her father always said whenever someone made fun of Claire, whenever anyone pointed out (her grandmother most of all) that in the United States of America there were over fifteen hundred such communal experiments in living and most of them failed. "Because of sex and drugs and ego," the grandmother would say, stabbing her listener with her piercing green eyes, her white hair rolled up like a crown. "I have two words: *Jim Jones.*"

"I can already see that the great experiment of America works perfectly," Cesare said beneath the bright lights of the watermelon stand. Beth lit up like a prize. He wanted to fly away with her right there, to rise up from the table in front of his friends to show them *she wins.*

When Beth first met Cesare's father, Giovanni Paolo, she thought he was the gardener. Cesare had driven her to Fiori not long after they met again. It was early fall. The woods were thick with fallen leaves and the sky was gray and somewhat sad. Giovanni Paolo appeared from what seemed to be a garden arbor still very green with all the ivy. In his left hand he carried a small rifle and on his right hand he wore a thick black leather glove. The glove seemed odd to Beth, somehow hard, yet also very workmanlike and worn, something a gardener would wear. She imagined it had a mate he had already taken off. He was a small old man with a fringe of thin white hair on his otherwise bald scalp, and a serious demeanor. With some trouble he placed the gun beneath his right arm and, sticking out his left, ungloved, hand for her to shake, said, *"Piacere."* He did not look her in the eye or even smile, and she assumed this was because the gardener was either tired and shy or rude. The exchange lasted less than a minute before he vanished back into the arbor, so quickly Cesare did not have a chance to say a word. She noticed that this old man's shirt had ripped at the shoulder and that sweat beaded beneath his eyes. Then he was gone. "Why does the gardener carry a gun?" she had asked Cesare.

"You mean my father." She blushed, mortified, and then just as quickly felt insulted. She pictured him zipping up to Bern with that small gun to save his daughter from the clowns.

"He doesn't like me?" she asked.

"He's scared of you," Cesare said.

"Of me?" Beth almost laughed. She looked down at herself, feeling quite small and young but also sort of powerful like an army, a country, Cleopatra. Not long after this first meeting, the father would start asking Cesare, in front of Beth, "Whatever happened to Francesca?" Cesare was always formal and polite with his father and would never have corrected him about Francesca, though Beth would have liked him to. Even when Cesare teased his father over small things or funny coincidences (for example, the pope had the same brand of skis as Signor Cellini and liked to ski the same Cortina slopes as Signor Cellini, the parallels made room for jokes, especially since Giovanni Paolo was not at all religious), he did so with trepidation, as if he did not know how his father would respond, as if he knew he must always be careful. Beth would come to learn that Signor Cellini had supported Mussolini (briefly) in his youth and that now he gave impassioned speeches about the secession of the north from the south.

The gun was for shooting *uccellini,* the small birds in the bird arbor, which the Cellinis ate every Sunday for *pranzo* on top of polenta that Cesare's mother stirred for an hour. Gentle Elena's nature above all was to compensate for her husband's hardness. When Beth first started seeing Cesare in Città after Greece, Beth had a chronic stomachache. Elena oversaw her cure, taking the girl (because Cesare loved her) to all the finest doctors and specialists, paying the bills without letting the girl know. Elena was also refined; she peeled all her fruit before eating it (including the grapes, of course) with a small knife and fork designed especially for the task. The skin slipped off to reveal the glistening, wet body of the fruit. Beth found the skill amazing in its intricacy, like the fine art of carving filigree. She couldn't imagine peeling her fruit; her father had taught her that that's where the nutrients were and on their farm they carefully grew produce organically, precisely so that the skin could be eaten. Chefs drove all the way from New York City, Philadelphia, and Washington for Claire's produce just because of the care with which it was grown. She remembered the chefs, their hands especially, how important the chefs had seemed as they handled the fruit, turning it delicately, their big hands prizing each piece, connoisseurs of the exquisite.

Signora Cellini, who was always busy with social obligations and some sort of volunteer work, had several maids, one from Sri Lanka, one from North Africa, and one from Russia. The Russian was quite old, but had been with the family since the children were small. The Sri Lankan wore a sari at all times and tried to teach Beth and Cesare's sister, Laura, to put them on, wrapping them in yards and yards—nine to be exact, as in "the whole nine yards"—of silk. Beth knew how to wrap a sari; Preveena had taught her at Claire. But Beth did not let the Sri Lankan maid know because the lesson and the knowledge seemed to be something that she prized sharing. "You're the luckiest girls alive," she said to them, holding her life up to theirs, "freed by your fate."

Funny thing was, in some ways Beth felt like the Sri Lankan maid: that is, Beth felt that Laura was the luckiest girl alive. Beth didn't have Laura's privilege or Laura's funny beauty or Laura's sophistication or even Laura's intelligence. The first time Beth met her, she fell in love with her. Laura had just returned from America, overweight as she had promised her brother, from all the hamburgers. "Too many hamburgers," she had said, pulling Beth into an intimacy. It was the way Laura smiled as well, laughing at her newfound chubbiness. She was chubby, but Beth had not seen her before. Beth admired that she was amused rather than frightened by the extra weight: too many hamburgers, simple as that. Her blond hair was cropped short at her ears and she smiled and laughed and her good humor was infectious. Her funny stories of America—those girls to whom she taught English in the trailer; the cops who pulled her over, their mirrored sunglasses; the fans at the Springsteen concert throwing themselves at the feet of the singer—animated Cesare in a way Beth had never seen before. "I owe all my adventures to Cesare," Laura said, giving her brother a big kiss on the cheek. "It was his idea for me to go to America." They were standing in the kitchen of the Città villa, smells of dinner heating up the room, the cook swishing in and swishing out, pinching Laura's cheeks between her fingers in a tender, familiar gesture. Beth marveled at this world of maids and service, a world which Laura and Cesare knew well how to negotiate, knew just how far intimacy could be pushed. Beth observed the Cellinis, every detail. She felt jealousy and yearning. She wanted more than ever to be a part of the family, to be Laura's sister. And because Cesare loved this funny little American, Laura adopted Beth, lending Beth her beautiful clothes (much more classic in style than Bea's of-the-moment fashions) and skis, inviting her to stay with her in Milan, including her with girlfriends on shopping excursions to Florence. Laura, too, was studying economics at the Bocconi. She was behind Cesare but catching up while also, simultaneously, studying fashion. Her ambition was to design stockings and tights for women. In her apartment she had dozens of mannequin legs dressed with sumptuous silk samples. She had an adoring boyfriend, whom her parents fawned over, sending them back to Milan with food enough to last a week so that they'd be well fed and not need to worry about interrupting their studies. Jackson would never have saved Beth from clowns—perhaps that was a good thing, but Beth couldn't help but envy the fact that Giovanni Paolo would drop everything for Laura. Beth watched their relationship, watched how this confident girl, filled with good humor, could melt the hardened man in a way that Cesare never could. Signor Cellini would never raise his voice with her; he would never doubt her abilities with her studies. Sometimes Beth wished that Laura could take the baton from Cesare and take over the family's march across time.

The Sri Lankan maid was in love with a middle-aged Italian man who still lived with his mother. Because of her brown Sri Lankan coloring, the mother forbade the marriage. They married anyway at a small church in the town of Porta dei Miracoli (Gate of Miracles) near the train station. Cesare served as witness and then paid for the banquet he had arranged in the station's *trattoria*. Bottles of wine were opened as trains rumbled by; the wedding party celebrated amid a flurry of passengers, everyone smoking. They dined on *risotto con funghi porcini*. A man played some romantic music on a guitar. Cesare presided with grace and like a brother because the Sri Lankan maid had had no one else. He lifted a glass of champagne to the bride and groom. "To outsmarting fate," he said. The train station had been the bride's choice; she wanted to be able to flee should her husband's mother try to intervene.

Elena, with her friends—Cat in particular, skin permanently tanned and bejeweled—spoke of the American, making predictions on the course the relationship would run. Elena was lovely with Beth because she was Cesare's girlfriend, but the possibility of Beth scared her, too. She was not afraid of Beth remaining in Cesare's life so much as of Beth somehow being capable of taking him away. What mother wants to lose her child? "She is a kind girl," Signora Cellini said. "Though her manners are atrocious." Elena felt at once bad and liberated for saying that. The girl would start eating before everyone else, catch herself, and stop; she would sop her sauce with a piece of bread; she would pull apart her bread so that crumbs left a mess at her setting. "Perhaps she doesn't understand the way we do things here."

"This relationship will pass," Cat said, identifying Elena's concern with the same precision and authority with which she identified the passion in Valeria's eyes in the Cellini fresco. "And if it doesn't pass, I assure you that son of yours will never leave Città. He is not capable. He has everything here. He is someone here. Do you think he wants to be an immigrant starting from nothing with nothing? Who wants to do that but unfortunates with nothing to lose?"

"Si, si, é vero," Elena would admit, encouraged by her friend. But Cat and all the friends wondered what it was that drew Cesare to the American girl, who was cute, perhaps, though a bit awkward, with features just a little too big for the face that held them.

From the finely spun and colored glass of the Venetian chandelier suspended above the Cellini's dining table dangled an ugly plastic buzzer that Signora Cellini pressed when she needed service. Service, Beth would come to understand, had a higher status than aesthetics. There was also a button hidden beneath the table that she could push discreetly with her foot. *"Prego?"* the maids would ask when beckoned. Accidentally, they were called when Signora Cellini learned that Beth was not christened. A nervous gesture, the button-pushing, and the maids descended and Signora Cellini crossed her chest and promised Beth that she would help her fix things. *"Cara mia, cara mia,"* she kept saying. All the commotion scared Beth, who hadn't quite understood (or couldn't quite believe) that christening could be this significant. "But what's wrong?" she asked, pushing her chair back from the table, truly stricken as if Cesare's mother had spotted the devil emerging from her. "Mamma, please," Cesare said, standing up to calm his mother with a wide embrace.

Beth was as susceptible as any girl to the desire to please a potential mother-in-law. Simply put, Beth wanted Elena to love her, love her like a daughter the way that Bea's parents did. But for all her generosity and innocence, Elena had a strong reserve. She didn't let people in very easily. Beth wanted to be let in. She wondered, once alone with time to think, if Elena would warm to her more if she were christened.

"I might like to be christened," Beth said to Cesare. When she really thought about it though, she realized that she didn't even know the difference between christening and baptizing (perhaps it had something to do with full immersion?) or if there was even a difference. Beth was woefully lacking in any religious education. And it is said that America is the most religious country in the world! She did know that babies were christened, in the Catholic Church anyway, to absolve original sin and that concept she couldn't abide by or get around. A little baby, sinful? And she told Cesare so.

"It's only a metaphor," he said, stroking her hair, wishing she wouldn't take this all so seriously. He didn't. He never went to church or thought much about being Catholic.

"A metaphor for what?"

"Non importa," he said. "This is not important. Just think, her name is Elena. Elena was the mother of Constantine who because of her made Christianity legal." What Beth didn't tell him was that she wanted to find a way to make Elena love her. Then she thought about her father, about his love for her, how he loved to allow her her freedom to shape herself, to see what emerged on its own. She missed her father. Sometimes she missed him so absolutely she thought she would fly home to Claire and never leave. Sometimes she hated Jackson for his stubborn inability to leave Claire and visit her. She wondered if she were to die would he come to her then?

Sometimes Cesare would look at Beth and try to imagine her on her farm with her father. Who would she be there? What would her father be like? Who would Cesare become there? He knew Jackson was a big man with a big presence, that he liked fun and drama and would loan his land to groups of people who would stage reenactments of battles from the Revolutionary War. Troops in red coats and blue coats shot off cannons and artillery in Claire's fields as all the people living there sat on the deck, cheering for one side or the other. Beth's grandmother cheered for England. Jackson always wanted to barter for the loan of the land the way he bartered with the Amish for butchering his livestock. Plenty needed doing at the farm. Beth, instead, would make the reenactors pay. It had been her job since childhood to see to it that her father didn't give too much away.

Jackson wrote his daughter twice a week without fail, sending her small things from the farm: a dried soybean, a chicken feather, a red maple leaf in the fall. She knew the only way to have a relationship with him that was deep and meaningful would be for her to make her life at Claire, and she knew as well that she could never do that; for her that choice was not freedom, and she knew as well that her father understood this quite clearly. As it was with the others who came and left Claire, the decision was hers, and he would not judge it or interfere with it. Not returning to live at Claire, Beth realized, was as clear a path to her as not leaving Città was for Cesare, though neither could fully admit that yet.

On Sundays, Signora Cellini stirred the polenta herself, tending the hot molten mass of bright yellow mush, stirring and stirring and fussing. They served it as a first course with either milk or cheese and then as a second course with the *uccellini* (bones and all). The first time Beth joined them for the Sunday meal she learned the subtleties of polenta. Trying to be polite and proper and to do everything right because she wanted terribly to impress and be something other than a silly (threatening) American who entertained them with stories of her eccentric family, Beth used both milk and cheese. Cesare laughed, then Laura, then the parents—an endearing lovable laugh that seemed to want to embrace this silly American. Beth blushed even so, embarrassment welling up from her toes. (On polenta, milk and Parmesan do not go together.) No matter what she did in Italy, Beth seemed to always get everything wrong. On her second-course plate, the tiny birds lay whole and butter fried, staring up at her, their eyes now like dulled silver. This was the first time she had ever eaten *uccellini* and she didn't know what to do and didn't want to watch the others or ask. The *uccellini* were delicious. The bones added texture. No one said a word, so she assumed the bones were meant to be eaten. The heads however were not.

And the black glove: it was not really a glove. Rather it was a hand. His father had lost his hand as a young man when firecrackers exploded in it. He had been studying to be a doctor, the first of the Giovanni Paolos and Cesares to study something other than economics. After losing the hand, he reverted to finance. Beth understood that he was a hard man, hard on his son who was not interested and thus slow with his studies, hard even on his beloved daughter for her fancy, silly dreams. But his desire to be a doctor and the loss of his hand would always soften him for Beth simply because it seemed that he, too, had once had the desire to step outside the plan. She had her father send her pumpkin and corn seeds from America so that she could give them to Giovanni Paolo, who spent hours in his garden. Those vegetables were exotic here and thus would be a challenge. The seeds brought him a patch of bright orange pumpkins and a row of sweet Silver Queen so bizarre and delicious he could not help but fall in love with *l'Americanina*.

———

This morning of the kissing in the summer grass, Beth had sat in a chair while Giovanni Paolo gardened, keeping him company. Signora Cellini hung up some laundry on the line and spied on her husband and Beth as he told her that Cesare had failed two more exams. "This is not good, not at all good," he said, looking into the dirt. He could never look Beth in the eye. Even so, each time he spoke to her she felt she was gaining acceptance, becoming real for him. He was telling her of Cesare's failure, she understood, because he assumed that she was the reason for Cesare's continued distraction. And if there were good reason for the distraction (say marriage) then he would abide as long as she helped Cesare get back on track. He plucked at weeds and snapped branches awkwardly with his left hand using the gloved hand to steady himself. She wondered what his stump looked like. She wished she could ask him about his dashed dream. She remembered the little Amish kids stealing apples from the gala trees at home. How they held the apples in their hands, turning them over and over like a discovery, before they bit into them and ran away.

"Cesare doesn't like the Bocconi," she said boldly. "He doesn't like finance and business and socks and shoes. He likes books, literature, writing." Big American big-mouthed gaff, but she would not be afraid of this man and she knew that was the only way to make him love her, knew that Laura was not afraid of him and that Cesare was.

"What?" he asked, looking up from his job in the dirt to meet her eyes.

"He needs a break," she said softly.

A professor from college shot to mind, standing in front of a blackboard explaining Kierkegaard's *Repetition* and the need to change experience through a rotation: read the play from the middle backward; finish the end of a book before reading the beginning. She remembered that Kierkegaard meant "church-yard" and that the professor had said the philosopher's most famous words were, "You must change your life." And what was she doing in Italy after all? She wanted to explain all this to Giovanni Paolo, but didn't, of course, because she was just twenty-one and didn't understand it all that well herself.

She helped him weed for a while and he instructed her on how best to get weeds at the roots. "See, like this," he said, jutting his hand into the soft earth, wiggling the weeds before plunging his hand again deeper into the dirt and then plucking the clump, roots and all, free. "Nature does not like gardens. It does not like to be controlled." Balancing on his right hand, he held up the perfectly extracted weeds for her to admire. His garden was nearly weedless: straight clean rows aligned like soldiers. Then for a bit they did not speak, and then they did. "We have never had an American in the family, never a foreigner of any kind, for that matter." And in that way he welcomed her. She felt warm and eager to please him, though she understood somewhere that her triumph did not involve her roots and she wondered if she really had the will to leave America. In fact, being welcomed, the whole notion of leaving America permanently made her nervous and then—once again, yet always surprisingly—sad.

From the garden, she looked down through forests to the lake, which spread out like a small whitecapped sea on which billowed many pretty sails. For five hundred years the Cellini family had spent weekends in this house in woods thick with maple and ash and some pine. The Fiori house was a stucco building with an enormous fireplace in the dining room in which all the cooking (polenta and *uccellini*) had once been done. In this room the fresco of Valeria had been made. In this room Valeria had flirted with, been romanced by, Benvenuto; in these woods they had stolen kisses, lain in the grass, hunted for mushrooms perhaps, dreamed impossibly for sure.

Each room of the Fiori house had french doors leading to a small patio. A porch extended from the kitchen to a trellised walk dripping wisteria in the spring. The azaleas and rhododendron thrived on the hill that rose to the winter cottage (where the bird arbor was and where they stayed once the weather turned cold because the cottage was small enough to heat) and in May when the bushes flowered, the hill turned vibrant with all their various colors. And every year the Cellinis had the big party to celebrate the flowering of the *azalee,* women in white gowns with gloves rising past their elbows, men in fine dark linen suits.

From the Renaissance to now, Beth thought. An epic journey, a colossal amount of time, slippery like an iceberg, that she was trying to scale, to fathom and understand. Great empires had risen and fallen; America had been discovered; Bernini had been born, leaving a trail of sculptures in his wake that made one weep. If a hundred years holds four generations, then five hundred years holds twenty. Twenty generations of Cellinis with fine Federicas on their arms—into and out of great gardens and porticos and churches and *palazzi,* into and out of peace and Garibaldi's unification, and more wars and peace again to here: the late-twentieth century with all its fancy spaceships to the moon and a young American girl with the potential to destroy it all.

Each generation of Cellinis had given the world a living breathing vibrant kissable Cesare with hopes of his own. She saw them all marching across time. Through the repetition of this life, it was to Beth now as if this family had somehow figured out how to achieve immortality. Her mother had died in a car crash in Turkey when Beth was three, and her father had re-nounced conventional life in order to live the dream he had dreamed with his wife when they pondered the heights of their future. Was this five-hundred-year-old Cellini family the pondered heights of one person's dream? She felt wicked for telling Giovanni Paolo that Cesare did not like the Bocconi.

"By my estimation you're approximately the tenth Cesare," Beth said, turning to face him. It was dusk now and the late summer air had cooled. Swaths of violet streaked across the sky. The sounds of dinner being made inside the house could be heard. On a faraway road a car honked and church bells rang for evening mass. The air filled with the musky smell of summer mushrooms, wet and soft in the diminishing light. He studied her, reading that something entirely too big was going on inside her head. "What little miseries are you concocting in there?" he asked.

"My roots aren't very deep," she said.

"They're wide," he said, "very, very, very."

"It doesn't make it easier for me to give up everything," she said. She knew that she was going home and she was losing faith that he would come. Something big pressed against her chest, something irreversible, something final that left her standing alone.

"I know," he said.

"Your father thinks I'm a weed," she said.

"A powerful weed," he said, trying to lighten her mood.

"This is real," she said. "Don't be lazy." She wanted to cry. He lay still, looking into the early evening. A thin moon shone against the indigo blue, and stars began to bubble in the sky. He thought of his paraplegics, trapped in their chairs, of how he loved to let them roll fast down gentle hills, how they shrieked with delight.

"What happened before five hundred years ago?" she said, reading the sky, too, as if it held the answer.

"I suppose some boy had his own name," Cesare said. For Beth, becoming a part of Cesare's family, with all its laws and time and its well-grooved path, would be like slipping into the cool sheets of a well-made bed on a tired night. She closed her eyes, feeling his fingers at her hips, on her back, tracing the arc of her spine. Surrendering can be so comfortable.

"You're not coming," she said.

"Don't be dramatic," he said.

"I can't compete with all this." She thought of the portrait of Valeria, of how her face alone held the story of before and after, of the exquisite love that led to despair. And all those oblivious partiers carried on, merrily ignorant of the real, the universal, of their own suffering and the ambiguous claw snatching all that was good.

"I want to marry you," he said, pulling Beth to his chest. He imagined America, the pull of it, and her strange little world at Claire.

"Then know the rest of me," she said, almost as a dare.

"Doesn't your father ever want to leave?" he asked, as if that were a key.

"Doesn't your father ever want to leave?" she countered.

After leaving Greece, Cesare did not see Beth again until they found themselves on a train traveling from Città to Milan. It was a dangerously foggy early October day—that fog of the Lombardy kind, suspended over the entire Pianura Padana. He was headed to the university to take an exam he knew he would fail, and he knew that by failing the exam he would make his mother anxious and his father angry. He would fail the exam because he had not studied. He had not studied because he wasn't interested. In front of him was an impenetrable wall that he could not see his way around. He kept failing the exams, one after the next, and it seemed he was going nowhere, though his direction was very clear. All he needed to do in life was follow the path. If he did, in one sense, he would be free from the burden of want and desire and longing and ambition, of having to make himself. He would be made already, given a jump start on life by being handed a position of prominence and power in a wealthy little town nestled into the foothills of the Alps, surrounded by emerald lakes. But the simple duty of studying he could not do and thus he became a disappointment to his parents. He feared they thought he was stupid. Rather he wanted to please his father in some other way. Prove himself. Show his father he could succeed. Write a book, say, and hand it, published, to him, for him to read and admire so that he would not think him stupid.

On the highways, flooded with lights like a football stadium, as if that light could penetrate the fog, two of his friends had died. His two friends had not been able to carry forward anything. He looked through the window to see if he could see through the fog. Instead, he saw the reflection of a woman sitting down next to him. She wore blue jeans and a pink sweater that made her blond hair more blond and her blue eyes more blue. She wore sneakers. Studying her reflection it took him a moment to recognize her. Once he did, he was afraid to turn, afraid that he would be wrong. He had hoped for this, that they would run into each other. He had been waiting for the moment ever since she vanished in Greece. He turned. She smiled. He smiled. She had known when she sat down who he was. She, too, had been hoping for a chance meeting, afraid to call him once she returned to Città because Greece seemed like a dream and she thought he might be angry at her for leaving without a word. Now she was on her way to Milan to register for an Italian class. She didn't know what to say. She noticed that he was reading *Slouching Towards Bethlehem,* so she slouched toward him and told him she was a child of Bethlehem, which, indeed, she was. She began to flirt effortlessly, looking downward in a slight gesture that suggested both vulnerability and abandon. Somehow it was as if they were meeting for the first time all over again. In response to something silly that he said about the nebulous *nebbia,* she laughed exquisitely. Her face fractured into a hundred shades of light. And he wondered, if silly wordplay can release her so entirely, what will love do?

Instead of going to the university, she went with him to the roof of the Duomo, where they picnicked on *panini* and drank a little too much wine. They were alone up there. Who would bother climbing all those stairs for a view of fog instead of Alps? The fog was so thick they couldn't see their own hands, so thick they couldn't see each other even if only a few feet separated them. They played hide and seek, emerging and reemerging, swimming through the fog, sneaking up from behind to scare each other, thrilling with anticipation—those splendid moments before the soft lips of a first kiss (all over again), when curiosity and expectation combine. She poured the wine generously into the plastic cups and took him on a tour of the ferocious gargoyles, showing him her favorite faces, teeth and fangs designed to keep away the devil. Then she disappeared again. Each time she disappeared he worried that the fog would swallow her, would suck her back into the void that existed before he met her. He tried to convince himself that he was not concerned. He had been raised to be tough and stoical. He tried to convince himself that it would make no difference if she vanished as quietly as she had reappeared.

That night he telephoned his parents and told them that the

exam had gone well and he would stay in Milan to celebrate. For three straight days he disappeared with Beth until waking up on the fourth he understood for certain that she was the other half of his life. And he understood for the first time the meaning of ambition.

Then she was gone and then he was here, standing in an immigration line at John F. Kennedy International Airport, listening to a recorded voice repeat "Welcome to the United States of America" with a pride distinctly and sweetly American. At Malpensa Airport in Milan no voice said *Benvenuto in Italia.* He thought of Beth as a little girl pledging allegiance to the flag in school, right hand pressed to her heart. She had explained that children all across America pledged allegiance to the flag each morning. He saw all those many teachers teaching love of country to immigrants from everywhere. In Italy national and civic pride did not need to be taught, rather it flowed with one's blood since they were and had always been Italian—remember, *campanilismo,* the pull of the bell tower as natural as breathing.

He noticed small differences like truths: the people most of all. Hundreds of other tourists and immigrants were having their visas checked. They came from all over the world. Even in the line for American citizens—fast moving and enviable—the faces came from all over the world. No distinguishing them from us, the melting pot clearly visible, all exotic, and he felt the beauty of anonymity, the past of who you are quietly erased if you choose. All these lives stood on the threshold of the hope for something more.

The customs official checking Cesare's bags was a big happy man with thick hands that sifted through Cesare's neatly folded clothes, packed by his mother's maids the night before as his mother ran around nervously going over lists of what Cesare might need—aspirin, shampoo, socks—as if they might not have these simple things in America. "You're coming back?" his mother repeated, while his father sat quietly in an armchair, reading the paper, flipping the pages with the black glove of his missing hand. Giovanni Paolo looked up just once, his gentle *"Cara mia"* dismissing the idea altogether. He knew his son absolutely. He knew the youthful desire to flee prescription, knew how age dissipated the need like a solvent. He remembered studying to be a doctor, the defiance and ambition he had felt in knowing he would make himself. And he remembered, years later, after age had gained its advantage, after his lost hand recorded his lost quest, his gratitude for so many ancestors working together to create history, albeit a private history, but history all the same. Giovanni Paolo knew his son, knew that Cesare, too, would come to appreciate the Cellini heritage. Hard he may have been as a father, but that did not mean he did not fiercely love and know his son.

Waiting for the official to finish with his bags, Cesare tried on different expressions, understanding that he was free to make himself; he was not known here. He was not a student; he was not the son of a prominent family from a rich Italian town. He could become whomever he liked. His slate was clean. The not knowing was what he adored about this culture of multiplying possibility. He was giddy, rolling fast down that gentle hill. The old rules would lose their grip. He looked down at his legs and wilted just a little, embarrassed by the creases in his jeans, pressed by one of his mother's maids; he wanted to be tough; he wanted, absurdly, to be a cowboy. Even to feel this possibility, if only for a moment, was like the anticipation of that first kiss.

The happy official plucked out presents wrapped for Beth. Cesare was afraid the man would open them, but he only asked what was in each package. The inspector drank an enormous coffee, twenty times the size of an espresso. More, more. The land of excess, of plenty, of dizzyingly big skies. "You're spoiling someone," the man said with a big grin, then carefully returned the presents to the bags. "I'm the last obstacle between the two of you," he added with an over-familiarity Cesare noted as another small American truth. "Free to go," he said, and pointed to the sliding doors of the main terminal. They opened and closed like a mouth, revealing as they did an abundance of chaos, noise, and a sea of expectant people upon which Beth floated like a raft. *Free to go:* a ticket to anywhere.

Five

Claire

In May of 1968 Claire died on that small Turkish road. She stood on one side of the road, Jackson on the other. Behind her was a stone wall that she had just climbed in order to see if something spectacular lay hidden beyond it. She lost her grip and fell to the ground, nothing serious, just a scrape, stood up, looked at Jackson, smiled, and wiped her hands on her jeans. The day was warm. They had been hiking in the hills above the Sea of Marmara, which spread out vast and blue beneath them. A few flowers struggled here and there to emerge from the dry earth. Claire had wanted Jackson to see a shepherd with his flock meandering across a field toward the sea. Just then a car cut between them, the only car to pass all morning. It screeched and skidded to a halt, sliding into Claire, scooping her up, rag-doll-like, and heaving her against the stone wall. Jackson reached his arms out toward her, started grabbing for her as if to stop this freak and absolutely unacceptable occurrence. Time froze, then accelerated out of control. Her body dented the fender. Her skull smashed into the wall and cracked like an egg. The driver was a small man with dark hair, a mustache, his face stricken with panic (he could see the situation was not good). He indicated with his hands, because it was clear that Jackson did not understand Turkish, that the sun had momentarily blinded him. Claire was twenty-five years old—a gorgeous woman with thick dark hair and big green eyes and dimples and a mole adorning her sweet round face, a face that could fracture light.

She was not alone, of course; many people died that year, as we all well know: Martin Luther King Jr. was shot; Robert Kennedy was shot. Steinbeck died; Helen Keller died; Tallulah Bankhead died. Sergio Leone, king of the spaghetti Western, made *Once Upon a Time in the West,* casting Henry Fonda, the quintessential American hero, as a merciless villain capable of shooting down a child point-blank—blowing away our notions of the good and the wholesome. Lieutenant Calley and his men were doing just that in a small Vietnamese hamlet called My Lai. And all the regular souls, all the yous and all the mes, died their ordinary deaths—their lives perhaps not effecting history like a King or a Kennedy, but affecting history just the same: private histories, yours and mine.

Claire's damaged head bled into her husband's lap, her blood warming his legs, and as the car that killed her drove to the nearest hospital, Jackson spoke to her about their dreams, and about their daughter (just three years old in New York City with her grandmother, doing all the naughty things that three-year-olds do, blissfully unaware in her self-centered cocoon of "no" and "mine"). Claire's black hair (tresses of curls that her mother used to tame with rags by tying each lock up tightly at night—it had hurt to move her head against the pillows—so that in the morning Claire would have perfect sausages bobbing about her face) turned blue with all the blood. Slowly, the color in her cheeks drained, and her body lost its heat. But Jackson kept talking. He talked to her all the way back to America. He didn't stop talking to her. He vowed he never would. And indeed he never did.

In April, the month before, they had gone to Pennsylvania to look at a college that had wanted to hire Jackson to teach philosophy. He had his PhD from Harvard and was in the job market for the first time that spring. He took one look at the school, with its quaint campus with all its oak trees and its tidy chapel and its homogenous student body reacting against nothing in a time when there was so much to react against, and he knew he could not spend any portion of his life teaching there. Instead of going to the interview, he went with Claire on a drive through the hills of Snyder County, and then they flew off to Turkey to a philosophy conference in Istanbul (something about the influence of East on West in modern times, a conference they knew from the start they would not attend much of). And thus he delayed the search for a job, postponing the task until they could understand something meaningful to do with their lives. They were dreamers, believers, optimists, visionaries— typical of their generation. They believed in better and more, in not giving up, in not settling. Claire had been a senior at Radcliffe when they met, a philosophy student herself. Jackson, who was just beginning his dissertation, taught undergraduate philosophy classes. He was not one of her teachers, but she saw him around. He was older and dangerous-seeming, with his loose clothes and his thick sideburns. He was not at all like the other men, neatly put together in their oxford shirts. Claire devised routes that allowed her to bump into him and she kept bumping into him until he took notice, and then she invited him for coffee, almost commanding him to join her, using her sweet bright smile to temper the imperative.

Whereas Jackson's work involved a little-known twentieth-century French priest, Abel Jeanniere, with radical ideas about sex and celibacy and the church (for a short while in his youth Jackson had considered converting to Catholicism), Claire was studying the sixteenth century's relationship to antiquity, focusing on Thomas More's *Utopia*. Her senior thesis concerned Plato's depiction of Atlantis, More's *Utopia,* and the role of women in both. Had she lived, she might have devoted her life to the study of feminism and More. When she died, however, she was at work on something more contemporary: she was writing a book with a group of classmates from Radcliffe on the subject of sexism in children's readers. Entitled *Dick and Jane as Victims,* the book took apart the Dick and Jane series in order to address sex stereotyping and its influence on children. Claire had a baby daughter, and she was determined that Beth have many options. Naive, yes; an idealist, yes—Claire was a girl herself, really, still fresh from childhood with an old-world order crumbling before her, a new one forming. Claire: her name means "bright," "famous," "clear."

On the drive through Snyder County, Amish and Mennonite country populated by the simple black-clad folk riding by in their buggies, on their horses, on bikes, plowing their fields by hand and horse, Claire and Jackson happened upon an apple farm that was soon to be auctioned. Flyers for the taking were stacked in a clear plastic box attached to a wood pole at the mysterious yet undistinguished entrance to a long, meandering driveway that seemed to rise to nowhere. They stopped because of the plastic box and because of the driveway, which Jackson thought might lead to an adventure. Already they had had an adventure with a Mennonite man while stopped at a roadside stand to buy honey from a little old woman with crumbling teeth and tattered black clothes and a very kind smile, her curly hair so thin you could see her scalp. The man appeared on the road in a black buggy pulled by a horse. He stepped out at the honey stand and acknowledged the woman, who smiled her broken-toothed smile, and then he turned his attention to Jackson and said, "We need to talk," as if he had known Jackson all his life. "The world is coming to an end," he said. "There is a meeting tonight at my farm and we would like you to attend." He scribbled down the name of his farm, gave directions, indicated that it was for menfolk alone, stepped back into his buggy, and drove off into the dales and hills. The sound of clopping horse feet trailed in his wake.

"I'll dress as a man," Claire said.

"I'd rather you not," Jackson said, without a hint of irony. "I'd rather protect my woman from news of the Apocalypse." And he scooped her up and carried her to the car like a bride. And though she knew he was playing with expectations and roles, she loved being carried and protected in his arms. She allowed her head to fall against his chest and somewhere she wished she were a heroine in a Trollope novel.

"Always carrying gracefully the burden," she said. And the old woman smiled curiously after them as if she were looking at two exotic creatures roaming the Serengeti.

At the mysterious entrance to the apple farm, Jackson looked at Claire and she curled her lips and everything at once was said between them: *Should we go? Absolutely. Onward, then.* Claire popped out of the car and grabbed one of the white sheets from the box and read Jackson the details as he maneuvered the Lincoln up the steep, rain-rutted road. (They had borrowed Claire's mother's car—always a Lincoln—a big boat but with power that easily negotiated the hazards of this road.) "Two thousand acres and one hundred of them are apple orchards holding about eight thousand trees," Claire read. "Each tree produces twenty boxes of apples and each box weighs forty-two pounds." Indeed, as they rose, terraced groves of apple trees spread out before them. The trees were just green with April warmth and the rains, and only on closer inspection could you see buds, even blossoms just beginning to open. Claire had never much thought about apples before. In five weeks the entire farm would be auctioned. She read that to Jackson and then looked at him and he looked at her and once again everything was said between them with the use of no words: *Let's come to the auction. Good idea. Maybe we'll even make an offer. But we don't have any money. So what?* They were living in a dark one-bedroom on Manhattan's Lower East Side. Jackson loved Claire for her desire to devour life.

The road kept rising, circling around a cone-shaped hill, cutting through the orchards then woods, moving up and up and up, seemingly into the clouds, which were thick that day, swollen with the promise of rain. On top of the hill were vast fields of long grasses blowing this way and that in a gentle breeze. The car bounced, got stuck, freed itself, then bounced some more until they pulled to a stop and got out and ran across the fields. "Think of apples," Claire said. "Do you ever really stop to think about apples?" There were no apple trees in sight anymore, but still she was high on apples. From up here you could see all across the world it seemed, far out over Pennsylvania anyway: hills rolling into more hills, and many farms in the distance like miniatures.

"John Chapman," Jackson said, "who spread apple seeds all across America."

"You would know Johnny Appleseed's real name."

"Apples float because they're 25 percent air. They're related to the rose family. Oh, and something about an apple a day." He began listing all the names of all the apples he knew: Jonagold, Red Delicious, Macintosh, Winesap, the dry red Ben Davis, Braeburn. "Shall I go on?" and he looked at her with his blue eyes and his half smile, and she loved him absolutely and felt delirious with desire for the two of them and for the things they would do together. He was a big tall man with those sideburns, the fashion of the day, slicing across his cheeks handsomely. He came from a good Christian family in Virginia (a hint of southern accent hid in his speech). Though his family had little, they encouraged him to apply for scholarships to the best schools in the Northeast; he had been a boy who liked to study and to think and to know, and he was generous with his knowledge— not one of those who like to make others feel stupid for what they don't know. His apple knowledge, of course, was just a lark. He had gone apple picking once in college and remembered some information. He continued, "They say three apples a day keeps three doctors away." Claire hit him playfully and he grabbed her and kissed her and she spun away from him so that he would continue to chase her across the fields.

His family was still in Virginia. His father was a retired mechanic and car salesman, and his mama, who attended church regularly and was upstanding in her community, had the defining characteristic of being obese. Claire's mother did not approve, never did and never would, of this union.

"He does not come from good stock," she had said to her daughter after meeting the parents.

(To Jackson's mother she had said, "I know of a good diet.")

"And your stock?" Claire had asked sharply. She had grown up in New York City in the rent-controlled apartment, attending the best schools, unaware of how intricately her mother balanced the finances in order to give the appearance that they had so much more than they actually had. Indeed, it wasn't until Claire was in college that she understood her family had nowhere near as much money as the girls she had gone to grade school with. "Never decline an invitation by saying that we cannot afford to do something," she once heard her mother admonish her father. "Simply say we are busy."

Stock: her mother chuckled a little as she would when her airs, those airs, were identified. But for her mother, anyway, it was as if she, and her daughter, were somehow exempt from the reality that they were not Rockefellers or Carnegies or Kennedys.

"At least I'm not obese. With fat like that, carrying all that weight around, she will not last the decade. And that man, that Johnson"—she enjoyed pretending that she could not remember Jackson's name—"he will never be rich. You need a lawyer or a banker or a doctor," her mother informed her. Her own good husband had been an engineer. When he died two years ago of lung cancer (caused by pipe smoking according to Claire's mother, who always had to have an explanation), he left her with an inheritance and a solid pension that would take care of her for life—not in grand style, but comfortably all the same if she were wise. She lived in the sprawling rent-controlled apartment overlooking the Hudson River, after all.

"All unworthy professions in classic literature. Doctors were scorned—life's gatekeepers," Claire said. Of course, Jackson knew of his future mother-in-law's feelings, but he was too confident to care much and too kind to take offense. Rather, he humored her and flirted with her and made her smile and laugh. What he didn't fully appreciate, because he was not vain or conceited, was that the thing that bothered her most about him was how sexual she found him to be. He oozed sexuality through his sheer strength and size and confidence. Try as she might, she could not stop herself from imagining her daughter in a variety of compromising positions of ecstasy.

"With him you will never be rich," her mother said, sharp eyes piercing, "and if you struggle your entire life you will not age well and that's a fact." At all this, Claire simply laughed and married Jackson and had a daughter soon thereafter and with Beth the dreams began in earnest, and now Claire danced across a field with her husband racing after her ready to tackle her. She wore an orange tweed suit that her mother had bought at Best's so that she would look the part of wife for the search commit-tee at the college. At this moment they were supposed to be there eating lunch with faculty inspecting Jackson (and Claire) to see if they would be a "fit" for the community.

"Just think of Beth in these fields. They'd seem endless for her. So much to explore," Claire said. And she wished her daughter were with them now, her pudgy little body in her arms as she ran across the field. "We'd build right here. The house should be right here to take advantage of the view." Claire showed him the flyer and the map it contained of the farm. On the map, a farmhouse from 1846 was indicated, but they had not yet passed it, as it was hidden in a grove of sycamores at the bottom of the other side of the hill. Upon seeing it later, they would declare it far too dark and depressing though they would decide it could be useful, if properly restored, as a store from which they could sell the farm's products. The old house had been lived in for many years by the old apple farmer and his son and was in a catastrophic state of disrepair with dog feces smelling up the place.

"We'd build it here—big and filled with rooms so that any-one who wants can come and stay and stay and stay, as long as they help the farm to thrive, as long as they contribute talent and ideas. My gosh it's big enough at two thousand acres." And even if this was, as it most likely was, just one of many idealis-tic notions that Claire would have had across the span of her younger years, Jackson took it as gospel after her death—talked to her of it as they drove to the hospital, as he flew her body home, as he stood tall and elegant and pained along with her mother at the funeral before the cremation. *Where anyone who wants can come and stay and stay and stay.* Talked to Claire of it as he held their tiny Beth in his big arms, comforting her as she cried for mama, Jackson not understanding, perhaps never understanding, how to tell Beth where her mama was. "She's inside of you," he would say later when Beth was a bit older but not yet old enough to understand metaphor. She would want to turn herself inside out like a shirt.

But that day, up there, everything was right and thus began the dream, with those few words and the rain clouds streaking by and the sun on distant hills. Claire took off her coat and she took off her shirt and she took off her bra. She did a little seductive dance for Jackson. And she took off her skirt and she took off her slip and she took off her shoes and she took off her stockings and her underwear and she looked at him with teasing eyes, pursed lips, and did another little dance with her slip as a prop, tossing it and then even her earrings (pearl studs) into the field, and once and yet again everything was said between them with the use of no words and the warmth of April and a lacy mist on their backs.

The whole drive back to New York City they built their house on top of that hill.

Five weeks later, an urn of ashes in his arms, Claire's mother and Beth at his side, Beth in a ridiculous tailored coat with velvet and fur purchased for the occasion by Claire's mother, Jackson bought the apple farm at auction, using a portion of Claire's mother's inheritance from her husband. There were only a few other bidders: an Amish man and a few locals with not enough cash. For collateral, the mother (her name, by the way, was Eunice, but no one really called her that—she was Mother, the

grandmother, Grammy, or to her friends Uni or Nice, pronounced like the city in France) took out a life insurance policy
on Jackson for $500,000, she being the sole beneficiary. (He
outlived her by many years, but long before she died he had
been able to repay her with interest, which she refused, from
Claire's earnings and from investments gone well.)

By himself Jackson walked up the long drive, over the vast
fields, and through the woods, scattering the chips and ash and
even a screw or two (the remnants of a childhood operation involving her spine) that were his wife. In the beginning, because
of necessity, Jackson left the farm. But once the house was built
(he mortgaged the property to raise the necessary funds) and
once his Beth was settled there, he did not leave again until
2017 when Valeria would take him to Washington to receive an
honor from the White House for his "significant contributions
to the advancement of hydrogen for fuel." Actually, Valeria
would force him to come, taking a stand, saying to him what
his wife had never had the chance to say and what his daughter had been helpless to ask: stop hiding. "For Mom, please. For
Claire," Valeria would finally say, just as simply as that.

Driving to Washington, out of the farmland and into sprawl
that gave way to more sprawl until all gave way to city, was not
as hard as Jackson had always feared, just as the shot is never
as painful as the child imagines, and cold water becomes warm
after the stab of entering it. It was in the ease of the journey
that Jackson found the greatest sadness because that ease described just how possible it would have been for him to go to
his daughter when she had needed him. He remembered her
pleading with him to come to New York, stricken by the end of
her relationship with Cesare; he remembered Preveena begging
him to come search for Beth in the days following the calamity.
How unyielding he had always been, how afraid he had been

of what he would feel if he left. His allegiance to Claire had allowed him to believe he was honoring his grief, that he was giving Beth her mother by being faithful to his beautiful wife. At what cost, he asked himself now? Peaceful, oblivious, the world drifted by outside the window of the car, just as it always would have and always will. The cost was Beth, of course, denied a mother by chance but a father by will, his own will to refuse to look sorrow in the eye.

In the beginning the people who came to Claire were friends. Jackson had no grand (or even grandiose) design. People came for the weekend and stayed and stayed and stayed. Of course, many left as well. The first person to come was Albarbar, a friend from Harvard, where he'd been a student of religion. He only visited for a week: having earned his PhD, he had a position at Columbia and quite enjoyed the city. Albarbar assumed that the idea of a community at Claire was a stage of mourning, a phase that Jackson would pass through, but in the meantime he would indulge his friend. In fact, Jackson might be able to help someone else he knew. Albarbar had been to Rishikesh in India and had met a woman there who wanted to come to America to see what it was all about and to escape a marriage she was not happy with. Her name was Preveena and she was eighteen years old. She had wide dark eyes and uncommonly short hair (for an Indian woman) and grand ambitions to be a scholar of English literature, which she studied in Delhi. Eventually she wanted to teach and write elaborate novels, long and windy like those the nineteenth century is famous for. But her subject, of course, would be India, the Indian family across religion and caste and occupation and time. (This dream of writing evaporated with her teenage years, but she never stopped loving to tell the stories of her large and crazy family.) Preveena came from money, married money, and arrived at Claire in a sari with her belly peeking through the folds and pleats. Gold trimmed the borders of the peacock blue silk from Benares and a red bindi shone on her brow. She came to Claire with a trunk of tattered, well-read novels and another trunk of silk and jewels, and she never left.

Preveena had a friend in Madras who had a friend in Rome who had a friend in Milan who had a friend in New York who had a friend in Dallas who had a friend in London who had a friend in Paris and so it went. They came discreetly, one by one. Discreet in that it wasn't a big deal; Jackson would never have tolerated recruitment or proselytizing. No one was trying to convert anyone to anything. You helped, that was all. Some stayed for a day; some a week; some, like Preveena, never left. Albarbar visited from New York, amazed to witness the growing dream, his bald head sparkling in the afternoon sun, an astonished question mark of an expression on his face. The price each person paid to live at Claire was work and work alone. You could come with nothing, contribute only what you wished, but everyone was expected to work. At first the work consisted of developing and expanding the apple farm, making it as profitable as could be. Those who had the talent for such learned to splice branches onto root stock (apple trees, like citrus, don't grow true to their seeds: if you plant a Braeburn you don't necessarily get a Braeburn) or concoct formulas that would keep pests away without poisoning the trees (or people). Claire became like any community; expansion required a variety of definite talents. People either knew how to build or learned to build; people either knew how to manage money or they learned. No one profited individually from their work at Claire; while there you contributed according to your talents and abilities and were provided for according to your needs, but no one left Claire with more than they'd brought there. All went back to Claire. After taxes were paid, Claire's profits became part of the estate, and the estate of Claire was not owned by Jackson, would not be left to Beth (or later Rada) upon his death. Claire— the land and the community's investment—would be left to the people of Claire, and upon the dissolution of the community, Claire would be given in trust to the State of Pennsylvania for the people of Pennsylvania as a park, all two thousand acres preserved. (Lawyers, you see, were necessary, too.) On the few occasions that people left unhappily, their departure had to do with money and feeling that they weren't getting enough. The complaints always boiled down to a certain suspicion and vexing greed. Once Claire was sued. You learn from experience, or so the saying goes. After that, people who stayed had to sign a contract waiving the right to sue.

Some people simply contributed thought: they thought of what else Claire could achieve. After apples the farm moved on to meats, bartering with Amish butchers for their services slaughtering cows and pigs and chickens and turkeys. Like the apples, the livestock was raised organically. The animals thrived without antibiotics and hormones, living as freely and naturally as possible. The community at Claire had the manpower and the time and the desire to do things naturally and well.

There were plenty of skeptics, of course: writers and journalists from New York City and Philadelphia would come posing as newcomers then leave. Cynical pieces would appear in a variety of magazines and newspapers from *Vanity Fair* to the *New Yorker,* from the *New York Times* to the *Philadelphia Inquirer,* poking fun at the endeavor. Jackson didn't care. He read all the articles with pride. Indeed he loved the *Times* and had it delivered daily to the foot of that mysterious driveway, which would always remain unmarked. It was his daily ritual and pleasure to walk the long distance down the hill to fetch the paper. The news was his link to the world. (A ritual that would end with Beth's death.) And, of course, locals were suspicious, too, until they learned the economics of the place (Claire's money went to local banks after all), felt its contributions, and knew, from time and experience, that it wasn't a hippie enclave of free love and LSD. (It should be said, however, that Jackson and the lot did enjoy a good joint from time to time—Moroccan hash, Asian weed.)

People came to Claire from all over America. One man came from China when it was still quite difficult to defect. They came from Africa. They came from Norway. They came and they came and they came. Even dogs and cats came; they came from neighboring farms. "They prefer life at Claire," Jackson would say. After meat came berries, after berries came vegetables, after vegetables came ideas: hydrogen for fuel, a passion ignited in Jackson by a Russian electrochemist, who was a brief member of Claire at the height of the 1973 oil crisis and was working on the idea of a hydrogen economy. He envisioned a world in which people's cars, homes—whole cities, entire countries— employed water as fuel. Unrealistic as this pursuit may have seemed at first, it sparked Jackson's imagination. He was never one to dismiss an idea for being impractical or unrealistic if it might lead to something new and marvelous.

As more people came, children arrived or were born at Claire, and the school was started. It reached out into the local community, welcoming those who did not live at Claire, offering an alternative to the public schools, and a few local kids were even brave enough to attend. Educators joined the community and the children thrived.

As Claire grew, the community's needs did as well, and new markets were found or created for Claire's products. Fancy

restaurants and gourmet food stores in New York City and Philadelphia were tapped as a market for Claire's meats and berries
and vegetables and apples. An Italian man at Claire made fresh
ravioli and *tagliatelle* like no one had ever tasted before. The
people of Claire decided to use those reporters and papers to
advantage, parlaying publicity into a lure for tourists. Guests
could stay at Claire for a night, all meals included, for one hundred dollars, and people came—though few of the tourists remained. Claire wasn't about shunning capitalism: if money was
needed, money was made, and once made, extra money was
used to grow more money. No shame in that.

During these early years, Preveena fell in love with Jackson,
and throughout their love affair he continued to talk to Claire.
He told her about how good it felt to feel love, about what it
was like to be alive, about how Beth accepted Preveena. And
Beth did. Preveena taught Beth bits of Hindi, told her long con-
voluted stories about monkeys in banyan trees and bathers in
the polluted Ganges. She described the funeral pyres and how
babies and bodies floated by in the river, and she told her how
the Ganges, long ago, came down from the heavens in a torrent
on the back of Shiva's wild hair. And, of course, there were ma-
haranis and maharajas riding bejeweled elephants on their way
to shoot tigers. Preveena, in her sari with all her stories and her
beautiful eyes, also had a talent for fly-fishing, which she shared
with Beth. They haunted the raging spring streams together, a
picturesque and unlikely pair.

Jackson was weaving the dream, but he was not in charge.
He didn't have that sort of ego or desire for power. Besides, he'd
have been no good at it. He wasn't interested in leadership as
a role. In fact, his penchant for bartering had to be kept in
check—a job that fell first to Beth, then to Preveena, then to
Sissy Three.

People fell in love and then fell out of love and there was conflict over that. Some left as a result, since even two thousand acres isn't always enough to escape a love gone bad. Others endured. Shortly after Rada was born, the love between Jackson and Preveena went bad. The new mother became more and more jealous of Claire, of Jackson's conversations with her, of his inability to let her go. He spoke more to Claire about Rada (a very dark-skinned girl with his blond hair and her mother's big eyes—a most alluring contrast in lightness and dark) than he did to Preveena.

But Preveena stayed. She taught everyone to appreciate elaborate Indian feasts. Beth loved her nine-curry meals eaten with your fingers—right hands only, please (the left was traditionally used for the toilet). Preveena conjured up pilaus and kormas and raitas and mango chutneys, spending days in the kitchen combining spices, toasting cardamom and coriander and mustard seed, crushing the spices into a dust with a pestle, teaching Beth the chemistry, answering the girl's endless questions.

Meanwhile, Jackson continued to speak to Claire about the dissolution of love, about his role, her role, wondering for the first time if time would have dissolved their love, pondering that notion with her, but only for a moment before banishing the idea because his world was built upon the endurance of their love.

As strong as Jackson may have been and seemed, his grief endured along with his love. Alone sometimes he would cry. Beth always knew what the long absences behind his office door meant. As a child she would sit outside the door and wait. She didn't care how long it took for him to emerge. It was her small attempt to defy her mother and claim her father for her own. She would sit there, legs crossed Indian-style (as they used to say), back straight, and stare hard at the door, so hard some-

times she imagined she could penetrate the door with her eyes
and see her father sitting at his desk, head resting in hands, sobbing and trying to speak to someone who was not there. The
inescapable ache paralyzed her father. When he finally did come
out, she would curl up beside him and brush his hair with her
fingers, feeling the great weight of his sorrow, feeling scared by
it. She hated her mother for dying, for stealing her father as
well.

"Don't hate Claire," he would say. He knew his girl. He
wanted to speak to Claire so that Beth could hear her mother
answer. He wanted Beth to know that her voice was beside
them, her wisdom with them, that she loved her girl. He wanted
his daughter to be caught up in Claire's arms, smothered with
Claire's kisses. "See your daughter, darling," he said. It seemed
to Beth he really was speaking to someone, but Beth couldn't
see that person. "See what a fine job we're doing here with her,"
he continued.

"But I don't even know this woman," Beth said. "And she
definitely does not know me."

"Don't say that," he snapped. "She does know you. She
knows exactly who you are. You have been the same since the
moment you were born. She knows your fierce will. She knows
your warmth and love. She knew exactly who you would become." He looked into the terrified eyes of his Beth.

They continued to come. Mash arrived in the mid-1970s from
New York City and before that Russia. He built teepees and
yurts and small cabins in the woods so that privacy could be offered and respected. He instructed others on how to help and
some people who wouldn't have thought of themselves as talented carpenters learned otherwise. In 1984, Hunter, the failed
investment banker, came from New York City (a lot of people

came from New York City). Somehow this one, with all his supply of champagne and his penny loafers (tucked with pennies), had been involved with Ivan Boesky and fallen for him quite some time before Boesky would fall. Hunter, adorable, dirty blond hair, relentlessly positive, knowledgeable about many things, great questioner, he would become Beth's husband—Valeria's father. But of course no one knew that yet.

Sissy Three came with her mass of reddish curly hair and her bright energy and her bossy nature, bossing everyone with her big plans as if she had lived at Claire since its inception and knew what was best for the place. She wrote a constitution. (To this day it remains buried in a drawer in a basement somewhere at Claire.) In fact, she became obsessed with the real Claire, poring over pictures of the woman—some even say she was trying to compete with Claire, trying to trump her zest for life with even more. Sissy Three spoke as if she knew Claire and soon this interest brought Jackson and Sissy Three together, though Jackson had no idea of the depths of inquiry and research Sissy Three had engaged in: weekends in New York with Claire's mother, flipping through old photo albums and Claire's notebooks from college, reading her letters from home. "She was smart," the grandmother said to Sissy Three, enjoying her attention and her interest. "Far smarter than I could ever have been. She had grand notions, but she was too smart to have wasted her time at the farm. She'd have written books. She'd have been at the forefront of this women's movement like—like what's her name?" She tapped her forehead with the heel of her hand as if she could knock out the name.

"Betty Friedan?" Sissy offered.

"She knew Betty Friedan—Claire knew her. Indeed Betty's even been to Claire." Then noticing Sissy's hands, she changed the subject: "You have the most exquisite hands." She lifted them up to admire. Sissy Three's distinguishing feature, oddly enough, was her hands, very long and slender. In Paris she had been a hand model. A Japanese chemist she had briefly dated in Paris brought her to Claire on a bright spring day. The chemist was involved with the hydrogen economy project. Sissy Three never left.

And always the grandmother came, arriving in her black Lincoln with a scarf around her white hair and a shawl upon her shoulders. She would sit on the deck overlooking the fields and forest and the distant farms. She would tell Beth about a better life in New York City, trying to convince her granddaughter to follow Claire's own path. She wanted Beth to attend a private school where she would learn Latin instead of Hindi, to come to New York and learn to appreciate French cuisine instead of Indian. (By 1979 the grandmother had won this battle.) And she would sit with Jackson, pretending to sip her champagne (she was not a drinker), and tell him he was a dreamer; she would all but tell him his dream was sure to fail as these experiments in alternative living always do. "Too much sex, too much ego, too many people with too many destinies."

"Now, Grammy," Jackson would say, offering her the "piping hot" tea that she had requested simply because she liked to ask him to do things for her. Jackson kept Claire alive for her, and though she would never admit it, she was drawn to the community, she came and she came and she came, sitting on that deck somewhere deeply enjoying the place and the views, and telling Jackson why it would never work. Irascible, she may have been, but she was not immune to the power of her daughter's myth. She sat there above the spot that Claire had declared as the site for the house, where Claire had danced a sweet striptease in an April mist. Rising on her forearms to look at Jackson, naked both of them in the grass, Claire had said, "The world can't possibly be coming to end if we can feel as good as this."

By the time Cesare arrived at Claire in November of 1985, brought out for Thanksgiving from New York City by Beth, there were over one hundred people living and working at the farm. Claire was not what Cesare had imagined. He had imagined a chaotic place with people living on top of each other and somehow all getting along in spite of themselves. He had imagined everyone eating and cooking and sleeping together, lots of odd people from all over the world walking around dreamily dreaming up ideas, kids running around wild and unkempt, and everyone with jobs that somehow got done, Jackson presiding over it all with a soft hand that his daughter (and various women) tried to make more firm. That was not Claire. What he found was an ordered place with privacy, routine, discipline even. Odd yes, different yes, but more like a village, a town of sorts, than Cesare's idea of what a commune might be. Although in one detail, Cesare's imaginings were realized: the kitchen in the main house was open, it seemed, to anyone at anytime. People both familiar and strange to Cesare helped themselves to the food in the refrigerator and the cupboards all day long. ("A revolving door," Grammy would say. "Feeding all those people will be the ruin of Claire.")

At Claire, there were dirt streets (made by Mash), which contrasted with the interiors of the yurts and huts, all impeccably decorated with gleaming white walls, antique beds, and breezy curtains, courtesy of a designer named Short (and, indeed, he was short, with lots of hair and long fingernails). Short's contribution to the community was his eye for antiques, and their ability to appreciate.

The community had a store for supplies and a store that sold goods to tourists; there were business offices, the school, and, of course, the house sprawling on top of the hill, made of glass and cedar—also decorated by Short. Cesare had never seen such a house, which seemed of no particular design but was spectacular nonetheless for the advantage the windows took of all the views and the way the wood united the disparate parts. A deck trimmed the entire house and each of the five bedrooms, as well as the living room, the dining room, and the kitchen had sliding doors that opened onto it. The house had never been enlarged. It was built all at once with the knowledge that the views would not change. It followed a vague plan drawn up by Claire as she rode beside her husband on their trip back to New York City so many years ago. "Glass," she had said. "Lots of glass. So it looks like water and so that nothing is hidden from us."

At Thanksgiving dinner Cesare was surprised to find fifteen or twenty people instead of all one hundred as he'd imagined. Even this was a large group, he was told, but it was made up of family and friends. The other people of Claire had either gone away for the holiday or were having it with their own families. Rarely over the course of the year that Cesare was in America and visiting Claire was he aware of all one hundred people. Just as in a town, the population isn't constantly at your table.

Jackson, Preveena, Sissy Three, and Rada struck him as an odd family: not freaky, but unfamiliar. Jackson, for example, did not have the two wives—Preveena and Sissy Three—that Grammy had warned him about. ("Two wives," she would say. "Three if you count Claire. And I mean the farm, not my daughter.") Preveena, who was more like a sister, carrying on playfully with both Sissy Three and Jackson, was involved with Mash, the Russian carpenter whose thick accent Cesare had a hard time understanding. In Italy families were so straightforward; Beth's family was unusual but also refreshing, and Cesare admired the attempt here to make a happiness, to create a situation (unconventional as it may have been) that worked as well, perhaps better, than traditional families, in which unhappiness was so often swept beneath routine. They were trying, simple as that.

Though Cesare wouldn't have acknowledged his quest as directly as this, he wanted to see Claire, to see America and Beth's world, so that he could understand her completely, know her thoroughly, know if their love could withstand their respective histories. For him it was safer to think of his experience in terms of America: since he was a boy he'd been dreaming of America, reading about America, in love with America, and now that he was here, he wanted to sink into it, become it, know everything he could and experience everything he could. In theory, he liked adventure. In theory, he was willing to lose himself and try on anything and everything to see how it fit, to see if he looked better, felt better, in some other guise. This was the essence of him, the thing about him that Beth loved most, that Beth tried to excavate and encourage.

Leaving New York City on the Wednesday before Thanksgiving with all the other undergraduates returning to their former lives, he felt American, like a college student going home. He loved the idea of college, of all these boys and girls independent of their families at such a young age, able to do and choose as they please; they learned the concept of choice simply by the range of topics they could pick from to study, and in doing so, they learned who they would and could become. In Italy, university was very different. You lived and studied at home (it was customary to live at home until you married), visiting school primarily to take exams. You had no real relationship with your professors and the university you selected was based on the job you would have once you finished, which was

already decided by family legacy. He was at the Bocconi because its focus was economics. You would not go to the Bocconi
if you needed to study law or medicine or language, say. A lib-
eral arts education was had during high school. His summer
trips to London had given him a small taste for independence,
but those excursions were tightly structured, well organized,
and taken with a large group of Italians. Here in America he was
like a chameleon. He could adopt the life of the American student, try it on for size.

On the road, the long straight I-80, driving west, filling up
with gas (very cheap, he noted) at those massive truck stops that
seemed to sell everything, driving over the small ribbon roads
that laced together quaint farms, with their cows and chickens,
and communities of houses that all looked the same, lit up
brightly (already) with elaborate odes to Christmas—Santas
and reindeer and blinking lights climbing up the houses, trees,
garages, entire neon crèches in front yards—Cesare felt especially like an American boy going home. When he arrived at
Claire that afternoon, a cold November day, leaves off all the
trees and grass stiff with a freeze, he threw off his jacket with
the confidence of one who belonged. He joined the small American football game on the front lawn as if he had played many
times before and as if he had known these strangers all along.
Beth watched. This was why she loved him.

"Welcome," Jackson said, smiling, his hand extended. He
was a tall, slender, handsome man with penetrating blue eyes,
bushy eyebrows, and a sharp jaw. (Cesare had envisioned a
heavier-set man.) His hair was thick, his sideburns cut across his
cheeks. He wore faded blue jeans and a flannel shirt with a
leather vest, reminding Cesare of Peter Fonda in *Easy Rider,*
which he had seen many times on television as a boy, gathered
with a group of friends all privately dreaming they were riding

free on motorcycles on those long American roads. Jackson seemed youthful, unlike a father, despite his forty-seven years. Cesare gave Jackson two kisses on either cheek and then kissed Preveena and Sissy Three. Rada jumped into his arms. An admittedly strange-looking girl, Cesare thought; her dark skin and blond hair were such a striking combination. Cesare would soon see that Rada, ten years old, was in love with Beth, like a puppy, following her around and wanting to be just like her big sister. As a result, Rada would flirt wildly with Cesare, telling him everything about herself that was just like Beth: "I don't drink carbonated things, like Beth. I only like coffee ice cream, like Beth…" She would sit on his lap at the dining table or in front of the fire. She would ask him repeatedly to be on her team when playing football. She would take him for walks to show him her secret hideouts. Beth indulged her little sister, teasing her about her crush, scooping Rada into her arms and tickling her in a way that delighted Rada far more than the gesture deserved. Cesare noted all this, deciding there was something sad in her desperation, as if she were trying to find a closer link to this world in order to compensate for the fact that one side of her, her Indian world, was so obviously unknown to her.

"That's ridiculous," Beth would say later when Cesare tried to explain. "That has more to do with you than Rada."

On the lawn, a football game had begun before their arrival. As they approached, Cesare was surprised to see Preveena in her sari and a sweater, football in her arms. "Isn't it hard to run in that?" Cesare asked. And she smiled at him, loving his directness. She was beautiful, perhaps the most beautiful woman he had ever seen. Her hair was very short and her eyes bright and dark but still somehow like lights, accented by the arcs of her dark eyebrows. Her face was broad. There was a lot of it, but all her features worked together to make a composition, a study in perfection. Beth had not mentioned Preveena's beauty. A small diamond stud sparkled in her nose. Her complexion was as even as milk glass except for one large freckle on her left cheek.

"So this is our Beth's great love. We've heard all about you," Preveena said. "And now we're going to want to hear everything from your perspective, all about this love affair in Páros."

"A third degree," Jackson said. "You'll have to watch out for us. We like questions." The lawn sloped toward dense woods, an intricate network of bare trees.

"Answers even more," Preveena said.

"And I have heard all about you but still have many questions," Cesare said, and the list dashed across his mind. Most of all he wanted to know how it was possible for Jackson to never leave Claire. He did not seem the type of man who could stay put. "He brings the world to him," Grammy would say.

"Beth can worry a little too much about us," Jackson said. "I hope she and her grandmother haven't told you too many stories." He smiled a big mischievous smile, his face alive with depth and mystery and gentle fun. For as long as Cesare could recall, Beth had never slighted Claire, only spoken of it with fondness, and at times, perhaps, Cesare imagined, for he did not yet know himself, a bit too idealistically. He wondered if she were different around her father. Jackson looked around for his daughter.

"Here I am," Beth said, running down from the deck to greet her father with a big hug and kiss. Cesare noted (he was noting just about everything) their obvious love, nothing formal about it. Jackson swept Beth into the air as if she were still a child and then set her down so she could kiss the others. The cold air steamed from all their mouths.

"Finally," Sissy Three said. "All these years Beth has been hoarding you."

"Now Sissy," Preveena said. Cesare was struck immediately by Sissy's beauty, too. The opposite of Preveena's beauty, Sissy's was a pre-Raphaelite vision, with her blue eyes and her long reddish tresses, her sharp and pointy nose. Her face seemed to be made of porcelain and just as fragile. She wore jeans and sneakers and a sweatshirt. He was impressed by these two women, whom Beth had spoken of so often. Here they were, come to life like characters resurrected from the pages of a book, vibrant, pulsing with blood. Somehow he never expected them to be only a few years older than himself. How strange to find these two living side by side even if there was nothing strange about it for them.

For a few moments they fawned over Cesare, offering him a drink, a smoke, a tour of the grounds. They asked Beth quick questions about school and New York, the pizzeria where she worked, teasing her, Cesare could tell, by the way she laughed and bowed her head. They seemed like three sisters. Rada jumped around them, trying to include herself.

Mash and Hunter were playing, too. They kissed Beth and shook Cesare's hand. They seemed nice. He looked at Hunter, recalling Beth's declaration of his wealth. He was dressed like the exact image of the American boy that Italian boys aspired to—khakis and untucked oxford shirt all in need of ironing, boat shoes. An Amish farmer and a pair of Amish boys played, too, as well as some others, the names of whom Cesare did not catch—friends from a neighboring farm that had nothing to do with Claire although they probably bartered some wares, friends from New York City, a rumpled professor with a name like Ali-baba. They huddled around kissing and welcoming Cesare and Beth. Beth listed all the treats she had brought from New York City—biscotti from the Bronx and olive oil and mozzarella and wines. She promised to make pizza and asked Mash if he would quickly build her a brick oven. "Anything for you, dear," he said, and winked. (And he did make the oven. Beth had that effect; people wanted to do things for her.) When Cesare's sister came home from Milan, she brought nothing. When she left, she had bags filled with steaks and pastas and cheeses and fruits, supplies enough to last her until the next visit. Cesare noted the contrast.

"It's getting dark," Preveena said. "I want to make my touchdown before it does." She tossed the football to Cesare and told him he was on her team. The football spun off her fingers and glided smoothly to him. He caught it against his chest and then he passed it back to her, rolling it off his fingers. "You're a quick study," she said. "I'm sure Beth didn't teach you how to play."

"He's befriended a group of football players from Texas at school," Beth said. "All they do on Saturday is teach Cesare how to play and then how to drink as many beers as possible."

"Texans?" Sissy Three said, as if Texan football players and New York City didn't make any sense. Just then Cesare looked at Beth, bundled up in a sweatshirt and sweatpants, down vest, and running shoes, and understood that she made sense here. Creases made by his mother's maids still lined his jeans. The creases made no sense.

"Watch out for those Texans," Jackson said, lifting his left eyebrow flirtatiously. "They don't usually play fair." Cesare thought of the day Beth first met his father, how he had been cool and stern, how her friendly welcoming manner hadn't been able to imagine the impolite man as Cesare's father, rather she had mistaken him for someone irrelevant who had had a bad day, who didn't need to be friendly: the gardener.

And the game carried on with Preveena in her sari making her touchdown and Cesare being kneaded seamlessly into the fold. This was the scene Cesare wanted to re-create, later, when after returning to Italy, he would gather his friends to play football in the big field at Fiori. He would want to collect a group of people coming from everywhere: his father, his mother's Sri Lankan maid, her husband, his windsurfing friends. He imagined throwing a football to his little old father, imagined his father catching it and then sailing it off his curling fingers, a smile on his lips. He imagined hugging his father, big and broad, the way Jackson hugged Beth.

The sun, falling into the hills, splayed its colors against the sky.

Thanksgiving, too, was an odd and beautiful ritual for Cesare to observe, all the warm faces gathered around a long table singing songs ("We gather together to ask the Lord's blessing" and the like), eating the largest bird he had ever seen (which had been raised and killed by them), heaping plates with potatoes and yams and greens and stuffing and sweet cranberry sauce and pearled onions—dishes he had never seen before, tastes he had never tasted before. Like everyone else's, his plate overflowed with a massive heap of food—nothing delicate or discreet. He thought of his very thin mother, of how she was almost afraid of food and only ate the smallest amount. He imagined her shock before a plate such as this, and he looked forward to describing the details to her, knowing how she would laugh. *Grammy's serving,* he would write, *was the largest and she ate every last bite, even helped herself to more. She ate like one of those Amish mules. All the foods ran into each other—cranberry against potato against kale against onions until it became pink and indistinguishable. The more it blended together the more she seemed to enjoy it, mashing it all together with her fork.*

Gravy dripped over everything. All of these jolly people gathered to say thanks. Thanks for what? Thanks for coming to this country, thanks for being together, for getting along? Italians had always been in Italy—they were long past the stage of being grateful for who they were. There was something innocent and naive and young in this ritual, which he would observe again at Christmas with all the caroling and the Santas everywhere and the adoration of the tree. At the table everyone talked at once, arguing and discussing passionately a list of subjects that included music and food and interior design and even the color of the dinner plates—cranberry with gold trim. "Plates should be white," Short declared in a discussion of aesthetics, "to show off the food."

"What if the food is ugly?" Hunter said. There was a confidence to this handsome young man, who was probably younger than Cesare, the confidence of privilege and a fine education. He came from Beacon Hill in Boston, wealth, blue blood. He had gone to Harvard, then Columbia for business school. Hunter's Boston Brahmin credentials (which Cesare learned from Beth, who listed them as though they were reasons why he should warm to Hunter, as if their wealth and familial prominence were enough to make them best friends) meant nothing to Cesare. Hunter would try to engage Cesare in arguments about corruption in the Italian banking industry and in Italian politics. What Cesare noted most about Hunter was his aggressiveness, his desire to let you know how much he knew about everything from Italian culture and history to music and food to literature. (What could an Italian possibly know about American nonfiction and the literary journalists? Hunter implied. Rather than engage—Cesare did not argue; that was not his nature—he changed the subject.) Cesare wondered again if Hunter had ever had designs on Beth, as he seemed to be performing for her, and somewhere Cesare understood that Hunter's elite upbringing—his money, his schooling, his knowledge of the world—seduced her. Hunter hovered over Beth, smiling, and flirting, telling her of grand travel plans and ideas for making money off of nothing for Claire. Beth seemed to blush, becoming bashful with his attention, the way that can happen when someone you like flirts with you—the way she had been with Cesare in Páros. ("You've got him all wrong," Beth said to Cesare alone, after dinner. "He's a gentle soul and your jealousy is making you see innocent questions as challenges." Pause. Then, "Do you want me to fall in love with him?")

"Food is never ugly in a house like this," Short said.

Reagan was spoken of and the stock market and the latest hot topics in the *New York Times,* which, every morning, sprawled across the dining-room table until thoroughly read by all who cared. Cesare imagined that no one was ever lonely at Claire, and then he wondered if that was why they were all here. Beth had told Cesare that Hunter's family came once a month to Claire to try to convince him to come away, telling him that fear was trapping him here.

"Thanksgiving is a designed holiday," Preveena said to Cesare. She sat to his right. "By a woman named Sarah Josepha Hale, in the early nineteenth century. She wanted a holiday that centered around women and their food and she promoted the idea in a novel that she wrote and in an enormously popular magazine she published that was filled with advice for making your home more perfect. She wanted to give a holiday to women."

"And the Pilgrims?" Cesare asked.

"They had nothing to do with it really. Myth, that's all."

"Preveena knows her Americana," Sissy Three said. Her face glowed in the candlelight.

"Sarah Hale again," Beth said. She was sitting across from Cesare, dressed in a long black velvet gown. Everyone had dressed formally. Jackson wore a bow tie and a tuxedo vest. His sideburns caused his smile to seem even bigger. Cesare wondered if he would be capable of growing sideburns. Rada sat on Jackson's lap, eating off his plate, which Cesare found mildly distasteful, as if she were some kind of unruly pet. "Lincoln made it a national holiday finally in 1863."

"Beth knows her Americana, too."

"She can tell you all about your national anthem," Cesare said.

"We've heard it many times," Sissy said. Grammy started singing the song. Rada joined her. Cesare knew that Grammy had a low opinion of Rada. ("She's so dark and odd with that blond hair. A half-breed. Neither here nor there.") But together they got the whole table singing. Beth smiled, a youthful smile—a smile he had seen often on Laura, a younger-sister smile, one that surrendered age and any wisdom. At Claire, Beth became a child in a way Cesare had not seen before. Yet at the same time she was also responsible and in charge: organizing the cooking and the table setting, negotiating deals for land use and apple sales and beef butchering—doing it all fast and effortlessly. Clearly she had been doing this for a long time and clearly Jackson depended on her, but somehow the need and the reliance were an unspoken given that she smiled off (in that smile to Sissy Three) in the guise of innocence. Looking at Beth, Cesare had a strong urge to protect her.

The meal began with a moment of silence (also a funny tradition) and a prayer (though none of these people seemed very religious) and ended, after dessert (smaller plates heaped with strange concoctions of pecans and pumpkins and chocolate and all very delicious, if unfamiliar, all melding together) with Sissy Three standing before the table and lifting her glass, her cheeks flushed with wine and champagne, for a toast to Claire. "Not the house Claire, but the dreamer Claire. Thanks for dreaming your dream."

In between Alibaba (Albarbar) argued with Jackson about the impracticality of hydrogen for fuel: "Natural gas is in short supply. Coal will be used perforce and it will do more damage to the ozone than oil." They all knew about the evils of coal. Snyder County was on the border of Pennsylvania's anthracite coal region. Albarbar was a small overweight man, stooped over and bearded with his rumpled tweed jacket, always short of breath—the sort of American intellectual Cesare had imagined when he read about New York intellectuals. He could imagine Albarbar's book-lined apartment, stacks of old newspapers he was afraid to throw away because he might want to refer back to an article on something or other. Albarbar liked to argue. Jackson didn't. He simply listened, lit a cigarette that was a joint, passed it to Albarbar, and told him not to get so excited. The conversation, though, grew heated. Mash and Hunter joined in, Hunter standing up now and again to pour everyone champagne, and the grandmother repeating her mantra about Claire failing. But Jackson remained steady. In fact, Cesare sensed a remoteness, as if only a part of him were truly there. As Cesare grew to know Jackson, that characteristic would define him most of all, and though Jackson was an ambitious dreamer, loving and kind, Cesare would wonder how good he could really be as a father at such a distance. As distanced as Cesare's father was from his son, that distance did not preclude Giovanni Paolo from having a well-defined vision for his son's future and thus his well-being. "He's with my mother," Beth would explain simply—something she had been saying for years and which she had come to understand as making sense.

After dinner Cesare cleared the table, did the dishes, swept the floor. His helpfulness was remarked upon. But lying in bed that night, having been in America just about six weeks, he felt for the first time just the slightest confusion ripple through him—a confusion he couldn't articulate, but the answer to which seemed buried in the image of Sissy Three (what kind of name is that?) standing before the table, flushed cheeks, flowing hair, lover of Jackson, toasting Claire, "the woman." Everyone had raised their glasses, nothing odd, as if they were toasting the president or God or Sarah Hale or the cook who made the fabulous meal. It rippled through him, a slow burn.

"Are you awake?" Beth asked, turning to him in the dark. He wanted to ask her about her mother, have her say something that would dissipate the confusion.

He said nothing.

"Do you like it here?" she asked, a question she was fond of asking, as if the question could take his temperature. Though she had a sense she knew the answer: He loved it here. He loved New York. He loved Claire. They loved him. She felt very happy as if everything were as it should be in the world. He pulled her against him and into him. He thought of Fiori, of the house standing there, occupied by his family for five hundred years. "You're so soft," he whispered. Outside the moon was full, glistening on the frosted grass, and the confusion continued its slow creep, baffling his desire to conquer America and the new and the unfamiliar until the confusion was erased by sleep.

Cesare would be in America for nearly a year, time enough to understand the confusion, which would recede and return like a tide. Each time it returned, however, the source of his confusion became clearer and clearer, like an image emerging from a Polaroid. He came in October of 1985. His year would cross into 1986. The America he found was quite different from the America Claire left behind in 1968. Cesare's time in America was part of a historic period oddly marked by eruptions and explosions that rocked the world. The list is long: the Greenpeace vessel, the *Rainbow Warrior,* was bombed and sank in Auckland Harbor; the volcano Nevado del Ruiz erupted in Colombia, killing over 23,000 people; the spaceshuttle *Challenger* exploded with the teacher, Christa McAuliffe, aboard. (As she and six others met their deaths, Beth and Cesare were skating at Rockefeller Center, trying out loops and figure eights). The Chernobyl nuclear reactor melted down killing thirty people and spewing radiation into the atmosphere. Across this canvas Madonna skyrocketed into the stratosphere, simulating masturbation as she toured the world promoting *Like a Virgin.*

Ironically, this time is remembered by most Americans as a peaceful one, one of prosperity. The dollar was strong. Reagan was president. Gorbachev became the Soviet leader. Ivan Boesky published *Merger Mania;* Michael Milken was the undisputed junk bond king, and the stock market soared—bubbling, erupting, ballooning. Studio 54 was the place to be; cocaine was the drug of the moment (best spot in the city to buy: 106th Street and Amsterdam). "Holiday" played endlessly; "Like a Virgin" played endlessly; "Material Girl" played endlessly. All Madonna, all the time. She posed for *Playboy. Desperately Seeking Susan* was released. And Cesare came to America—a handsome Italian boy filled with grand notions of possibility, following his American girl to New York City across which he loved most to drive late at night in the grandmother's Lincoln, cruising the avenues and the canyons of Wall Street, making himself believe in the impossible.

In New York, Cesare lived with Grammy (none of that monkey business). Beth lived with two of her friends from NYU, downtown on Sixth Avenue in an apartment crowded with furniture harvested from the street, a notion that took Cesare a while to adjust to. The idea of sitting on a couch, eating at a table, sleeping on a mattress (here he drew the line) that had been used in unknown ways by unknown others was grotesque at first. But before long he, too, was helping Beth haul home a chair or two for the dining table. "It's perfect," she said, finding a red velvet chair on the street. One of the legs was cracked and a tear cut across the velvet on the seat. Otherwise, it was fine. *L'America,* he thought. He thought that all the time with an amused smile. For curtains, Beth hung old sheets, tying them back during the day with ribbons from last Christmas's packages. The arrangement of other people's things implied forethought, even effort. Unusually shaped wine bottles were used as vases to hold flowers bought at Korean groceries, which were open twenty-four hours a day on all corners of all streets. The flowers wilted immediately in the heat of the apartment. Even so, they remained in the vases for days. "I like them dead," one of Beth's roommates would say. "That way they last longer." Beth would cook elaborate Italian meals for dinner parties on a dirty and very old stove, inside of which it was not uncommon to find a cockroach or two or three scurrying out to escape the sudden heat. She made her own gnocchi and her own *gnochetti alla romana* and her own tortellini and her own ravioli and her own lasagna. Lasagna noodles hung on the backs of chairs, from towel racks, from hangers. By candlelight a table of friends would talk and argue about Reagan and Koch and then move on to music and then philosophy—Nietzsche and nihilism and Hegel and tragedy. "Hegel said that genuine tragedy is a case not of right against wrong but of right against right." Heady thoughts picked up that afternoon from their philosophy classes that along with the wine and endless cigarettes made them feel grown-up. (On weekends that parents visited, all evidence of such parties was deeply hidden and more bows were tied around more curtains.)

Watching all this, Cesare would remember Beth in Italy, how their dinner parties were the times in which Beth felt most to belong. Always Beth's friends would turn to Cesare and ask him about Italian politics. "How many prime ministers since World War Two?" Always, in the beginning, they'd mispronounce his name—*Say-zar-hey, Say-zar, Cheese-ar-a*—until finally, giving up, they called him Caesar, a name that Cesare found both ugly and endearing, endearing in that hearing himself called by it he imagined that he had really become an American boy: Italy and his life there as neatly hidden as the cigarettes and the wine bottles on parents' weekends. On parents' weekends, of course, Jackson never came to town. "You know he can't," Beth said to Cesare, though somewhere he wanted her to fight her father on this, to break him. Jackson's refusal to come to Beth angered Cesare: Jackson was acting like the child that Beth was born to mother. "Your father is no different," Beth would say. "I don't see him or your mother racing over here to visit you."

"Oh come, Bet. You know it is not part of Italian tradition."

"What?" she would ask, screwing up her face to indicate that his logic made no sense. A little fight would be ignited, a little fight hinting at the deepest fissure. Americans were vagabonds. Italians were not.

"My father takes an interest in what will become of me."

"My father wants me to become what I want to be," Beth snapped back. And then they were really fighting. Oh, she could fight. "Your father just wants you to spend your life preserving the past. He doesn't care about your future, only that you uphold something dead."

Cesare insisted that she did not understand. "Bet, be reasonable. Bet, be reasonable." But Cesare knew that Beth was right, that if he lived permanently in America, his father would never visit him.

———

Cesare watched Beth's roommates move about her apartment, as if he were watching a show, studying a new species. One of them was a girl into leather with a whip; the other was heavy-set, with pink hair and a penchant for lots of jewelry and ripped tights. Both wore severe black makeup. Yet they were nice girls who liked Cesare because he teased them playfully and made them laugh at their own eccentricities. They would take him out to clubs when Beth was too busy with school or waitressing, guarding him protectively though somewhere both girls had wild crushes on him. Their names were Veronica (the leather girl) and Jane (with pink hair). The three of them went odd places—a church turned into a disco, a gay club on many floors with transvestites dancing on podiums before an oblivious crowd, a bank vault turned disco, too. All Madonna, all the time. In the bathrooms people snorted-up ravenously, nostrils white with the stuff—Jane and Veronica, too. They offered it to Cesare. He demurred. Then they talked fast and endlessly to him about their families and his: "What's it like to be five hundred years old? Beth says you're five hundred years old." Or, "Is everyone fat in Italy?" asked by the pudgy Jane (who didn't think of herself as pudgy), shouting above the music, partying masses crushing against them. "Enormous," Cesare answered, with a wink. And he learned that Veronica's family was very wealthy—her grandfather invented the ball bearing or something like it. Jane was, in her words, "an army brat," a term that needed defining for Cesare. They, too, called him Caesar. Late at night he would see them home, sneak into bed next to Beth, and watch her sleep, imagining her life before he arrived in New York City, envious of all the boys whom he believed admired her.

It had taken him nearly two months to come to America after their late-afternoon conversation in the long summer grasses at Fiori. For those two months they had written their letters, declared their love—he more than she, afraid as he was of all these college boys and of the things they would do with and to Beth. Cesare would wait impatiently for the mail each day, dreadfully morose when a letter did not come. He would think of her brushing her teeth, her hair, think of her being watched in this casual ritual by a boy, a college boy into the music that she liked—the Talking Heads, the Ramones, the Police. He would imagine her resisting the boy at first, putting him off with stories about her Italian boyfriend. Then he would imagine the boy's persistence, her inevitable surrender to the delights of desire—fingers delicately tracing secret spots, working her into a lather of confusion until she could do nothing but plead, but beg, but ask for more. He could see it, as if he were sitting there, in one of those armchairs found on the street, watching for himself. Her letters said little, the distance like a yeast, a culture that caused his love to swell until it hurt, until it ripped him up inside. Then her voice on the phone—sweet American voice—asking simply: *"Vieni?"* Are you coming?

When he could stand it no more, he told his parents he was leaving and, putting all school and career obligations aside, he bought his ticket, packed his bags, and flew off to New York. As the plane landed at JFK in the late afternoon, the sun a scarlet disk sinking behind the buildings, all he could see in all those buildings was promise and its relief.

When he first arrived, it seemed she made love in a new way, a way he imagined she learned from those college boys. The notion intoxicated him with its pain. She was somehow sexier, more free, more eager. And he would wonder, realize, then believe this change was a result of a confidence he had not understood so clearly in her before.

And now here she lay, exhausted by work and school. He could look at her all night long, marvel at the depth of her sleep, at the peace in her lips. He didn't wake her; just being here, gazing at her could be erotic enough. In the morning he would deflect Grammy's queries concerning where he had spent the night. He knew. She knew. But queries and lies, nonetheless, were obligatory.

Cesare made friends easily. He had met the Texan boys at the dining hall one evening while Beth was at work and he was using her meal card, pretending to be a student. They took him in, taught him to play football and to guzzle beer. Cesare even developed a little beer belly of which he was strangely proud. He embraced everything, including junk food. He gorged on heroes and hoagies and pizza and meatball sandwiches and sloppy joes with the Texans. Beth enjoyed observing these friendships, friendships with boys she had hardly noticed before. They taught him to pump iron, develop well-defined biceps. Cesare wanted to become big like the football players. The boys invited him to Texas for the Christmas holidays. (Beth put her foot down.) They arranged for him to audit a creative writing class with a sweet young writer who had let the Texas boys do anything they wanted as long as they turned in their work. He wrote a short story for the sweet teacher with the crooked smile and crooked teeth (probably younger than himself) all about a town in northern Italy famous for its relationship to feet and the money it made off of them. The story was a parable about greed in the manner of Italo Calvino. The teacher, unfamiliar with Calvino, thought the story of feet and greed brilliant. Cesare loved it in America.

Solo, or with Beth, he went to hear jazz at the Village Vanguard, at Sweet Basil, and at Birdland all the way uptown. He walked the streets. Beth's schedule was busy. She wasn't free the way she seemed to be in Italy. She had four classes and the waitressing job at the pizzeria. She had grand designs for this pizzeria, AMALFI PIZZERIA blazing in neon, and her passion for it threatened Victor, the Albanian pizza maker, who preferred the status quo. She wanted to make thinner crusts, wanted the owner to invest in a wood oven, wanted to use sauce made from fresh tomatoes, make smaller single pies, charge more for better quality. She made test pizzas for the owner, Bruno, a short man from Naples. Cesare came in to help. "You're my sous-chef," she said. He donned an apron and a white chef's hat and for a while loved the idea of making something from nothing. Never in his life would he have imagined himself baking pizzas in New York City, much less making an Albanian immigrant mad at him for his efforts. This would be a good story back home, a good story as long as it remained just that.

Bruno loved the new pizzas. "Like in Italy," he said—*Eee-tal-lee*. And he kissed his fingertips. Beth used the best mozzarella hunted down in the Bronx, the finest olive oil, and basil brought from the hothouse at Claire. First, she and Cesare made pizza Margherita—named for Queen Margherita because she desired to eat pizza like the common folk and one was invented just for her, using the colors of the flag. Then Beth wanted to put complicated things on top of her pizzas and Cesare convinced her to keep them simple.

"That's another difference between us, between Italy and America: you like abundance, too much; we like spare, too little," he said.

"Stop noting the differences," she replied.

Beth's efforts were a resounding success: these pizzas sold. People couldn't get enough of them. Bruno was thrilled. (He even installed the wood oven after a while.) Victor was not. Jealous and angry, he tried to make Beth's job harder, tormented her because she was terrible at remembering people's orders.

She took it all so seriously, crying on Cesare's shoulder, feeling humiliated and exhausted from too much work and school.

"Bet," he would say soothingly, and he would pat her head and rub her toes and then hold her away from him in order to look at her with levels and layers of feeling. First love, love for her determination and ambition, her fearlessness, her willingness to do anything. Then the lurking confusion. He had had fun with the pizzas certainly, but in the end, what did they really amount to? And why in the world did she care about an Albanian? Then he would think of Sissy Three toasting Claire, "the woman," and her dream. He could see something, some vague scrap, a clue: Beth was at the beginning of her dream. She was just beginning to put the yarn on the needle, didn't even realize she was doing so. What were his dreams? Was he even, really, allowed to dream?

"I'm still your Bet," she would say to Cesare. Somewhere she wondered, but she never stopped believing: he was in love; she was in love. The vast divide didn't seem so vast. He was her Cesare, her Caesar, her emperor. A pause, then she was seized again. She wanted to make and to do and to create. A part of him wanted to take her away from all this and that same part of him couldn't get around the notion of her having to waitress and of her having ambitions that revolved around food, pizza no less. How proud she looked when Bruno savored her pizza, her face lit with meaning and purpose and consequence. Ambition.

Cesare, though he didn't admit it to Beth, hardly acknowledged it to himself, felt humiliated for Beth when she proudly counted her tips, more than a hundred dollars in cash and coins made from waiting tables. "We're rich," she had said. All he could think about was how dirty the money looked, how dirty it was making her hands. That part of Cesare wanted to take her back to Italy and buy her things and keep her safe and protected and give her everything she had never had: together they would make a simple family—two children, a dog.

It was easy, though, to be caught up in the ecstatic energy and pace of Manhattan, the electricity, the lights. Peep shows; girly shows; Men Only; XXX; prostitutes on the West Side Highway; Broadway; a man showering, naked, in front of a full-length window, full-length erection; everyone seemed to have some kind of leather accoutrement, funny hair—colored or spiked or shaved. Cesare's letters home were endless, so much to describe.

Eventually Dario visited him. Skinny Dario with his exquisite inability with the English language—he made no sense in America. He wanted his espresso, *"Corto corto, come in Italia."* He wanted his pasta, *"Al dente, come in Italia."* He wanted his big meal at midday, *"Come in Italia."* He wanted everything to be as it was in Italy. Catching the football nearly knocked him over. At Claire, where Cesare took him for a week, he complained about all the odd people. He didn't so much complain as continually comment on the fact that there was an Indian and a black woman and a Chinese guy, commenting by way of not-so-subtle jokes. In Città only the maids came from other countries. Then he started complaining in earnest about constipation and blamed it on all the strange foods he was eating at Claire—all those curries Preveena made them eat. He didn't want to do any work there because his stomach hurt. (There was nothing people disliked more at Claire than someone who didn't help out.) Mostly, however, he wanted to see Sylvia. He had been thinking about her ever since she left Greece. He asked until finally Beth begged her to come for a visit from Boston where she went to college. She blew in with her flirty smile and all her plans but absolutely no romantic interest in Dario. "What was I thinking?" were her exact words to Beth. Beth turned her own impatience on Cesare. "Why do Italians think so much about their bowel movements?" she demanded. Even she had not been spared detailed accounts of Dario's incessant intestinal antics and it had made her remember that more than one dinner conversation in Italy had revolved around people's bowel movements. Bea's sister had constant constipation and ate sticks of licorice, administered by her father, with the hope that it would release her bowels. When Dario left, Beth and Cesare were both relieved. "Let me know if I ever become like that," he said to her.

Then he would step out of Beth's world and into the grandmother's, with Beth putting on a pretty chiffon calf-length dress, black pumps, a strand of pearls around her neck, studs in her ears. Before him she transformed into a prim girl almost unrecognizable: a girl made for an expensive life that should be handed to her and not sought. Suddenly Beth was not the ambitious girl he knew. Seeing her this way he understood the role the grandmother wanted him to play, even if Beth did not. As they rode uptown in the cab, Cesare left the one reality for the other, knowing which one he preferred and which one he would choose if only he could.

The grandmother's reality was marked by crystal chandeliers and benefits at the Met (the Museum) or "hearing" an opera at the other Met. "My local theater," she was fond of saying. The big event of the season was the production of Wagner's *Lohengrin,* "From which the Wedding March originates," the grandmother informed him. For this event and for the party she would host "to introduce him," he needed a tuxedo, which she bought for him herself at Paul Stuart, "Where my husband bought all his clothes. Just feel this material," she said, fingering the fine wool of the tuxedo pants, inadvertently tickling Cesare's leg as he stood before her in full black tie. She sat before the many mirrors in the upstairs lounge of the formal-wear department, her image reflected for Cesare to infinity. In Italy there were not such big stores as this. An Indian salesman who had been at the store for years, and who had been the personal shopper of Grammy's husband, helped them find the right suit. Grammy knew everything about the salesman (wife in India, three daughters, no sons, tremendous regret, sends money home, family won't consider coming to America), but she did not know his name. She told him Cesare was an Italian prince. "Betrothed to my granddaughter. A big wedding as soon as she finishes college. Of course, we'll buy an even better tuxedo for that occasion—which will be celebrated at the Pierre, nothing less. Unless, of course you'd like to marry in Italy?" she asked, suddenly looking at Cesare, catching the Indian up in the drama of expensive matrimonial decisions, making him, Cesare noted, nearly pant with expectation for financial gain.

At her party to "introduce" him, he was the prince as well, and he obliged, indulging the grandmother. "Made in Italy," he said, making all the ladies laugh, and he spoke to each one of them, answering their numerous questions about banking and socks and shoes and the subject of his dissertation, which concerned the history of dyes, how the commodity became bankable. They were privately suspicious of his Italian origins and had discussed it with the grandmother previously. "He's a Catholic after all," one woman had warned. They associated Italians with the Mafia or with the gondoliers who rowed them peacefully over the canals of Venice or with their daughters' stories of being pinched while strolling through the Forum. At all this the grandmother had laughed and declared him a prince from a noble northern Italian family. "I've seen the villa," the grandmother had said. Verification. Proof. "Do you realize his family owns the only existing fresco painted by Benvenuto Cellini, perhaps the only painting ever made by his hand?" The ladies were well cultured. Culture was their currency. This detail inflated Cesare in their eyes as Grammy knew it would. They were fluent in the language of money and so was Cesare, though his ability with it was far more subtle and discreet.

At the party, elegant matrons swirled around Cesare, vying to impress him. One, with a blemished apricot complexion and auburn hair piled atop her head, attempted to engage him on his dissertation topic. She wore a particularly lovely dress with a brocade bodice in gold, and though she was not young, she was youthful. Her name was Gimbel, her husband was, "in retail" as she explained, but the detail of who she was was lost on Cesare, just as a Bianchi would have been lost on her. She sipped a flute of champagne and ate hors d'oeuvres continuously, plucking them from passing trays proffered by young waiters in white with gloved hands and bow ties. "Did you know that one of our presidents, William Howard Taft, had a son who died because dye from his blue sock got into a cut on his left foot? As a result there was a revolution in the sock dyeing industry here." Cesare had heard something like that, but he wasn't certain it was Taft's son or if a revolution had occurred. "Progress," Cesare said. "And penicillin."

Other ladies asked him other questions, telling him about their grand tours to Venice and the Amalfi Coast, about Positano honeymoons, trips to Cinque Terre ("Cinque" mispronounced with a soft *c*), Florence (one said *Firenze* with a flourish), and Pisa.

Grammy's apartment had big picture windows overlooking the Hudson, upon which floated one enormous and heavy barge. Cesare watched the barge and briefly wondered how it was that some of the richest people in America lived in rent-controlled apartments in New York City. Beth had explained to him the complicated system of rent control, which had been designed to benefit low-income families but was enjoyed by the rich. It reminded him of the complicated infrastructure of Naples that allowed the wealthy to flourish and the poor to remain poor.

Beth snuck up behind Cesare and kissed him. Throughout the party, he had watched her floating among the ladies, making small talk, graceful like a swan. He wished his mother could see her. She was elegant. He remembered his mother trying to tell him without being insulting, but being insulting just the same, that Beth's manners were atrocious. There was nothing atrocious about her. She was pleasing her grandmother by pleasing her grandmother's friends. At a party for *Carnivale* hosted by his parents at the Città villa, he recalled how she had tried to talk to his parents' friends but then seemed to give up and hardly spoke to anyone. At the time he had imagined it was because she was shy around the older more formal people. Now he suspected that his parents' guests had made no effort, having no idea what to say to her. So much interest was shown to him here, but in America they were more familiar with the foreign, infatuated even, eager to impress. "My childhood," Beth said. "One half of it anyway." Schizophrenic, he imagined, thinking of the other half, of Claire.

And then they would be at Claire. Beth's father never called to ask her to come, but his gravitational pull was strong nonetheless. At least every other weekend they went to Claire. Sometimes Cesare went by himself. Beth studied the farm's books, helped do the things that needed getting done in the spring with the apples. She and Cesare hauled strawberries to New York restaurants in June, blackberries in July, raspberries in August. Cesare grew to understand how all the various pieces fit into Claire's operations: the goats for goat cheese buttons; the bees for honey; the tourists for a night's stay and cash; the reenactments for cash; the slaughtering of the beef, the pigs, the chickens, and on and on.

At the grandmother's party, Claire, the woman, and Claire the place were both spoken of. On a wall in the living room hung an oil portrait of Claire when she was a girl, a lovely girl with strong eyes and dark curls; her fierce intelligence seemed to emanate from the very paint like rays of sunshine. Looking at it, the ladies would say, "An odd end for the dearest girl." Something they surely said each time they saw the portrait, never accepting or reconciling themselves to her fate, haunted by it themselves even though they had outlived her already by a lifetime.

At Claire there was one snapshot of Claire, taken moments before she was hit. She is smiling, her head turned to look back over her shoulder. She has climbed the wall and Jackson has said her name and she has turned knowing he will take a picture. The smile says, "I've seen what's on the other side of this wall and you haven't. I know what lies beyond. I want to take you there." Sissy Three caught Cesare studying the photograph. "It is not a coincidence," Sissy said, "that this is the only picture of Claire Jackson has." Beth was in New York and Cesare was visiting Claire by himself this time. He had been in America about eight months. He had heard Sissy Three speak on more than one occasion about Claire's dreams. He had not yet been able to penetrate Jackson, to get to a level of intimate conversation. Cesare understood he never would, that Jackson's own daughter never would, that Jackson wasn't designed like that—because of who he was or because of fate. Jackson, for the most part, kept busy with the chores of the farm and with his letters to Washington, working at a vast and dark desk late into the night. On the walls of his office were indecipherable charts and graphs and diagrams. Endless clippings from magazines and newspapers scattered the floor. Jackson still spoke to Claire, and Cesare was beginning to understand that if Jackson's own daughter couldn't find a way to talk to him about the futility of these conversations neither could he.

Cesare looked at Sissy's beauty pouring from her eyes and lips and asked her quite simply, "Why have you devoted your life to the casual dreams of some other woman?" Day in, day out, they ran this farm and made it work. Cesare had come to enjoy working with his hands—milking the goats; picking the early summer apples, the strawberries; fertilizing the fields; talking with Jackson about a day when America would not depend on the Middle East for fuel, predicting the grave dangers of doing nothing. Claire even sold berries to New York restaurateurs, negotiating keenly the price per pint. Sissy looked Cesare in the eye, held him with her gaze, and answered, "We all need to believe in something."

"It's not clear though if this is really what Claire would have pursued," he said.

"Yes it is." She flexed her hands in front of her. They were slender and long and beautiful. Better a farm than hands, he supposed. She could have spent her life believing in her hands.

"How do you know?" he pressed.

"Because I believe in the idea and I believe that her life has to amount to something, that lives have to amount to something," she said. And that is all she would allow on the subject. *She's crazy,* he thought. *They're all crazy.* But then he banished the notion, fearing it would break a spell.

Filippo Tommaso Marinetti writes about history consuming itself, regurgitating itself, repeating itself endlessly. We're tricked into believing in history's linearity. But it circles and circles and circles around on itself, learning little, trapping itself like the snake that eats its own tail. Fishing on Claire's swollen spring river, Preveena casting her line easily with the gentlest snap of her wrist, sari drenched and bunched at her ankles, resolved Cesare's confusion unwittingly and quite simply: "Jackson is stuck, like one in quicksand, in the past." She cast again. For a long time they were silent, casting, catching nothing, their flies skipping gracefully across the rapids. Then Preveena said, "Beth, however, is not. Jackson has somehow managed to set her free."

With her words the Polaroid image emerged, fully focused, and Cesare could finally see his life and Beth's with inescapable clarity. He sees Sissy Three toasting Claire at Thanksgiving. He sees Preveena fishing. He sees Beth concocting grand schemes out of pizzas. He sees Fiori. He sees the Cellini fresco with the outsized lovelorn girl. He sees his father in his garden working at the weeds. He sees Jackson tethered to the ground of Claire, chasing the smile of a beautiful girl. He sees history eating its own tail. He sees five hundred years of Cesares and Giovanni Paolos. He sees. He sees. He sees. He sees Claire, the farm, an elaborate homage to a personal past. Fiori an elaborate homage to a personal past. Jackson freed Beth. Cesare's father did not free him. Cesare had wanted to save Beth, or so he had imagined. What he really wanted was to free himself.

Cesare had left the Indian and Paul Stuart with the tuxedo, the shirt, the cummerbund, the bow tie, the cuff links, suspenders, and vest, thinking about Beth's roommate with her pink hair and ripped tights and of the Indian salesman who lived in Queens, his family in India, and of all the juxtapositions—dizzying and grand and simple—of Claire. All these worlds coexisting, integral and not, overlapping really, yet independent and aloof, the world in microcosm, all here to find linearity, to escape the past.

In Italy, men do not wear tuxedos. But Cesare enjoyed how American the fancy suit made him feel. Months later, a late summer evening, he wore it out, not for any occasion, just to drive those avenues and through those canyons, his arm draped effortlessly over the back of the front seat as if he were some grand character—a Gary Cooper, say, or a Cary Grant—in some romantic comedy from the 1940s. In New York he had the sense that even if one made one's self, one would still remain anonymous and there was something a little sad, a little terrifying in that: each person his own country held together by private, rather than collective, ambition. By this summer evening Cesare had been in America well over nine months, and though he had pursued many things, really, he realized, he had pursued nothing. He had spent his time stepping out with Veronica and Jane, playing with the Texans, drifting off to Claire to help on the farm, dabbling at one short story, writing those long letters home, roaming the Strand, reading, and receiving money wired from Città, courtesy of the Cellini bank. There was little that he had accomplished in terms of trying to understand if he could make a life here. He did not discuss this with Beth. But she knew. Italy, the predictability of his small town, the soccer game on a Saturday afternoon, windsurfing on the lake, a job held for him for centuries seemed very far away but completely possible.

Somewhere, somehow, for no understandable reason, he wished that Beth were the sort of girl who would dye her hair pink and cause trouble, that he were that sort of man, that together they could throw everything to the wind. Right now, cruising the heart of Wall Street, dark and late and no one about, he wanted to leave—wanted to pick up Beth and drive across America, drive to Las Vegas and get married, drive into a story, a novel, something bigger than both of them.

He drove to her apartment. She was asleep. He sat and watched her as he liked to do. The sirens of Sixth Avenue hollered. Lights swirled through the window. Her roommates were out. He thought of Grammy and her parlor games with her ladies, trying at once to be European while disparaging Europe with the notion of all Italians as carefree bottom pinchers, all Swiss as on time, all French as mean, all Germans as officious. He remembered stopping at the gas station on his last drive home from Claire, a massive truck stop somewhere in New Jersey. The gas station attendants all in a row pumping gas came from a dozen different countries. They had come for the Promise. Now their children spoke unaccented English. Now their children dressed in Levi's and ate fried chicken and Hamburger Helper. Now their children disparaged the countries of their origin as dirty and poor and filled with disease. Now their children were well educated, ambitious. Now their parents' pasts were absorbed neatly into the fabric of this culture—the fabric that permitted all and everyone to celebrate the Chinese New Year, Hindu Holi, Kwanzaa, Yom Kippur, and whatever else there is. Cesare thought of Fiori. He thought of socks and shoes and feet and of how flat the prospect of that work made him feel; he thought of Beth's pizzas and the delight on her face at their success. He wanted to feel in himself Beth's passion and ambition—the ambition she had once made him feel.

"Cesare?" she said, opening her eyes in the dark. "Are you wearing a tuxedo?"

"Do I look like a movie star?"

"My movie star." Red lights from the street striped her face. Her hair was messy, her teeth unbrushed. Then suddenly sitting up: "What's wrong?"

"I want you to get dressed," he said. "The car's waiting downstairs."

"Where are we going?"

"Las Vegas."

"To do what?"

"To get married." He had a good friend from Città who fell in love with a duke from Milan. When she was twenty-four, the duke flew her to America, to Las Vegas, and married her in a little chapel there. It was a surprise. Beth had always found the story very romantic, and Cesare knew that.

"What's wrong?" she asked again. She had the sense that something big was coming. She was afraid. She was wide awake now. She had the urge to yell at him, to tell him he had been lazy, that he had not tried, that he had never given it a chance. She knew him absolutely, knew where he was headed.

And then he said very simply, "I don't know who I am."

Much later, the year 1997. Beth is eight months pregnant with Valeria. She's sitting in a row of three seats at a discount store. The store is not far from Claire in Pennsylvania. Beth and Preveena are Christmas shopping. Preveena has asked a saleswoman to check the price of an untagged item she wants to buy: an Italian knitted newborn outfit for Valeria. "It's only worth it if it's cheap," Beth has advised, and Preveena disappears to find the saleswoman. Beth now is sitting by herself near the cashiers. Sun streams through the glass, warming her neck. She's wearing a floor-length sheepskin coat and black pants with large white flowers all over them, boots, and a black sweater that neatly covers her belly. She is tired from the weight of the baby and its incessant kicking.

"Are you Italian?" A tall older man appears before her, looking down at her. He has a closely shaved face spotted with nicks and tracks of dried blood. He sits down. His breath is bad.

"No," she says. But she is flattered.

"You look Italian." She wants to ask what it is about her that appears Italian. She thinks, All those years made me into something that I am.

"Parlo Italiano pero'."

"Di dov'e' Lei?"

"Ho passato qualche anno a Città la Venice quand'ero giovane."

"When you were young?" He laughs. "You're young now." She smiles, flattered again. "I grew up in Trieste in northeast Italy but I left after the war. Nearly fifty years ago. There was no work there."

"More time here than there," she says. She turns her head slightly away from his because she doesn't like looking at his shaving scabs and smelling his breath.

"Città is near Milano," he says. "I'll tell you a dirty joke in Milanese, but I won't translate it for you." He begins his joke. It comes out fast in an unfamiliar dialect. The only words she recognizes are "woman" and "snow." When he finishes he looks at her and laughs. "I won't translate it. You're too pretty to hear it." Again she's flattered. "I got a job two days after arriving in America," he says. "Working for the government. I speak four languages: German, French, Italian, and English. In Columbus, Ohio." She wonders what he's doing in a depressed shopping mall in Snyder County, Pennsylvania.

"Do you ever go back to Italy?" she asks.

"Every two years," he says. "I want to go back there permanently. I miss Italy."

"That's one country that is easy to miss," Beth says. A short while ago she ate a clementine and her hands smell of the fruit and the smell alone brings back all of Italy, of eating them endlessly at Christmastime, the silver bowls of them, of skiing in the Alps, in the Dolomites, of bars made from snowdrifts with bottles of alcohol chilling in them, of skiing for a week and never on the same trail, of the huts high in the mountains serving goulash and polenta, of waltzing in ski boots in the early evening, chilled and stiff from the slopes, warming up with hot toddies.

"My wife's American and her sister is handicapped so unless she dies soon we'll never be able to go back. She needs us. She can't move a limb. Completely paralyzed. She can't do anything without us."

Beth wants to ask what happened to her, but doesn't. "I'm sorry," she says instead, and looks around for Preveena. At the register a long line has formed.

"During the war I was in a concentration camp," the man says, and turns to Beth so that she can't avoid looking away from him, so that his eyes latch on to hers. She feels the baby move, kicking her little feet into her belly, pressing her head against her bladder. Beth shifts in her seat. The sun continues to prick against her neck.

"In northern Italy I was in the camp. My father didn't agree with Fascism, wouldn't support Mussolini. My father was killed. He would never tell us who we were. I still have a sister over there. My brother was killed by the Germans. My town has recently erected a statue honoring my brother, and I want to go back and see it."

His breath is horrendous. He still has her eye. The baby continues to kick. Beth's not sure what she is listening to.

"I don't know who I am," he says, not in an existential way. Rather he says it directly, as a matter of fact. She thinks of Cesare in her small New York City apartment years ago, there in his tuxedo, wanting to cry, wanting her to somehow be the answer, thinks of herself in Italy.

"I want to go back and ask questions. I want to know who I am. My father and brother were killed by Nazis. I was in a concentration camp. My father hated Fascism. He didn't want us to know who we are. I don't know who I am. America has allowed me to hide."

The line at the register is now very long. Beth hopes the

little knitted suit for Valeria will be too expensive because she doesn't want to wait for that line.

"I think we're Jewish, but our father didn't want us to know that."

Women pluck at the racks and racks and racks of discounted clothes. What is this story? She thinks of Cesare again. "I don't know who I am." She wonders if Cesare knows who he is today. Is this what he would have said fifty years later, after a lifetime in America? Preveena appears, beautiful as ever in her sari.

"They even sell olive oil here," Preveena says, flashing Beth a bottle.

"It'll be no good," the man offers.

"Surely," Beth agrees.

"But it says first cold-press," Preveena says.

"It says," the man mocks, but not in an unkind manner.

Scented soaps stack a table near the door. "I'll be right back," Preveena says. Preveena will be the closest thing that Valeria will have to a grandmother. Again, she disappears into the mess of the store. So much ugliness, Beth notes. After Beth dies, Jackson won't even be able to leave Claire to come to the memorials in New York City. Preveena will. Years later, thinking of Preveena, Cesare will understand that she set herself free. Ironically, Claire allowed Preveena to do so.

"Beautiful woman," the man says.

"She is," Beth acknowledges.

"We got our revenge. We got it, indeed we did. I could be Jewish but our father needed to protect us from that. If we didn't know it, we wouldn't have to pretend. We got our revenge up there in northern Italy in a part of Italy that's now Croatia. Those Germans came." He says the name of a place, but the name is unfamiliar to Beth.

Why is the man telling her his story? Cesare's father never let him forget who he was; the whole family kept itself alive with its history.

"They came and we mowed them down with our guns. We shot every single one of those Nazis. We didn't take any prisoners. Not a one. We killed them all. Killed them with the guns and when they were dead…"

Preveena appears with the little knit jumper, a fine knit for summer with a linen collar. On the collar are little figures— bears and boats. She's smiling triumphantly.

"Only five ninety-nine," she says softly, and gives a can-you-believe-it expression. The man is still talking; the shoppers are still shopping. Preveena gets into the long line. Beth shifts uncomfortably in her seat. The sun burns her neck.

"We got our revenge. They all died. We weren't going to take prisoners."

She thinks of Cesare. He did not have to leave his country for a job. His father, for a short time, had been a Fascist. Was it to escape, a means of survival, a way to preserve all that history? Indeed, had Cesare left Italy he would have had no job. Where would she be if she had moved to Italy?

"We didn't even bury those men. We wouldn't have let their bodies come near our graveyards where our good people lay. Not even a chance. You know what we did with them? You want to know? We threw their bodies like trash into the woods. Into the woods above the hills of grass where we shot them. Dumped them like trash. Not alongside our bodies would they lay. Not a chance. I'll go back and ask questions and I'll understand who I am. *Sei bella, veramente.*" You're beautiful, you are. He traces her cheek with his thumb, a fatherly gesture of tenderness, the way Bea's father used to do.

———

"I don't know who I am," Cesare said that night, looking dashing in his tuxedo, his dark hair receding at the temples. He undressed her, lifted her nightgown over her head. She undid the buttons of his shirt, slipped off his vest, unfastened his cuff links. She took his limp penis and sucked it until it filled her mouth. He imagined this was how she did it with all those boys. He touched her the way he imagined all those boys had touched her. He rolled her over almost violently, made her cry a little by withholding his fingers. Her front side pressed into the mattress, her arms splayed out above her head. He lay on her back, came in from behind, the way he imagined the boys had done. He wanted to hate her. She loved what he was doing to her. More, she pleaded. The summer night was not too hot but warm and sticky anyway. She wanted him. She was eager. She would do anything for him. It was this behavior he imagined she had learned from some of the college boys, daring, free American boys who didn't need to know who they were yet, who had time to figure it out, had choice to help them. Cesare told her what he saw her doing with other boys. He wanted to know the details. He asked her to tell him. He wanted to hear about her with others. They made him want her more; he needed reason to want her more.

September 2001: Cesare sits in the velvet chair beneath Cellini's fresco. The light in the bulb suspended above the painting goes out slowly, the light rising from floor to ceiling until it vanishes completely, causing the illusion of the cloud seeming to suck the figure of the artist into it, seeming to swallow him whole.

Isabella sleeps. Leonardo sleeps. In the morning Isabella will oversee the construction of a pool at Fiori. Delays have guaranteed that the pool will be ready in time for winter. The room is utterly black now. At the edges of the curtains the night is a shade lighter, adding not light but definition to the area. Cesare imagines his wife and son. Leonardo snuggles into the warmth of his mother's back. His small arms wrap around her thin waist. They're breathing each other in. Her dreams are filled with concerns about the pool. Even the idea of a pool had been forbidden when Cesare's father lived. Isabella is walking the line of preservation and perseverance. She knows the importance of continuity, but she adores her husband, his whims and ideas. She has the role and responsibility now to carry forward the Cellini line. Cesare sees Beth. She is poised at the top of a ski slope in a maroon down jacket, one size too big, about to begin her first race. She has only recently begun to ski. She is eighteen years old. Her hair is in braids peeking out from beneath an old wool hat that is orange and clashes with her jacket. He thinks he will buy her a hat for Christmas.

In Cesare's chest is a ball. The ball has dimensions. It is large, basketball-size, possibly awkward—football-size. Heavy. Impossibly heavy, made of lead. It sits there, anchoring him to the velvet chair. He thinks of Isabella in the morning, fresh from a peaceful sleep, peeling her fruit. He thinks of Leonardo eager for the day, all expectation and boisterous energy. His little guy doesn't yet know the meaning of fear, of anything beyond desire. His little guy looks like Cesare with his thick dark hair and his bright, hopeful eyes. His little guy, he knows, will be a solvent for the lead in his chest, following Cesare around as he does, all ambition to learn. His little guy—Cesare had not known the possibilities of love, the contortions and odd shapes it could take and make.

He thinks of Beth on the ski slope in Cortina in the L. L. Bean jacket. She is embarrassed by it, he imagines, perhaps because he is embarrassed himself by it. Her father gave it to her when she was ten, a few sizes too large so she would be able to grow into it, have it for a while. She has had it for eight years and has not fully grown into it. They are staying with Francesca and her fiancé in their slope-side villa. Ski in; ski out. No need to carry skis. Francesca has an Ellesse ski suit and the latest up-to-date skis, K2s. For after ski, *dopo sci* as it is called, Francesca has a floor-length sheepskin and big white furry boots to keep her feet warm. She looks as cute as a button, more fur about her face, mink shaped into a hat. Beth will admire her on the eve-ning streets of Cortina, alive with Austrians waltzing in their ski boots and drinking hot lemons, a light snow just beginning to fall. Standing there in the same maroon jacket she had used for skiing, Beth will observe Francesca with those keen eyes, com-pare herself to Francesca, then she'll pull the zipper of her coat up a little higher and stand a little taller. Watching Beth, Cesare will also want to buy her a floor-length sheepskin. He'll want everything for her—new skis, new clothes, new coats, new jew-elry. He'll want to transform her, make her feel apart, make her Italian, make her like Francesca—not because he wants her to be Francesca, but because he wants her to deserve the same.

But now Beth is on the slope at the race's starting gate. This is her first race. It's a foggy day. He can see her from where he stands alongside the gate and he can see the top portion of the course and a few of the posts she'll slalom around. She's using his father's old skis. The race begins. She starts off well. She's fast and determined, well positioned, tucked and low to the ground. She picks up speed easily. He wants to get her new gloves as well; she's wearing a pair of his sister's gloves. What does it mean to Beth to be staying with his old girlfriend in her mountainside villa, watching her in all her privilege?

In the morning Isabella will talk about the details of the pool. Just a few days ago Beth had a thriving career in restaurants and food and cookbooks. He's searched her on the Internet, read reviews, learned about financial gains and fiascos. He's seen recipes from her books, one in particular, *pasta carbonara*—his recipe from Greece long ago, made with bacon because *pancetta* could not be found—makes him smile. In all this he understands how permanently Italy and he himself are in her. He can no longer see Valeria or the party hanging above him, just a darkness that has two shades to it. In the morning he will take Leonardo to school, go with Isabella to Fiori, and then to work, where he will attend to the business of making more money off of feet. In the morning Beth's Valeria will rise to another day without her mother. So long ago he wanted to steal Beth, protect her from her dreams, make her his own. A thief, he had wanted to rob her of ambition and desire. What if he had? What if? Those two little words.

He saw then as she went down the slope, vanishing into the fog that swallowed her, zipping around those posts (she came in second, by the way), he saw again as she walked to the restaurant that evening beside Francesca, who was wrapped in all her fur and wealth, that what he had admired in Beth was her abandon, a willingness, an eagerness, a need, a desire to abandon everything and all for what she wanted, for what she set her mind on. (For a while she had set her mind on him.) It was somehow written on her simply in the coat: the coat was given to her by her father; she loved her father; it kept her warm; she didn't need to look like Francesca—she needed to look like herself. It was this abandon of pretension, of self, that he cherished, and he knew, as he saw her disappear down the hill, that he would be forever envious of, always wrestling with (indeed, hiding from), the desire to surrender to that abandon.

She drops him off outside the TWA terminal at JFK. She kisses him. She holds on to him tightly as if she can pull him into her forever, but he has pulled away like old paint peeling from a wall, somehow stuck but not stuck. He is rising into those clouds, pulled by the ugly claw and whatever you want it to stand for. He tries, unconvincingly, to reassure her. The night in her apartment he cried. Once he stopped crying it was as if he had made a vow to himself that he would never cry again for her or for childish romantic notions.

A reserve spreads across his face now. He seems eager to be gone. His demeanor shapes into something formal and foreign. "Good-bye," he says. "Good-bye?" she asks. The way he says the word is like *addio,* a final farewell—to God we go. She hangs on to him. He tells her it's going to be fine. Then he is gone, his back to her as he disappears into the odd wave-shaped terminal. And she knows that having had their dream, they will not meet again. It is their fate, just as the train dividing in the Spanish night was their fate. Every one of us has our bitter stories.

But he would come back. He would come back for Christmas bearing a green silk hat made by his milliner lover. All spring he would write Beth letters asking her to come to Italy.

But she would meet James. He would tuck his poems between the handlebars and the bell of her bike. His smile would cause a thousand butterflies to flutter about in her chest. Instead of flying east to Italy, she would drive west across America, understanding not at all why, pulled by some invisible force away from what she thought she wanted most. And why? Why? Because he did not love her anymore? Because of ambition? Because she was a dreamer? Because of Claire? Because she was Claire's daughter? Claire smiles, seducing the camera, Jackson, and the viewer with the possibility of what lies beyond—for what lies beyond is infinite and she is not capable of believing otherwise.

But always, for the rest of her life, Beth would ask the question: Does he love me still?

Six

Possibility

She was a part of him, like an organ. A part that hurt, ached in the center of his chest, in his head, his arms, his feet, the smallest bones of his toes. Yes, the pain dulled with time, but the ache, some memory of it, would remain, a scar from a long-ago surgery that throbs in the cold. Surgically, you could say, he removed her from him. Excised her with the knife of hate, the obvious antidote to love. Excised her with betrayal, humiliation, lies, until he couldn't stand her for her weakness, for her unstoppable love, that American will believing it could conquer all, the hubris. See her there crying? See her there desiring him still? See her there with her heart torn open by hope? The depths of hope, its deep recesses, its bottomless wells. Five years, that's how long it took. Even so, he loved her still.

In the late summer of 1986, after nearly one year in America, Cesare returned home. He kissed his mother. He kissed his father. He kissed his sister. He kissed the maids. He unpacked his bags. And then he started telling stories, stories that made them all laugh—stories about the commune, Jackson in his dark office surrounded by clippings; stories about selling berries, about being a merchant for a moment, negotiating stiff prices; stories about the grandmother and her Indian and the tuxedo (Cesare modeled it for his family), about the grandmother promptly falling asleep at the opera after the rising of the curtain and the first aria of long *Lohengrin*. Before the opera the grandmother realized that Cesare didn't have the proper shoes. Rather than let him wear any old shoes, she had their taxi stop at a pharmacy where she bought black velvet slippers. *"E vero?"* the sister asked wide-eyed with her smile, her curly blond bob pulled back by a gold ribbon, flapper style. It seemed Laura was as amazed by the notion of a pharmacy selling slippers as by wearing slippers to an opera. Cesare escorted the grandmother into the grand hall with the enormous Chagalls and all the people in their elegant dress. She played the part of old patron, noticed Gregory Peck and pointed him out (indiscreetly) to let Cesare know that they were among the best. Cesare showed his parents and his sister the flimsy velvet slippers, passed them around to be admired. *"Che ridere, che buffa, come ridicolo."* And the sister laughed, of course, the mother laughed, the father laughed big and brilliantly, a laugh larger than his small size. Cesare told them stories of eating Indian food with his fingers, of all the greasy excuses for fast foods. He told them stories of the furniture hauled off the street, of the kids opening fire hydrants in order to cool off in the summer heat, of the mixture of people, of the all-night stores, of the limousines and the dogs (yes, the dogs) that are chauffeured around in them (Mrs. Gimbel's poodle had his own car and driver). And they laughed more and couldn't stop. His father's laugh was magnificent to witness, breaking his face into warmth and tenderness, the laughter sparkling from it like a crystal in sunlight. His laugh made the mother laugh all the more. For a good long stretch they laughed, the laugh of relief because Cesare was home and because he was laughing (even if fondly) at America and because they knew the dream was finally over.

After settling in, windsurfing with his friends on the lake, a quick trip to Elba with his parents, cruising Città on his American bike (he bought it in New York, put a bell on the handlebar, and rode it all over the city), after an attempt or two to encourage his friends to embrace football, he got down to the work of completing his exams. He moved to Milan, lived with his sister, attended classes at the university every day, studied for and took his last exams, passed them with the highest grades he had ever received. He began work in earnest on his thesis, wrote it in three months, the words spilling from him as easily as water running from a faucet. In November, he started officially at the Cellini bank in Città. The hat lady, Greta, was his first client. She was Florentine with red hair and a big infectious smile. She came to him with a dozen hats, silk and velvet and leather with feathers and without, with and without fur, with felt cutouts and crystal beads in a rainbow of colors. She tried the hats on for him and then she tried them on him, adjusting them in front of the mirror. Her long fingers drifted gently across his cheeks and neck, and her big smile held his in the mirror for an instant. He looked charming, inviting in a fuchsia bonnet with a big fuchsia bow tied beneath his chin. Admiring her reflection, he kept thinking, She's Italian—as if that fact alone were amazing and precious and utterly inconceivable. Soon thereafter they began sleeping together and soon after that he bought Beth a hat—the green silk pillbox that reminded him of the one Valeria wore in Benvenuto's fresco. The purchase was his first cruelty. At Christmas he flew to New York to give it to her himself.

She met him at the airport, standing there with her hopeful smile, in a pair of white drawstring pants for summer, a sheepskin coat he had given her, and bright red pumps. She had been anxious about what to wear, had borrowed from the roommates, had tried to get it right. Her lipstick matched the shoes. She looked ridiculous. Any fashion sense she had gained in Italy she had lost as if her anxiety over the fate of their relationship had undermined her confidence and weakened her judgment. He could only think of Greta and her fingers and of the hats she liked him to try on and the undeniably beautiful fact that she was Italian with big Italian eyes and a big Italian smile and the fine Italian sense of design. He stayed one week. Everything he had found romantic before he found distasteful now: the furniture, the cockroaches living in the stove, the traffic noise, the incessant sirens and their red forbidding lights. He even noticed this time, had not before, the stalls in public bathrooms—how people's ankles and feet could be seen as they publicly performed a very private act. He had no interest in going to Claire. The people there somehow seemed ridiculous to him now, Jackson who would never leave, Sissy Three in competition with a dead woman, Preveena unwilling to let the saris go, and poor little Rada.

"Your family," he said to Beth after she asked him if he'd like to go to Claire. Just the way he said the words indicated how he felt. And the slight shift of his head, that particularly Italian gesture, dismissed her entire family as odd. She felt both deeply offended and deeply injured; as though he had finally seen the thing she had feared most her entire life. She had known that feeling as a little girl playing in the normalcy of Sylvia's house, enacting dramas of normal lives with Sylvia's Barbies and all their convertibles and their campers and their dressing tables and clothes and Kens. Sylvia's family was nothing like hers: Dinner on the table at 5:30 sharp. Mother alive, mother at home, mother who packed lunches each morning for her two girls, who sent her good husband off to work with a kiss. Beth had never allowed herself to think of her family as odd; her family was simply her family, but she had always been drawn to families like Sylvia's and Bea's and Cesare's. Now Cesare sat in a chair from the street, ripped floral pattern, the window behind him open even though it was cold and winter, because the steam heat was just too hot. The sheet-curtain danced in the cold-hot air. "Your family is completely crazy."

When Beth opened the small oval hatbox decorated with drawings of important Florentine buildings and saw the delicate green hat nestled in white tissue, she knew everything—that on her head she was to wear the designs of her love's lover. She saw how Cesare watched her as she held the hat, meticulously looking for signs, trying to read in her expressions what she gathered, inferred, understood. She saw how he watched her with both pain and glee and how though he would not have been able to admit it so directly he wanted to cause her grief and sorrow. He wanted the hat to say everything that he could not. He wanted the hat to say, How could you think that I would leave Italy, my family, my life? Wind up here like any other immigrant to hear the news of my father's death over the phone in the middle of the night as my children, lying in their American beds, dreamed American dreams? How could I ask that of you? Trap you in a world that would ridicule your interest in pizza, in restaurants?

She knew what he wanted the hat to say. She would not let him do this to her, to them. So her face remained cool, expressionless, steady with that confidence he loved, the confidence of the maroon coat. She turned the hat around in her hands, noticed the label stitched into the interior bowl of the hat: Greta Ceseretti. She pictured the woman. She went to the mirror, placed the hat on her head, tilted her face to the left, admired

herself in the mirror. His eyes were still trained on her. The ra-
diator hissed. The apartment was cold. The mirror, too, she had
found on the street, had spent hours restoring the elaborate
wood frame, filling in wounds with wood putty, painting it
gold. She turned to him, more beautiful, in the hat, it seemed,
than he had ever seen her. Her hair hung long and full, flowing from beneath the hat, which crowned her pale winter face.
"It's lovely," she said.

For the next five months he wrote to her, he called her,
pleading with her to come to Italy.

Spring passed, then summer. James waltzed into her life with his
sweet poems and his spontaneous plans for a trip west, with all
the confidence of a handsome boy fond of a precious girl. He
took her words, her declarations of love (in the field of sunflowers) as truth. He had no experience to teach him not to
trust, to consider deceit. In his head he made elaborate plans for
her to come with him to Los Angeles. He could see her there as
well as anywhere pursuing a life of food.

All across America, in every campground they visited, on
every overnight hike they took, they made gourmet meals by
the campfire. He had a special bag with tiny canisters devoted
to herbs and spices. "I love you," she said again, after one such
meal. The meal, cooked at twelve thousand feet in two pots
above a campfire, the peaks of the Rockies purple in the fading
amber light, was called *Khoresh-e-Fesenjan,* or chicken stew with
pomegranate sauce served with barberry basmati rice. Beth had
learned the recipes from a woman at Claire, Nasim, who left Iran
in 1978 during the revolution because she had protested a bit
too much as a student. She was a sweet yet severe woman with
short curly dark hair and a large black mole to the right of her
lips. Beth did not know her well since Nasim had only recently

found her way to Claire, but Beth had been drawn immediately to her ability with rose water and rose petals and pomegranate seeds. Her fingers worked those ingredients like magic. James had bought the barberries and the rice from an Iranian market in New York City before leaving. Then beneath the stars, so thick it did seem feasible there were more stars than grains of sand, Beth declared her love again, admiring everything free about this man and his singular ability to cherish her passions. She was in love with his love of her. They lay together in the conjoined sleeping bags, limbs entwined. It was very dark and very bright, somehow simultaneously, and the sky shimmering with the morning stars and the morning planets. They lay together in this way, her eyes wide while he slept, waiting for the old moon to drop beneath the horizon, for the morning to rise, silver, like water draping the earth.

After the explosion at Old Faithful, however, James turned the Lincoln east and they headed home. It took them one day to break up; that was all. She cried. He cried. She hated seeing him cry. He said, "It's hard on the ego to accept you don't love me." He said it with his charming eyes smiling and a confidence that made Beth almost fall in love. "I'm sorry," she said, not bothering anymore to deny anything. In fact, what she wanted was to finally tell him everything: How it ached, how it hurt. How she didn't understand why she wasn't able to let go. How she believed unstoppably that she and Cesare were meant to be together, as if it had been predetermined, written by fate, by the hand of Brahma on their newborn foreheads. (She had learned from Preveena about this Hindu myth.) How she did not understand, not a thing, how people casually let people into their lives and then just as casually let them go. James was a kind man. He would listen. He would offer advice. "You know it has nothing to do with you?" Beth finally said. They were seated in the car somewhere in Wisconsin, near cornfields. Signs for cheese were everywhere. She never wanted to return to New York. She wanted to be on the road forever. *"Sh-sh,"* he whispered, and leaned across to seal her lips with his index finger, indicating *I know.* He knew. She knew.

Somewhere in Indiana, in a cheap Motel 6 with faded curtains and a lumpy mattress made more lumpy by the Magic Fingers mechanism that rocked the bed with a quarter, she developed such a bad stomachache she put herself into shock. James had to take her to the emergency room of a local hospital. Doctors swarmed around her (it was not a busy night), sticking needles and tubes into every orifice of her body. "It could be an ectopic pregnancy," a doctor in blue scrubs suggested, looking at James with an expression that indicated a desire for confirmation, as if James could rubber stamp the doctor's diagnosis. Beth's face shaded with panic, all its variations contorting her round cheeks and eyes, her large forehead. "But will I lose the baby," she asked. "Will I?" she kept asking. "Will I lose the baby?" She looked at James with terror in her eyes. She was all concern for the baby, wanted the baby as if it would answer some inexorable question. But it wasn't a pregnancy of any sort. It was simply fear, gripping her in the gut and twisting itself around her insides like a vine around a tree, choking the tree. She was released from the hospital. Nonstop he drove her to New York. He helped her unload her suitcase and backpack at her apartment on Sixth Avenue and then he drove her uptown to her grandmother's garage in front of which he kissed her hard on the cheek in a brotherly way. She watched him walk down the street with a hollow feeling because she knew he was a loving kind good smart man. She watched him leave, afraid all over again at the hardness she was capable of and of how suddenly and unequivocally alone she was with the buildings rising all around her and people rushing past, brushing her this way and that as if she were nothing more than one of those stray bags caught in the bare branches of a tree.

She had to give up the apartment on Sixth Avenue, but through Sissy Three she found a studio on York and Seventy-fourth: a walk-up four floors above a dry cleaner, the fumes of which wafted through her window day and night. She breathed in the sweet chemicals wondering, not caring, what harm it would cause at some later point. On the roof of the apartment across the courtyard, workers would whistle, seeing her through the curtainless windows. The apartment belonged to a friend of a friend of Sissy Three's from her hand-modeling days. The tenant didn't want to give it up because the rent was only three hundred dollars a month. The tenant left Beth a series of twelve signed checks in the exact amount of the rent. It was Beth's responsibility to deposit the rent each month in an account this person, Georgia Lazar, had established solely for the purpose. Then Beth would need to wait ten days for the check to clear. At that point she could mail Georgia Lazar's prewritten check to the landlord. After a year they would renegotiate. Georgia Lazar, Beth knew, had married and moved to a million-dollar home in Connecticut, but she had lived in this apartment for ten years while she struggled in New York. It was as good as hers and she wasn't going to give it up. If she gave it up she would be giving up all possibility of ever returning to New York City. (Years later, when Beth thought of New York's hold on people, she pictured Georgia Lazar: a slender fierce woman, unkempt hair flying about her face, fists clenched, sharp-jawed, pushing her way through the crowds, holding fast to her piece of the promise.) Before Beth at least three other people had lived in the apartment pretending to be Georgia Lazar. "In New York,"

Sissy Three had said, "real estate is everything. Keep that in mind and you'll do fine." Even though Beth had lived in New York for years, it suddenly became a new and unfamiliar world with a network of schemes and games she wasn't sure yet how to negotiate. While in school she had been oblivious to and protected from the intricacies of surviving in the city. Though the apartment was what it was, small, dark, filled with fumes, she found herself wishing the lease were in her name. And that desire alone seemed to be her initiation into the longing that is the fuel of those schemes, the longing which either causes one to leave New York or to thrive there.

With the remains of her street furniture and a few things from her grandmother (a set of silver for dinner parties, lace tablecloths, fine cotton sheets, and an oriental lamp with a ripped shade depicting a bird in flight), Beth brightened the place up. Even so, it remained dark. Her grandmother would call now and again. Usually she inquired after "the Italian." "Don't let him get away," she would warn. On the stereo Beth listened to Claudio Baglioni and Lucio Dalla and Lucio Battisti and wondered what Cesare was doing and wondered what in the world she wanted, what she would make of herself? She was truly alone, for the first time in her life. Her best friends from college had moved away, as had her roommates Veronica and Jane; they'd scattered across America, to Boston and Chicago and Los Angeles and Detroit, even. Bea was in Italy and it had been a long time since Beth had heard from her. She had married and vanished into a new life. Sylvia stayed in touch with letters and postcards from trips she would take with various boyfriends. She lived in San Francisco, attending Stanford's graduate program in creative writing. Occasionally Beth received short stories in the mail, describing their adventures in Greece. In her dark apartment, Beth felt very alone. Often she wanted to call James, fly to L.A., and make a life with him there, cooking Persian food and listening to his lectures on the geology of America. Friends she didn't know as well had gone to Wall Street, worked in banks, making far more in their first year than she would for a long, long time to come. She would run into them at awkward moments. Sometimes she'd find them at a table in the Amalfi Pizzeria where she still had a job. They would be finely dressed in suits, gold around their necks, pearls in their ears, the occasional diamond engagement ring glowing like the very sun. "I thought you'd made it," one might say (as in, *I thought you'd made something of your life*), while Beth stood with her pad and her pen poised to take their order. Beth would say, "The pizza here is very good," taking no credit, paying no heed. "So we've heard," they'd respond. "That's why we're here. I read that it's the best in New York, outside of Italy. We were in Rome this summer and…"

She'd bring flowers home—tulips flown in from Amsterdam on a 747, the airplane filled solely with flowers, an image she enjoyed—put them in a vase, turn on her Italian music, and make lists of what she had: her job at the pizzeria; the money from it; the success of the pizzas. Indeed, Italian tourists had started frequenting the place. It was written up in an Italian guidebook as the one place in Manhattan for authentic Italian thin-crusted wood-oven pizzas, *Come in Italia*. And then she would make a list of what she wanted: to be a cook, a chef; to write a cookbook; to own a restaurant. That's what she really wanted; that was why she was here.

Sometimes he would call, the international beeps rippling over the lines declaring him: *"Sei ancora perfetta?"* he'd ask simply, bringing back all of Greece. *"Sono ancora perfetta,"* she would respond. And that would be that, the call receding with the days until he would call again. The Italian music always made her sad, made her remember the Città life, the one she believed now she could so easily have lived.

She took a job for a famous chef, chopping vegetables in his kitchen, julienning lemon peel, mincing rosemary, dicing pancetta, chopping endlessly. Blisters developed on her hands. Her hands smelled perpetually of garlic. Her hair smelled of the kitchen. The kitchen buzzed with the activity of a dozen prep cooks, the pastry chef and his sous-chefs, the chef and his sous-chefs. The staff was large so that each task could be done efficiently and perfectly. Sometimes, if Beth was lucky, she was allowed to plate the food. But you had to be fast for that task, and no mistakes. No sauces on the rims. The food had to look like a million dollars before it was sent out, had to look so perfect the diner wouldn't want to cut into it. Flaws were not tolerated. There was a lot of heat, a lot of yelling, though oddly the chef never spoke. The restaurant was called Lago ("Lake") and it got three stars in the *Times* for its exquisite northern Italian cuisine. The big deal was that it deserved four stars but only got three because, along with Julia Child, the critic did not believe that Italian cuisine demanded the use of enough technique. Four stars were reserved exclusively for French restaurants. The famous chef of Lago, American, was famous as well for never speaking. He never did interviews, and those close to him were not allowed to speak on his behalf and had to sign an agreement not to before working for him. This was the late 1980s, the very beginning of the era in which chefs became superstars, garnering publicity and ardent followers, and raking in cash for celebrity endorsements of Viking Range appliances, say, or Calphalon pans. Indeed, Lago's chef was among the first of this species—though he never did endorsements. He was a purist. The press knew him and referred to him simply as Leo.

Lago was the hottest restaurant in town even if it was not French. In fact, people loved that it was not French; they were tired of French and curious about authentic Italian. It took a minimum of three months to get a reservation at Lago, and Leo was firm on no insider deals for earlier dates. Beth felt lucky to have landed a job there. All the other kitchen staff at Lago were aspiring chefs. A few other young women worked alongside her, eager, disciplined, ready to give everything. The waiters, on the other hand, actors or artists, all gay, all male, and all northern Italian, seemed to have more authority than those in the kitchen—except, of course, for Leo—and would snap at the kitchen help if a dish had even the slightest flake of parsley in the wrong spot. They seemed to belong here, in New York, un-questionably. After the restaurant closed for the evening they loosened their ties, put up their feet, joked with Leo for not talking, poured themselves a drink, lit cigarettes—did things that the kitchen help would never have felt comfortable doing. Then they would disappear into the night and the city as if it had always been theirs. Unlike Cesare, they were able to leave Italy because they had nothing there and it was easier to be gay in New York than in Milan.

"All that education to work in a restaurant?" the grand-mother asked. And then, "What has happened to my prince?"

"Your prince?"

"Well, your prince?"

The chef had a wife. Her name was Cosella and she was at-tractive in a fierce way, very tall, with short hair dyed blond, platinum really. Her natural color was jet black, and she liked for the roots to show. The abrupt contrast, along with her long nose, were her defining characteristics. Bones protruded from her willowy body, making her angular, adding to her ferocity. She came from Lago di Garda in northern Italy, and it was ru-mored that she was the real talent behind the duo, that late at night she was the one in the kitchen. (Beth would later come to understand that mystique and myth had everything to do with fame.) During the day, however, Cosella was the sole face of human resources, did the hiring and the firing and was known not as Cosella but as the Bitch (as in, "the Bitch this…"; "the Bitch that…"). She made every single person who worked for them cry on one occasion or another, often multiple times. The crying was done in the walk-in refrigerator—a cool chrome world of vegetables and meats and berries and desserts—and was usually the result of having been made to feel stupid and inadequate or just plain incompetent. For example, "You don't know who Escoffier is? Who Jacques Pépin is? My six-year-old son knows who Escoffier is." It's an Italian restaurant, Beth wanted to counter, but never dared. "It's all food, all for the preparation of great fine food. And these are the masters," Cosella would have answered in her thick Italian accent. She always had an answer for everything. "I must be in charge of everything," was her refrain. "No one pays as much attention to detail as I do." She would look at you, peering down her long nose from behind her vast desk. If you sank a soufflé, if your chocolate separated, if you accepted the delivery of imperfect vegetables, you would hear about the talents of her six-year-old son again and any of the talents you were hired for disintegrated in her mind as well as in your own.

When she hired Beth at $14,000 a year, Cosella was stunned to learn, after Beth said she didn't know how she would survive on that salary, that Beth had no trust fund. Cosella, looking at Beth with genuine puzzlement, said "Can't you dip into your trust fund?" It had never occurred to her, it seemed, to wonder how her employees survived on the small salaries— Beth would learn that they were lucky to even have salaries, since most restaurants paid hourly. If they couldn't afford to live on the offered salary, she assumed they had trust funds. She wouldn't have imagined the dark holes they lived in, piled up on top of each other to make the cheap rent even cheaper. She had always had money, always lived among people with money, and had no idea what it meant to do without. "But you look like you come from a good family," Cosella said, as if in apology. Money defining good.

"I don't have a trust fund," Beth said. Cosella held Beth with her eyes for what seemed to be the longest and most awkward moment Beth had experienced thus far in life, as if Cosella were seeing in Beth something she had never seen before. Cosella, though Italian, had moved to New York when she was fourteen and spent her teenage years in a brownstone on Fifth Avenue. Central Park was her front yard. She had gone to one of the best private schools and then to Barnard. Her father was in finance, her mother into spending money on Cosella and her three sisters. Cosella wore a mink coat throughout the fall, winter, and the spring. She had villas in Garda and on Sardegna, an estate on Nantucket, too. Her diamond engagement ring was ice-cube size. It was given to her after Leo became famous (and wealthy). Before that her parents had disparaged her choice of husband, believing their daughter would not be able to adjust to a life of lesser means. In fact, Cosella and Leo became so rich they liked to say that they were "able to sell their brownstone to buy an apartment," quoting a famous writer who hit the jackpot with a novel and was thus able to buy an apartment with twice the square footage of his enormous brownstone.

"It was all because of me," Cosella would later say. "I knew how to make money make money. Left to Leo, we'd be paupers." She seemed to like the notion of having just narrowly escaped pauperdom in the way people like Sylvia's Chas fondly remember their brush with poverty on youthful trips around the world.

Finally Beth averted her eyes and the silence ended with Cosella saying simply, "I'm sorry." She was sincere, sorry for

Beth's lack of fortune and the hardship it entailed, though not so sorry that she'd consider paying her more. Other than the detail of no trust fund she knew very little about Beth—knew nothing of Claire (the mother, or the farm), nor that she had gone to NYU, that her grandmother was a patron of the Met, that Beth was wildly in love with a man she could not have for reasons she did not completely understand. Somewhere Beth wanted Cosella to know all about her, wanted Cosella to have more sympathy for her and to fall in love with her and adore her as a mother would. Beth wanted to win her, have her see how bright and sharp she was, what a fabulous cook she was. She wanted her warmth to melt Cosella's iciness. It would feel like a victory, she imagined. Indeed, Beth wanted all older women to love her like a daughter—Bea's mother, Cesare's mother, Preveena, Sissy Three, even.

There were times though when Cosella would surprise Beth, make it clear to Beth she had compassion, that she was capable of love, that she was not the Bitch. (She knew how she was referred to.) She would show Beth that she understood that she was struggling, that she knew Beth was giving a lot to the restaurant, and that she was appreciated. Cosella would call Beth to her office and give her a check for a staggering sum, over a hundred dollars, and send Beth to her salon to indulge in a haircut. The salon was like nothing Beth had ever seen— spare, burbling water fountains, prancing borzois, Farrah Fawcett and other superstar patrons smiling from the slickly framed covers of *Elle* and *Vogue* and *Harper's Bazaar* that adorned the walls. The stylists glided around the salon with the insouciance of the rich and of those who cater to them, their hair all sorts of colors and styles and their clothes hip and of black leather involving chains and exceedingly skinny legs. For all of her grandmother's pretension and Paul Stuart tuxedos, Beth had never been in a place like this. The tip was more than Beth spent on food in a week (she ate at the restaurant and had ramen noodles at home, three packages for a buck). Beth had to write the stylist a check in order to offer a tip and then hope that the stylist wouldn't cash it before Beth's paycheck hit her account. To compensate for the unexpected expense she paid her electric bill late. She was too proud to ask her grandmother for help.

After one punishing episode in Cosella's office (scolded for dropping a lobster in a pot of boiling water without first killing it with a sharp jab to its head: "Scalded in boiling water? Can you imagine? The most painful way to die. Do you know how long it takes for the water to come back to a boil, thus to kill the creature? Do you? Do you? You had no business handling the lobsters. They aren't your territory. You stick to celery, carrots, scallions, shallots. Stay away from the lobsters."), Beth broke down and cried right there in front of her. "I can't keep this up," she said. "I'm exhausted." In the beginning, Beth kept her job at the pizzeria, waiting tables three nights a week after sixty or so hours chopping vegetables and beating egg whites at Lago. Running between jobs, literally, had taken its toll. In the bathroom of Lago, Beth would change into her waitressing uniform (tan pants, white shirt), put on black running shoes that doubled as her waitressing shoes, and run three blocks across town and thirty blocks downtown to Amalfi Pizzeria. She could always see the restaurant's flashing neon sign far in the distance as she ran down Seventh Avenue: the sign, a beacon of tackiness, made her think of the critic of Lago giving it three stars because it was Italian cuisine. (Each time, running down Seventh, she would remind herself to tell Bruno to upgrade his sign.) Arriving sweaty, she would wash her face in the bathroom, pinch her cheeks, brush her teeth, and wait on tables until 2 A.M. At 8 A.M. she would begin the entire routine over again. She sat in Cosella's office sobbing.

Instead of firing her, which Beth believed Cosella would do, she sent a masseuse to Beth's studio, not once, but four times. Lying beneath the hands of the masseuse, on a table the masseuse had lugged up all four flights, Beth fell in love with Cosella. At the end, when she tried to tip the masseuse, Beth was told that everything had been paid for. The following summer Cosella gave Beth her house on Nantucket for two weeks while she and Leo went to India on vacation. Despite the kindness, the gifts, Cosella remained demanding: ever vigilant for the smallest sign of incompetence, she never hid her anger at Beth's or anyone's mistakes. And Leo always remained an enigma. During the years Beth worked at Lago, he did not speak one word to her. But Beth penetrated Cosella, pried her open like an oyster, forcing Cosella, in all her privilege to see (and admire) raw sloppy ambition at its inception. Cosella's ambition had had a head start; she had always had the plush cushion of wealth.

Eight months into Beth's job at Lago, Bruno fired her from Amalfi Pizzeria for not being on the ball. (The news of Beth being fired delighted Victor, the Albanian *pizzaiolo*.) Beth was not surprised. Rather, she was relieved. She had gone as far as she could go there. It was only a pizzeria, after all. Now her ambition was to someday make the critics see that Italian cuisine was equal to or better than French. Beth found herself wishing that instead of a massage or a haircut Cosella would give her a raise. But the thought of Cosella, entrenched in her dark office behind her vast desk, looking at her subjects by raising her head and sliding her eyes down her long nose, made the asking of a raise all but impossible. And chopping carrots, there was little way for Beth to measure her contribution or make a case for the essential need of having her there. And there—Lago—was definitely one of the best restaurants to be working in if food was your dream. A list a mile long of people who wanted to work at Lago waited on Cosella's desk, a fact that everyone knew well.

Late at night, lying on her bed, Beth would wonder why she wanted this. She would wonder where she would be if somehow she had been able to go to Italy. She would look at the phone, will it to ring. Cesare had written her a letter after their Old Faithful argument, a letter telling her to take responsibility for her part, reminding her that she could have come to Italy, if only just to see: that she had owed that to their relationship. Telling her that Greta meant nothing, a nice woman, sure, but not Beth—not warm like Beth, soft like Beth. Greta was hard and fun, but not serious. He needed Beth. Telling her that this interruption in their relationship was the challenge they had needed to get beyond for their great love to thrive. She would read and reread the letter, wondering if he was being fair or if he was just trying to pass the blame. Exhausted, she would breathe in those sweet fumes, eat take-out Chinese in bed for a splurge, and watch the fat man in his underwear in the apartment across the courtyard scratch his butt and balls before settling down in an armchair to his dinner and the blue glow of the television. She would fall asleep with the lights on, the remnants of the Chinese food on the floor by her bed. She would dream of the apartment growing bigger, doors opening onto rooms she didn't know that she had, rooms that then opened onto more rooms until she had so much space she could waltz endlessly from room to room to room. In the morning the shower would scald her if someone anywhere in the building flushed a toilet. Even so, walking to work she would feel elated by the dream of all those rooms.

She did have some fun, too. Hunter moved back to New York from Claire, took a job working for a hedge fund (Beth could never understand what that meant no matter how many times it was explained to her), made tons of money, and took her out to fancy restaurants and the theater on her days off. He took her dancing and to comedy clubs and jazz clubs. At a thrift store, he bought her a dress for these occasions, a black dress with a thousand silk string tassels. When she moved, the dress shimmered with all the elegance of money. Beth thought, How easy it could be to surrender to Hunter, to succumb to his wealth. He enjoyed spending money. "Money is meant to be spent," he would say. But he liked to spend it on objects and situations that could tell a story. At an antique store, he bought her a Persian ring from the fifth century, sold by a wizened man in his upper years with a cane and a bent back who still traveled the world in search of treasure. The stone was red jasper and Hunter placed it himself on the middle finger of Beth's right hand, scaring her as she felt a pang of desire. The muted hammered gold and the sparkling stone were fifteen hundred years old. She loved wearing that history, loved imagining the other women before her admiring the ring on their hands. At ABC Carpet he bought her a Persian rug, a Kerman with a garden design. She learned that Iranians were among the first rug makers twenty-five hundred years ago and that originally the rugs' designs were a form of writing for illiterate tribesmen, a way of setting down their fortunes and their troubles and their joys, dreams and sorrows. The rugs came from places she had never heard of, grand names like Khorassan, Baluch, Quchan, Shirvan, Lilihan—places she would never visit or know but that Hunter talked about bringing her to as if in doing so he could open up the world, make it just a little bigger than Italy. She would pull out the atlas and try to find the towns on the map. About Hunter, there were things, his vast knowledge, that desire to know and to share, that reminded Beth of what her father might have once been.

At the Persian grocery (which James had found) she selected (and Hunter paid for) pomegranates and barberries and rose

water and saffron and a spice known as *advieh* and candied orange peels and cartons of rice noodle sorbet. She practiced Persian cooking, making feasts for Hunter, turning her interest in
Persian cuisine into a passion. (She had already mastered Indian
and Italian.) And sitting in her small apartment with the candles
flickering and some Mozart playing quietly (chosen by Hunter),
Hunter spoke to Beth about her father, remarking on his ambitions and how he was a grand, if mysterious man, and Hunter
praised Jackson for saving him simply by allowing him to be
nothing, a blank slate that Hunter alone had the authority to
color in. (Hunter, for a long time to come, would serve as an in-
vestor for Claire, offering financial advice.) Beth loved it when
people admired her father. But somewhere, deep inside, she
wished he could be for her what he seemed to be for all these
other people.

"What was it like to be his daughter?" Hunter asked. The
question startled Beth for an instant. It was an intimate question, in a way. She looked at Hunter. He was a good five years
older than she was, heavier than Cesare—a man who had spent
too much time drinking beer and at a desk. She could see he
had a hairy chest; hair pushed up at his collarbone through the
neck of his T-shirt. She could imagine Bea saying, in her charming accent, each word carefully enunciated, "I do not like hairy
chests." The mess of their dinner littered the table. She had always thought of Hunter as a privileged, confident man, but
looking at him now he seemed vulnerable, and that vulnerability took away from his confidence. At the same time it made her
feel she could say anything to him.

"It sucked," she said, surprising even herself because it had
not sucked. It didn't start sucking until Cesare described her
family as crazy, until she saw her father's weird experiment
through Cesare's eyes and felt branded as its primary guinea

pig. "Oh, I don't mean that. It's ambivalence, is all." She paused for a moment. "The ambivalence of age." She was thinking of Cesare, wondering if he would still love her if she had come from an ordinary family.

"All your age," Hunter joked. "Your very ancient age." He placed his hand on hers. Little pangs of desire shot through her, but she quickly swatted the feelings away. She was in love with someone else. She did not want to feel this; she was not capable of allowing herself to feel anything for another man. James had proved that to her.

"Everything is on his terms. For god's sake, he's my only parent, and he won't ever come to visit me, see me in my world. Blah, blah, blah. My mother, my father, my mother, my father... I could spend my life on a couch. No thank you. I love him. He's my father." And with that she put to rest, for now, the am-bivalence she had just allowed herself to feel.

On weekends sometimes Hunter would drive Beth to Claire for a visit. During the long drive home they would continue the conversation, compare the freedom of her childhood to the structure of his. Hunter was always curious about her. He asked her so many questions, took such an interest. She grew used to having him nearby.

"You left," Beth said, meaning Claire. "Does that mean your parents won in the end?"

"Won?" Hunter asked.

"They wanted you to leave." Beth had met his parents on a few occasions. Her impression was cursory—enthusiastic people who loved adventure as long as it remained in its place. For example, they would have loved Claire if it did not involve their son, if they had known Jackson as a friend who remained safely at Claire, someone to tell stories to their friends about, to enliven dinner-table conversations. They had tons of money and did not work hard, the mother not at all. She didn't even do charity work. As far as Beth could tell, she slept all day and in the evenings organized dinner parties to entertain herself. Indeed, the father prided himself on earning an enormous salary and working very little—he was in something to do with finance, which, like hedge funds, Beth didn't pay enough attention to to fully comprehend. Hunter's father spent his days collecting things. He collected original maps from the eighteenth century and even earlier, maps drawn by Guillaume de l'Isle, say, or Samuel de Champlain or Nicholas de Fer—names Beth had never heard, but Hunter's father spoke with such authority and enthusiasm about them you seemed fairly to be missing out on life's great pleasures if you did not own a few yourself. "Maps freeze time, history," he said. "And owning the map you get to ponder that frozen moment, daily." The maps were indeed beautiful, etchings and engravings and lithographs, watercolor and gouache, pen and ink and aquatint, satin and parchment. Hunter's father, Palmer, was a short man and handsome like his son with a boyish face and a deep-dimpled smile. He prided himself on his vast knowledge and could speak with authority on almost any subject. At Claire he went around admiring the antiques bought by Short, familiar with their origins and market values. He lifted pillows, upturned mattresses, poked his head under tables—just the way Hunter had done when he first admired Claire's antiques. Watching Palmer, Beth suddenly understood Hunter, understood that his great need to know was sparked by competition with his father—to be wiser, know more, so that his father would never doubt his intelligence.

Hunter's mother had had a little too much work done on her face and the result was not a good one. She, like the maps, looked frozen, but instead of perpetual youth, her face revealed a certain fatigue, that of a sixty-year-old woman tired by life and

by having borne five children. She appropriated her husband's interests in maps and in collecting as a goal and as a principle. "We can leave a mark if we leave behind a significant collection," she was fond of saying. (As it happened, she was also fond of talking about friends of theirs who had become terminally ill.) Hunter's parents assumed everyone collected something and wanted to know, upon meeting Jackson and Beth, what it was they collected. "People," Beth said. "We collect people."

"And food," Jackson added. "My daughter collects food." Beth looked at her father with warmth, felt a flush of love for him with his long sideburns, his bright eyes. It always surprised her that he understood her interests because the two of them so rarely discussed them. But he knew just when she was devoted to pizzas or pastas or Persian food or Indian. She loved that he watched her so carefully even if from afar. This knowledge added to the complexity of her feelings for him, making her feel that the distance between them was not as great as she often imagined—as did meeting Hunter's parents, who made her realize that there are people out there crazier than her own family. She wondered what Cesare would make of them.

"They wanted me to get back on my feet, thought I was afraid after the Boesky fiasco," Hunter said. The drive along I-80 took them through rolling farmland and then vast stretches of pine, as they rose into the Poconos and slipped down to the Delaware Water Gap. "I certainly didn't leave because I suddenly became unafraid."

"So you were afraid?"

"I fell really hard. You make a lot and then you have nothing and everyone thinks you're a scoundrel when they used to love you. It's hard on the ego."

"Why did you ever leave Claire then? Why did you ever go back to Wall Street?"

"Because I wanted to be near you," he said. She shivered, the truth so blatantly acknowledged.

"Near me?" she said. But I'm in love with Cesare, she thought, though she said nothing.

"I know," he said, reading her mind. And she looked at him, sweet blond man with all that hair pushing out of his shirt and his ferocious need to know all about everything to surpass his father who knew maps deeply and everything else quite well. Somewhere, however, she wanted to know what it was about her that he wanted to be near. "Simple: you're not afraid," he would have answered.

In New York, he dropped her off at her apartment, seeing her into the building. Surrounded by the strong scent of cat piss and garbage in the vestibule, she gave him a quick kiss and then disappeared, fast, up the stairs, frightened by what seduced her.

American Express gave her a credit card, which made her feel instantly rich and unwise. She promptly used the card at her favorite store, a French boutique on Madison, to buy far more clothes than she could possibly afford. The clothes made her feel like a doll. She bought little cashmere suits and flared pants with matching jackets with enormous buttons in white, sheer shirts she would only wear a lacey bra beneath so that you could just see it shimmering against her chest. She threw out all her old clothes. She didn't care if she went into debt. New York could do this to you. She got a Visa card and transferred the balance from the American Express because it had to be paid off every month whereas the Visa did not. After the breakup of Ma Bell in 1984 telephone companies vying for customers were paying people to switch carriers and Beth quickly learned to profit from it. Before long she was switching between companies on a monthly basis in order to take advantage of the of-

fers—fifty dollars from one, one hundred dollars from another—feeling quite proud of all she was saving, making even.
Finally, she got rid of her street furniture, replacing it with
castoffs from her grandmother and from Claire. She wanted her
world to look beautiful. Always, she bought flowers from her
Korean grocer on the corner. The saleswoman there had come
to know Beth, loved her smile, and gave her little extras—
apples, dried mangoes, bananas. The credit freed Beth and she
accepted no more presents from Hunter. She told him that she
loved him like a brother and asked him to be just her friend.

"So it was the money you were after," he said, teasing her.
He scooped her up and kissed her on the cheek. "Like a good
brother," he explained, adding: "If you don't want the money,
I'll quit my job."

"No, no. Don't quit your job. You're going to have to get me
out of debt someday." He laughed and she laughed and their
relationship was resolved and she felt happy to know that he
was there (as a brother).

"Wait until he finds a girlfriend," Sylvia said to Beth over
the phone all the way from California (a free call, thanks to
Beth's schemes).

"That would be a relief. When are you visiting?"

"When I sell my novel. And you?"

"Once I open a restaurant and it gets a great review."

"Trapped by the poverty of youth."

"I miss you."

"He loves you."

She started having dinner parties with friends from work,
with friends from college who had returned to New York after
having had their post-graduation flings with other cities, with
friends of Hunter's though she always (mistakenly) believed she
would have nothing to say to the investment bankers, would

have no idea how to talk their language. She made elaborate meals, Persian, of course. She learned the names of the dishes: *kashk-o bademjan* and *borani-e esfenaj, kukuye sabzi, run-e bareh*. She wanted her apartment to be like a culinary salon. She became extravagant, hunting down Persian caviar, beluga and sevruga, serving it with vodka and champagne (Dom Perignon supplied by Hunter, of course). For atmosphere, she would put on some Persian music and place all the food in the center of the table along with platters of fresh herbs and rose petals scattered here and there.

Indian feasts were another of her specialties. Wanting people to know the pleasures that lay beyond the familiar pilafs and curries and vindaloos, she introduced them to more authentic, exotic dishes like *idli upma* and *bhel puri, kararee bhindi,* Malabar salmon and *Gobi lahsuni* (she loved the names), to chutneys with sour pears and tomatoes and coconut. She was eager, if asked, to explain the subtle science of their spices, of cilantro and tamarind and mustard seed and cumin and coriander. Her apartment always smelled exotic. Regularly she would make nine-curry meals and ask everyone to use their fingers, explaining why. Beth relied on lessons picked up from Preveena and Nasim, supplemented by urgent calls to them at Claire. Beth and her friends would have long conversations by candlelight late into the night, talking about books and politics and local restaurant gossip: who had been reviewed, what young stars were shooting up, who was writing a cookbook, what advance she had been paid, what new food store was opening. The food people—friends from Lago primarily, kitchen help like Beth, all of whom took food seriously and wanted someday to be the chef—rarely tried to hide their jealousy of the latest young chef who was rocketing toward the culinary stratosphere and they were endlessly critical of any new restaurants even if they hadn't tried them.

"Zoo is a zoo and what a name."

"I'm more talented than that guy. I can tell you that, even at my worst."

"It's because of who he is."

"Who is he?"

"Jake McFundy's son."

"He's male. It's because he's male." Out for the evening, away from the restaurant and Cosella and silent Leo, they would all feel a certain freedom as if they owned themselves again, as if their futures really were their own. Inevitably though they'd start talking about Cosella and the latest insult she had thrown at one of them. Old stories and new stories, Beth's story of the trust fund, would come bubbling up; even off work, they weren't free of Lago.

Someone would change the subject. A relief. They'd argue about French cuisine and the techniques—clarifying butter, beating egg whites in ice, beating egg yolks in a bath of warm water—using Julia Child to support themselves or dismissing her entirely as elitist. "I don't agree with her, but elite she is not." And then she'd be described by someone who had met her, even if briefly, perhaps even just a handshake. (Secretly Beth had decided she wanted to become the Julia Child of Italian cuisine.)

They talked until there was nothing left to say and they felt glutted and a little dirty and futile. Hunter would pour glasses of Armagnac and change the subject to the theater and the ballet and the opera and the latest exhibit at the Guggenheim, none of which the foodies could afford or had much time for, but they would be relieved to no longer be fixated on the successes of others, and they would listen to the bankers talking about the arts and making comments (not mean) about the size of Beth's studio, enjoying the intimacy, the idea of slumming it.

After the meals Beth would give each of them a finger bowl and drip rose water into their palms. She loved entertaining:

loved the days of thought and preparation; loved choosing what to wear, making the meal, setting the table with all the silver and all the candles, hanging (ironed) linen towels in the bathroom, lighting dozens of votive candles, placing them here and there; loved especially the appreciation afterward. "I want to marry Beth," someone would always declare. She would not let the size of her apartment stop her from what she wanted to do most. Most of all, she loved the romance of food, especially of Persian and Indian cuisine, the deep history, the sensuous quality of the flavors and of using your hand and a piece of nan or a branch of fresh dill in lieu of a fork. But Italian was always her strength.

Through Hunter she heard of another illegal sublet on the Upper West Side. With two bedrooms, a living room and a dining room, this one had four times the space of the studio, and, best of all, it cost only five hundred dollars per month. Beth had grown wise to the ways of the city: with a roommate to pay the rent, she could live rent-free and not need to worry about finding another waitressing job. So she did just that and more. Instead of giving up the apartment on York Avenue she sub-sublet it, illegally, of course, for double what she paid to Georgia Lazar, and thus she was not only not paying rent, she was making enough money each month to be able to live on her Lago salary. Promptly she went to her French boutique on Madison and bought another outfit, a pleated black skirt covered with the finest white polka dots and a matching shirt. She bought a black leather jacket and a pair of shoes. She went back to the salon with the borzois and had her hair bobbed to just above her chin. She looked French. In her new apartment she hosted a Persian dinner for ten. She loved New York.

A year later she lost this apartment because the building belonged to Columbia University and she was renting it from pro-

fessors who had long since left Columbia. The school had finally caught up with them. Hunter set Beth up with a realtor
who adored her the instant she met her simply because of Beth's
determination to attain the unrealistic: "I want to find something
big and beautiful and cheap," Beth declared.

"I have just the thing but you'll never be able to afford it,"
the realtor responded. "Unless, of course, you can get that cute
man who's in love with you to pay for it." The realtor was a
large woman with thin reddish hair and a slight smile that
seemed almost a smirk. She had had three husbands consecu-
tively and from each husband she had a son. The husbands were
Turkish, Israeli, and Spanish respectively. "I'm making my way
west," she explained. "The next husband will be American."
What she really wanted was to be a painter.

"Tell me about it?" Beth asked referring to the apartment.

The apartment was several blocks south of where she lived
now, three times again as large, with windows facing south,
views of the Empire State Building, views to the west of the
Hudson, three bedrooms, a formal dining room, and a large living room. The rent was not much, but still beyond her budget.
She calculated in her head, as she wandered from room to room,
lingering at the windows to admire the view, that simply by getting two roommates and by having them pay the rent she could
live rent-free again in grander style still.

"I want it," she said.

"Fifteen thousand cash in a paper bag," the realtor replied,
with that knowing smirk of hers. The real estate deal involved
placing all those thousands in the paper bag and handing it off
to a man in a long dark leather coat on the corner of 103rd and
Broadway near the one line. He, in turn, handed Beth a large
envelope in which, she hoped, she would find the lease (rent
stabilized) in her name and the keys. He had the longest, most
delicate fingers she had ever seen on a man. His fingernails were

manicured. Only reluctantly did he let go of the envelope. Then
he vanished down the stairs into the subway station and she
never saw him again. She had borrowed the money from Hunter
(he did not advise this transaction), agreeing to pay him back
each month with the money she earned off of her York Avenue
apartment and from her tenants. (Eventually Hunter referred to
the various tenants as "Beth's mules.") The night she got the keys
she invited him over. The apartment was still empty, the late sun
poured through the windows (it was summer). She plugged in
a boom box, slipped in a cassette of Chopin, put on her shimmering black-tasseled thrift-store gown and waltzed from room
to room until Hunter arrived with champagne. He opened all
the windows and a gentle breeze rushed in from downtown.
She kissed him that night. One small kiss, that was all. One
small kiss that did not make her feel shocks and stabs and jabs,
that did not leave her hungry. Rather the kiss, small as it was,
seemed to wrap around her like water, like that gigantic Colorado sky draping the earth. "I'm sorry," she said, pushing back
from him.

"For what?" he asked.

"Because I can't do this," she said.

"Why?"

She said nothing and he knew why.

"You should have come to Wall Street," he said after a bit,
sweeping his arm in a grand gesture around the living room to
acknowledge her accomplishment. "You don't mind risk and
you understand probability. By now you'd be a multimillion-
aire." And he raised his glass to her.

Always, she thought of Cesare. And always his calls came,
far apart, yes, but like sporadic tracer flames they lit up the
darkness.

———

At Carnegie Hall with Hunter one night, there to watch some friends of his from Germany play in a quartet, she became smitten with a small violinist named Hans, and he with her, much to Hunter's disappointment. Beth's infatuation would lead Hunter to a romance of his own that would become quite serious. The girl's name was Dina, and she was a model for Bloomingdale's, who, with her long legs, wore miniskirts easily. Beth would lie in bed at night, imagining them out on the town, spending all of Hunter's money, Dina unappreciative of his exotic excursions to thrift stores and Persian rug marts. At least, though, Beth felt freed from guilt.

Beth and Hans met after the performance, stayed out all night, walked through Central Park to her apartment at dawn just as the joggers and the businessmen were starting the day. In her kitchen she undressed him. On the side of his jaw where the violin pressed into it, a tough leathery patch had formed. She touched it. It was black and ugly like an enormous mole. He was her size. She did not need to look up to him, rather she could look straight into him. She began to kiss the leather patch, the back of his neck, each eye. She loved that he was her size. She kissed his collarbone, his nipples, his belly button. At his penis she lingered for a while until he lifted her to him and undressed her, throwing off her cute French clothes, pushing back her cute French bob. And they spent the day in this way in her new apartment, her roommates safely at work. They did this whenever he flew in from Germany, in his hotel above Carnegie Hall, in a taxi, in the park. Sometimes he would lie her naked on the bed and play Mozart for her on his violin until she could bear patience no longer. From Germany he wrote her long desperate love letters that made her laugh. She loved being admired, she loved that men were attracted to her. It made her want more men, many men.

Men appeared from everywhere. She dated all the time. She never slept. She went out with a Brazilian architect who liked to eat tongue and get her stoned and fuck her on his architectural drawings and on the children's furniture he had designed. Through him she met a woman who made a lot of money in Hollywood because she had the unique ability to mimic weird sounds. She could crow like a rooster, howl like a siren, purr like a cat, growl like a hyena. Beth had a fast and delightful affair with that woman's husband, who was elated that she didn't mimic the sounds of beasts upon climaxing. All these men drifted across her life, gliding by as if on a conveyor belt before disappearing. She dated other people's boyfriends; she dated other married men. They took her to fancy restaurants; they picked her up late after work. They offered her fine wines, some drugs, gave her pretty presents, invited her on trips to faraway places they happened to be visiting on business. She had an affair with a man twice her age who had three children, the oldest of whom was only three years younger than she. Her involvement with all of the men was never emotional. She did not care when they left or she left. They were fun, that was all. She enjoyed being adept at letting go.

With the help of Cosella, who now knew all about Beth's life at Claire, her dead mother, and her Italian love affair, and who as a result had adopted Beth as a sort of daughter, Beth started a small catering company, catering parties for Leo and Cosella at their Fifth Avenue apartment. Leo, when not at work, never wanted to cook. For them, for their parties, Beth liked to cook anything but Italian. She was not afraid to try other cuisines, but often she made her elaborate Indian meals and Persian feasts, encouraging Leo and Cosella to encourage their friends to eat with their fingers. Their friends were important people and it gave Beth a thrill to feed them: politicians, actors, singers, famous writers, a jazz musician or two. (She even cooked for Bill Clinton—before he ran for president.) Beth had either heard of Leo and Cosella's friends or knew that if she hadn't heard of them she should have, simply by the way Cosella said their names. These dinners led to other dinners and before long Beth was able, with the consent and goodwill of Cosella, to quit her job at Lago. By this time she was sous-chef in pastry and this was as far as she would ever get at Lago. She knew it; Cosella knew it. The higher positions would never be vacated, so Cosella gave her a chance in another way. It was the elaborate displays Beth created, the exquisite details, that people loved— those finger bowls and the rose water, the barberries (which they had not known to have existed) and the ambrosial rice noodle sorbet. Beth would always emerge from the kitchen at the end of the meal to drip the rose water on the guests' palms herself, radiant in some splendid outfit with a clean white apron tied around her waist and her hair pulled back with a bandeau or up in the smallest chignon. Cosella would stand at the head of the table, raise her glass to Beth, and make a toast, ask Beth to take a bow. All the famous guests would clap.

Out on the cold street, wrapping the cashmere coat from her boutique tightly around her waist and neck, knotting her scarf high beneath her chin, pulling her hat down over her ears, feeling the bite of that January air, looking south to the buildings high above the park, seeing her breath, watching a taxi scream down Fifth, admiring a couple strolling home late and a little drunk hand in hand, walking to Madison to catch the bus north, admiring the lit-up windows of the fancy stores, all the pretty prospects they promised, an enormous check for her dinner in her pocket, Beth would get a rush. She could do this, she believed. Whatever *this* was, she could do it.

———

A childhood friend of Cesare's came to New York. He took her to a famous steak house and ordered a four-pound lobster for them to share and she showed him just how to eat it, just how to get every last little piece from the head, how those pieces are the sweetest and most tender. (She did not tell him that a four-pound lobster was a ridiculous notion and bound to be much tougher than a one-and-a-quarter-pound lobster.) Told him how you kill a lobster, told him that originally lobster had been the food of indentured servants and slaves and in colonial days that they had had an uprising to protest the incessant meals of lobster; they wanted something different; they wanted meat.

"How in the world do you know so much about lobsters?"

"I'm a chef," she said with a blue-eyed twinkle. Just saying the words felt like she was cheating a little, like she was stealing something. But she loved saying it anyway, the first time she ever had: *I am a chef.* Always people were asking you to list your accomplishments, detail your résumé to prove yourself. *I am a chef.* She blushed a little with the confidence. It was easier declaring this to an Italian; she knew an Italian wouldn't care.

This man, Gianni, was Cesare's oldest friend. They had met as boys ice-skating on a frozen pond on the outskirts of Città. They had been five at the time, and had been good friends ever since. Gianni was a doctor, engaged to be married. Beth had met his fiancée in Città, her name was Grazia and she was tall and slender with lots of hair and a bright toothy smile. She was incredibly sweet, if not too smart. Grazia towered over Gianni and teased him often about his height, but in a nonthreatening way that somehow made her size seem maternal, as if she would mother him well for life because of her height. Her ambition was to be Gianni's wife, mother of him and of his kids—an ambition, Beth surmised, that made Grazia's life simple: all she had to do was remain slender and sexy and soft with Gianni, curl up to him like a cat and make him feel comfortable and safe. Gianni was a small man with a round warm face and sharp eyes. His professional specialty was blood and he had come to New York for a conference at Sloan-Kettering that concerned the relationship between a rare T-cell lymphoma and mononucleosis and something to do with Japan. In Città, Beth had always had more questions for Gianni than for Grazia, endless queries about his research and the makeup of blood and the cures for the various kinds of leukemia. Blood was a subject that Grazia did not want to hear about. Thus she did not come with him to New York.

Eating the lobster, pulling the tender bits of meat from the tiny crevices, Gianni asked Beth to feed him the meat. She did. Then he fed her a piece of the tail. He let his index finger linger on her lip, just long enough for her to become curious about his intentions. The candle on the table lit his face. The waiter approached to ask a question, but faded quickly back into the swirl of the restaurant. Beth showed Gianni secret crevices in the tail and fed him those bits, just flecks of meat on her finger, which he sucked off. He poured her another glass of wine. They spoke Italian, which she loved because it had been a long time since she had had a chance to. He reminded her a little of the violinist in his size and confidence. She thought, it flashed across her mind delightfully and painfully, that there was not a person in the world she could sleep with who would wound Cesare more. She wanted to wound Cesare. Gianni ordered a chocolate dessert, a mixture of cake and soufflé, oozy warm interior, a fashionable cake, popular in New York. He fed her spoonfuls of the chocolate, which she ate slowly, pretending to be innocent of her own seduction. Never once was Cesare mentioned. Gianni paid the bill and took her to his hotel and made love to her very gently and very carefully (as if he were handling delicate china that did not belong to him) beneath the cool pressed hotel sheets. Slowly enough, patiently enough, thoroughly enough that she couldn't do anything but explode with pleasure, until it began to dawn on her, horrified and too late to stop the inevitable, the notion itself working like an aphrodisiac, that this was just what Cesare had wanted.

Afterward, as Gianni's fingers drifted the lengths of her back, her bare arms, she pressed her cheek into the soft cool pillow and allowed herself to feel the burning sensation in her eyes and nose. She lay there, silent, for a long time. Gianni fell asleep. The hotel's thick windows kept all the noise of New York out. But she could see through a gap in the curtains that it was raining outside. She lit one of his cigarettes and smoked it and then another, watching the rain come down. She was not a smoker, never had been.

"Did this unfold as planned?" she asked Gianni before leaving. She half expected him to take out his wallet and pay her.

"He loves you," Gianni said.

"I hate you," she said to Cesare on the phone, glad somewhere for the excuse to call him.

"No you don't," he said.

"Why?" she asked. Then she started to cry. No one said a word for a while. She could hear the static in the line hissing and shimmying all the way across the Atlantic, all the way across Spain and the Mediterranean, beneath the Alps to Città.

Because I'm some part of you. I'm what you didn't have growing up. I'm your dead mother, I'm your father as he would have been, I'm the life you would have had had your mother not died. I'm impossible. I'm the Atlantic Ocean, another world. Because you are some inextricable part of me, my ambition, my possibility, my potential. You embody it, promise it, answer it. Because you refuse and I refuse to believe in the power of history and time.

Campanilismo, Beth thought. Valeria came to mind, looming above the crowd at the Fiori party, her stricken face reaching desperately for the leg of the artist as he rises inevitably into the cloud as if she were trying to pull back time.

Benvenuto only lived in Florence. Think of how far we've come, she thought. Cesare can be with a Florentine. In three hundred years perhaps he'll be allowed to be with an American. Then she thought of Benvenuto fleeing love for what he wanted most, for what he wanted more than Valeria. Then Beth thought about herself, her own inability to leave America, her own allegiance, what she wanted most. *Campanilismo,* she thought again, picturing all the many skyscrapers of Manhattan, their spires shooting into the heavens. Her bell towers.

"Why do you need to torture me?" she asked. "Why do you need to humiliate me?"

"Because I want you to stop loving me," he said.

"I hate you," she said, contempt becoming seduction in their mad dance.

"Come visit me," he said.

"Pay for the ticket," she said.

"Certainly," he said.

"This feels like an addiction," she said.

"It's worse," he said. "It's a belief."

He sent her a plane ticket. They met in France at the Lac d'Annecy. Beth had never seen water that shade, emerald like the jewel. They met in Paris. They met in Milan on her way to visit Hunter (and Dina) in India. Her visits were secret. He never told his family. She did not tell Bea. The trips were fast, a few days, and awkward. At first, hope filled Beth. But she soon realized that distance had transformed them both into strangers and within only a few hours, a day, her hope would vanish. Cesare could not stand what New York had made of Beth, someone

inelegantly scrounging for money through a complicated network of shady real estate deals that didn't even involve equity,
someone who bought and spent on credit, someone desperate
for more, chopping vegetables and believing she was becoming
something. For Beth, Cesare had settled, settled into a life as a
banker, loaning money to support other people's dreams. He no
longer carried a book. Indeed, he never read, never wrote. She
felt sad; she did not know him anymore. Even so, for a while
they stubbornly believed that somehow they could return to before, make time stop, that they could still save each other from
their lives.

Then his father died. He died late at night in his bed at
home. His wife and daughter and son were there. Cesare stood
by the bed, holding his father's hand, rubbing it to give comfort, silent tears about his eyes, silent promises about his lips.
"Put out the cigarette," the father said to his boy. His boy felt
very much like a boy—a reprimanded child—not a man saying good-bye to a man, but a boy who wanted to grow up and
be admired by the one person who would not be there to appreciate the transformation. It was his turn to take the mantle,
leave folly behind by annihilating Beth once and forever and,
in doing so, annihilating himself. For what? "Put out the cigarette," his father had said, and soon thereafter he died.

Years later, Cesare sits beneath the fresco in the bright dark
of that late-September night. For what? For what? He can see
nothing but the tenderness of night, the daring of morning trying to push through the part in the thick velvet curtains.

The next meeting was in Città. Beth stayed four days and then
flew home to New York knowing the love affair was finally
over. Cesare was now a new and completely unrecognizable
man. He detested Beth from the moment he saw her and it
seemed he brought her to Italy simply to show her all the ways

in which he now could not bear her. He would not kiss her; he feared she could have AIDS. He said he never would have married her, even at the height of their romance, because he knew she would never be able to bear him a son because her mother had only had a daughter and her father had only had daughters. "Leave my mother out of this," she said. He said that she was so disorganized she would lose her children on a street somewhere. He would not take her to Fiori. He would not take a day off from work to spend with her. Rather, he left her in his apartment (he had moved away from the family villa). It was an ugly modern apartment with views of the town and its mocking bell tower. Finally at the airport, as he dropped her off, he took her hands in his and held them warmly and said as if conceding something that he would be here for her as a brother, nothing more, but always as a brother.

"I don't hate you," she said to him, looking him sharply in the eye. Travelers streamed around them, all the sounds of an airport. A plane took off.

"You, your eyes, reminded me of your grandmother just then." For an instant he seemed tender. Then, as if trying to cauterize any weakness he said, *"Addio."*

Such a cold word, *addio,* it jabbed her as he intended it to. Looking at Cesare, she could see only his father. But she did not say that. She said again, "I do not hate you," because she would not let him win. Everything inside of her ached, throbbed actually. She turned her back and disappeared into the terminal. She would not let him win because she was not talking to Cesare but to some impostor who had possessed the Cesare she had known because of circumstances that were far larger than and deeper than her ability to comprehend.

She flew home to New York, crying the entire way, banished, exiled, bereft. Suddenly somewhere over the Atlantic, waves way beneath like clouds, the water like sky, she sat upright.

She would call her father. She saw him in front of her, holding her hand—her little hand warm in his big hand. She was four years old and he was playing with her; she was riding on his shoulders. "Run, Daddy, run," she used to say as she made him dash across the fields at Claire. She would interrupt him at work, in his office, in the fields, in the orchards, and make him get down and play with her, and he would. He always would. She had never really asked him, asked him with urgency, to come to her. Her requests had always been halfhearted; she'd never expected him to come. Now she would be urgent in her demand. She designed a plan. A fat old man sitting next to her on the plane asked if he could eat her meal. She had not even realized the meal had been sitting in front of her for a long time. Sunlight poured through the window. Her father. She would call her father. Simple as that. She would talk to him about love, about her mother. He would come to New York City and visit her. It became crucial that her father leave Claire for her. She was all hope, a muscle of hope and optimism.

"But you know I can't, darling," he said into the receiver.

"But I need you."

"It's all right to suffer, sweet girl." She had never asked him so completely and so eagerly, with so much resting on his answer. She had never asked him because she had not wanted to be rejected. It was easier for her to never ask than it was to ask and be told no. She imagined her mother tethered to her father's leg, anchoring him as if with ball and chain and lead and cement to Claire. Once again she hated her mother.

"Please," she whispered into the phone. "Please," she said again. She would not let him know how hard she was crying. In a nearby apartment, work was being done; a jackhammer was demolishing something large and tough. Jackson was silent. She could imagine all the beauty of Claire spreading out around him, the far and distant hills with the little farms glowing like miniatures, like prizes; the quiet songs of the birds, a tractor in the field. Silence. A golden silence. Silence that held potential, a remedy for all. Her father would drive in to New York City in the pickup, visit her in her apartment, bring her fresh lamb and eggs and apples from Claire, make a delicious meal with her, talk to her late into the night about love and love gone bad and love stopping time and the awful leap that occurs once time starts again, how time speeds up as if to make up for stopping, the horrendous shock of the real and the inevitable. He would give to her all the beauty of his pain and knowledge, everything she had been deprived of. He would stroke her hair, kiss her gently on the scalp, rub her back—his sweet girl, his little daughter three years old again when everything was as it should have been and she was in the blissful self-centered state of the age. He would look south out her windows and say, "What a wonderful world you have made for yourself." Perhaps he would say, "You're so like your mother." The potential of that silence, the thick cloud of it that held everything and nothing.

"Please," she said, so quietly the word could barely be heard.

"Don't," he said. Don't make me say no again.

A few days later she searched her apartment for those long-ago lists of what she had and of what she wanted. She updated them and soon thereafter set to work.

The 1990s—the steady rise of the stock market, of the dollar, of the Internet, of wealth. Bill Clinton became president. He appeared on late-night talk shows making fun of himself in very unpresidential ways. He could blow a saxophone along with the best of them. Newt Gingrich. The New Republicans. O. J. Simpson. The Unabomber. Oprah. Julia Roberts. Yoga. The self. More and more and more. Princess Diana died. John-John Kennedy died. Chefs became indisputable superstars. Lucent and Cisco and eBay and AOL and Intel and Amazon. The cell phone. Bill Gates. (It was claimed that he earned so much money it wasn't worth his time to bend over and pick up a five-hundred-dollar bill. Some of Hunter's Wall Street friends would take this as a challenge, calculating how much their time was worth, how much they could forgo for the sake of the value of their time. "Gross," Beth said. "Pathetic.") America was on an upward trend, rising, rising to meet the need of more and more.

When Beth was a little girl she loved chocolate. Of this Jackson was well aware, Beth knew. Especially, she enjoyed trying to understand the brownie—how to make it moist as if from a box but from scratch. Six, seven, eight years old, standing in the kitchen at Claire, she would practice and practice and get everyone involved, giving her tips, helping her with recipes. Her brownies were awful, hard as rocks. People chipped teeth on them. Some of the kids used them as ammunition for their slingshots. A window was broken with a brownie of hers. But Jackson wanted to encourage the interest. He didn't want her to give up. He loved her curiosity, her drive, her ambition to understand. For her birthday he ordered her a case of Duncan Hines brownie mixes so she could consistently make successful brownies—a compromise, yes, but he wanted her to succeed so that she would gain confidence. "But they're not scratch. They're cheating," she said, looking at him. His daughter was a purist, in search of the authentic. He admired his girl, his proud smile indicated as much. He would tell the story to anyone who would listen, "My daughter's a purist," he would say. "My eight-year-old girl has rejected *the mix*." His pride propelled her. She wanted him to acknowledge other special things about her. She couldn't get enough.

He tried a new approach to the brownie. He sent away for fine Belgian chocolate and French cookbooks with recipes for flourless chocolate gâteaux. He sent away for and gave Beth a double boiler and a rubber spatula and a springform pan and whisks in a variety of sizes and a set of measuring cups and spoons and mixing bowls all for her own. And he helped her negotiate the recipes, helped her learn the essential detail of patience, helped her understand the finicky nature of chocolate, of eggs. By nine she had perfected *Gateau au chocolat:* le Diablo from *Simca's Cuisine* by Simone Beck, partner of Julia Child. He remembered, she remembered a long table of people savoring her chocolate cake by candlelight, looking at the little girl who made it. She had a white apron tied around her waist, a big smile on her lips, for she knew she had succeeded. No doubts or second thoughts, knew it unequivocally. "I am good," she thought. "I've got a talent."

By ten Beth had mastered Julia Child's creamless mousse. She had mastered the soufflé and the truffle. By eleven she was an understudy for Preveena and her curries. She was hooked on food, handled all of the produce at Claire as if she were handling a new baby, remembering the big hands of all those chefs who handled her father's produce. She had a respect for food, an appreciation, an understanding, an empathy that only someone who cared deeply could have. Her father loved to watch her, could watch for hours, sitting in the glass dining room with the *New York Times* spread on the table in front of him, his little girl wrapped in her white apron busy melting and blending and sifting and concocting in the kitchen, bringing him now and again something to taste and to judge. And it was his eyes on her that propelled her forward. As she too rose along with the effervescent decade, as she updated her lists, as she contemplated where she had come from and where she wanted to go, it was her father's eyes on her, his belief in her, that sent her forward. And the obstinate hope that if only she achieved enough, he would someday come to her.

In the fall of 1992, a few months after Beth's final return from Italy, Bea arrived. She called a few days before in the middle of the night to say she was leaving her husband, that he didn't know it, that he wouldn't know it until she was gone, that she was coming to live with Beth in New York City, was it all right? They hadn't spoken in a long time. Bea had been mad at Beth for coming to Italy en route to India without letting her know, and as a result she had given Beth the silent treatment for so long that Beth hadn't dared call her when she was in Città. Beth was surprised to hear her friend's voice. "I knew you'd been mad," Beth said to Bea over the phone. "Then I was too embarrassed to call."

"You knew I wouldn't have approved. You knew I would have made you stop wasting your time on him." And, of course, she was right. Sometimes Beth had thought their friendship was over, outgrown or abandoned or simply lost to time and change the way friendships of youth often are. Hearing Bea's voice now, she realized that that would never happen.

Bea arrived with several suitcases and all her bossy enthusiasm, ready to fix her own life and Beth's. She unpacked her bags, hanging her perfectly pressed clothes in Beth's closet, placing her folded shirts and neatly pressed underwear and bras among the things in Beth's bureau. Though all of the details of her wardrobe remained the same, Bea's face and body had changed entirely. Her long nose had been bobbed, her thick black hair, so long she could sit on it, had been streaked blond, her brown eyes had become green, and her full body was as thin as a twig.

"I hardly recognize you," Beth said.

"Imagine. Next he wanted me to fix my boobs." The *he* referred to her husband. "That's when I left."

Bea approved of all of Beth's French clothes. She didn't approve of her hair, which had grown out of its bob, and before long Bea cut it and highlighted it and taught Beth (once and for all) how to style it with a blow dryer.

Since Beth had two roommates, Bea made herself at home in Beth's bed. Late at night she would tell Beth about Giorgio, her awful husband. She had met him in town through a friend and had been attracted to him because he was an artist who designed shopping bags for department stores in Milan, Florence, and Rome—a lucrative job. Initially, Bea had hoped—believed even—that they'd get out of Città to a bigger life in Milan or Rome. They were married for three years, and never left Città, but toward the end of those three years he kept making appointments for her with the plastic surgeon and at the tanning salon. He started buying only diet food for her and gave her special low-carbohydrate diet cookbooks. He did not mind when he discovered that she was bulimic. At the tanning salon she met a married man with whom she fell in love simply because he made her laugh. "He was not attractive, a short little guy with bad teeth, but everything he said made me smile." He promised he would leave his wife. He gave Bea a ring. They ran off to Venice ("which isn't as romantic as they say because the canals smell and it is crowded with tourists") to Florence and Rome and the island of Giglio. "Giorgio never noticed," she said. "I'm sure he had his own affairs." After a year the married man, Marco, still had not left his wife, so Bea called Beth and fled. Her husband had no idea where she was. She wrote him a letter at 37,000 feet and posted it upon arriving in New York.

Listening to Bea, Beth felt as if they were sixteen again, talking about the boyfriends of their teenage years who would soon become irrelevant, like having a sister, an older sister who knew all the answers even if her own life didn't seem to indicate it. When Bea had exhausted the subjects of Giorgio and Marco, the conversation would turn to Beth and her affairs and of course to Cesare. Beth told her about the past five years of breaking up and how cruel he was to her in Città and then all about the one-night stand with Gianni. "Good riddance," Bea said of Cesare. She propped herself up on the pillows and looked at Beth, her eyes chatoyant in the dark, the ceiling fan creaking, stirring up the air. "He was never going to be for you. He was stupid, Beth. A stupid Cittadino who couldn't see beyond the shadow cast by his bell tower."

"Those damn bell towers. It's a surprise, really, that more of them haven't been knocked down."

"It would not be worth the effort," Bea answered. And there late at night in Beth's bed, Bea's own ferocious ambitions, trapped for so long, came bursting forth. And there late at night they began to scheme and concoct and dream of ways to realize their desires. Bea wanted to be a buyer for a big department store, fly all over the world finding irresistible objects and clothing, to adorn women and make them feel new and perfect and pretty.

Bea would, in fact, start looking for work, using her family's connections. She would find a job and live in America for the rest of her life. After Beth's grandmother died, Bea would take over Beth's apartment and Beth would move into her grandmother's. (Grammy died in her sleep of heart failure, ninety years old, in 1995.) Eventually Bea would meet and marry an American and have a thriving career at Lord & Taylor's. She would become Valeria's godmother and adopt her, in spirit, anyway, after Beth was killed, making herself available to Valeria at any time of the day or night. Bea would never have any of her own children but she took care of her friend's children with a fierce devotion. Even Cesare would be in touch with her later on when his son Leonardo came to New York for his PhD in art history at Columbia. Cesare would call Bea and ask her to watch out for him. A call from the blue and a call that would change a certain perception Bea had of him—a perception vivid and clear and strong as she lay in bed with her heartbroken friend.

But that was all later. Now Bea could see her friend needed as much fixing as she herself needed. It was easier to work on her friend than on herself. Beth showed Bea her lists and Bea crumpled them up and threw them in the trash and told her to keep nurturing her catering business and start writing her cookbook, told her it should be more like a memoir of her time in Italy with recipes as ornaments decorating the experiences—*pasta carbonara* made by a beautiful Italian man with whom she would fall permanently in love on a hot Greek night with a full and silver moon, the secret of their love still a mystery even for themselves.

Beth did as she was told and sat at a desk in her bedroom and day in and day out for a year she worked on the book. When she wasn't writing she was catering, sometimes with Bea's help. When she wasn't writing or catering, she was trying to fix Bea up with Hunter, who had left Dina. They all met up for Mozart and wine at the Met and giggled and told stories about the escapades of years ago. Hunter watched the girls with fondness as they described sleeping in the Athenian park, leaving their luggage on the street, or Beth's attempt at waxing her legs—that one hairy leg, Bea begging Beth to finish the job. "It made the waxed leg look prosthetic." Hunter asked questions and the girls spoke with memory and passion and Bea observed Hunter with a careful eye, that discerning eye of hers that would be so good at picking the prettiest shawl out of a stack of shawls one hundred high. She watched Beth as she tilted her head and curled her lips and blushed ever so slightly, as she glanced at Hunter for approval, to see if she made him smile. Then Bea engaged Hunter directly in a conversation first about himself and the hedge fund, then about Beth and her cookbook and her famous dinners and her desire to open a restaurant and he described Beth's parties in detail (the rose water and the petals and the conversation, the dresses she would wear and the music she would play and the people she'd invite). Beth lifted her hand to show Bea the Persian ring he had bought for her long ago. Bea admired it, holding Beth's hand up to the light, turning it around, believing her friend to be a fool. She looked at Hunter, "You bought it because she has romantic ideas about Persian food? Clever." She tightened her lips and nodded her head ever so slightly, understanding perfectly the entire situation. From the ring to the rugs to Sylvia to Claire to Jackson and then back to Beth. Before long she had him helping her figure out the financing for Beth's future. During discussions of finding a silent partner and collateral and loans and all the rest, his conversation became as animated as his face.

Walking home through the park, a full moon in the twilit sky: "He's so clearly in love with you," Bea said to Beth. They strolled arm in arm around the reservoir, over the bridle path, past all the playgrounds with the playing children fading with the day and rollerbladers, bicyclists, and the ubiquitous joggers rushing by. It was fall and warm, a warmth that somehow promised spring.

"I know," Beth said, as if it were a burden.

"Then I suppose what you don't know is that you're in love with him?"

"Don't be silly," she said, but their kiss filled her mind, that kiss in her empty apartment, brand-new to her and like a mansion, that kiss warm and protective if not passionate, like the sheltering sky. "He's like a brother," she added. And then she explained more about his years at Claire.

"He's cute," Bea observed.

"You think so? I can't see that anymore."

"We can renovate him," she said. "Of course, he won't become Italian. He is very American. But we can remove the pennies from his shoes." They both began to giggle at the grandiosity of the silly idea of renovating Hunter.

"Don't underestimate the power and allure of being cherished," Bea said, suddenly serious. She turned her head abruptly as a speeding cyclist rode by. All her hair followed, like a spray of silk tassels, like the dress Hunter had given Beth long ago.

The cookbook sold, did relatively well, and led Beth to a friend of Hunter's—a bond trader, a bear of a man called Bear. Though his name was Henry, he'd become Bear because he liked a bear market. He liked as well to make big bets and big dares. He dared Beth to come to Wall Street, told her if she gave him eighteen months he would turn her into a bond trader. "Anyone can do it," he said, then asked if she had ever studied calculus. "Calculus?" she asked, horrified. Nothing sounded more dreadful to her than eighteen months on Wall Street. It was the subway, too, the idea of riding it every single day all the way down there. But secretly, somewhere, there was something intriguing about making so much money. She thought of Henry James's description of the American scale of gain, one that stopped at nothing, would sacrifice anything, for so much money that it would all be worthwhile. Beth had scrabbled so hard and for so long that the notion of making more money than she could possibly spend had a certain appeal to it. How lovely it would be to be like Cosella, a triumph on her own terms with a life perpetually cushioned by money and all that it could buy. Bear and his wife were a bit like that. Bear made five million dollars a year. His wife made a million. "It pays for the babysitter," he'd say with his jolly smile, his big belly jiggling, and his red hair seemingly on fire. For Bear, the bets never stopped and the projects never ended: the things he wanted to fund and finance and back kept growing. Beth became one of his projects. She liked being his project. Since he was a young boy he had wanted to be a cook. His apartment had a state-of-the-art kitchen, including a Wolf Range cooktop with six burners and a griddle, and a Sub-Zero refrigerator. A temperature-controlled cabinet of glass, twelve feet high, stood in the center of this kitchen, filled with premium wines—nothing under seventy dollars a bottle. A ladder, twelve feet high, slid around the cabinet on wheels. Bear's goose fat was flown in from France, along with his foie gras; his olive oil and parmigiano were flown in from Italy; his chocolate from Belgium, and so on and so forth. He had a woman whose only job was to keep the copper pots and pans sparkling clean, which wasn't hard because the kitchen was rarely used. He had no time and his wife hated to cook. Even if she had wanted to, she had no time, either, since she was an internet stock analyst.

He loved Beth's book and decided to invest in her restaurant so that he could live vicariously. He gave her the money that allowed her to turn a ramshackle storefront on Avenue A into a trendy, well-reviewed hot spot where people could taste the fresh simplicity of northern Italian food. A glass wall divided the kitchen from the dining area so that the guests could watch the grand opera occurring before all the chrome of the stoves and ovens. The chef (who had been a sous-chef when she hired him away from Cosella) and the kitchen staff worked busily in their white hats and aprons.

Bear held court at the mahogany bar, imported from Italy, and ate his dinners—*Tonnarelli con la Belga e la Pancetta Affumicata, Risotto con Carciofi, Filetto di Bue alla Moda di Como* and the like—with his Wall Street pals during their late night schmoozing sessions. He brought them all here. Bear would offer Beth suggestions in front of his friends to show them just how involved he was, ideas concerning the lighting, the seasoning in certain dishes, the wine list, and even ridiculous suggestions like importing fruit from Rome. She'd smile indulgently and pat him on the shoulder, give him a kiss, telling him in this way that she was the one in charge. Even so, "I made it happen," Bear would shout above the din of all the happy diners.

This was as close as he would ever get to his own restaurant. He had two children, would have two more, the wife, high overhead with his multimillion-dollar apartment, his kitchen, his wines, tuitions, college, retirement—funny how fast six million a year will go. He couldn't take the risk himself. Instead, he traded mortgage bonds high up in the North Tower where eventually he would die, with Beth—an act more intimate, when done with someone else, than making love.

In the summer of 1996, after two years of dating, thanks to Bea, the matchmaker, who understood perfectly the entire situation, Beth married Hunter—easy all-knowing Hunter standing right in front of her on the vast lawn at Claire. Beth wore her mother's wedding gown, a big white dress with one hundred buttons running down the back to meet a bustle. It was silk satin with a full organza slip. The silk had turned cream-colored with age, even so, the dress remained beautiful with its puffy capped sleeves and lace about the bodice, and it fit Beth perfectly. She was exactly her mother's size. Wearing the dress, Beth felt close to her mother in a way she had never experienced before, as if

Claire were standing there with her, a real woman—not an abstraction or a dream or a farm. Her mother had been ten years younger than Beth when she wore the dress before two hundred people in New York City (at the Pierre), with Grammy secretly apologizing to her friends for the obesity of her son-in-law's mother. Beth thought as well about her grandmother, how she had helped Claire select the dress at Bergdorf Goodman's, insisting on formal and traditional as if the dress alone could have changed Claire's choice of groom.

Beth wished her grandmother had lived to see her marry Hunter because Grammy had approved of him: he was charming, he came from the right family (crazy as they were), he earned a fabulous living, and he had quietly paid her bills so she could have the best medical care as she got old, even arranging for a maid to care for the details of her life that she could no longer handle (when Beth discovered the checks she felt a little more of her heart give way to him). "He comes from good stock," Grammy was fond of saying. "Don't let this one slip through your fingers." She said that the day before she died. Standing in her mother's dress Beth imagined she would have become Claire for Grammy, starting out anew all over again. The dress had remained vacuum-packed and stored in a gold-colored box on a high shelf in a deep closet in the grandmother's rent-controlled apartment. The box had a clear plastic window so that a portion of the dress could be admired, which of course Beth had done many times—first at her grandmother's instigation and then on her own, as if she were admiring some part of her mother, peering in at her through the small plastic window, watching her change shade and character with time. After the wedding Beth returned the dress to the gold box to save it for the daughter she knew she would have someday.

Life rolled on swiftly, moving like the river that it is. Hunter would never be the love that Cesare had been, the desperate, suffocating, addictive, gorgeous, impossible love—a torrential love that stopped time. Rather, it was a quiet love that flowed steadily, growing with and through time like morning glories or some other beautiful unstoppable vine. Nothing fragile about it, as solid as that sky.

The hedge fund Hunter worked for collapsed when a disgruntled employee told stories that got the SEC involved and the company lost 80 percent of their investors. The man whose company it was, once worth billions, was left with (relatively) little, and Hunter was let go. Instead of finding a new job he decided to help Beth with her second cookbook, another memoir, this one all about Claire (her mother and the farm) with recipes like ornaments, from India and Iran and all over the world (including one for camel stew, ingredients: one large camel; ten medium lambs; thirty medium chickens; etc); some of the recipes were Preveena's or Nasim's or her own, others were left behind by the various residents of Claire. This book did better than the first and helped fund (along with Bear) the initial investment for Matera, Beth's southern Italian answer to Como, inspired by a photograph she had seen of Matera's *Sassi,* the rock-cut settlement sculpted out of the tufa hills upon which the town lies. Her design now would be the same as it had been with Como: find the chef, start the restaurant—she preferred being a businesswoman (a nice Cosella) rather than a chef—and once successful, sell it. She planned to sell Como too now.

The year after Beth and Hunter married, Valeria was born, named for a woman of strength whose face captured the essence and passion of life in its fine mixture of exquisite pain and her desire to steal time, grab it from the sky. Valeria's newborn eyes were ferocious in their passion, claiming Beth immediately and

entirely, infusing her with love that swelled to enormous pro-
portions, that obliterated all other love for a while and in so
doing infused her with more than a bit of fear. "I am yours," the
eyes said, "I am yours for life," staking claim to Beth's heart as
no man ever could. Looking at Valeria, perfect in her newborn
beauty, Beth knew that every choice she had made that had led
her to this moment had been the right choice.

By the summer of 2001 Beth was working on the business
plan for her third restaurant—Preveena—trying to persuade
Bear, who was not as fond of Indian food, to help her once
again. There was more risk involved now. Though the first two
restaurants had been very well received and well reviewed and
even won a prize or two, they had sadly not been financial successes and Beth had not been able to sell them. A third restaurant, Indian-inspired no less, and started by an American, a
woman no less, was not an easy venture to embrace. But Beth
did not care. She wanted to open Preveena. She believed in Preveena, the menu, the food, its ability to be popular; she envisioned a salon of sorts in a townhouse where people could come
to a grand bar and eat whatever was being served that evening.
She was determined. She was all will. No one was going to stop
her. Bear *would* help her. (This was when, all these years later,
she imagined Georgia Lazar, the woman who sublet Beth her
first apartment, clinging to her piece of New York, hands fisted,
face fierce and angular, pushing through the crowds.) On a six-
week trip to Italy planned by Hunter (Beth had not been there
since 1992), they spent a week in the south of France to help
persuade Bear, following him and his family to the small town
of Saint Rémy where he had a château in the hills of Les
Alpilles, not far from Les Baux, in the weird and wild desert
landscape of Provence, so scrappy and beautiful in its nakedness.
Beneath a sky of shooting stars (2001 was a good year for them

in Provence), sipping cool whites from Bellet, from Mas de Daumas, Gassac, the children running around in their noisy way, Beth would seduce Bear with her plans for Preveena. It would happen. The desire gripped her; it went beyond the idea. It was a need. She was hungry with ambition. She was determined and fierce and bold. She wanted more: another restaurant, another book, a food store, another baby. It didn't matter that the other two restaurants had not been financially successful. This one would be. She knew it, like you just know some things. She was potential. She was possibility with the ability to reinvent, become something, something better. She was more. She was gain on an American scale. She was America.

Seven

Lachesis

The accordion nature of time—it bellows. The present pushes up against history to kiss it and all that is in between lies flattened. The air rushes out so that all that is now meets memory, undiluted by the clutter of the intervening years. A friend of Beth's from Claire, a Seattle fireman who came to live there for a year or so, once told her of being on a navy ship during the Vietnam War. The ship ported in Japan and he got off and took a bus back to the air force base he had lived on as a child. It was dark as the bus made its way to the base, a black that revealed nothing, but even so the fireman knew exactly where he was; he knew each turn, each bend, each curve, each bump, each straight stretch of road. He was a seven-year-old boy again riding the familiar route at the end of which stood his dead parents, waiting for him to return. He was trying to grab something back, hanging on to escape the undertow.

She always knew that she would see him again. She knew the moment would come when she expected it least. For a long while she imagined the moment, on an exotic trip somewhere, riding camels in the hot desert of Jaisalmer, riding elephants on a beach in Puket, imagined what they would say to each other, imagined nothing would have changed: whether they were in their thirties, forties, fifties, or sixties even, they would fall into the familiar embrace. She would dream of that embrace—see it vividly in a flash, an instant, a nanosecond. He sitting there, somewhere, holding her. She could not see his head or hers. She could not see his legs or hers. Simply, she saw her torso inclining to meet his, felt his arms wrap around her, a study in surrender and in power, out of time and space and body, in perpetuity. The image would shoot across her dreams like a slide out of sequence, flash by as she recognized it, then disappear. Awake again, she would feel hope. She would not tell Hunter, of course. She loved him too much, but it was a different love: a practical love, an arranged love, solid and steady and capable of duration, void of fizz and passion. Other times, she imagined she would see Cesare and they would simply talk and in that moment all the explanations for why they were not together would finally make sense, defining how a love not finished can even thus be over.

She saw him again in Provence in the hot summer of 2001. She saw him sitting in a cast iron chair at a table beneath a canopy of plane trees reading a newspaper and drinking an espresso. She saw him sitting there by himself. On the table in front of him rested a green notebook, which she imagined was a journal, and she imagined he had started to write again and that made her happy. He was wearing khaki military shorts, the kind that she and Bea bought in the markets in Milan, where there were stacks and stacks and stacks of them, cast away by boys whose service had been completed. (Beth remembered being surprised that there was a man so small that his shorts fit her.) He wore a white T-shirt and docksiders and his black hair was just as black, receding just as faintly at his temples. A summer tan gilded him with an aura of health. He had not changed. So powerful was the jolt, knifelike, it caused her to flee his line of vision, darting into the dark hotel lobby. She had been walking back from the pool across the vast lawn of the hotel, carrying her daughter's doll. The limp doll had a smile on its cloth face that seemed to represent all that was now. He, sitting over there beneath the shade of the canopy, a chorus of crickets humming white noise, was all that had been. Time flattened. She needed to breathe. This was not as she had ever imagined it.

The lobby had high ceilings, a dilapidated grandeur, peeling paint and plaster, regal portraits of long-forgotten royalty, gold paint flickering in the dull light, a marble staircase with a red velvet runner. She stood there, small, hoping he had seen her, too, hoping he would follow her inside, swoop her up in his arms, and all the clutter of the past nine years would vanish, turning the moment into what she had always imagined. She waited for what seemed to be a long time but may well have been only a minute or two. Though it was hot outside she shivered in the cool lobby. When she walked back to the pool he was gone and she wondered had he seen her, too?

A year like every other: George W. Bush had become president of the United States of America in one way or another. He was speaking about tax cuts and Star Wars and Iraq. The economy was in a slump. An earthquake in Gujarat, India, had killed nearly twenty thousand people. The FBI agent Robert Hanssen had been arrested for spying for the Russians; Slobodan Milosevic surrendered to police to be tried for crimes of war; Tony Blair was reelected; for the first time a blind man reached the summit of Mount Everest; in China, Zhonghua Sun was put to death by the People's Republic because she refused to be sterilized. In June there was a total eclipse of the sun. In July, Hunter, Beth, and little Valeria, four and a half years old, flew off to Italy.

The trip was a present to Beth from Hunter and her first return to Italy since 1992—the year of her final break with Cesare. They stayed for six weeks, traveling in a rented car to a fifteenth-century castle converted into a hotel in Spongano, Puglia, surrounded with orchards of lemon trees and bordered by a pool the size of a small lake. The owner, a friendly man, loved Americans and made Beth and Hunter and Valeria elaborate dinners of local fish every evening. They ate beneath the stars, the table lit with citronella candles to keep away mosquitoes. There were carafes of local wine, *vino bianco un po frizzante.* They spoke of politics and Bush and Berlusconi and of the American taste for large bathrooms. "I had to design the rooms with big bathrooms in mind, all first-class comforts, if I wanted to attract Americans," the owner told them.

They were alone at the castle, but Beth wondered what kind of Americans these guests would be, marveling at that defining characteristic. Later she asked Hunter if he cared about the big bathroom. "It's better than a small dirty bathroom," he had said, lounging in a tub with a whirlpool. He patted the water. His smile invited her to join him. The memory of sleeping in the Athenian park flitted in front of her, of the bordello in Barcelona, of the dirty, small bathroom located down the hall shared with all the other guests. How long ago was that? Nineteen years? It was hard to accept that she could be of an age where she could talk about nineteen years ago.

The castle at Spongano, the owner told them, had been owned by his great-grandfather, a man with twelve grandchildren. It was bequeathed to his eldest son, as was the custom. The son died childless and so it went to the next eldest son (two daughters lay between the sons). This man, too, remained childless, but he had a dog that he loved more than any child he could have had. He would have left the castle to the dog, but of course that was not possible. Instead, one of his younger brothers had a son who had a special affection for the dog, fed the dog prime cuts of meat and prepared risottos for him in a way the dog liked, with fresh butter and sage and parmigiano. Upon his death, the man left the castle and all its land to this nephew. This boy (a teenager when he inherited the property) was the father of the man telling the story.

"No wonder you love Italy," Hunter said, walking through the groves of lemon trees, the castle glowing in the moon's light.

Having been told that Puglia's coast was among the most beautiful in Italy if seen from a boat, they hired one to ferry them along it, and admired the black rocky shores glistening in the strong sun. "The Amalfi Coast without the Amalfi," one friend had said of a particularly hilly and scenic drive skirting the coast. And Beth remembered Cesare, knew she would not see him here. Remembered the giant ferry moving away from the Brindisi docks, remembered that she had commented on the beauty of the coast they were leaving in their wake as the ferry moved toward Greece on one of their many trips there. "*Terroni* vacation there," he had said. *Terroni:* a pejorative term describing those from the south of Italy, those of the land, who worked the land, ate from the land, were the land. It was a moment, she remembered, when Cesare had defined himself, a small part of him, in a way she found unflattering. His comment revealed the truth beyond his seeming graciousness, revealed his belief in hierarchy, and it had made her suspicious of him for a moment— if this was his attitude toward an Italian, what about an American? A clue, she could see in retrospect, to their future. The rocky coast had big *grotti* the boat could enter, dark caves that echoed their voices and the slap of the swells that smashed against the caves' walls, rocking the boat violently.

From Puglia they traveled inland to the Sassi of Matera, where from their bedroom window they watched the sunset lighting up the small canyon of caves. It was Beth's first trip there even though it was the name of her restaurant. Lying in bed with Valeria asleep and a full moon lighting up the night, Hunter said, "I had to bring you here." That was Hunter, always thinking of what ignited her imagination. So in love with making her happy was he that she could take his love for granted and long for the impossible, protected by the slow and steady creep of that beautiful vine.

From Matera they drove to the medieval town of Castellabate, where they stayed in a hotel a thousand feet directly above the Tyrrhenian Sea. From their patio the panorama included a vast expanse of sea, the islands of Ischia and of Capri, and the Amalfi Coast shrouded in mist, in the thick summer haze. The view made Beth think of Sylvia, still in California but working for a start-up in Silicon Valley, ultimately too practical to rely on an income from writing. The islands floated off shore like myths. After Castellabate came Herculaneum with its well-preserved Roman ruins, temples looming magnificently in the heat, drenched in sun and creeping oleander, and then the Amalfi Coast with, indeed, too much Amalfi. "It's a shopping mall," Beth declared, though a part of her wouldn't have minded drifting the streets to admire the shops. But Hunter would have none of it, so they pushed on to Pompeii, from Pompeii to Maremma, from Maremma to Giglio—a small island just north of Sardegna and just south of Elba.

There, they discovered a small hotel with little bungalows perched on the edge of a cliff, each one hidden by eucalyptus trees. A splendid spot you could get to only by boat, and once there you never wanted to leave because the setting was magical—a cliff rising from the sea to a terrace for sunbathing and eating and drinking, rising to a restaurant, rising to a Jacuzzi, rising to a sloping field upon which roamed goats that were the source of the milk used to make the hotel's own fresh goat cheese, served every evening with *miele di castagna* (chestnut honey). This was an entirely new Italy to Beth. In this Italy she was a tourist. Her old Italy was another country in which she had been called *Signorina* and in which she was decidedly a member, a citizen. But she still spoke Italian and Hunter adored watching her negotiate everything for them while he understood little of what was being said.

"I hate that I'm called *signora*," she told him, looking at herself in a hotel mirror, in one of those American-sized bathrooms. She traced her eyes with a finger, gingerly touching the lines of age. Valeria stood next to her doing the same thing. "My eyes," Beth said to Hunter, holding him in the mirror with her eyes. "My eyes, Daddy," Valeria said, mimicking her mother. But that's all she said to him about the nineteen-year gap, the divide between her Italy and this Italy. She still felt like a girl with possibility lying just in front of her, just within her reach. She bent down and kissed Valeria on the head, "My little monkey," she said. "My little sponge."

"You're my *signorina*," Hunter said, and kissed Beth's ear. His breath sneaked into it and she flinched. She loved him, she did, she told herself. She turned around to kiss him.

"The first time I went to Rome was with Bea and her grandmother," Beth said. "I was sixteen." The memory had just bubbled to the surface, long forgotten. "Bea's grandmother's sister was a very small, very old nun, and she lived in a convent and we went to visit her. It seemed we were there for hours, in a room of old nuns, in their habits speaking in Italian, which I didn't yet understand. The old nuns pinched my cheeks and laughed at me sweetly for understanding nothing and for being American, like I was some sort of rare pet. When they realized I wasn't baptized they weren't exactly scared, actually more curious about how to save me. They were just going to arrange a baptism. They wanted Bea's grandmother to extend their visit so they'd have the time. But that wasn't possible." She thought of Signora Cellini's fright upon learning that she was a heathen.

"So close yet so far," Hunter said, and kissed her sinful forehead.

"You've always loved me, haven't you?" she said.

"Since I first met you."

"Persistent."

"I knew you'd love me."

"Tenacious."

"I took the long view."

"Do you miss earning your own money?"

"So many concerns, my love." He put his hands in her hair and she felt the quality of his that she loved most—his easy adaptability—and how this freed him.

Swimming from the cliffs of the Giglio hotel, a particularly handsome, though older, Italian man joined Beth. He dove in just after she did and followed her a distance out, far enough so that the people lying on the rocks in the sun seemed small. Beth thought that it was strange that this man chose to follow her. He had not been friendly, though most of the other guests at this small hotel had been, and thus he had stood out. All meals were shared and cocktails were enjoyed together at sunset. His wife, a tall aging blond woman with weathered skin, never offered even the slightest smile, though Beth had seen her reading an American novel and suspected her to be American. In the water, however, her husband was clearly following Beth. Beth smiled, treading water, admiring the beauty of the cliffs. *Ombrelloni* for shade had been erected here and there, poking up among the rocks like exotic trees. A child with a snorkel swam about close to shore, lifting his head to shout out the names of creatures he had seen below. On the terrace, a hundred feet up, preparations were being made for lunch, Beth could hear the clatter of silver and glassware. "*Americanina*," the Italian said, and Beth nodded. She imagined, seeing his dark receding hair and his clever eyes, that Cesare would be like this at sixty. "This place is a jewel," he continued in Italian. "It is," Beth agreed, wondering if she had been mistaken about him, if perhaps he was friendly. "I've been coming here for years," he said. "No one knows about this hotel." They bobbed in the water, gentle waves pushing against them. This would have been her life. "A secret," Beth smiled. "Don't tell any Americans about it," he said with a sudden sternness as he swam up quite close to her. For a moment she thought he might try to drown her. "What?" she asked. "Americans, they'll ruin it. Don't go back to New York and tell them all about it. Look what they did to Tuscany after that book, that Tuscan Sun abomination. Destroyed."

Beth swallowed a gulp of seawater and started coughing. She remembered being in Spain a few years back and an old man had recognized Hunter as American and the old man told Hunter that he hated Americans and then he looked at Beth and said, "You're Italian. Italians are good, they make me laugh." She had been proud to be confused for an Italian, but she wanted to apologize for all Americans, their big-bathroom needs and their loud consumptive mouths. Then she hated the little old man for his categorical hate as she hated the presumptuous swimmer now at her side.

"What do you do?" he asked, friendly now, as they swam back to shore. It felt as if she were swimming across some great divide, the impossible. She stopped swimming, looked him in the eye, turned on her back and floated beneath the sun. "I'm a writer," she said.

———

In Pisa, she remembered driving fast in the Maserati, kissing Miki on Forte dei Marmi's jetty—his big hands and his big feet and his big penis. All the surprise of Greece floated unknown in front of her. How fun it had been to be eighteen, driving fast to Parma to eat tortellini and fresh parmesan, knowing nothing of the divide.

Pisa was as far north as she would go this trip. Instead, they turned south again and headed to Florence and a week in a friend's villa in southern Tuscany, in the small town of Cetona: lazy days of eating well and reading and drinking more *vino locale un po' frizzante* broken up by day trips to local markets, and to Assisi and Orvieto and Montepulciano. She surrendered to her new role of tourist, letting the old *signorina* go, and before long the present stopped its kiss with the past.

Then, sitting on the patio of the Cetona villa beneath a grape arbor, looking across a valley to the small hillside town of Città della Pieve, she heard her cell phone ring. It was Bear, calling from Provence. "OK, little darling," he said, upon hearing her voice. "You're in Europe and you're coming up to my little shack in Provence. You're coming just as soon as you can and if you give me any lip I won't help you fund a thing. You're gonna come up here and sell me on Previn or whatever the silly name is, and you're gonna cook me those Indian concoctions and potions and you're gonna seduce me." Bear somehow always reminded her of a Texan even though he was decidedly not a Texan. Rather, he was born and raised in Connecticut and had never set foot in Texas. But he had been a political science major and had studied Lyndon Baines Johnson in particular and, Beth suspected, had adopted some of the president's bravado and swagger. She smiled. Bear knew her too well. "I can just feel you smiling, Beth," he blustered, "and so I know you're coming."

"It's glorious here," she said. The patio sloped down to meet a terraced vineyard beneath which stood a grove of olive trees that gave way to a rolling field. In the middle of the field glistened a pool where Valeria and Hunter swam.

"Six weeks is enough time in Italy," Bear said through the static. "Time for a little French influence and time for that daughter of yours to be corrupted by my brood." There was silence for a moment. "C'mon, darlin." With that, she realized her vacation was now officially over and that she would have to go to France or give up on Preveena. Bear had been in Provence for about a week, just long enough to be somewhat bored by Elaine, his wife, and in need of new company to show off in front of so that they could be admired by those who had less— a recreation that Bear's wife loved as well. And Beth understood fully that by playing the role of friend-of-lesser-means, doing all the requisite admiring, she would earn her restaurant.

"Preveena," Beth said. "It's called Preveena."

"Oh, OK, sweetheart. Whatever you say. We'll talk about that name." And then he clicked off, his voice sucked up to the satellites.

"Hunter," she yelled down to the pool, "Valeria." She slipped into her flip-flops and ran down the hill of olive trees with the cell phone in her hand to let them know they would be off to Saint Rémy to see Bear.

The hotel was a rundown château in the center of town surrounded by vast gardens, plane trees, and a big green lawn with a pond in which large goldfish swam about. A little stone putto spurted water from his mouth and tiny frogs leaped here and there while the incessant cicadas sang their endless song. The château stood four stories tall. In the direct center on the second floor, like a mouth, was the glassed-in balcony of the master suite, which belonged, of course, to Beth and Hunter—paid for by Bear because he believed they'd be more comfortable in a hotel than at his villa with the kids. "The gesture only seems extravagant, my pet," Bear had said, and then informed them that the rooms were "dirt cheap." "Never forget the importance of illusion," he said to Beth, giving her his dimpled knowing smile. Since the hotel had yet to be renovated, it still had low prices and tiny bathrooms (and, incidentally, no other Americans). At the edge of the grounds was a riding stable and every day Bear's four kids and Valeria took lessons while Bear and his wife and Hunter and Beth went on excursions to L'Isle-sur-la-Sorgue to buy antiques, to Avignon to learn about the popes, to Arles to see the views that van Gogh had painted, to Aix to roam the meandering streets and to shop and to see the views painted by Cézanne. To the Camargue, through fields of lavender and wheat and coquelicots. Wine tastings at Châteauneuf-du-Pape, in Beaumes de Venise, in Mas de Daumas. Saint Rémy they learned was famous for three things: it was home to one of the oldest archeological sites in Europe—the ruins of Comptoir de Glanum, from the third century B.C. before control passed to Rome under Julius Caesar; it was home to the asylum where van Gogh lived the year before he killed himself; and Nostradamus was born in the town in 1503. Through all of this Bear swaggered, shedding dollars and francs and euros with his big smile and his French that did not even attempt to affect the correct pronunciation.

Valeria loved being with the "big kids" and learned to love to ride even though the lessons were conducted in French, which she didn't know, of course, but somehow understood. At the end of the lessons, Bear's children would swarm around the adults (who always arrived from their own adventures late) and tell them of Valeria's accomplishments. She fell asleep on the

pony; she fell off the pony…and got right back on; she trot-
ted; she cantered; she learned to make her pony stop. Never
once did Bear mention Preveena. But Beth knew she was doing
her job. She admired all the armoires and chairs and divans that
his wife bought in L'Isle-sur-la-Sorgue. ("We filled an entire
container last year," Elaine told Beth. Their New York apartment
was so big that even fully furnished it still had room for another
container's worth of antiques from Provence.) They wandered
the roving markets, each day in a new location, purchasing hon-
eys and soaps and bags and hats and fresh cheeses and breads
for picnics, and Beth dutifully listened to how cheap everything
was: the dollar was strong that summer. Bear's "shack" was a
sprawling two-story, seven-bedroom (five bathrooms—all very
big, indeed, Hunter pointed out, sneaking Beth into one so that
they could laugh) villa in the heart of Les Alpilles. Despite
the parched landscape, Bear's garden was green and filled with
flowering roses in all shades. His near-Olympic-length swimming pool brimmed with cool water, beneath a grove of cypress.
The focal point of the entire downstairs was the kitchen with
its thirty-thousand-dollar Le Cornue stove, trimmed in copper
to match the pots. Beth wanted to cook on that stove, but Elaine
would always say that it was too hot, and she would suggest
Oustaù de Beaumanière or some other favorite restaurant for a
dinner beneath the stars, and they would find a babysitter for
the children and off they would go to dinner and conversations
about the antiques purchased that day, the bargains found, the
extravagances to be indulged in. Elaine tried to sell Beth on the
merits of a ninety-euro straw hat. "It's designed," she said.
"You're paying for the design." "But does it last longer than an
ordinary straw hat?" Hunter responded, causing her to crack a
half smile—an instant in which she could appreciate her own
absurdity. Beth much preferred her husband as an entrepreneur,

making his way with her, than as a financier, and often counted her blessings that he had been fired. She knew, though, that sometimes Hunter longed for those excessive days when money seemed to fall from the skies like so much rain, knew that making money had made him feel more male even if he never would admit it. She told herself that she never missed the indulgences that money could buy, though of course that was not entirely true.

Bear and Elaine would ask Beth about her European days, which she loved as it made her feel she had an important past, a past that defined her. They would ask her to repeat a story they had heard before. Beth had been with Bea's family on Favignana. Bea and Beth had eaten dinner by themselves and Signora Nuova wanted to know what Beth had eaten, had she eaten well? "I said I had eaten *pompini* for dinner," Beth said. She had meant to say *polpettine* to Signora Nuova—"meatballs." *Pompini* was something else entirely. "You had blow jobs for dinner," Bear said in his big way, slapping his knee, tickled by the mistake of this woman who seemed to him incapable of such a lapse, imagining her as a suntanned teenager on an Italian island and what she might have done, what experiences she might have had that would cause her to learn such a word.

They would talk about their next vacation and how old the kids needed to be before they could "do Asia." The biggest topic every night at dinner was Elaine's fortieth birthday. Should it be Moroccan or Persian? "Oh, Beth, you could do the Persian. A Persian theme! Or Indian or Chinese. No, no, not Chinese, can you imagine?" They planned to have all the furniture removed from their apartment for the evening no matter what the theme. Beth thought about the Italian man on Giglio trying to catch her as she swam, trying to stop her from doing any harm, begging her to leave it all alone, to preserve it, untouched. The other thing she had felt, floating on her back in the water, was power—a sudden jolt of it.

Later that night Beth would ask Hunter if the idea for Preveena was a bad one, "Am I just another tour guide taking people to the exotic, an exotic I don't actually know?" "Is your interest genuine?" he asked, knowing the answer. And she saw Preveena at Claire making a curry powder for chicken, roasting the cumin and mustard and coriander seeds on the stove, remembered how it seemed she was making a magic potion, how she loved the chemistry of it, what the flavors did to the chicken. Beth thought about her father, about how Claire collected people. They had come from everywhere by chance, sharing a desire to do something other with their lives—if only to start fresh and figure out for themselves who they were. Beth had grown up feasting on the differences of people as if that were normal. Didn't they all—Bear, his wife, Hunter—to some degree? She had the strong desire to return to Claire and live with her father and make it work. "Let's do," she said to Hunter later, appreciating, it seemed for the first time, the beauty behind her father's ambition.

But that was later. At dinner, talk moved back to Asia where Bear's wife had a friend in Bangkok who had "cheap, so cheap" live-in help "twenty-four/seven" who "cooks and cleans and cares for the kids. And she's a fabulous cook. Imagine if we could have Beth twenty-four/seven." Bear gave her a warm, adoring smile, a smile that acknowledged his wife's silliness. But Hunter couldn't help himself: "Imagine if we could have you twenty-four/seven," he said to Elaine, "as our live-in party planner and interior decorator?" Elaine laughed at herself and gave Beth a kiss, all good fun and fantasy. "Bear will fund Preveena," Elaine declared, with her pretty smile shimmering on her face like a star. Elaine was nice looking in the way unattractive women can be if they have money and confidence. Her face was long and horselike, but she had vibrant green eyes, thick long black hair with tight, elastic curls, and a smile that rounded her long cheeks. With Elaine's support, granted because of her faux pas, Beth knew Preveena would open within the year.

And then she saw him. A stab. Like the first time she saw him standing on those steps in the sun, negotiating in ancient Greek with the landlady who understood not a word. He was sitting there beneath the plane trees with his espresso, his torso leaning elegantly toward the table. She felt sick to her stomach. In the cool lobby she asked a maid for a glass of water. She asked in her awful French and loudly enough that he might hear and recognize her voice and come to her. He would come to her. He had to come to her. Her voice sounded brash and demanding, impetuously American. Bet, I am Bet, she wanted to scream. As in to gamble everything. She had been right all along. She would see him again at a time she least expected. She had the urge to run back to the pool and tell Hunter and Valeria. She had the urge to walk stealthily up to him, wrap her fingers across his eyes and whisper *"Indovina chi sono." "Sei Bet sei,"* he would answer because there was only one possibility, only one Beth.

But he was gone when she reemerged from the lobby in the hot July sun. She walked back to the pool and she thought of the fireman and she thought of the past six weeks in Italy and she thought of his journey along the dark road, how he knew every curve and every bend, and she realized now that she, too, had known all along that she was on a familiar route leading her back, just as that train dividing in the Spanish night had brought her to Cesare. She felt sick with anticipation. She walked fast back to the pool, back to her life. She was brimming with hope and longing and promise. Glee curled her face.

How ridiculous, how absurd, she thought. How inevitable. Of course.

He had seen her, too. He had seen her first as she walked across the lawn from the pool to the hotel. She was wearing a bikini with pink flowers. Around her waist she had wrapped a red sarong, which fell to her feet. In her hand she carried a girl's doll. A clip scooped up all her hair. Lipstick darkened her lips. Too dark, he thought. She was more woman now than girl, but otherwise she was the same. Same gait, same determination, same strong body. He could tell she was on a mission. At first he thought she was heading right for him. His heartbeat quickened. He smiled. He made to rise then noticed she was not looking at him. She had not seen him. He turned to his paper and pretended to read. He sat very still, seemingly absorbed. He wanted to know if she would recognize him as she passed, what she would do. He was steady, though he sweat. How long had it been? He felt her through the corner of his eye as she passed. She had come to Italy last and he had been cruel to her in order to drive her away for good. His mission had been successful, but of course he had not stopped remembering her. She vanished into the hotel and again he was alone. He breathed deeply, disappointed. Then he heard her voice asking for a glass of water—her same American accent stumbling over foreign words, stabbing them with American consonants and vowels. He remembered their first kiss in the late night streets of Páros, hiding from the others, how important and urgent it all seemed. *"Tu sei perfetta,"* he had said, and she had repeated the phrase with that accent of hers, that had made her seem at once fragile and innocent and demanding, full of the ambitious drive of one who is taught from birth to dream, that accent that had made him want to protect her and save her from the fragility of dreams and all that was wrong with the world. How he had wanted her to save him, too.

Cesare had come to Saint Rémy with his son and his wife because she had been interested in a festival celebrating a rare pear found only in the vicinity of the town. Cesare did not know the name and would not ordinarily have come on such an excursion, but had because his son had asked him to and he did whatever the boy wanted. They were in Saint Rémy for three nights and the pear in question was one that his wife wanted to taste to see if it would be worth the expense and if it would add to the variety her family business of exotic fruits and vegetables was famous for. All day she and Leonardo had been at the festival and when they returned they went for a swim. Cesare, in the garden, awaited them. But when he heard Beth's voice, he slipped away to his room. From his window on the second floor he watched Beth walk back to the pool.

Why do we go back? Can we go back? Should we go back? At the end of his travels on the dark but familiar road, the fireman, of course, had not found his dead parents. He found instead unfamiliar faces living unfamiliar lives in a home that had once been his. He knocked at the door of the house lived in by his family. A man had opened the door. It had been a Saturday morning, the night after the bus ride, and the man was standing there obviously expecting someone else. The fireman wanted to be welcomed, brought inside and shown around, wanted this man's life to somehow reveal something about his own lost life. But the man, in his pajamas, simply looked confused. "Not a good time," he said. "My wife's sick and the boy and girl are upset." He shut the door and the fireman took the bus back to the ship and the ship back to Vietnam, unable to escape the undertow.

———

Beth stubbed her toe walking back to the pool. A frog leaped in the pond with a splash, and a butterfly settled in her hair. The cicadas sang, the heat pooled in her eyes, making her whole head swim. Her daughter ran back and forth from the pool's stairs to the shower with some little friend she had made. Beth didn't pay attention. Hunter kissed her. A few other people lay on chaises beneath umbrellas, sleeping, reading, smoking. "I'm so hot," she said. "You are?" he asked teasingly, flirting. He kissed her again and she hated him. She turned away. His breath smelled. She tried to read a novel but couldn't concentrate. She tried to read a book about a woman's life told through stories about food but found it irritating and unbelievable. She jumped in the pool and felt refreshed but no more calm. She wanted to see him. She would leave to find him. A beautiful woman dangled her long legs in the pool. Her lotioned body seemed to absorb the heat. She deftly smoked a cigarette and read *Elle*. Beth wondered if that were Cesare's wife. She knew his wife's name, Isabella. Beth wanted to say out loud, "Isabella," wanted Isabella to respond, wanted to swim over to Isabella and pull herself up next to Isabella and have a conversation with Isabella. Valeria and her new companion were screeching with delight, splashing each other with the cold shower water. Beth would say to Isabella, "I am Beth." And Isabella would know exactly who she was, and the knowledge would make her nervous, would threaten her serene beauty and calm. And Beth would learn from Isabella how not a day passed that Cesare did not think of her; she would learn that he had a shrine devoted to pictures of her on his office wall. Isabella would say to her that he should have married her, that it would remain the one big regret of his life. "Really?" Beth would ask, surprised by this truth, but not really. Hunter tried to talk to her, but she could not hear what he said so anxious was she with love. She wanted to tell him that she had seen Cesare, ask him what to do, deflate it, make it normal, not that big a deal. Perhaps they could all have dinner with Bear. Cesare could see how far she had come, that she had made something of herself. She felt ridiculous for thinking this, but imagined Bear, shedding his cash, would be proof that she were someone. "If only you didn't want to be a cook," Cesare had once said to her, as if that one desire were the cause of their divide. She stood up and wrapped her red sarong around her waist and told Hunter she was going to lie down before going out with Bear, who was coming to collect them in an hour or so for another night of rich food and wine. She would find him. She was all determination and belief. She would see him again. She would make him speak.

If you were there, standing in the middle of the lawn, looking toward the house you would have seen that all the windows on the second floor but one were shuttered. You would have seen the glass room jutting from the facade like a miniature crystal palace. You would have seen a woman inside in a silk slip, sitting in an upholstered armchair with big flowers in gold brocade, a vase of cut roses standing tall on the coffee table upon which rested her feet. If you had zoomed your lens in to get a closer look, you would have seen that she was crying, faint tears that could easily have been confused for sweat. But at her chest, you'd have seen there, love fairly palpitating, swelling the rise of her breast. You'd have seen a woman caught, frozen in a summer heat, caught in the divide, the grand chasm. If you were observing even somewhat keenly you would have seen the man in the one unshuttered window to the right of the glass palace. You would have seen that his eyes were trained on the woman's back. If you were godlike and could feel what this couple felt, you would know that she felt those eyes on her back and that

it was the sensation of them that froze her to the brocade armchair. He was speaking to her. She was speaking to him. They
were saying what they had always wanted to say. I love you still.
I have never stopped loving you. *What has haunted you, what have
you longed for and missed and dreamed of?* She was asking a million
questions. *Do you know who you are now?*

Bet, he said with his beautiful accent. Bet, you are always
the same.

You are mine, she said. Silence.

You married Hunter, he finally said, that old tinge of jealousy.

You knew I would. Just as I always knew you'd marry a
woman from Città. Only, I thought she'd be big and fat and
hideous.

He laughed. I didn't like to think about who you would
marry, he said.

You had a choice. You chose laziness, she said.

You chose, too, he said. But chose not to believe that you
were choosing.

And they fell silent again for a while the way you do when
having difficult conversations. The pause became like a breath.
She contemplated the statement. Had she made a choice? Had
she chosen something else over him? That's not the way she remembered it. He chose a Florentine who made silk hats, one of
which he cruelly gave to her. The afternoon light was turning
golden. A light breeze stirred the heat. On the coffee table by
her feet were two empty jars of strawberry jam, licked clean by
Valeria, who did not like the French cuisine and was eating only
jam.

I could not compete with your ambition, he said. And I
could not stop it.

I wasn't ambitious, she said. Only for you.

Be honest, Bet, he said. Give that to yourself.

You're being so pragmatic, she said. Didn't she already
know all of this? What they wanted was to live something un-
livable, step inside the lost chance.

Out the windows Beth could see her daughter twirling
across the grass with her companion from the pool. She knew
it just then—that was Cesare's son. They stopped at the frog
pond, started poking it with sticks. And the pretty woman with
her long legs dangling into the pool was his wife.

That's Leonardo, she said.

And Valeria? he asked.

The perfect ending, she said.

Always a romantic, he said.

Are you happy? she asked.

Are you happy? he asked.

Valeria and the boy dashed across the grass holding hands.
The boy had long dark ringlets that shimmered around his
round face. The sunlight came through the glass and pricked her
on the shoulders.

She feels his eyes on her back, continuing their slow burn.
The children dart through sprinklers, fanning cold water across
the unnaturally emerald grass.

Do I have a choice now? She remembers their first kiss. The
children pause to inspect something, side by side, heads close,
they look carefully into the grass at some treasure they find
magical. What language are they speaking? Valeria bursts up
like a fountain suddenly turned on and runs away from the boy
with the treasure in her hand. He chases her and she throws it
at him and then leaps into the sprinkler again. Her daughter's
body is strong and agile. Beth loves that body, loves scooping it
up in her arms, pulling Valeria to her chest to hear the constant
of her heartbeat.

How could I have asked you to do what I could not? he says.

Tears in her nose and at the base of her throat. Her chest is swollen with them. You should have asked me. That should have been my decision to make.

Hunter now appears on the lawn. He seems somehow small, stooped, old. Valeria runs into his arms. The little boy stands at Hunter's side, looking up to him. He kneels down and begins to help the children with something. The sun is slipping off the day, casting light, spraying the room with gold. She stands up. Hunter disappears.

Cesare wills her not to turn. If she turns just now she will see him. He knows she knows he is there. He can see her in her pink slip. He can see the sharp angles of her shoulder bones. He wants her to turn and not to turn. If only she would turn. He wants to see her face once more, see some signal on it. Now the children catch crickets in the palms of their hands.

A maid knocks on the door, then enters. In her soft French she says she is here to prepare the room for the evening. She turns down the bed. She clears off the empty jars of jam from the coffee table. She begins to pull the heavy curtains across the tall windows. Beth asks her to leave the curtains open. *"Pardon,"* the maid says, *"pardon."* Beth hears the children squealing outside. She wants to see him. Just for an instant. She wants to know if he is there, if she is right. Has he been speaking to her? She feels those eyes; they are there, his eyes. She wants to ask the maid to tell her if a man is sitting in the window, the one with the open shutters? Is he there? What is he doing? Is he looking this way? He is telling her not to turn. She starts to turn. She pleads with him to wait. I want to touch you again, she says. I want to see you, smell you, breathe you, feel you, be you. She is invincible, golden in the golden light in her glass palace. The sensation is exquisite, the sensation is life in all its depth and beauty, all blurry with chaos and confusion and longing and will. It becomes a game almost, with her will. Just one quick glance back. She hears the boisterous voice of Bear downstairs, gently commanding. She hears the children. She sees Valeria, sees her thick dark hair, wet from the sprinklers, whipping against the grass as she turns cartwheels. The boy is no good at them, but he tries. She thinks of the fireman and his dead parents and she remembers him sitting at the table at Claire telling her the story. "Before I got there, before I saw the man in the door of my house, standing there telling me to go away, it had been real. I had seen my mother. I had seen my father. They'd been alive." She sits down.

In the morning they all flew home.

Eight

L'America

Morning comes as it always does. Pale blue at first, but you can tell it will be a beautiful day, one of those cloudless September days that make it seem the whole world is clear. The sun, creeping into the sky, burns off the night's thick fog and though it is early, the sun is high enough already to light the snowcapped mountains, to make them shimmer, miragelike. If he were to stand up and part the curtains, the mountains in the distance would greet him, floating islands in the sea of sky. But he sits still, in his velvet chair, waiting. Waiting for his son to rise, for his wife to stir, for the momentum of the day to begin, to push him along. But the light leaking through the velvet curtains spells with certainty the nature of the day. This light catches in Valeria's longing, pleading eyes. *The brilliance of the artist,* Beth had said. *He leaves it up to us to interpret, and how we choose reveals just a bit more about ourselves.*

He contemplates the painting now. Not the outsized girl or her love or the party carrying on around them, but rather the small details: the bell tower at the edge of the town, the hill of flowers, the road (no more than a thin line) running down from the town toward the lake. He will drive that road today. He thinks of how little the landscape has changed in five hundred years. He will drive that road today with his wife to speak with construction workers and a designer and a stonemason, all people involved with the construction of the pool. Once it was a day's drive by horse and carriage from Città to Fiori. Now it takes half an hour by car. The pool, once finished, will be where his father's vegetable garden is, jutting, it would seem, from a wall of rock, giving the illusion of being suspended in the air high above the lake. The pool, once finished, will be the first change to the landscape in five hundred years. The idea sweeps across his mind, as it has many times before, but now, instead of triggering a pang of guilt, it makes him bold. What else will he do? Where will his son be in twenty years?

On the table beside him is a phone, beside the phone is an ashtray, in the ashtray are a dozen partially smoked and stubbed out cigarettes. Behind the table are the drawn curtains with light leaking through, behind the curtains are the snowcapped Alps, beyond the Alps lies the rest of the world dappled with the multitudes of unhistoric lives, with the yous and the mes living our hidden myths, offering our small kindnesses. The piece of paper holding the e-mail message falls from Cesare's hand to the floor. He hears the soft sound of his child's feet shuffling to the toilet; he hears the child pee and then flush the toilet. He hears his wife call after the child telling him softly and with love to do what he has already done. Cesare smells the ashes in the ashtray, feels the smoke in his lungs. He is not a smoker, but it feels good to feel it there now.

Valeria married the year after Benvenuto left. She married a man figured in the painting. He is the only guest whose eyes address the viewer, but is so small you might not notice him. They had three children and he prospered as a lawyer working for many of the industries thriving in the already rich town of

Città. They lived together into old age and then he died and then she died and then her children died and then her children's children died and so on and so forth. And now Cesare sits beneath her, able to realize for the first time in the forty-three years he's been lucky enough to contemplate this painting, that this moment, falling so precisely in the center of After and Before, captures not only her entire life but that of twenty generations of her family—spells it, the pleading desire to be free and not free.

"Babbo?" Leonardo calls. He stands in front of Cesare rubbing the sleep from his eyes. He climbs into his father's lap to nestle. Leonardo smells like sleep. His little body is warm. Cesare holds his boy tightly, feels the rhythm of his breath. He runs his fingers through the child's thick black hair, inhaling the sweet scent of him. Valeria, looming tall in her fresco, presides over them with her question of freedom. The child grows bigger and bigger and bigger in his arms. He is a teenager who wants to study in America. He is twenty-three years old and wants to teach in America. He is thirty years old and wants to marry an American and build a house with her somewhere in Connecticut. He is forty years old with three English-speaking children living in rural America. (*Married to my Valeria?* he imagines Beth asking. *Always a romantic,* he imagines answering. *Is that what you want for your son?* he could imagine her asking. *For him to live the life you didn't get to live? Are you sure?*) Cesare holds the boy now with everything he has and only then, only after the night and the fog and the story of it all, after five hundred years culminating in an American dream, only then does he begin to cry.

"Babbo? I'm speaking to you. I want to come to Fiori today, *Babbo.* Please. I don't want to go to school." He hears his wife turn on the faucet in the bathroom. She will be splashing her

face with cool water, brushing her teeth. Then he hears her turn
the faucet off. He hears her walking down the hall and then
down the stairs to them. "Mama says I can come if you approve.
I want to come." His voice is whiny in that five-year-old way.
And then his wife appears. She looks somehow brand-new,
strange and unfamiliar with her big dark eyes and her porcelain
skin.

"You didn't sleep last night, *tesoro?*" she asks. Her long black
hair is tied in a bun at the back of her head. Her eyes are rested
and bright, ready for the day. Her white bathrobe is tied at her
thin waist and she wears pink ballet slippers on her feet as she
always does in place of ordinary slippers. She always has something on her feet. She never goes barefoot. She does not want
her feet to get dirty. She will go into the kitchen now and make
herself a coffee, one for Cesare, too, if she is feeling generous.
She will choose a few nice pieces of fruit and set to peeling
them for herself. Then she will start with the calls: calls to her
sisters, calls to her parents, calls to the army of people coming
to Fiori to discuss the plans for the pool. Leonardo squirms in
Cesare's arms, shouting at his mother about coming to Fiori and
having the day off from school. He is electric with possibility
for the day: a day away from school, a day with his parents
doing grown-up things that have wonderful implications for a
child. He imagines next summer splashing in the pool with all
his friends. Isabella pulls open the curtains and sunlight floods
in, bouncing off the marbled floors, soaking the room with the
brilliance of the clear blue day and all of its implicit hope. Cesare's eyes are shot with blood and dark circles weigh down his
brown eyes. She notes the cigarettes but says nothing. She does
not ask for explanations, only desires to be told what he needs
and wants to tell her. She bends down and picks up the piece
of paper lying on the floor and gives it a quick scan and says,

"*L'America,*" with a little tinge of dismissive impatience, but also an indulgent smile. She knows her husband, has been encouraging him in his interest in doing business with an American from Baltimore. In her elegant hand the white piece of paper flutters delicately like a tissue, nothing more. She leans to kiss him softly on the forehead. The paper rests on his shoulder. She has no idea what it says. She whispers, so that Leonardo cannot hear, asking Cesare if they can spoil the boy, bring him along, he has been so eager and curious about the pool. The boy understands implicitly the great hurdle this pool represents— knows it the way kids can sometimes, wise beyond their small number of years. She moves her face away from Cesare's and cocks her pretty smile and he smiles back agreeing and Leonardo, understanding, leaps out of his father's lap and tears off to get dressed, squealing with delight. Isabella goes off to the kitchen still carrying the paper, unaware of what she holds in her hand, unaware that Cesare has been crying, all business and efficiency, ready to begin the day. And what would this news mean to her? A sudden jolt would shock her. She would feel for a moment her husband's sadness (of course, she knows who Beth is); she would sting with her new proximity to the calamity. But most of all, he knows, she would feel the horror, but only briefly, that it would ripple through her and then just as easily ripple out of her as such emotions always do in people who have escaped someone else's tragedy. So he says nothing.

He hears the coffee being made, hears the selection of the fruit, hears the calls begin. She would have shared the news with her sisters, another piece of gossip to feed upon—and nothing wrong in that. Gossip is just another form of storytelling, another way to understand those things which make no sense, to tease them and pull them and mine them for contrast and comparison to one's own situation. The sunlight blots out the fresco, reflecting off the protective glass, turning the picture into a white void. The day has begun. Soon they will be on the familiar road and this, too, will be incorporated, kneaded into the fold, worked and processed like sea glass found on the beach made smooth with time, by the endless repetition of rolling against sand in the waves.

There she was: two moments: the first and the last. A Greek island. A strong, blinding late afternoon sun. He was standing on steps leading to an apartment, talking to an old Greek woman clad in black. He was trying to negotiate with her a price for another room. She spoke no Italian or English so he attempted to speak with her in ancient Greek. She did not understand that, either. Then he began to gesture with his hands. He rubbed his fingers together, shrugged his shoulders. He was a good mime. She understood. They were making progress. He smelled rosemary and lemon blossoms. The strong sun bit into his tanned arms. His friends arrived with their American girls. He turned to greet them, and there she was, small blond American with her cherubic dimpled smile. She blushed, averted her eyes, looked at him again, her determined eyes piercing into him. And he knew he was on the verge of something enormous, something grand. He felt vertigo, feared he would fall down the stairs. For nineteen years he had been remembering her there, dressed in something that did not suit her, something ridiculous belonging to Bea, something orange and awkward, that on someone else might have been stylish, but not on her. She averted those eyes only to cast them back in a way that at once captured her ability to be both shy and confident, that made him want to fall down those stairs and land at her feet, take her hand in his and begin the walk, the echo of which sounded still against his mind, reverberated still with each breath.

And then her back to him, his eyes penetrating her back, the straps of a pink silk slip gracing her slender shoulders. The beauty of her tanned back, the sharp lines of her bones, jutting like wings—were she a bird and could take flight. The conversation in the French hotel, their children gallivanting on the lawn, discovering the small things—a leaping toad, a clover, a cicada, the big worm-eaten leaf. Dancing in the dappled shadows of the plane trees. There was motion in those shoulders. She wanted to turn. She wanted to see him once again, a last time. This small story the myth of their lives, of his life and her life, inflated within them, these words their monument as the fresco was a monument, as Claire was a monument. For a moment they had the ability to defy time and history, to be a story for their children and their children's children and so on and so forth. *I am trusting you,* she said. Her back firm now, unyielding. No Orpheus was she. The afternoon sun illuminated her with haloes of light. *And damned if I look back.*

He rises from the velvet chair to the day that will carry him on and away from this with nothing and everything changed, carry him through the same patterns of remembering, of working in his bank, coming up with and supporting new ideas for socks and feet, of dreaming another destiny, of reprimanding and adoring his child and being impatient and loving with his wife, of trying to tame fear with a laugh, of drinking his aperitif in town before dinner on the carless cobbled street filled with shoppers buying their bread and their pastries packaged in waxed paper with bows, greeting each other with smiles and stories of their tangled dramas as they have for so many years and generations, same as they do everywhere, ordinary people engaged in ordinary lives that amount to everything.